Legends of Deceit

(Legends of Deceit Series Book One)

Rebekkah Ford

First Edition June 2017
ISBN: 978-0-692-89664-8

Interior Formatting by: Tugboat Design
Cover Design by: Airicka Phoenix of Airicka's Mystical Creations
Editor and Proofreader: Chase Nottingham

Table of Contents

Other Books by Rebekkah Ford

Beyond the Eyes trilogy
Beyond the Eyes
Dark Spirits
The Devil's Third
Tangled Roots: (a companion to the trilogy)
Ameerah: (a Beyond the Eyes spin-off)

Thank you for purchasing *Legends of Deceit*.

Get a FREE ebook when you join Rebekkah's mailing list. Plus, get notified on upcoming releases and exclusive contests. Get sneak peeks, top secret information, and advanced reader's copy. Rebekkah doesn't share, sell, or spam newsletter subscribers.

http://bit.ly/RebekkahFordList

Acknowledgments

I'd like to thank Laura Farmer, Debb Lavoie, Bonnie Schuster, Crissy Sutcliffe, and Karlee Lawrence for being my beta readers and a huge support of my books. You girls rock!

I'd like to thank my street team for your support. I appreciate it. You're awesome. Love ya!

I'd like to give a shout out to my cover artist Airicka Phoenix from Airicka's Mystical Creations, my editor Chase Nottingham, and my formatter Deborah Bradseth from Tugboat Design. All three of you were a huge help in making this book what it is today, and I appreciate you and your dedication. You're awesome!

Also, I'd like to thank my fans. I appreciate you more than I can say. Y'all rock!

"Who in the world am I? Ah, that's the great puzzle."
~ Alice in Wonderland

Chapter One

Guilt and grief were the worst feelings anyone could ever experience. I should know. I had the misfortune to come home from a four day, fun-filled trip to Vegas with my bestie Kimmie, only to discover my parents were slaughtered hours before I arrived. If only we hadn't flirted with the hot guys from San Francisco at the charming café we ate at after our plane landed in Seattle or took the scenic route home, I would have been there before the bastard murdered my family. Maybe I could have stopped him. But who was I kidding? Could I really have subdued a blood-thirsty killer who was probably jacked up on drugs and stark-raving mad? Probably not. The guilt, though . . . the fucking guilt and the all-consuming grief screamed inside my entire being that regardless of the situation, if I had been there, they'd still be alive. Somehow I knew it to be true, a fact comparable to the sun setting in the west. There was no argument, no bullshit reasons to disprove. I was the cause of their death, but why? My question would be answered soon enough after *they* confronted me.

~Six hours beforehand~

Insanity. What was it really? What sort of behaviors qualified a person to be a prime candidate to wear a big, shiny gold badge embossed with her name and below it a contrived yet simple statement such as "I'm loony tunes" to warn others they weren't conversing with a *normal* person? I pulled my phone out of my purse and looked *insanity* up on Wikipedia while my BFF Kimmie and I were driving home from the airport in Seattle. The bright August sun was glaring through the windows. I raised the cell upright to read the definition, shielding the screen with the cup of my hand.

My heart sank.

Psychosis which basically meant loss of contact with reality. People with psychosis were described as psychotic. The term was very broad, I read, and then the word schizophrenia jumped out at me like a bright neon sign. I picked the word. Common symptoms: false beliefs, hearing voices, and unclear thinking. All three described what I'd been experiencing since I turned twenty-two a month ago.

"What are you reading?" Kimmie asked as she took the exit off the highway. She was driving my car. It didn't take much for me to convince her to do so. I hated driving in heavy traffic or the city for that matter. Kimmie on the other hand didn't mind and loved my 1967 Chevy Impala. It was the same car Dean "swoon-worthy" Winchester drove on the TV show *Supernatural*. Yes, we were huge fans. We grew up watching *Supernatural*, and my father had taken it upon himself when I was fourteen to purchase this kickass car on the condition I helped him restore it. Of course, I agreed and by doing so, I now knew how to rebuild an engine, a carburetor, and everything else that entailed ensuring I had a reliable ride. My father didn't want me to be reliant on a man for anything, so he and my mother raised me to be self-sufficient, which I was grateful for. Add a healthy dose of stubbornness and determination, and I was a force to be reckoned with. Just sayin'.

I turned off my phone and frowned. "I was reading about schizophrenia."

"Why? Do you think I'm nuts?" Kimmie laughed and tucked a lock of brown hair behind her ear. She had a cute bob style that framed her round face perfectly. "I did act pretty crazy the other night while we were at *Tao*." She tapped her chin with the tip of her finger. "Actually, I acted pretty nutso the whole four days we were in Vegas, but I blame it on the alcohol and all the hot guys we met."

Forgetting about my worries for a few moments, I thought about how much fun we had and the free drinks we kept receiving. Kimmie and I both danced with several smokin' hot guys at the clubs we went to, and I won three thousand dollars playing blackjack our first night there. Half of my winnings were now gone, though, because I treated us to some entertainment like seeing the Aussie Hunks at the *V Theater* who were trained dancers. Boy, was that a lot of fun. Their smooth, chiseled, muscular bodies swayed and gyrated to the beat of the music in languid and effortless movements. Yum. The mental visual that memory conjured had me wondering what it would be like to have sex with a guy with a physique like the strippers had. I bet it would be mind-blowing. I bet I'd–

"Earth to Haven," Kimmie said, interrupting my thoughts. "You didn't answer my question."

"What question was that?" I was lost. My mind quickly searched for the answer. It came to me, but Kimmie beat me to the punch, and just like that, my worries were back.

"Do you think I'm nuts?"

"Of course not."

"Why were you looking up schizophrenia?"

I wasn't sure if I wanted to tell her the truth, but I needed someone to talk to about this because it was bothering the hell out of me.

I ran my fingers through my long dark hair and took my sunglasses off. "What I tell you stays between you and me, okay?"

Kimmie steered to the side of the road, parked, and cut the engine. Good thing we were taking the scenic route home. I wouldn't have felt comfortable parked out in the open where people had the opportunity to gawk at us as they drove by. She pushed her shades down the bridge of her nose and met my gaze. Her brown eyes sparkled with curiosity. "What is it?"

"You have to promise me you won't tell anyone."

She stuck her pinkie out and curled it like we used to do when we were kids. "I swear."

I hooked my pinky with hers and took a deep shaky breath. "I've been having dreams."

Her mouth formed into an O. "Pornographic dreams. I love having those. In fact, I've been having them since we–"

"No," I said. "I mean, yeah, I've been having those, too, but no, that's not what I'm talking about."

"Then what?"

"Well, throughout my childhood, I've had dreams of another place, but they've been few and far between, not enough to alarm me because back then they weren't clear. Yet at the same time, they seemed familiar to me."

"Even though the dreams were fuzzy?"

"Yes. Anyway, after I turned twenty-two last month, I've been having those dreams again. Only now they're vivid, and I can swear they're real. I've been there."

Kimmie's eyebrows knitted together. "So you think you're crazy because you believe your dream is of an actual place that you've been to?"

"Yes, but I'm not done. It's a fantastical land, sort of like the Shire with bright green grass, rolling hills, deep forest, and mountains in the distance. There's also mythological creatures such as a unicorn, a baby dragon, fairies, and werewolves." I watched Kimmie closely to gauge her reaction.

She rolled her eyes. "This is your big secret?"

"No, I'm not done yet."

"Haven, you're dreaming those things because of the movies and TV shows we watch. Shifters and fairies don't exist. At least, not in our world. Maybe in another time they did, and that's where the stories originated from. Maybe you're dreaming of a past life when those things were among us. I don't know, but sweetie, you're not crazy."

What she said made perfect sense. Of course I'd be dreaming that stuff because of the brain candy we mentally fed ourselves. Okay, I could live with her reasons, even though the dreams seemed so real that when I woke from them, my heart ached with a longing comparable to being homesick. But what she said didn't sedate all my concerns. There was more.

"You could be right," I admitted, "but I've been hearing hushed voices, too. Explain that."

Her face screwed up. "Voices? Like how? I need more detail. Describe."

Kimmie had always been the reasonable one. I realized now I should have told her about this a while ago. I shifted in my seat and stared at my lap, then met her gaze. "It's more like whispering, but I can't make out what they're saying."

"When do you hear them?"

"At night when I'm in bed right before I go to sleep and sometimes in the morning after I wake up, and I'm lying under the covers thinking."

"It could be demons," Kimmie said and laughed when she saw the horror on my face. She placed a hand on my shoulder and squeezed. "I'm kidding."

"Thanks a lot." I scowled. "When it happens again, I'm going to be thinking they're demons, and it's going to freak me the fuck out."

"They're not demons. Think about it. You sleep with a fan on. If you listen to it, sometimes you can hear it make weird sounds."

She was reaching for an answer and the excuse she used certainly wasn't it. I was tired of this conversation and didn't want to tell her I knew what I heard. Her demon comment made more sense to me than the fan did, and it creeped me out.

I needed a distraction, like our trip to Vegas was the perfect remedy for my schizo problems. While we were there, I was fine, but ever since we stepped off the plane, those two issues we'd been talking about had been weighing on me.

I stared out the window into the prairie where a boarded-up farmhouse was being swallowed by a sea of vines and grass. A rush of sadness came over me. I found it heartbreaking to see what could have been once a wonderful house left unwanted.

I opened the door and stepped outside. The warm sun felt great on my skin. The sky was the same dark blue as my eyes. Wisps of smoky white clouds dotted the heavens above. The fresh earthy smell of dirt and prairie grass wafted in the air.

Kimmie got out of the Impala. "What are you doing?"

I pointed to the shabby farmhouse. "I want to check it out. I won't take long." Before she could reply, I jumped the ditch separating the road from the prairie and hurried across it.

Kimmie jogged behind me to catch up. "What if there's a bum living there?"

I shrugged. "I guess we'll find out." Worry crossed her face. "It'll be okay," I assured her and patted my tan cargo pants. "I have pepper spray."

"That makes me feel better," she mumbled.

"Where's your sense of adventure?"

"It's back in Vegas where those hot strippers are. Besides, you're the one who wants to be an archeologist because you love to explore. I'm not into that or this." She waved her hand in the air, indicating at the dilapidated structure in front of us.

"And I love history," I added with a grin, ignoring the objection in her eyes.

We reached the front of the house. The white paint was cracked and chipped from years of neglect. Half of the wooden porch had collapsed, and the rotted floorboards told me we had to watch our step. A couple planks of wood were placed crosswise in front of the door to keep intruders like us out, and the large windows on either side of the entrance had boards nailed over them. I reached through the gap and turned the doorknob. To my surprise the door swung open, releasing a sharp creaking sound.

"Not a good sign," Kimmie said with a hint of caution in her voice.

Without saying a word, I ducked beneath the boards and entered a narrow foyer. A dank, moldy smell burned my nostrils. The dull wooden floors were coated in a thick layer of dirt and dead flies. I wrinkled my nose and moved forward toward a steep staircase covered in debris. Kimmie was hot on my heels and bumped into me when I paused to decide which way to go. I turned right and went into a room with a square rough oak table and three matching chairs. One of them had a broken leg and was tilted at an odd angle against the wall. The huge picture window was streaked with a black residue. Rays of light filtered through the filth, swollen with dust particles. I speculated if the substance was from the broken stone fireplace on the far wall. There were piles of garbage and broken pieces of timber covered in soot scattered across the hearth.

"I wonder who used to–"

"It's her. It's the king's daughter!"

"You wonder who used to what?" Kimmie asked as she picked up an old *Playboy* magazine with the tip of her fingers, her face scrunched up in disgust. "Ick. I think we're not the only ones who decided to check this house out." She dropped it on the floor. "What were you going to say?"

I shook my head. This house was creeping me out. I could have sworn I heard a voice. It had to have been my imagination. "I don't remember, but I think we should leave just in case someone is squatting here."

"You don't have to tell me twice," Kimmie said, crossing the room and then screamed when a mouse darted in front of her across a pile of garbage and broken plaster. She ran from the house.

I laughed. "It was only a mouse."

Kimmie made a face. "You know how much I hate rodents. They're nasty."

"Alaris."

What the? I knew I heard it this time. I repeated the name in my head, and oddly enough, a heartbreaking sadness overwhelmed me.

"What's wrong?" Kimmie asked. "You look like you're going to cry."

I grabbed her arm, causing her to stop. "Did you hear it?"

"Hear what?"

"The voice."

She glanced around. "What voice? I didn't hear anything."

"Okay, I'm officially a fruitcake . . . You seriously didn't hear it?" I was secretly praying she was messing with me and actually heard it, but by the confused, weird expression on her face, I knew she didn't. I headed back to the car in quick strides.

"No," she said, falling into step with me. "What did it say?"

I jumped the ditch and got into the Impala. When she settled herself behind the wheel and pulled onto the road, I answered her. "It said, 'Alaris.'"

"Alaris?" Doubt crossed her face. "Are you sure you heard someone say that?"

I nodded. "The words were as clear as you speaking to me now." I chewed on my fingernail, not knowing what to do. Should I tell my parents about it and maybe seek professional help?

"I don't know what to tell you, Haven, except if you were crazy, you wouldn't be questioning your sanity."

"Maybe so," I said, watching the orange reddish sun slowly dip into the horizon as a duality between doubt and reason encompassed my thoughts.

* * *

I dropped Kimmie off at her house and headed home, trying not to think about the possibility of me being crazy. I thought about us getting our own place, which we could have done after we graduated high school, but Kimmie was the voice of reason, and I was glad I listened to her. Why waste the money we made working at the Full Moon Café on rent, utilities, and all the other expenses that came along with living on our own, when we could be staying with our parents and save the money we earned and also help pay for college? Our folks thought it was an excellent idea, especially mine. We weren't rich like Kimmie's family, and I knew my mom and dad were worried about how they'd be able to afford paying for my tuition. When I heard them one night discussing putting a second mortgage on the house so I could get my master's degree, I decided then I wouldn't allow them to go into debt for me. When I confronted them about my decision and stressed how much they'd given up for me throughout my childhood, my mother cried.

I turned onto our street, reliving in my mind that moment. I'd never forget for as long as I lived the relief on my parent's faces and how proud they were of me.

Our ranch style house was nestled in the center of a grove of trees at the end of the street, away from the other houses due to my father purchasing two lots on either side. We liked our privacy, and my father loved his workshop on the south side of the house. I was glad to be home, looking forward to sleeping in my own bed. I noticed all the lights were off, including the one on the porch. Mom always left it on when I was out after dark. How odd. Maybe they went to a movie I guessed as I pulled into the driveway. I turned the headlights off and cut the engine.

Silence.

The air was even still.

My stomach dropped.

Something wasn't right. I could feel it in my gut. I stepped out of the car. A thick, earthy concrete scent engulfed me—a sign of rainfall. As I approached the front door, I reached in my pocket for the pepper spray, pulled it out, and opened the front door. "Mom. Dad. I'm home." The whole house was dark. I pulled my cell from my pocket and turned the flashlight app on so I could see. There was a lingering burning smell like burnt plastic. I crossed the short hallway, the bright beam from my cell pointed straight ahead, brushing over the family pictures on the wall. I stepped into the kitchen that branched off to the left and flipped the switch on and off several times.

Nothing.

What the fuck?

"Mom, are you home?" I called, moving my phone in front of me so I could see. Ick. There must have been a dozen dead flies on the tiled floor, reminding me of the ones in the abandoned farmhouse. I stepped around the island in the center of the room. The toe of my shoe caught something. I tripped but grabbed the edge of the counter while jerking my cell down, illuminating the floor. I screamed and jumped back. In an instant my throat tightened and the tears flowed. "Noooo!" I quickly backed across the room and collapsed to the floor. My heart raced and broke all at the same time. With shaking fingers I dialed 9-1-1. Several sobs escaped my lips.

"Nine-one-one. Can I help you?"

My shaky fingers fluttered to my lips, the tips pressing on them.

"Can I help you?"

"I'm Haven Evergreen and . . . and . . ."

"It's okay. Take your time."

My heart split in half, and I bawled. "I . . . I . . . I just came home from Vegas and f-f-f-found my mom in the kitchen . . . on the floor . . . without her head."

Chapter Two

The dispatcher didn't reply. A flash of white light lit the dark room, briefly illuminating the kitchen and my mother's decapitated body lying in a heap on the floor nearby. A peal of thunder caused me to squeak and jump at the same time. The house shook.

I sucked in a sob. "Hello. Are . . . are you there?"

No response.

A frightening thought entered my mind. What if the murderer never left? He could still be here. I pushed myself off the floor, refusing to look at my mom. Lightning strobed through the kitchen window. Tears ran down my face. A disturbing thought poked through my desire to flee.

Dad.

Where was he? More than likely he'd be in his shop. He practically lived there building custom furniture. What if he were still alive? I had to check, but before I did, I tried to call 9-1-1 again.

No reception.

Damn phone. I made a move to leave the room, using the light app on my cell to see in front of me, when two tall men wearing hooded cloaks appeared what seemed to be out of thin air. Their bodies were half-transparent. I screamed and aimed my pepper spray toward their shadowed faces.

"Alaris," the one on the right hissed, sending chills down my spine.

"If you come any closer, I'll spray you. I'm not kidding." I waved the canister back and forth so they knew I meant business.

"I bet her blood tastes sweet," the other one said. I could hear the smile in his gravelly voice. As he took a step closer, his cloak billowed out from behind him as if it caught a draft of air. The radiance of my cell showed his black leather knee-high boots covered with tiny silver spikes.

I backed into the corner of the cabinets. I didn't know who the hell these people were and why they'd be here.

My pulse pounded in the side of my neck.

Why would he say that about my blood?

Vampires didn't exist.

The TV shows I watched weren't real. They were fiction.

Was I really nuts?

I could be imagining this, but then the other one spoke, joining his partner's side, jarring me out of my mental tirade.

"Scrumptious, I say, but we have our orders, and if we don't abide by them, we'll pay a heavy penalty."

"Just. One. Taste," the first one said. "No one will know but us. It's worth the risk. The other two didn't satisfy me. The male tasted . . . bitter."

They moved forward. Choking back a sob, I pushed the nozzle on the pepper spray down. He said other two which meant they killed my father as well. Oh, God!

Nothing.

The damn thing wasn't working.

In panic, I shook it.

What the fuck?

I threw the canister at them and dodged to my left.

Lightning flashed through the window, illuminating the granite kitchen counters and stainless steel appliances. One hooded guy moved to my right, the other flanked my other side. They were swift and appeared to be gliding across the room. Red eyes glowed from the shadowy depths of their hoods. I was toast. All I could do was force my mind and body to remember the taekwondo moves I learned while growing up. Hell, I was a black belt. Was. After graduating high school, I lost interests in tournaments and got lazy. I should have listened to my mom and–

Mom.

Dad.

I cupped a hand over my mouth, releasing muffled sobs. Once again the tears flowed. I didn't have the strength or resolve to fight. Whatever those beings were, whether they were a figment of my imagination or not, they won. I was done. I dropped to the floor into a sitting position and at the same time someone whistled. The sound came from across the room. A tall silhouette figure stood behind the entities moving toward me. They paused and turned. Flashing light from the thunderous storm provided glimpses in intervals of a dark-haired man wearing upper body armor the color of walnut molded to his chest and waist. The shoulders were protected with the same leather material with three thick pieces riveted together. The top was an upright wing attached to the next piece with an ornate metal buckle on each upper shoulder. There was more detail on the central part of the armor, but I couldn't see through the tears; however, his outfit reminded me of something out of a steampunk novel.

"Larkin," the hooded being to my left whispered in a high, creepy tone.

Larkin held a flat, round, pointy object in both hands, pinching them with his fingers. They glinted silver when he angled them toward my assailants. He raised his arms, bending them at the elbow, and in one swift flick of his wrists, he released the weapons. They flew across the room, striking the murderers through the throat. A horrible high-pitched screeching sound filled the room, causing me to cover my ears. The hooded creatures vanished.

On instinct, I hopped to my feet. The kitchen light came on, causing me to squint. My eyes were burning from the onslaught of tears. I blinked and refocused. Larkin was about twelve feet away, staring at me with what appeared to be an astonished expression on his handsome face. His piercing green eyes were locked onto mine, and for a split second, a sense of familiarity poked at the back of my brain. But then reality settled in, and I saw this moment as my cue to run. I made a move to do so and stopped when he spoke. "It is you." He sounded dumbfounded. "Alaris. You are alive. The rumors are true."

"I don't know who in the hell this Alaris is," I said, "but I'm Haven Evergreen. I just lost my family." The thought of never seeing or conversing with my mom and dad washed over me. A choking sob escaped my lips. I held my stomach, bent over, and bawled. The dark curtain of hair hid my face, but I could see him through my peripheral moving toward me in slow even strides. "I don't know why this is happening," I cried, rocking back and forth. "I don't understand . . . I don't understand . . . I don't understand."

"Your questions will be answered soon enough," Larkin softly said. He cupped his hands on my shoulders. I was too emotionally exhausted to stop him, and his warm touch was of comfort, not aggression. "You need to come with me, Alar . . . Haven."

I shook my head in protest and straightened my posture. "I'm not going anywhere. I don't even know you. You need to go. I called the cops before my phone died, and they might be here any moment. If they see you dressed like some kind of mythical warrior, they're going to arrest you."

He stepped away and pulled what looked like sharp silver stars out of the wooden cabinet doors. He stuck the weapons inside a pouch in his leather hip belt and turned to me. "Those two entities who were here and killed your parents are headhunters, also known as revenants, which are spirits not bound to a tether, unless some sort of sorcery is at play, and I have no doubt there is."

"This isn't real," I whispered. "It can't be. Maybe this is a horrible nightmare I can't awake from." I recalled a *Buffy the Vampire Slayer* episode where she was in a psychiatric ward because of the belief she was a vampire slayer when really she was crazy. That could be me now and everything I'd witnessed tonight was only an illusion, a figment of my imagination. If it were true, then my parents were still alive. Hope sprang forth within me, but then sank when Larkin frowned. He didn't need to tell me I was bullshitting myself. I knew I was, yet I couldn't wrap my head around the events that occurred tonight or him being here for that matter.

Larkin leveled his eyes with mine. "I assure you, this is real"—he touched his chest, his muscular bicep bulging as he did so—"I'm real."

"Fair enough." I wiped the tears off my cheeks, "but I'm not in the right frame of mind to–"

"You can't walk away from this." He sounded both desperate and demanding at the same time which pissed me off.

"I can do whatever the hell I want," I said, the back of my neck heating from the sudden anger rising within me. "I'm not leaving here. I have to bury my parents and take care of everything else that follows."

"You don't have a choice."

"I have a life here, Larkin, and I do have a choice. No one can dictate to me how I'm going to live my life. Period!" I wanted him to leave and this whole nightmare to end. I picked my cell off the floor, prepared to call 9-1-1, but then he spoke, causing me to pause.

"You don't have a choice," he reiterated, "because the headhunters are not going to stop entering your world until they kidnap you, or you come with me where you'll be protected." When I didn't say anything, he continued, "Do you really want to risk them killing someone else you love in an attempt to reach you?"

My heart dropped and my stomach twisted. A fresh set of tears followed. "You're telling me if I were here when those headhunters arrived, my parents would still be alive?" I choked out.

He held up a hand, his wide-eyed expression clearly saying he should have thought before he spoke. "That's not what I meant. Honestly, their behavior tonight was something they normally wouldn't do unless there was a purpose behind it which I plan to find out. However, because their actions were peculiar, if I were you, I wouldn't want to risk them harming other people I love."

Kimmie and her parents came to mind. They were like my second family. There was no way I'd take the chance of them getting hurt, so I had to go with Larkin. On any other day, I'd be thrilled to be with him. He was smokin' hot, better than the strippers in Vegas, but right now, I didn't give a shit. I realized then I had no idea where he was from and what brought him here to me. Why me? Despite his effort at relieving my conscious from the burden of being responsible for my folk's death, the guilt weighed heavily on my mind and heart. All I wanted to do was curl up inside a hole and die mourning the loss I could have prevented. But now wasn't the time.

"I don't want to put anyone else in danger," I confessed. I could hear the exhaustion in my voice, the defeat. "Where are we going?"

Relief crossed his face. "We're going to Atheon. It's one of the many outer planes beyond this realm, but I'll be taking you to the rural Midlands first. It's a place largely removed from the kingdom, and they have little control over."

"Kingdom?" I recalled hours ago when Kimmie and I were in that abandoned farmhouse. I heard a voice saying, *it's the king's daughter.* What the hell was going on? Could the voice have been talking about me? I highly doubted it.

He nodded. "I understand you're confused, but I promise you"—he touched my arm in a sympathetic manner—"you'll know everything soon enough." His eyes never strayed from mine. He was serious. I couldn't stop staring into the green abyss of his gaze. In the far edges of my subconscious mind, a spark of some kind of memory fired—a déjà vu of some sort where I'd peered into his face before, only it was of a boy instead of a man. His hand went to my cheek, but then he dropped it to his side and cleared his throat. "We have to go." And just like that, the memory dissolved.

I blinked. "How?"

He offered his hand like someone would in a friendly greeting. There was a silver ring on his index finger I hadn't noticed before. The band was thick with ornate swirly designs, and set on top was an off white round stone with fiery red and blue veins throughout, reminding me of an opal. He rubbed it with his thumb. I took his hand. Warmth filled my body. The kitchen around us rippled as if it were made of water and a stone had been tossed into it, and then the room disappeared along with the life I knew.

Chapter Three

As quickly as we left, we arrived in a vast meadow in the middle of the night. The pitch black sky was scattered with thousands of brilliant twinkling stars, and to my surprise, two white moons, not quite full, yet bright enough for me to see my surroundings. There were three men in leather armor similar to Larkin's astride powerful gray horses with flowing manes and tails. A large opulent carriage constructed of shiny dark wood and gold trim with glass windows stood nearby. It had four lanterns that appeared to be made from crystal, planted in the front and back, each one illuminated a buttery glow from within. The temperature felt like it was in the low seventies, and the air carried an aroma of freshly-cut grass. Larkin was still holding my hand and pulled me closer to him before letting go. He stiffened beside me, and the momentary awe I felt from the experience of teleporting to a different realm fizzled.

"What's the meaning of this, Draylan?" Larkin asked the dark blond-haired guy who kept staring at me. In fact, all three of them were gawking at me from their horses.

"The king requests her immediate presence," Draylan replied, reluctantly shifting his attention off me onto Larkin. "We're under strict orders to retrieve her."

Why would the king be eager to see me?

"Tell Merrack she needs time to adjust. Tell him she's been through a traumatic experience. The headhunters killed the humans who were taking care of Alaris and then went after her. She needs time to recover before anything else gets sprung on her."

"Headhunters?" the brown-haired guy asked, his voice pitched in surprise. He pulled the reins on the horse, shifting himself closer to us. "What the hell were headhunters doing there?"

Larkin rubbed the side of his face. "I don't know, Narik." He sounded concerned. Worried.

"Regardless," the one on Narik's left harshly said, "we have a job to complete. Everything else will have to be sorted out later." He jerked his head toward the carriage door. "The journey will be comfortable and allow you to visit with Alaris so you can—"

"What if I don't want to go?" I had enough of the testosterone. I was tired, and a piercing throb started above my right eyebrow. On top of it all, my heart was heavy, and my patience ran thin. All four men shifted their attention to me. The one who I interrupted had an annoyed expression on his pointy pale face. An odd look to him made me wonder if he was human. "None of you are my boss," I continued. "And news flash, Sparky, my name is *not* Alaris. It's Haven Evergreen. Take notes if you have to so you don't forget it."

Mr. pointy face laughed. It was a hollow mocking sound that immediately fired me up. My hands balled into fists. "You don't have a choice, Princess," he said. "I've never failed in my duties, and I'm not about to break my perfect record on account of an ignorant spitfire like yourself."

"I don't know who you think you are," I said, taking a step toward him, "but you can fuck off. I'm sick and tired of being told I don't have a choice. First, it was Larkin, and now it's you telling me the same damn thing. I'm not a Stepford wife, ya know?" After I said that, I realized they probably didn't know what I meant. Their blank expressions confirmed it. "A Stepford wife is subservient and obedient to her husband," I amended.

Larkin stepped in front of me, his back to me. "You're out of line, Farran, with your disrespect. I suggest you make a conscious effort to remember who you're talking to and humble yourself in her presence. If you had any wits about you, you'd apologize to the lady and try to understand our precarious situation. I thought you out of all people would."

Larkin was blocking my view of Farran, so I couldn't see his face, but I heard the derisive snort he made.

"We all know your history with Alaris," Farran said, confusing me. *History?* "Merrack even knows it. Why do you think he allowed you to go retrieve her?" When Larkin didn't answer, Farran continued, "He knew you'd do everything in your power to protect her and bring her safely to him. You've succeeded in your task, yet you're defying him by allowing your emotions toward her rule over your loyalty to him."

"If Merrack were knowledgeable about the situation of what Haven has been through and *lost*," Larkin stressed, "he'd agree with my decision to keep her here until she was emotionally capable of meeting him."

"Maybe so," Farran said, "but I'm not leaving here without her."

"I guess you'll be here for a while, then," Larkin said, stepping beside me. When I swayed to my left almost toppling over him, he caught my arm and steadied me on my feet. "Are you okay?" Concern entered his eyes.

"She's exhausted," Narik said. "She needs to rest."

He was right. I was tired, emotionally and physically. I also didn't want Larkin to get into trouble with this king guy whom I suspected I was connected to in some bizarre way. Besides, why prolong the inevitable? I was more of a let's-do-it-now-and-get-it-over-with type of gal anyway. I just didn't like tyrants and wouldn't put up with being disrespectfully ordered around. However, to keep the peace for Larkin's sake, I'd go on one stipulation.

I rubbed the back of my neck and yawned. "Narik is right. I am exhausted." I moved closer to Farran to address him. His pale blue eyes were cold and brimming with an arrogance that gave me the sudden urge to knock it right out of him. He folded his hands and leaned forward on the saddle. I squared my shoulders, refusing to allow him to intimidate me. "I'll come along on one condition."

He smirked. "And what might that be?"

I glanced over my shoulder at Larkin who had his arms tightly across his chest, closely watching Farran. "Larkin rides in the carriage with me and remains my escort while I meet this king of yours."

"Do you remember, Larkin?" the blond guy, Draylan, asked.

I made a face. "No, why would I?" Then, I remembered Farran mentioning Larkin's history with me. None of this made any sense. How could we have known each other, and what was my connection with the king? Farran called me princess, and the voice back at the abandoned farmhouse said she found the king's daughter. They couldn't be talking about me. But then I remembered the vivid dreams I had, the ones I told Kimmie about. Could they have been memories of this place? My sluggish mind tried to process all the questions racing through it, but I was too beat to focus on them. I waved a hand in the air distractedly when Draylan opened his mouth to reply. "Never mind. Larkin can fill me in. Right now, all I want to do is sit and relax." I headed to the carriage. As I walked by Larkin, I gave him a sidelong glance. "Are you coming?" He did a curt nod and turned on his heel. No one said a word, but I could feel them staring at me and hear the hoofs of the horses turning around.

Larkin stepped in front of me, but before he opened the door, I stopped to admire the coat of arms emblazoned on the panel. It had a golden dragon and mysterious Celtic knots and symbols around it. With the tips of my fingers, I traced the dragon design with great fondness.

"Does it mean something to you?" Larkin asked in a low voice next to my ear, causing my heart to race from the warmth of his body heat touching my bare arm and how sexy his voice sounded.

"I don't know," I answered, staring at the picture while trying to rein in my erratic emotions. I stepped inside the carriage and was immediately amazed at how luxurious it was. The interior was lined in a white silvery silk and upholstered in light blue velvet. The windows were dressed in taffeta curtains in the same hues as the plush couches. I sat next to the window, sinking comfortably into the cushions. I ran my hand along the soft velvet fabric, enjoying the feeling against my skin.

Larkin closed the door behind him and took a seat across from me. "I apologize for Farran's behavior. Sometimes he takes his duties too seriously."

"You don't need to apologize for him," I said. "He's an overbearing asshole. Plain and simple."

Larkin laughed. "I can't argue with you there." He paused, and at the same time the carriage lurched forward and wheeled across the meadow. "How are you holding up?"

I stared at my lap, and an image of my mother's headless body flashed in my mind. A lump formed in my throat. My vision blurred. "I'm tired, I'm confused, and most of all"—I glanced up at him. A tear slipped down my cheek.—"I'm heartbroken."

Sympathy softened his handsome features. "I'm sorry for your loss." He leaned forward and rested his forearms on his thighs. "There are no words to dull the trauma or heartache you're enduring right now, but please try to find some solace in knowing I'll do whatever is in my means to discover why this happened and to–"

"You already told me why my parents were murdered," my voice cracked. "It was because the headhunters were looking for me, and my mom and dad happened to be in their way." I took a deep trembling breath, allowing the tears to fall. "*I'm* the reason they're dead." I dropped my face into my hands and silently sobbed.

"I didn't mean to suggest you were the cause of their demise." He placed his hand on my knee, causing me to look into his pleading eyes. "Please don't entertain such thoughts because if you do, the guilt will rob you from a life of happiness and contentment."

"Then why?"

"I don't know," he said with a troubled look, "but I assure you, I'll get to the bottom of it and justice will be served."

I wiped the tears off my cheeks and nodded. He sat back while I lay on my side, facing him. I rested my head on a cream colored velvet pillow with golden tassels. "Why am I here?" My limbs felt as if someone poured lead into them, and my brain was on the verge of shutting down. But despite the extreme fatigue, I needed Larkin to answer a few questions.

"That's a loaded question."

"I want to know." When he looked away, possibly debating on where to begin, I quickly decided to make it easy on him. "Start from the beginning."

"Very well," he said, meeting my gaze. "I'll give you the short version, because you need to sleep. Then, I'll fill you in on the rest later. Is that a deal?"

I stretched my hand out. His eyes darted to it and back to my face. The corner of his mouth curled. Through the tiredness and grief that had been chaining me down since I stepped into my house today, my stomach managed to flip. He took my hand in his, and I shook it. "Deal."

Chapter Four

He sat back and cleared his throat. "Do you mind if I ask you some questions first?"

"Not at all." My heart raced from the sudden dose of adrenaline coursing through my veins, temporarily subduing my weariness in favor of curiosity. I sat up and brought my knees to my chest, wrapping my arms around my legs.

"Have you ever had any odd memories or dreams?" he asked.

My first thought was: *How did he know?* The dreams I'd told Kimmie about instantly came to mind. I nodded. "Dreams. They were so vivid I could swear they were real. To be honest, I thought I was losing my mind."

"Tell me about them."

"They were about a fantastical land with dark green rolling hills and a thick forest where I'd wander and play." I paused, trying to recreate it in my mind, but the vague images paled in comparison. "There was a unicorn. I remembered watching it roam through the forest. It was white, but when the pockets of sunshine gleamed down upon it, its hide shimmered a bluish color."

Larkin was studying me, hanging on my every word as if it was critical for him to devour each syllable in order to survive. "Anything else?"

I had the feeling he was anticipating for me to say something specific, but I had no idea what. "Not really. All the dreams were basically the same, but then again, I can't remember all of them." I rested my cheek on my knee and mindlessly spoke my thoughts without bothering to censor them. "I've had a pretty good childhood, but despite it all, I've always had a quiet sadness within, like how a person gets when she feels out of place but keeps it to herself. I never understood it, but . . ." Then it dawned on me, and I gaped at him.

"But," he prompted.

The pathways in my brain expanded, allowing the wheels of indirect information I'd been receiving since this evening come together and roll through my mind. "Wait a minute. It's starting to make some sense why I'm here." I scratched my head, tilting it to the side. "Well . . . sort of."

He was watching me with an intense expression. "Tell me what you're thinking."

"No," I said. "It's your turn. I'm not going to share anything else until you tell me why I'm here." I crossed my arms, determined to keep my trap shut until he shed some light on my situation. "And don't sugarcoat it, either, and I don't want none of this short version bullshit."

He took in the stubborn jut of my jaw. "Very well," he said, heaving a heavy sigh, "but I don't think it's a good idea considering what you've been through tonight."

"I'm a big girl. I think I can handle it," I answered while secretly wondering if I could and braced myself just in case he was about to rub salt into the gaping wound I had in my heart.

He locked his eyes on mine. "Your life on earth was a lie. The Evergreens weren't your biological parents."

I laughed. "Yeah, right. You're full of shit."

"I'm telling you the truth."

A flash of anger went through me. "No, you're not." When he opened his mouth to object, I continued, "I remember being four years old and my parents throwing a birthday party for me in our backyard. I recall it like it was yesterday."

"Planted memories," he simply stated.

I shook my head in irritation. "What? What the hell do you mean by *planted* memories?"

"At the age of twelve, you were compelled to forget about this place and new memories were planted in your head . . . memories of your host family."

"Yeah, right." I tightened my arms around me and rolled my eyes. "This is ridiculous." I stared out the window into the night. The forest we passed was bathed in the white glows of twin moons, their rays highlighting leaves, throwing double shadows of their majestic sizes onto the ground. I wondered what lurked within those timbers. I pointed to the window. "Now you're going to tell me there are werewolves out there, right?" I was being facetious, my words colored with sarcasm. When he raised his eyebrows and had that do-you-really-want-to-know look, I pursed my lips. "You're a nice guy," I said now massaging my temple, "and I appreciate you saving me from those headhunters, but I know about compulsion. I watch *The Vampire Diaries* and *The Originals*. The vampires in those shows sometimes uses compulsion to suit their purposes."

"Like in your case," he commented.

"No," I said, my voice elevated. I stuck my hand out and chopped the air with each word. "It's fiction!"

"Listen to me." He scooted to the edge of the couch and leaned forward on his splayed knees. "The TV shows and movies you've watched featuring magic and mythical beings have some truth to them, but the creators don't realize it."

"How so? Don't tell me they're under a spell, too. Hell, the world . . . *My* world . . . is under one, right?"

He nodded. "In a way, yes." When I narrowed my eyes, giving him a clear signal I thought he was bullshitting me, he raised his hands in a halting manner. "Hear me out. Have you ever heard of Atlantis?"

"I have. Plato wrote about it and archaeologists, and historians think they found parts of the city in coastal Spain." One of my goals in life was to take part in those expeditions. I read that Plato's grandfather heard the story about Atlantis and relayed it to Plato. He was told it happened 9,000 years before their time. Whether it was all true or not, I didn't know, but I'd love to hunt for the lost city.

"Before Atlantis, there was Atheon. Atlantians heard of us and tried to emulate our utopian-type society. What they didn't realize, though was we were far from perfect and by trying to recreate an outlandish version of our way of living, it ended up being their downfall."

The racing thoughts in my head stilled as if each one were a sentient being holding its breath. I sat up, captivated by what he was telling me. If it were true, then one of the most sought-after mysteries to be solved in my world was being unraveled to me. Of course, I was skeptical, so I asked, "How do you know this about Atlantis, and what does the people on earth being under a spell have to do with what you're telling me?"

"We know about Atlantis because of this." He raised his index finger with the ring adorning it. "This is a portal ring that allows the wearer to teleport from our world to yours. Only a few have been made, and each is designed specifically for the owner, meaning no one else can use it. To answer your next question, figuratively speaking, humans on earth are under a spell because soul memory, as we call it, recalls the ancient mysticism that once dwelled in their realm. It's part of their eternal history. It's part of them. Writers, producers, directors, painters, and the like, are more attuned to that nature of their existence. Therefore, without consciously being aware of it, they're actually tapping into that well of knowledge which in turn, trickles through onto paper, a canvas, and whatnot. Why do you think stories such as *Harry Potter* and *The Hobbit* are extremely popular?" He was on a roll and didn't wait for me to reply. Instead, he answered his own question. "Because it pulls at people's heartstrings and something else deep within them. A longing. Sometimes a sadness that they don't understand because the memories of those times are locked away within their true essence."

I nodded, knowing exactly what he meant. "I've had those feelings before."

"Exactly," he said.

"So you're telling me unicorns, fairies, trolls, and dragons exist?" It felt weird asking him that question because I was having a difficult time wrapping my head around everything he was telling me, even the bit about the Evergreens not being my biological parents. But I had to admit that deep down in the recesses of my entire being and in the far reaches of my mind, there had always been a wavering question mark concerning my relation to my folks. I looked nothing like them. Both had blonde hair and brown eyes, whereas my hair is black and my eyes are dark blue. They were tall, and I was five-foot-five. Differences such as those caused me to wonder a time or two if I'd been adopted. I even asked my mother once. She laughed, shook her head, and hugged me so tight I lost my breath. "No, sweetheart," she said and pulled back, holding me at arm's length. Her brown doe eyes were full of a fervent love that made me feel guilty for even questioning it. "You're our daughter," she adamantly said. "Your daddy and I love you with our whole hearts. You belong to us, and we didn't adopt you." I'd never questioned my relation to them again and actually forgot about it until this moment. A sudden, haunting feeling filled my chest. Oh, God. Larkin was telling me the truth. The Evergreens were my host family.

"They do," he answered. "But we can get into more of that later." He leaned forward and touched my knee. "Are you okay?" He studied my face, his eyes dancing across it. "You look pale."

"I need sleep," I said, lying again on the bench seat, turning my back to him. This was too much for me to handle. Maybe if I nodded off, I'd wake up in my bedroom to the smell of bacon and eggs my father liked to cook on Sunday mornings. I closed my eyes and surrendered myself to the misty regions of dreamland, all the while secretly praying for clarity, strength, and to have what happened tonight be nothing more than a nightmare.

Chapter Five

Someone was calling my name. The hushed tone was like a soft breeze navigating through the cracks of my deep slumber. Only the name wasn't Haven. It was Alaris. I jolted awake, half expecting to be back in my bedroom. I sat up and swung my feet to the floor. The light blue curtains were drawn over the windows. Damn. I was still in the carriage. Larkin must have closed them when I fell asleep. Everything that happened last night was real. Now what?

Larkin was rubbing the side of his face, his sleepy moss-green eyes meeting mine. "We're almost there." He massaged the back of his neck and yawned. "The king–"

"He's my father," I whispered, staring at nothing in particular. Everything that happened last night came rushing back at me. Larkin didn't specifically say the king was my father and neither did any of the other guys, but puzzling all the information from last night's events made it obvious to me. My stomach rolled from the realization that my life had been a complete lie, and I didn't know who the hell I was. The Evergreens were my parents. They loved me, nurtured me, and raised me in a good home. Had they known all along I wasn't their offspring? Were they part of this sick charade to trick me into believing I was someone else, living someone else's life? Why?

"Yes," he answered, "Merrack is your father."

I pushed the curtains aside to take in my surroundings and possibly get lost in them for a few moments. We were traveling on a narrow road between a sloping mountainous valley carpeted on either side of us in dark green grass and foliage. There were rocky, jagged plateaus high above us, crowned with immense, thick trees, obscuring from prying eyes what dwelled within its depths. A cave that housed a dragon, maybe. The thought of a dragon existing and the possibility of me ever seeing one stirred an array of feelings within me: excitement, love, and sadness. Last night, when I was admiring the one on the coat of arms, I'd never fathomed they might be real until now. I closed my eyes and stilled my thoughts in an attempt to thumb through my memories for an answer to why I felt that way. The sound of the clippety-clop of the horse's hooves and the muffled voices of the guys talking outside made it hard for me to concentrate. I opened my eyes and sat back. It was no use. Besides, my feelings were all over the place which made it difficult for me to focus on one thing at a time anyway.

"What are you thinking?" Larkin asked at the same time we stopped.

"Are we—"

There was a knock at the door.

"Yes," Larkin said.

The door opened. A stream of light poured into the carriage. Narik stuck his head in and looked at me. His brown eyes softened beneath his heavy lids. I bet the poor guy hadn't slept all night. A stab of guilt poked me. "Are you hungry?"

Actually, I was. My expression must have given it away because before I could answer, he stepped back. Larkin leaned over to see what Narik was doing.

A wicker basket with a red and white checkered cloth covering the contents appeared in the doorway. "We were passing a village during the night," Narik told us. "Brunhild was patiently waiting along the side of the road to give you these baked goods she made especially for you." He handed the basket to me. "There's also Orange Bliss in there."

Larkin make an appreciative sound. "I love Orange Bliss."

I set the basket beside me. "What's that?"

"It's a drink," Narik answered, "made with a special kind of oranges, cream, vanilla, sugar, and something else, but I'm not sure what. It's really good, though."

"Sounds like a creamsicle." I removed the cloth, releasing the wonderful aroma of cinnamon and caramel. "Mmmm." I breathed in the delicious smell. There were bite-sized cinnamon buns in a light blue crystal bowl that had scalloped edges and would be considered vintage in my world. Beside it was a glass bottle with a cork on top of its neck. It was filled with light orange liquid. "Did you guys get to eat?" I asked Narik, making my mind up right there if they hadn't I'd share with them. There was enough to ration out between the five of us.

He nodded. "We have. Thank you."

"How did Brun . . ." I forgot what her name was and looked at Larkin for help.

"Brunhild," Larkin and Narik answered in unison.

"Yes, her," I said. "How did she know I was coming, and why would she do this for me? She doesn't even know me."

"Time to saddle up," Farran said to Narik. "We need to keep to the schedule."

Narik looked in Farran's direction, held a finger up, and turned to me. "There are rumors about you flowing through every village and nook and cranny for months now. The king and queen haven't confirmed the rumors so people's curiosities continue to grow. Brunhild saw us a few days ago traveling near her home while she was out scavenging for herbs. She's an intuitive old gal, so she must have picked up on what we were doing and decided to whip up the items in the basket for you."

I heard and understood everything he said, every last bit, but what caught my immediate attention was one word: *queen*. If the king were my father. If (I still was having a hard time believing what Larkin told me last night, even though in my heart I knew it to be true.). The queen was my mother.

I could feel the color draining from my face. "The queen?" I didn't want this, I decided. The Evergreens were my parents, not Merrack or the queen, whatever her name was. Just because we were blood didn't mean they were Mom and Dad. They gave me up, but it was worse than that. They had me fooled into believing I was someone else and for years I lived a false life. My stomach twisted, and the hunger I felt moments ago vanished.

Narik shared a look with Larkin. There was no need for them to voice the message they were silently relaying to one another. Their expressions told me there was more, and Narik must have thought Larkin had shared that piece of information with me by the way his lips parted, and his eyes widened in a you-didn't-tell-her kind of way. Larkin slowly shook his head.

I had enough. "What the hell? When were you going to tell me I was going to meet my mother as well?"

"I'll let you discuss this in private," Narik said. He closed the door, leaving Larkin and me in silence.

I raised my eyebrows. I wasn't going to leave this alone. "Well?"

He ran his fingers through his dark hair and met my demanding gaze. "She's your step-mom. Datura is her name."

"Where's my birth mother?"

"After she had the memory spell cast on you and handed you over to the Evergreens, she died from a broken heart."

A weird, choking sound escaped my lips. "What?" I covered my mouth and bent forward as a sudden bout of tears flowed. My chest and throat tightened. I couldn't breathe.

Larkin jumped up and kneeled before me. He cradled my face in his hands, forcing me to look him in the eyes. "I'm sorry. I know this is a lot to take in and deal with, but I'll help you get through it." His thumbs brushed across my cheeks, swiping the tears away. "You need to calm yourself. Slowly breathe in through your nose and out your mouth . . . exactly. Good." The grip around my upper body loosened, and I was finally able to breathe normal again. I sat back, and Larkin returned to his seat.

"Why . . . why would she give me up?" My voice mirrored my feelings. Raw. Broken.

His forehead wrinkled. "I don't know. It's a question even Merrack can't answer, but he's determined to find out."

"How do you know about my mother dying from a broken heart?"

He had a sullen look on his face. "Our mothers were best friends. She held your mom's hand while she died."

"It doesn't make sense," I whispered. "If she loved me so much, why would she take drastic measures to get rid of me?"

He sadly shook his head. "I don't know."

"Wait a minute," I said when a thought occurred to me. "Merrack had no part in giving me up?"

"No, he didn't know he had a daughter until a few months ago."

My mouth dropped. "Are you serious?" My head felt like it was going to explode with all of this twisted information that didn't add up, and my feelings were running wild. I couldn't rein not one in so I could feel something other than sudden numbness. "Why?"

He pointed to the basket. "Can I have a drink of the Orange Bliss?" I handed it to him and watched as he uncorked the bottle and took a swig. He closed his eyes and sank back into the couch. "Ahhh." He licked his lips and looked at me. "This is some amazing stuff." He sat up and leaned forward, offering me the drink. "Try it. There are some magical properties in this stuff to relax you, and it's delightful."

I narrowed my eyes. "Are you going to answer my question?"

"I will after you try this."

"Fine." I accepted the bottle and cork from him and gingerly took a sip. The orange, creamy taste awakened my taste buds in a pleasant oh-so-yummy manner. I took a deeper drink, surprised I liked it so much since the liquid wasn't cold at all. The taste totally reminded me of a creamsicle but creamer and smoother. "Mmmm, this is yummy." I corked the bottle and placed it back in the basket. The tension in my body lifted, and I sighed at the groovy relaxed feeling that followed.

The corner of Larkin's mouth curled into a lopsided grin. "See, I knew you'd like it."

I smiled. I couldn't help it. He was so cute the way his face and green eyes lit up. I could see the boy in his handsome features. A sudden dose of familiarity sparked through me again. *History.* Farran said Larkin had history with me. But he needed to answer my first question before I went off onto another topic. "So why didn't Merrack know he sired a daughter?" I pressed.

"Because your mother Karrina left–"

"Her name was Karrina?" I repeated her name in my head thinking maybe it would unbolt the lock to my memories. Nothing. It was no use. When Larkin nodded. I gestured for him to continue.

"Karrina left him," he went on, "when she discovered she was pregnant with you. She fled to the Midlands where she was from and gave birth to you there. The reason for her hasty move was her fear in what Merrack was becoming. Once his father died, Merrack became king and the power went to his head. Darkness was taking hold of him."

"What do you mean?"

Larkin rubbed the back of his neck and sighed. "He began rattling on about elemental magic. If one were to possess all four, he'd have the most powerful magic in this realm which would be disastrous. His sudden obsession led him to dark places, seeking answers on how to accomplish such a lofty goal. During this time, his behavior grew darker and the changes in his appearance frightened Karrina, so she left and kept you a secret."

"Wow," is all I could say as my imagination went wild with fabricated scenarios that would have driven Karrina to take such drastic measures to abandon her relationship with Merrack. I had a hard time referring them as Mom and Dad, and I wondered while envisioning a dark shadow creeping inside of Merrack, if I'd ever be able to do so.

"Thankfully," Larkin said, "after Karrina broke his heart, he drank heavily. The alcohol numbed his senses and in turn caused him to discard his prior notions to seek ultimate power in favor of living a hedonistic life that nearly destroyed everything his father had worked hard to build."

"Why didn't he try to get Karrina back? If she was the love of his life, surely he would have realized why she left him and tried to make things right with her again." I knew I would have if I were in his shoes. What he'd done was counterproductive to the love he felt toward her, unless he wasn't truly in love but thought he was. Ya know, in love with the idea of being in love. I had a few friends like that who ended up wasting years of their lives with partners who they kept around more for comfort than anything else. Of course, their relationship eventually ended, and both parties were thrust back into singleville after years of having a companion.

"Can I have some more Orange Bliss?" He scooted to the edge of the couch and leaned over when I handed it to him. He took a drink while I bit into a mini cinnabon, savoring the luscious cinnamon and caramel combination. So yummy. "Merrack wasn't in the right frame of mind to try and win Karrina back," Larkin continued. "The excessive drinking and partying and his philandering ways trumped everything else, even his feelings toward her."

"That makes sense," I said more to myself than him. When I was in Vegas with Kimmie, we drank and partied most of the time we were there and thought of nothing else but having fun. "How did he—"

The carriage was slowing. Larkin peeked out the window, then looked at me. "We're here."

Shit. I wasn't done grilling him with questions that I wanted answered before I met Merrack and Datura. There was another one I wanted to ask him. What was it?

History.

Oh, right!

"Farran said you had history with me," I anxiously blurted in fear he wouldn't have a chance to respond. "What did he mean by that?"

Larkin maintained eye contact with me. I noticed they softened as well as his voice when he said, "We were best friends."

Stunned. I blinked at him. The door opened, and I knew my life would never be the same again.

Chapter Six

"The king is waiting," Farran said as he opened the door wider. I swallowed hard, twisting my hands in my lap. I knew I had to get up, but I couldn't take my eyes off Larkin's. In another life, we were best friends which explained the feelings of familiarity I had earlier. I tried with all my might to remember him, but I kept running into a blank wall. "I can't recall," I finally said.

The corners of his eyes crinkled. "It's okay. It's not your fault."

"Can the spell be broken?" I was thinking about *The Vampire Diaries*. In the show, if you were compelled when you turned into a vampire, the charm broke, and the person gained back her memory. The show was fiction. I knew that; however, what Larkin said last night about TV shows such as TVD had some truth to them.

"Yes," he answered, "and I suspect Merrack will want to break it so he can find out why you were sent to the earth realm in secret."

"Your mom was her best–"

Farran cleared his throat loudly, earning a dirty look from me. "You can save this conversation for later." In a swooping motion, he gestured for me to step out of the carriage.

I was about ready to tell him where to stick it when Larkin placed his hand on my knee. "My mom doesn't know why Karrina went to drastic measures to have you lose your memory and then pluck you from our world . . . at least, it's what she says." He rose and jerked his head toward the open door. "C'mon. I'll escort you."

Hesitantly, I followed Larkin outside, blinking against the bright rays of sunshine, wishing I had my shades. We were on a narrow cobblestone road lined with thick hedges. In front of us stood an elaborate gateway with pointed gables. Gray stone, dulled from age, shone through the green moss that covered its structure. A Gothic kingdom is what this reminded me of, giving me a sense of foreboding, yet at the same time, the archaeologist part of me, the student, was too much in awe to give into my reservations. There were two small turrets on each side behind the front peak and two decorative grayish green spires nestled on either side of the peak like two sentries, daring intruders to challenge it. Below it was a large arched entranceway with weird Celtic knots and what looked like rune symbols running up and down the length of the thick steel gray stone. A latticed black metal gate slowly rose, releasing a clanking, tired sound as Farran told me he thought I'd like to stretch my legs and walk up to the palace to get some fresh air after being cooped up all night. The carriage passed us as he was telling me this. I noticed no one was steering it, only two large beautiful chestnut horses with black manes and tails.

"I thought there was a coachman driving the carriage," I said to Larkin when Farran mounted his horse and road ahead of us with the other men.

"There's no need to," he said, glancing at me. "I have an affinity with horses."

We walked beneath the arch of the gateway. As soon as we passed through, a sharp metallic sound behind us caused me to look over my shoulder. The gate dropped with a loud angry thunk. I jumped at the harsh sound and bumped into Larkin's side.

"Easy there." He placed his hand on my arm to steady me.

"Sorry." I pulled my arm from him and wrapped it around myself. "I wasn't expecting that."

"It's understandable," he said, stepping in front of me and placing his hands on my shoulders. He had to be at least six four, his muscular frame shielding me from onlookers. My stomach flipped from the serious concern in his face and how close he was to me. He bent his head as if there were people within earshot, and he didn't want them to hear what he had to say. He spoke in the low tone of voice that I found sexy. "I can't imagine what you're going through right now, but I've seen the turmoil, the heartache, the anger, and uncertainty in your eyes. If I had the power to release those burdens from you, I would, but I don't. All I can do is assure you I will seek justice for the Evergreen's death and help you the best I can to adjust to your new station in life."

I bit my lip and nodded, surprised by his fervent pledge to me. I could have questioned his loyalty. I mean, hell, he didn't really know me. Sure, according to him we were the best of friends before Karrina ripped me from this world after she had my memories of Larkin and my life placed in some sort of a cryosleep—a state of suspended animation within the depths of my consciousness—but I didn't question it. So far he'd been nothing but kind to me, and I had to admit, I did feel comfortable around him. I could see us becoming good friends again.

He dropped his hands from my shoulders and stepped aside, allowing me to take in the large courtyard. A high wall built of heavy gray stone encompassed the acres of lush green land filled with many tall, full trees, except for a large break in the wall that opened into the mouth of deep dark forest. Set high on a craggy grass hill was a stone castle-like palace the color of baked-yellow, worn but hearty in structure. A large round turret with squared notches was attached to the front. Twenty or more steps descended from its top to the ground. I guessed it to be an entrance. The four peaked towers on each corner of the building had dark, shiny bluish gray pointy roofs that reminded me of a witch's hat and arched windows below it. The backdrop of the forested, sloping landscape set an amazing fairy tale contrast to the seemly imposing palace. I imagined standing inside one of those towers looking through the window over the peaks and valley that stretched across the horizon. What an awesome sight that would be.

"One day this will be all yours," Larkin said as we walked beneath a canopy of trees on the cobblestone road that led to the palace.

My stomach lurched when he said it. "I don't want this," I said and meant it. "I don't want all the responsibility." The thought of being in charge of other people's lives sickened me. The only life I wanted to be responsible for was my own. I realized then I didn't know what type of government Atheon followed other than a monarchy, but regardless, I had no interest in ruling.

"You don't have a—"

"Don't you even say it," I said, cutting him off. We stopped, and with my fingertip I playfully jabbed his chest, even though he couldn't feel it beneath the leather armor he wore.

Larkin laughed and raised his hands, palms facing me. "What?" He was playing dumb, but he knew exactly what I was referring to.

Someone giggled. The sound was light and airy, like a tiny tinkling bell. I looked up to the right where the sound came from—or so I thought—but didn't see anything.

"You know what?" I challenged, biting back a smile. "I do have a choice, Larkin. Like I told you earlier, it's my life, and no one can dictate to me how to live it. I have plans."

The humor slid off his face. "You can't go back . . . at least not right now."

"I know." A lump formed in my throat, and my eyes misted over. A stray tear escaped. It slowly trailed down my cheek, hot and wet. I looked away when I saw the immediate sympathy enter Larkin's face. I walked across the courtyard toward the palace, all the while forcing myself not to think about what happened to my parents. He was by side, falling into step with me. I could feel his awkward silence, struggling for words to ease my pain. To save him the trouble, I cleared my throat, silently hoping my voice wouldn't fail me when I spoke. "If you're genuine in your promise to find out why those headhunters came into my world, killed"—I swallowed hard and took a couple deep breaths—"um, brutally destroyed my family, and went after me . . . I'll do my best to adjust to this realm; however, I want you to capture them." I looked at him, feeling the anger and determination harden my face. "When you do, I want to be there to question them." My mind was made up. I didn't even have to think about it. The idea came from a sudden flash conceived from the turmoil of my loss and then born from the silent rage that had been growing inside since last night.

"I can't promise," he said.

"Why?"

"Because you're the future queen. I can't endanger your life," he answered matter-of-factly.

I laughed from the absurdity of his statement. "Datura is the queen, not me. I could give two shits about it. Once the headhunters are taken care of, I want you to return me to my own realm. Like I told you before, I have a life there. I worked hard in school to get where I'm at, and I'm supposed to go to a university next semester, but most importantly, I'd like to put my parents to rest. They deserve it, and I need to do that for closure. Do you understand what I'm saying?"

He nodded. "I do, but you have to realize your parents will be put to rest before you're able to return, and there will be the question of your disappearance. I'm sure there's a search party for you as we speak."

My heart sank. I never even considered those things. Kimmie came to mind, and I wondered how she was dealing with the situation. I'm sure she was being questioned by the police and FBI and was beside herself with worry. I felt like shit for putting her and her family through this, but there was nothing I could do. I came here to protect them. Otherwise, I would have never left. I had to get back home as soon as possible. I had to convince Larkin to help me. "I never thought about that," I said. There were birds chirping and singing all around us. I looked up into the trees but couldn't see them. They must be higher up on the branches, I thought. "But regardless, I plan to return after we find out why the headhunters did what they did to my parents and why they're interested in me."

Larkin cocked an eyebrow. "We?"

"Yes, you and I," I said, motioning between him and me.

He shook his head. "Not happening."

I was about to object when a man and woman exited from the round tower that projected vertically from the front of the palace. They proceeded down the stairs. From a distance, I couldn't make out what they looked like, only that he was tall, and she was probably two or three inches taller than me. My stomach rolled with nerves.

I nodded toward the couple. "Is that Merrack and Datura?"

"Yes," Larkin answered. "Merrack made sure no one would be around. He wants to keep you a secret until the time arrives to announce your presence. He also didn't want you to endure being a spectacle in front of hundreds of critical and curious eyes. I imagine he'll do the best he can to make sure you feel as comfortable as possible in a situation such as yours."

Hundreds of eyes?

My nerves frayed at the thought of a crowd of people staring at me. I hated being the center of attention, except for when I was drinking and having a blast. Then I didn't care. I thought about Kimmie and me going to parties in college, drinking jungle juice, playing quarters, dancing, and laughing. The memories caused a fierce ache in my heart. I missed my best friend. I missed my life where I took my studies and job seriously yet had a good time all the same. I was responsible and always looked out for Kimmie and my other good friends, but now these strangers— because let's face it, they were strangers—expected me to rule someday. No. I refused to live a life in charge of hundreds if not thousands of souls.

As we got closer to the palace, I couldn't help but admire the regal crowned bronze gas lamps that were posted a few feet apart along the rest of the cobblestone path. The oaks thinned and expanded across hundreds of acres of land to where we were no longer beneath its cover. I squinted against the bright sun, once again wishing I had my sunglasses. In the distance I could make out stone houses dotted between the oaks, with thatched roofs and what looked like rectangular windows. My heart squeezed at the sight, and I had a déjà vu moment, like I'd been there before, but that couldn't be right.

"Have I been to one of those houses before?" I asked Larkin.

"No, why?"

"Because I feel like I have."

He rubbed the side of his chin and looked at me. "Those types of houses are common in the Midlands where you and I are from. You have a similar house, only bigger and more cheerful."

"What do you mean I have a similar house? I don't own a house." Maybe he meant I lived in one, once upon a time ago, when I was here with Karrina.

"The house you were born in and grew up in . . . well, until you were sent to the earth realm . . . is yours, Alaris. My mother has taken care of it for all of these years."

"Haven," I corrected him. "My name is Haven, and why would your mom do such a thing?"

He sighed. "I understand you're used to the name Haven, but your birth name is Alaris. You need to get accustomed to it because it's how everyone here is going to refer to you. On the matter of my mother troubling herself with another house to upkeep, I always found it a fruitless act to perform, and I've mentioned it to her more than once. Her answer was always the same: she promised your mom to preserve it in her memory."

He was right on the Alaris part. I didn't like it, but hell, I had to face the fact I was in a realm where people knew me or of me by that name. So I sucked it up and told myself I'd go along with it. Then I thought about his mom. How odd she would do that, but then again she was honoring her BFF's wishes. Wouldn't I do the same thing for Kimmie? Of course, I would, especially if that was one of her dying wishes.

"Okay, Alaris it is," I said under my breath as we approached the palace.

Merrack and Datura were walking toward us now. I took a deep breath, trying to control the hammering in my chest, silently telling myself I got this. My goal was simple. I'd play along and do what I had to so I could go back home.

Chapter Seven

My attention immediately centered on Datura. Her straight platinum blonde hair fell down the back of an elegant flowing dark blue velvet dress. The front was made of brocade gold-colored fabric. At the end of the long sleeves, the cuffs were decorated with gold patterns. Her porcelain skin was flawless on her heart-shaped face that bore high cheekbones. My God, she was beautiful. I suddenly felt like a plain Jane with my khaki cargo shorts, white boyfriend T-shirt, and brown Dr. Marten sandals. Don't even get me started on my hair. I was sure it looked like a hideous rat's nest. Ugh.

"This feels like a dream," Merrack said when they reached us, his mouth agape in astonishment, tearing my attention away from Datura who sent me a pleasant smile. She seemed friendly, easing my nerves a bit. "You look exactly like your mother."

My mind observed him in a quick analytical way, trying to find similar physical attributes I shared with him. He had a short, well-trimmed beard and chestnut eyes the same color as his thick head of hair that ended in loose curls on the back of his neck. My eyes were dark blue, and my hair was straight. He was handsome, though, and well-built, but the only resemblance I shared with him was the shape of his eyes were round, almost heavy-lidded—bedroom eyes is what some people called it. I possessed the same feature. In fact, Kimmie used to tease me about how sexy they were which always made me laugh.

"Alaris, this is Merrack the king and Datura the queen," Larkin said, gesturing to each one as he spoke their name. "Your father and step-mother."

I didn't know whether to bow or curtsy, so I was relieved when Datura offered me her hand. Her fingers were long and slender, nails perfectly manicured, and she wore several jeweled rings. When I took her hand, it was cold against my sweaty palm. I should have discreetly wiped off the dampness on my shorts first. I silently chastised myself. I was so out of my comfort zone that it was horrible. Thankfully, Datura didn't display any hints of disgust. Instead, she shook it gracefully, and her crystal blues eyes held a welcoming sparkle.

"It's a pleasure to know you, Alaris," she said, her tone smooth and sweet like melted chocolate. "I'm sorry we had to meet in the throes of your misfortune. I wish it could have been under better circumstances."

"A misfortune for all of us," Merrack corrected.

"But of course." Datura released her grip from mine, her charming smile never faltering.

"I take it Farran filled you in about the headhunters," Larkin said more as a statement than a question.

Merrack tore his eyes away from me to address Larkin and nodded. "Indeed he did but only a loose version of what transpired since he didn't witness the attacks. Therefore, I'll expect a full report from you tonight after dinner."

Larkin dipped his head in acknowledgment to Merrack's orders.

"I can tell you what happened," I said, hoping to save Larkin the trouble of writing a personal statement on the matter, even though I preferred not to talk about it.

"You may," Merrack answered, "when you feel ready to do so. There's no need to rush things."

"Yes, there is," I said, wondering if he even cared about what the headhunters had done to my family. Larkin lightly cleared his throat beside me as if to signal for me to shut up. I ignored it. "We need to find out why the headhunters came into my world, destroyed my family, and went after me. Then I should decide what their punishment will be."

"Let's walk while we discuss this matter"—Merrack gestured toward the palace—"but I prefer we do it behind closed doors."

"That's fine," I said, realizing he was right. This was a family matter and needed to be dealt with privately. "I think it would be best to talk about this in the comforts of your home."

A warm smile crossed Merrack's face. He was pleased with my response. "This is now your home, too."

I was about to object in a gracious but firm manner, but Larkin shot me a wide-eyed look. He was walking beside me on my right while the other two were to my left, so they didn't catch his silent message: *Keep your mouth shut and play along.* A glimmer of hope rose within me that Larkin was going to allow me to take part in his mission to capture the headhunters, resolve the situation, and then take me back home. I kept quiet and nodded instead.

"I prepared a room for you," Datura said. "I trust it'll be to your liking."

"I'm sure it'll be fine," I answered. "You didn't need to trouble yourself over me." I had to admit I was surprised at how warm and welcoming they were toward me, especially Datura. I wasn't even a blood relative of hers, and I was sure it was hard on her to all of a sudden be a step-mother to someone she didn't even know existed until recently. Did she even want me in her life? Would she feel threatened? Jealous? Would my presence in the palace stifle her and throw her whole game off? Hell, I didn't know. I'd have to make a point to assure her I was no threat to her, I could take care of myself, and I wasn't starving for fatherly attention or compliments. I had an awesome father who loved me and taught me how to be self-reliant.

Had.

My expression fell at that heartbreaking reminder. My eyes prickled. We reached the limestone steps to the palace. Merrack led the way. I followed behind Datura while Larkin picked up the rear. I was thankful they couldn't see my face because I was sure it was blotchy from the emotional strain I was desperately trying to get a handle on.

"It was no trouble on my part," Datura answered as we climbed the steps. "I've always wanted a daughter and was delighted to learn Merrack has one. Now I have someone to preen with before a ball or a big event. To be frank, Alaris, it can be dull at times being the only female in our household."

"Well, I'm not here to steal your thunder, and I appreciate your kindness."

"Oh, I never thought such a thing," Datura said over her shoulder punctuating it with a lighthearted laugh. "Stealing my thunder. No, dear, I imagine you would rather be in the earth realm than here; however, fate brought you to us, and now you have a new path to follow, one of greatness and glory."

I swallowed the words on the verge of rolling off my tongue and tightened my lips. I wanted so badly to tell her fate could piss off. I chose my own path, and this wasn't it, but I didn't.

We entered the tower through a shiny arched oak door set into the stonework. I couldn't help but admire the wrought iron hinges and the two decorative bands across the top and bottom of the woodwork. It reminded me of a tree turned sideways with thin branches curled inward in a spiral pattern and sparsely spaced ornate leaves placed across them. It was gorgeous. With a start, I realized I was anxious to see what the inside looked like.

"In your world, this is called a mudroom," Datura told me when we stepped into a circular chamber. Soft beams of light filtered through arched stained glass windows high above us. A couple granite benches sat across from each other, and cast iron gas lamps were anchored to the stone wall. "You'll find," she continued as we entered the palace, "we have similar amenities as you do. We're far from being barbaric."

We halted in a vast room with shiny blue and cream checkered marbled floors. An immense crystal chandelier hung above us. There were several wooden doors in shapes of teardrops on either side of the room. Straight ahead was a grand wrought iron staircase with beautiful circular designs. The top curled and then swooped upward. The stairs branched off the landing, leading to the second floor.

"Upstairs are the sleeping chambers. Each has a master bath," Datura said. "To the left of us, through the first door is the kitchen. The second is the dining room, and the third is what you refer to in your world as the living room. On your right, the first door is the library. The one after that is the study, and the third is the restroom. Merrack's office is behind the staircase. Obviously, you can't see it from here, but that's where he holds his meetings." She turned to her right, and we all followed her. "Let me give you a quick tour of the bottom floor."

She showed me the rooms, and I couldn't help but be impressed by the architecture. Each one had a whimsical sort of Gothic feel with pointed arched doorways, curved ornate oak furniture, and long, heavy curtains that draped elegantly over the windows in colors of deep blue and gold. The kitchen, on the other hand, was the black sheep compared to the rest of the palace I'd seen so far.

"As you can see"—Datura made a sweeping gesture—"the kitchen is much different than the other living spaces."

She was right. It was spacious and had a witchy, country rustic flair I absolutely adored. The stone fireplace with a cauldron hanging inside was neat. Above a worn timber island in the center of the room were copper pots and pans. I continued to drink in my surroundings. Drying herbs hung near the deep porcelain sinks beside a black wired basket filled with garlic. I thought the glass-front rustic green wood cabinets, open shelves, and pine countertops were cool. I felt as if I stepped into a fairy tale kitchen and was surprised to see a huge black and chrome refrigerator and a cast iron stove with two ovens and eight burners. Wow. I think I loved this room as much as the library.

"Why is the kitchen different than the other rooms?" I noticed a piece of paper stuck to the front of the fridge and wondered what it said? It looked like a list of some sort. Grocery?

"Because," Merrack answered, "our kitchen and laundry help prefers an earthier environment to work in, whereas our other help couldn't care less."

Datura noticed me staring at the fridge. "If you want something, a certain food or beverage, write it down, and place it on the refrigerator before you turn in for the night. Our nightly worker will do his best to get it for you or an item similar. All you have to do in return is leave a bowl of cream and some fresh bread over there"—She indicated to the round table built from rough timber toward the middle of the room. There was a bowl of fruit in the center—"as a gesture of appreciation. And whatever you do, never ever criticize his work."

My eyebrows pulled together as I wondered what type of help she had. "Why?"

"The little bugger," Merrack answered with a half-smile, "will undo what he did and leave our household, and let me tell ya, it's hard finding a replacement."

Little bugger?

"You look confused," Larkin said with an amused expression on his face.

"Um, yeah." I looked at Datura. "What if I wanted a Snickers candy bar from my world?"

"Then he'll do his best to retrieve it for you," she simply answered.

"How?" This was so weird. What and who in the hell were we talking about? Obviously, this "worker" had the ability to teleport between worlds. I wondered if he owned a ring like Larkin's. But I thought Larkin mentioned earlier only a few were made. I was confused on every level imaginable.

"You have a lot to learn about our world my dear," Merrack said. "Once the spell cast on you is broken, you won't be nearly as perplexed as you are now."

My heart lurched at the thought of uncorking memories of my past. Would I be able to cope with the overwhelming flood of recall on a life stolen from me? What type of feelings would I encounter during the process? Right now, a bitter and angry taste remained in my mouth about the whole thing, but I was also aware I didn't know the reasons behind Karrina's hasty and life-changing decision to rip her child from her life and world. I reminded myself I had to first give her the benefit of the doubt before I allowed resentment and other dark feelings roost inside me.

"When will that be?" I asked as we headed back to the great hall and paused at the foot of the stairs.

Datura tucked a lock of hair behind her ear, and with a start, I noticed for the first time its top was pointed like Spock in *Star Trek,* only her ear was smaller than his.

What the fuck?

I shifted my attention back on Merrack before Datura caught me gawking at her. Out the corner of my eye, I saw Larkin looking at me. He must have caught my surprise. I ignored him and focused on Merrack.

"I'd like to do it as soon as possible," he replied. "However, the decision as to when is up to you. Tell me, and I'll make the preparations."

"What if I don't want to?" I had every intention to go through with it, but I wanted to see what he'd say if I chose the opposite. Would he respect my decision, or would he force me to comply with his wishes?

Datura stiffened next to me. "What if you don't want to what?"

"Go through with breaking the charm."

"Why would you not want to?" Merrack asked in surprise as if the thought I might refuse never occurred to him.

"I don't know. Maybe because I'm afraid of the things I'll remember. What if afterward I develop psychological problems and become a basket case? Maybe I don't want to risk the chance."

Merrack stroked his beard in contemplation. "I've never thought about the possible side effects."

"Alaris," Datura said in a calm syrupy sweet voice, "you'll be fine. In fact, it'll probably be the best decision you've ever made."

I didn't think so. The best decision I'd ever made was breaking up with Brody. I wasted two years with that cheating, lying sack of shit. One night his drunken ass backhanded me, and then I surprised him when my fist met his nose with a loud crunch. I ended our toxic relationship right there and never turned back.

"Well," Merrack interjected, disappointment plain on his face, "if Alaris doesn't want to–"

"I'll do it," I interrupted, appreciating he'd respect my decision either way, "but after we discuss the issue regarding the headhunters."

Merrack smiled and clapped his hands together. "Splendid. Datura will show you to your room so you can get some rest. Tonight after dinner, we'll meet in my office, and you and Larkin may fill me in on what transpired last night. In the meantime, I have another matter of importance to discuss with Larkin that needs to be addressed right away."

Larkin furrowed his brow which made me curious about what seemed to be a crucial matter. It appeared the same thought ran through his mind, as well. He dipped his head in acknowledgment and followed Merrack to his office, sneaking a peek at me as he walked by, leaving me alone with Datura and a nervous stomach.

Chapter Eight

U pstairs was a large elaborate hallway with a rounded ceiling dressed in the same earthy green wood as the kitchen cabinets. The matching wainscoting along the walls with the damask golden wallpaper above it whispered of hidden secrets and mystery. There were two rooms on either end of the corridor and half a dozen spread out in between. Teardrop-shaped gas lanterns hung from cast iron spirals mounted to the walls. Its frosted glass glowed a sunset orange from the hall lamps.

Datura turned right, and I followed her as she told me her and Merrack's bedroom was the one on the far left down the hall. The other rooms were for guests. She pushed opened the heavy oak door. "This is your room. I hope it's to your liking."

I walked in and immediately fell in love with everything. The chamber itself was massive. A four-poster bed with sheer curtains draped around it, sat in the center. Victorian style furniture made me feel as if I stepped back in time. I went to the antique vanity that was a cream colored wood and made the mistake of glancing at my reflection in the round mirror. I looked awful. My dark hair was a mess, my shirt wrinkled, and the whites of my eyes were bloodshot. No wonder Merrack told me I should get some rest.

"The restroom is here." Datura opened the door a few feet away from the vanity. "There are fresh towels, soap, toothbrush; everything you need."

I poked my head in. Holy cow. The large bathroom sported a round sunken tub, an enclosed shower, a nice shiny black granite countertop, a fancy oak linen closet, and a toilet.

Datura opened the closet door that was on the other side of the vanity and flicked on a light. It was full of clothes, alarming me. She stepped back as I walked inside.

I took a white boho style blouse off the hanger. Medium. I turned and narrowed my eyes. "How did you guys know my size?"

"The witch we employed to find you told us."

"Who?"

"Brunhild."

"The one who made the Orange Bliss and mini cinnamon buns for me?"

"Yes."

I hung the blouse back up and turned the closet light off. "How did you and Merrack find out about me?"

A slow smile crossed her lips, but then it disappeared as quickly as it came. She frowned. "Larkin's mom Fiona was ill. The poor dear picked the wrong berries and ate them, mistaking the fruit for an almost identical kind. Unfortunately, they were poisonous. Shortly after, she ran a high fever and became delirious, talking rubbish. Alarmed, Larkin asked for our help. Of course, we immediately came to his aid since his loyalty to Merrack has never wavered, and he's one of the best warriors we have. As we assisted in the matter, Fiona's hallucinations grew. She thought the healer who was working to cure her was Karrina. Fiona spoke what at first we thought was nonsense about Karrina having a daughter of whom she was quite fond of, begging her not to send you away to another realm." She paused and stared passed me in thought. I was afraid she wouldn't tell me the rest, but then she met my questioning eyes. "When Larkin became upset, we decided to pursue the possibility Fiona was telling the truth."

"What happened to Fiona? Is she okay?" I thought about Larkin and wondered how he felt when he discovered his mother knew all along what happened to me but never told him . . . or maybe she did. I wasn't sure. The conversation in the carriage seemed like a distant dream. I couldn't recall him saying anything to me about him knowing where I was before Fiona's delusional confession to the king and queen.

Datura stood in the doorway now, clearly ready to leave me on my own. She tucked her hair behind her ear like she done earlier, revealing her pointy ear. "She's doing fine now."

"Merrack didn't punish her for never telling him about me?"

"No, he didn't." She turned to leave.

"Wait," I said, stopping her. "Can I ask you another question?"

"Yes, of course." She clasped her hands in front of her, giving me her full attention with a patient, almost motherly expression on her beautiful face.

"How come you have pointy ears?" There! I asked. I was a blunt and bold person. It was better for her to find out now than later. I hoped I didn't offend her and became relieved when she smiled and absently touched the tip of her ear.

"I'm a fairy from the Solas clan."

My eyes widened. "Are you serious?" I inwardly cringed after those words flew out of my mouth. *Of course she's serious, dumbass. Look where you're at. Toto, I've a feeling we're not in Kansas anymore or in my case, Washington state.*

Amusement broke across her face. "I am."

The room shifted out of place for a few seconds. All the things Larkin told me about magic and mythical beings were true. Forget about Dorothy, I was Alice, and Atheon was fucking Wonderland.

Datura reached her hand out and stepped forward as if she was going to come to my aid. "Are you okay? You look pale."

I blinked and waved her off. "I'm fine. This is a lot to take in." I felt so out of place here and longed to turn back time. I wanted to be home with my parents. We might not have been blood, and even though I didn't know what part they played in this twisted scheme to toy with my life and warp it to suit whatever purpose, I still loved them. They were Mom and Dad.

"Yes, it is," she agreed. "I thought maybe Larkin had already told you about me."

I rubbed my forehead in circular motions. "No, he didn't tell me you were a fairy. I thought if fairies did exist, they were small like Tinker Bell."

"We are different types. Some are small while others are human size such as myself."

"Okay." All I could think about was how was I going to acclimate to a world I knew nothing of, while desperately wanting to be back in my own? An image of my mother's headless body flashed in my mind. I winced and felt as if I were kicked in the stomach. I wrapped my arms around my middle and told myself I needed to get a grip on my emotions, at least in the presence of company. I would seek justice for the slaughter of my parents and then return home.

"I suggest you bathe and get some rest," Datura said. "I know Atheon is different from your world, but soon your memories will be restored and you won't feel so out of place and confused." She turned and left, closing the door behind her.

I'd never felt so sad and alone in my entire life.

* * *

After I cried my eyes out in the elaborate spa-like shower that took me what felt like forever to figure out which knob did what, I got dressed. The antique bureau was full of pretty brand new, lacey undergarments. They fit me perfectly which bothered me. How did Brunhild know what size I wore? She had to have been the voice I heard when Kimmie and I were in the abandoned farmhouse. It made sense, but how she saw me, I didn't know. I decided on wearing the white boho blouse I'd picked up earlier and a pair of brown stretchy pants. I found some makeup in the vanity drawer and was about to apply some when there was a knock at the door.

"Yes," I said, crossing the room to answer when a second knock followed the first.

"May I come in?" a masculine voice asked.

I opened the door and recognized him right away. Draylan. He had a silver tray in his hands with a croissant sandwich of some kind on a vintage blue and white china plate. A teacup sat on a matching saucer beside it. Worry stained his honey-colored eyes. I wondered why and at the same time realized this was the first I'd seen him without his armor. My gaze skimmed his black pants and T-shirt before reaching his face.

"Datura thought maybe you wanted some lunch and requested I'd bring this to you."

"Oh." I moved out of the way, so he could step into the room. "You can put it on the desk." I motioned to the right side of my bed and watched as he crossed the room. He was tall and muscular like Larkin. In fact, all the guys I'd met so far were. I guessed they had to be in supreme shape in order to be part of an elite group of warriors here in Atheon. "It was nice of Datura to think of me."

"She was concerned about you." He set the tray down as I moved beside him to see what exactly he brought. "She can empathize with what you're going through regarding what happened to your family."

I jerked my head up from examining the sandwich he brought that looked like a chicken salad with red grapes and walnuts. "How so?"

He scratched his head, mussing his dark blond hair, and frowned. "Her family was slaughtered as well."

I gasped and covered my mouth. "Oh, my God! By who?" My heart broke for her, and I had a newfound feeling of warmth toward her.

"By a band of Murks."

I made a face. "Murks. What the hell is that?"

"They're dark beings," he answered, "like the ones who haunt children's dreams."

I barked out a sharp laugh and shook my head. "Wow." Not knowing what else to do, I went to the vanity on the other side of the room and grabbed an elastic from the top drawer. My hair was still damp from the shower, so I raked my fingers through it, then pulled my dark tresses into a ponytail. I think I was in shock, wondering how far this rabbit hole was going to go.

"What?" Draylan asked, his forehead wrinkling.

"The more I learn about this realm," I said, licking my lips from the sudden dryness in my mouth, "the more I feel isolated from reality. I feel as if my sanity is hanging by a thin string, and any moment now someone is going to clip it." He moved out of the way when I returned to my spot next to him. I pointed to the teacup. "What's in this?" I seriously needed a drink. I picked it up and sniffed it. The milky liquid smelled like butterscotch.

"An herbal tea called Ashwagandha, with sugar, milk, and honey. It'll help with your stress."

I cocked an eyebrow. "Really?"

"Yes," he answered confidently. "We always drink it if we had a bad night while out on patrol. The taste isn't fantastic by any means, but it's palatable and does the trick. It also helps you sleep"—he glanced at my eyes that I knew were still bloodshot and now swollen from crying —"which looks like you can use some more of."

"You can be honest and tell me I look like shit," I said. "It won't hurt my feelings because I know I do."

He laughed. "You're far from looking like crap. What I mean is you're tired and secretly mourning the loss of your parents, which is an emotional strain on the mind and body on its own. Not to mention your memories of Atheon are sealed from your conscious mind so everything you're learning here comes as a shock to you."

"You're a perceptive person." I took a sip. The tea was warm and tasted kind of earthy, but the milk, sugar, and honey made it tolerable. When I swallowed, a warming sensation trailed down my lungs and into my chest, spreading across it in a soothing manner. Yeah, this tea wasn't all that great, but I could tell right away the herb was doing its trick. The tension in my neck was subsiding. I flashed Draylan a lazy smile. "This is working."

The corners of his mouth curled. "Good. I'll leave you to your lunch and rest then."

"Don't go yet," I said when he turned to leave. "If you don't mind me eating in front of you, I'd like for you to stay and visit for a while. I want to know more about the Murks and what you and the other guys do, unless you have to be somewhere." I liked Draylan. He seemed like a nice guy and around my age. I wasn't ready to be alone with my thoughts and secretly hoped he'd stay and keep me company.

"I would love to," he replied, "but I have to go workout and train."

"Oh." I looked down, trying to disguise my disappointment. I really didn't want to be alone right now. "I understand." I took another drink of the tea, chugging it down this time in hope it would put me to sleep for a while so I wouldn't have to sit in my room by myself with thoughts that would depress me.

"I'm sorry." He looked guilty, making me feel bad.

"No, no. It's okay." I set my cup on the saucer with a clink and forced a smile. "I'll be fine. I just wanted to know more about Datura and the Murks you were talking about. They sound scary."

"They can be," he admitted. "However, my cohorts and I have been training since childhood on how to protect others from them, so quite frankly, it takes a lot to rattle our chains."

"I'm sure." My eyelids were getting heavy, and I had no desire to eat. I blinked hard to stay focused on him.

"It looks like the tea is working its magic."

"I think I'm going to lie down now." I moved the sheer bed curtain aside. "Maybe I shouldn't have drunk the tea so quickly."

He let out a humorous laugh. "I was wondering about that when you gulped it down." He dipped his head like Larkin had done with Merrack. "Farewell, Princess, and sweet dreams. It's been a pleasure."

"Thank you. See ya later." I crawled into bed and slipped under the covers, feeling relaxed and extremely tired. The door clicked shut as I was closing my eyes, all the while hoping I wouldn't have nightmares about those Murks—whatever they were—and would wake up feeling refreshed and ready to do what needed to be done to get the hell out of here.

Chapter Nine

I woke to the sound of lip smacking, chewing, and grunting. At first I thought I was still dreaming, but the noise continued. I opened my eyes. The sun must have been setting because the bedroom was drenched in a pinkish purple color. The top edges of the walls were darkening by the minute.

"Mmmm, good this is. Buttery and sweet. Tasty is the meat."

Slowly, I rolled to my side toward the scratchy withered voice. Through the sheer curtains I saw a guy small in stature with short and curly reddish-brown hair, a shaggy beard of the same color, and crude brown clothing as a peasant would wear in medieval times. Like Datura, he had pointy ears. From his profile view, his face appeared to have deep wrinkles.

Was this the little bugger Merrack talked about when we were in the kitchen earlier?

I pressed my lips together to keep quiet when really what I wanted to do was speak to him. But then again, maybe it wouldn't be a good idea. What if he got pissed off and tried to attack me. My heart raced. *Stay still, Haven. Don't make a sound. He's almost done with the sandwich.*

"Nice. Nice of the princess to leave this for me," he said between bites. "Never knew me would like something else other than cream and fresh bread. Surprise I am."

A knock at the door startled me. With a *pop!* the little guy vanished.

I pushed the curtain aside, swung my legs over the bed, and rose. Ignoring the other knocks, I examined the last couple of bites left on the plate.

"Alaris?" The door cracked open, and Larkin poked his head in.

"Yes."

"It's almost dinner time."

"Okay."

His eyes darted past me, resting on the little bit of food left on the plate. "You already ate?" He opened the door wider and looked at me.

"No, this was from earlier." I wanted to tell him about my little visitor but decided not to. When he raised his eyebrows, I continued, "Draylan came by earlier and brought me some tea and lunch. Wasn't that sweet of him?"

"Why would he do so?" He sounded surprised and a tad annoyed.

"Well, actually," I said, "Datura told him to. He was only acting on direct orders." Come to think of it, as I said that, it dawned on me Draylan was only being courteous to me and nothing more. He wasn't trying to be my friend. It was all business.

Tight-lipped Larkin nodded.

I had a feeling there was something he wasn't telling me, but I wasn't about to ask him. If he wanted to tell me, he would. Obviously, he didn't which irritated me.

"I'll be down in about twenty minutes," I abruptly told him.

"Don't you want me to escort you?" he asked, closing the door behind him.

I crossed the room to the vanity. "I can manage on my own."

"But I'm your warrior."

"What?" I turned to him, not sure if I heard him correctly. My gaze swept over all six-foot-four of him. He was wearing what looked like the same black pants Draylan wore, but the T-shirt Larkin had on was white and fitted tight across his muscular frame. His dark hair was messy on top, and his chartreuse eyes held a glint of uncertainty in them. My stomach fluttered as a mental visual of him kissing me entered my mind.

"I'm your warrior," he repeated, the unsureness still hovering in his eyes.

"My warrior?"

"Yes."

"I don't need a warrior."

"You need protection, Alaris. As of right now, we don't know what the headhunters want from you."

"True," I said, understanding his point, "but who decided for you to be my warrior?"

"I requested it when we found out you were alive and well. The decision was from the beginning."

The fluttering in my stomach returned. Only, this time it felt like there were now a swarm of butterflies inside my belly. "Oh." A new mental image of him holding my arms above my head, my back pressed against the wall, and his lips on my neck emerged. I looked down and rubbed my temple.

Get a grip on yourself, Haven. You have more important things to do than fantasize about Larkin. Besides, he only chose to be your warrior because you were best friends once upon a time ago. He probably sees you as a sister and nothing more.

The thought of Larkin only seeing me as his BFF made the steamy thoughts and images of us disappear.

"Do you have a headache?"

I dropped my hand. "No, I'm fine . . . so your job is to protect me?"

"Yes, and to come to your aid when needed."

I placed a hand on my hip. "Don't tell me you're going to be my shadow or babysitter, because I won't have it. I don't care what the hell my status is in this family and if my life is in danger. I will not live under that yoke." I wouldn't either. Yeah, having Larkin as my warrior gave me a secret thrill, even though it was all business; however, to have him chained to my side—forget it.

The corner of his mouth curled. "You're just as sassy and headstrong as you were when we were kids."

"I'm serious, Larkin." I purposely ignored his remark because it was becoming clear to me I was nothing more than a fond childhood memory. He probably thought it was his obligation to be my warrior because he blamed himself for not protecting me when my mom made the decision to rip me from this world.

"I won't be around you all the time," he said. "I have training and patrolling I have to do, among other things."

"Like catching the headhunters?"

He nodded and glanced at my bare feet. "You should get some shoes on. Dinner will be ready in about ten minutes or so."

"I need to put some makeup on first." I moved toward the vanity.

"Leave the makeup alone. You don't need it."

"Don't tell me I don't need it," I snapped, glaring at him.

He scowled. "What's your problem?"

"My problem is you've"—I pointed at him—"been telling me what to do and what not to do since last night."

"You need to quit being so defensive."

"Yeah, well, you need to quit being so bossy."

"It was meant as a compliment, nothing more."

"What was?" My mind was spinning with frustration that I didn't know what the hell he was talking about.

"The makeup," he said, exasperated. "You don't need it, but if you think you do, by all means put some on."

"Thank you," I said, realizing now his earlier statement was meant as a compliment like he said. I sat on the chair in front of the vanity and proceeded to apply black eyeliner. "I'm sorry. I'm on edge with everything going on." I glanced at him in the mirror and caught the tightness in his face relaxing.

"I don't mean to be overbearing. I only want you to be safe."

"Because you're my warrior."

"Yes."

"Nothing more."

He didn't respond, which solidified my earlier assumption he chose this job out of guilt. Fine. I could live with that. Besides, I didn't plan on staying in Atheon for long anyway. What bothered me, though, was his intentions were only genuine to himself, not to me. By protecting me and making sure I was okay, he'd be redeeming himself for not doing the same thing when we were kids.

"Can you get me a pair of socks out of the top drawer over there"—I gestured to the bureau—"and then a pair of shoes in the closet while I finish up here?"

"Of course."

I was done fixing my face when he handed me the socks and placed a pair of black leather ankle boots on the floor next to me. I thanked him, then asked him about patrolling. What exactly was his job? He told me he and the other guys watched out for any trouble going on around the kingdom and nearby villages. Most of the time, it was Murks causing disturbances or doing something sinister in which case he'd have to act accordingly. As we were talking, we headed to the dining room, chatting away down the long hall. While we were descending the large staircase, he told me Murks were ghouls, dark elves, fairies, succubi, leviathan, shifters, and the like. I shivered and hugged myself from the scary thought of ever having to see one of those creatures, let alone fight them. Draylan wasn't kidding when he said earlier Murks were creatures that haunted children's dreams.

Merrack and Draylan were the only ones sitting at the claw-foot dining room table in the center of the room. It was already set and laden with food, several bottles of wine, and a pitcher of water filled with ice. I wondered where Datura and the other guys were and asked as I took my seat and poured water into my glass.

"Narik is on duty," Merrack said, placing two slices of roast beef on his plate. "Farran is escorting Datura to Brunhild's house and bringing her here, so she can lift the spell cast on you."

My pulse raced when I thought of regaining all my memories tonight. Tonight. Would it change me? I had no doubt it would, but my fear was those memories coupled with the ones I had now might breed feelings I wasn't ready to face.

"Are you having second thoughts?" Draylan asked while handing me the bowl of mashed potatoes.

"I'm nervous," is all I said, which I was. It wasn't a lie.

"Of course you are," Merrack said and then went into a coughing fit. Draylan handed him a glass of water.

"Are you okay?" His complexion looked almost ashen. I wondered if he was getting the flu.

He waved his hand in the air distractedly as he took a sip and nodded. Clearing his throat, he said, "I'm fine. I think it's all the excitement of meeting you, knowing I have a daughter, and worrying about you."

"Worrying about me?" I echoed, taken aback that he'd be concerned about me.

He pierced a piece of roast beef with his fork, then dipped it in his mashed potatoes and gravy, surprising me because I'd always done the same thing. "Yes," he admitted shamelessly, "You've been through a lot. I can't fathom how taxing it might be for you. I only want you to be healthy and happy, and I aim to make it happen."

A lump formed in my throat. He was genuine. I could tell by the earnest look in his eyes.

"I know we were going to wait until after dinner, but my interest and curiosity has got the better of me. Tell me about what happened with the headhunters," Merrack said, addressing me and no one else. Sympathy marred his features. "I know this is difficult for you." His voice was low and caring. "If you want to wait until another time to talk about it, I wouldn't have a problem with it."

"No, that's fine," I said. If I were to wait, it would take that much longer to catch the bastards. "I'll tell you now."

As we ate our dinner, I told Merrack, Larkin, and Draylan everything. I didn't leave any details out.

Merrack steepled his hands, resting his fingertips on his lips in thought. All at the table remained quiet. The sound of forks and knifes clinking against the plates as we finished our meal echoed around me. I wondered what Merrack was pondering, and for some reason, what type of father he would have been if things would have worked out between him and Karrina? I took a sip of red wine. It was sweet with a rich grape taste. Yummy. I could get used to drinking this. The thought of Kimmie and me doing shots at a bar in Vegas and dancing afterward made me instantly homesick, but then Merrack went into another coughing fit, pulling me back to the present. After he drank some more water and assured us he was okay, he looked at me with concern, alarming me. "The headhunters said they had their orders, and if they didn't abide by them they'd pay a heavy penalty?" he asked me, recounting what I'd told him.

I nodded. "Yes, and they wanted to taste my blood. Why is that? Are they some kind of vampires?" The thought of one of those creepy bastards sinking his teeth into my neck raised the hair on my arms. I rubbed them to subdue the sudden chill in my bones.

"They don't need to consume blood to survive," Larkin said next to me. "However, it gives them great pleasure to drink it off the living."

"That's comforting," I mumbled.

"What bothers me," Merrack said, "is they're revenants which is a spirit not bound to a tether, unless–"

"There's sorcery involved," I interjected. "Larkin already told me."

Larkin pushed his plate aside and folded his hands on the table. "They're the puppets so who's the puppet master?"

Merrack pointed at Larkin. "I was wondering the same thing and why?"

I looked at Draylan who hadn't said a word during this conversation. Maybe he was too engrossed and didn't have anything to add. He did appear interested by the way his gaze darted between us. "What do you think, Draylan?" I asked, curious to know his thoughts on the matter.

He glanced down, then met my questioning eyes. "I agree with Larkin and Merrack; however, since they didn't complete their mission, whoever was controlling the revenants probably punished them. I think if Larkin were to try to hunt them down, he'd be chasing his tail, so to speak."

"It is quite possible you're right," Merrack said.

"What?" My mouth dropped at the possibility no one would make an effort to track those murders and capture them. All three guys stared at me, surprised by my outburst. "You have to find those assholes. They brutally killed my family." My voice and the glass of water I held shook from fear, anger, and sorrow rolling through me. I suddenly felt hot. Beads of sweat formed on my forehead. My palms were burning. Bubbling sounds came from the water glass I held. Thick puffs of smoke rose to the top. Merrack and Draylan shot up from their seats.

"What the Devil?" Merrack gaped at me.

"Calm down, Alaris," Draylan excitedly said.

I was confused. I didn't know what was happening. The heat in my body was too great. The only thoughts I could hold onto were full of anger and fear.

Larkin leaned over and whispered in my ear. "It's okay. I give you my oath. I'll find those bastards, and they'll pay for what they've done to your family."

I relaxed. The water stopped bubbling, and my body temperature went back to normal. Larkin took the glass from me. "Have you ever experienced this occurrence before?"

"No," I answered, dazed. I dotted my face with a napkin. "I don't even understand what happened."

"What were you feeling at the time?" Merrack asked at the same moment Farran appeared in the doorway and announced Datura and Brunhild were in the study waiting for us. He looked from Merrack to me with a puzzled expression.

"I–" I stared at my palms. They were damp. The lines in them glistened in the light.

"Tell the queen we'll be there in a minute," Merrack said to Farran who was watching me with great interest. He gave Merrack a curt nod and left.

"I don't understand," I said, dumbfounded. I rose from my seat to emphasize my point. "I swear this has never happened to me before. At that moment I was overwhelmed with several feelings at once."

Merrack placed his hands on my shoulders. "I want to give you my sincere condolence for your loss last night." I blinked to stave off the tears, surprised at his sudden heartfelt admission. "I already spoke to Larkin about what needed to be done in this most unusual circumstance. Try not to worry yourself. We will take care of this situation and justice will be served."

"Okay." My voice sounded brittle and about to break like how I felt at the moment while I stared into his soft, caring eyes. This man was my biological father, I told myself, still trying to wrap my head around that fact. His feelings toward me seemed genuine. Maybe I should get to know him and his . . . *our* family history before I go back home.

"What we witnessed," Merrack said, "is something we'll have to investigate, but for right now, let's get your nasty charm lifted."

My heart pounded hard against my chest as I followed the guys into the other room, lacing my fingers together to stop my hands from shaking. Larkin had told me there were memories planted in my head of my earlier childhood on earth. Fake memories. What in the world would my real memories be like? Good? Bad? I didn't know and silently prayed things would work out in my favor.

Chapter Ten

The study was bathed in a soft golden light from an array of lit candles placed around the room on low bookshelves, the white stone fireplace mantle, and oak end tables. Draylan stayed behind, and there was no sign of Farran. I had to blink several times to adjust my eyesight. The thick scent of pine coated the air. When my vision cleared, and I was able to focus on my surroundings, I spotted Datura in the corner of the room talking to a much shorter woman, wearing a black hooded cloak. Brunhild, I guessed. My stomach twisted with nerves, and I tried to distract myself by looking about.

Datura caught my eye as I was admiring the dark wooden ceiling with a series of sunken panels in the shape of squares. The walls even appeared to be made from the same timber with intricate carvings on top. She smiled warmly and waved, indicating for me to join her. Larkin was by my side, and when I glanced at him, I caught the guarded look, but it was quickly replaced with a friendly expression. I wondered what that was all about and came to the conclusion maybe he was worried about Brunhild's ability to break the charm. What if she failed? Or worse . . . fucked something up? Shit. I never thought about that. I was basically giving her permission to toy with my mind.

When I approached them, Brunhild lowered her hood. To my surprise, she had pointy ears like Datura. Only, hers were longer and more pronounced, sticking out from her bushy brown hair. Her skin had a grayish tint to it, and her right eye was a dark watery brown while the left was pale blue. Her long hooked nose was the one thing on her face that wasn't puckered from age. She certainly didn't have the appearance of a fairy. While trying not to stare at her eyes, I wondered if she was really an elf.

"So this is Alaris." Brunhild smiled, revealing a black front tooth. She offered her hand to me. Her wrinkled fingers were spindly, but her nails were perfectly manicured with sparkly blue nail polish.

I shook her hand, feeling bad for her because honestly she got the shit end of the stick in the looks department. I absently wondered if there was a beauty spell she could use on herself, but then I thought if there was one, she'd already had done that by now, unless she didn't possess the power. It was a shallow thought. Looks shouldn't matter, but in all reality, they did. "Thanks for the Orange Bliss and cinnamon buns. They were awesome. Me and the guys appreciated it. It was very kind of–"

She jerked my hand, pulling me closer to her, startling me. Peering into my eyes, she said, "There's a great secret locked away inside you. The magic seal is a powerful one. Someone went to a lot of trouble to protect this secret that dwells within you." She released my hand. "Good thing I'm capable of breaking the spell, and it was my pleasure to make you those tasty treats."

Stunned, I stayed glued to my spot, wondering what the secret I harbored might be and how did she know? Well, shit, she knew how to find me, and she knew what size clothes and shoes I wore, which still baffled the hell out of me. She must have a crystal ball like the wicked witch of the west in the *Wizard of Oz*. I doubt she had flying monkeys, though, but the way things were going, I wouldn't be in the least bit surprised. Then I wondered if she was evil, but if she was, Datura and Merrack wouldn't be associating with her. According to Draylan, she'd then be considered a Murk.

"Since I now know how potent the glamour cast on you is"—Brunhild was now leaning across the coffee table in front of a plush maroon couch with overstuffed pillows, digging into a black cloth bag that looked like something you'd carry on a plane—"I know what to use to break it."

I threw Larkin a nervous look. He was watching her, appearing deep in thought and too engrossed in her actions to catch me staring at him. Merrack was standing in the shadows quietly observing. Datura had an anxious, excited look. When she caught me glancing at her, she crossed the room and softly told me it would be okay. Gently, she guided me to sit. I did and chewed on my nails while Brunhild organized the paraphernalia on the table. We quietly watched as she took some herbs and placed them in a granite mortar and used the pestle to grind them, all the while chanting under her breath in a language I didn't recognize. She took a vial of purple liquid and added a few drops to the mix. I looked up at Larkin, worried. My stomach was rolling with nerves again, and my heart was pounding something fierce. This time he caught my eyes. My feelings must had been etched on my face because he crossed the space between us and sat next to me.

"I need you to close your eyes," Brunhild said, "and think of the earliest memory you have. Once you have it, hold onto it."

The earliest memory I had. Hmmm. I was four . . . on a beach building a sandcastle with my dad while my mom took pictures. I twisted my lips to the side when I realized I'd never seen those pictures, but then remembered they burned in a fire.

"You need to concentrate more," Brunhild ordered.

I sighed and focused on that scene. It was a warm sunny day with a clear bright blue cloudless sky. There were other kids playing on the beach, screaming and chasing each other, all in fun.

"Don't lose your concentration." Brunhild's fingertip touched my forehead. It was cold and wet. She drew a swirly symbol while chanting once again under her breath in some foreign language.

In the picture behind my eyelids, I was smiling while building a wall of a sandcastle, happily chatting with my dad, the sand gritty and wet on my small hands and fingers. "This is where the princess lives," I told my daddy while compacting the sand.

"Is she waiting for her prince?" he asked with an endearing smile, working alongside me.

I rolled my eyes and snorted. "No, she's too busy with her own stuff to wait around for a boy."

My father laughed.

The scene faded, and a carousel of quick moving images from my childhood before the age of twelve with the Evergreens spun.

My heart dropped.

They *were* false memories. I knew this because as those memories whipped by in my mind, another one appeared below the others, steadfast, sharp, and luminous. I was eight years old, playing in the woods with Larkin. We were climbing a large oak. He was sitting on a thick branch above me, offering me his hand to pull me beside him. I reached up, and he grabbed it. "Hurry, before the Murks get you," he said, acting like he was panicking, hefting me higher.

My stomach was on the branch, feet dangling. "There are two ghouls circling the tree." I pretended to be scared while quickly pushing myself into a sitting position. "They look like they want to eat us." I pointed down to our imaginary monsters. "Look at their sharp teeth and nails. They can rip us apart."

"Not if I cut their heads off first." Larkin feigned pulling a sword out from behind his back.

I copied his gestures. "I have one, too. You kill the one on the right, and I'll take care of the one on the left."

He laughed. "Girls can't be warriors."

I glared at him. "Says who?"

Another scene followed. It was two years later. Larkin and I along with other kids around our age were swimming in a waterhole that was tucked away in a jungle-like mossy valley with beautiful cascading waterfalls, some multi-tiered. The water was a clear turquoise blue. We were all having fun, splashing each other, laughing. The next scene skipped another two years. I was twelve, roaming the forest when I–

Oh, my God, my dream!

The one I had about the unicorn.

It was real.

I remembered watching the creature wander through the forest like I told Larkin. The unicorn had a white body, but when the pockets of sunshine gleamed down upon him, his hide shimmered a bluish color. Quietly, I followed him through the trees, listening to the birds chirping around me, enjoying the woodsy, earthy smells. After a while, the unicorn stopped. He dipped his head, looked over his shoulder straight at me (he knew all along I'd been tailing him), and took off run–

Brunhild's chanting stopped. "The memories are coming to you slowly because I haven't broken through the heart of the charm. It's a doozy. I sure would like to know who cast it."

I kept my eyes closed and answered, "I'm not certain yet, but please continue." I was trying not to get annoyed, but for one, I was discovering firsthand the life that was stolen from me and for two, when Brunhild paused, so did the recall and visions I was having. The unicorn was showing me something, and I wanted to know what it was. Dammit.

Brunhild placed her fingertips on my temples and resumed her mantra, her voice low and methodical. I was back in the forest, staring after the unicorn. What a beautiful creature. It was rare to see one, let alone get as close to it as I had. I knew this, even at such a young age, and I felt both excited and honored by the encounter. I looked down to where he'd bowed his head and discovered a large teal blue egg the size of a baseball with brown speckles lying in a pile of dried leaves. I glanced around. There was no sign of a bird, and I wondered what type of avian would lay an egg such as this one. There was no protection around it. No nest. The mother must have abandoned it. I picked it up, wrapped the end of my shirt around the shell, and tucked it in my arms. I decided not to tell anyone, even Larkin. Besides, he was away from home training to become a warrior like his father was. He wouldn't be back for a month or so.

"What do you see?" Datura anxiously asked.

Brunhild stopped her chanting and dropped her hands from my head. The scene in my mind faded.

Fuck.

Larkin released an annoyed sigh under his breath. I had the sudden urge to open my eyes and look at him but didn't. The thought of him being in my presence warmed my heart. My warrior. My stomach flipped. Now that I was regaining memories of him and me, something shifted inside me. A bond between two souls that had been subterfuged for a purpose I had yet to discover but was on the brink of knowing.

"Wife, please," Merrack said from across the room, "don't interrupt the process Brunhild has to go through in order to have Alaris' memories restored. She will tell us once the enchantment has been lifted."

"My apologies," Datura said. "Carry on."

Brunhild released a slow breath. I could see behind my eyelids the shadow of her hands edging toward my face. Like a vise, she clasped them on each side of my head, her fingertips pressing on my scalp. In a deep and powerful voice, she launched right back into her incantation.

The visions came quickly this time, along with memories, thoughts, and feelings in between. The knowledge of Atheon I knew at that age. My mother Karrina. She was beautiful with long dark hair like me and had bluish-green eyes.

I loved her.

She was good to me.

We baked and created a garden together. She was an herbologist and healer. She'd collect medicinal plants and would quiz me on each one. "What plant is this one?" She picked up a large green serrated leaf off our kitchen table that was one of many different kinds laid out before us.

With the tip of my fingers, I pushed my bottom lip down and thought about it. "Ah, peppermint."

She nodded and wrote something in a black book beside her. "What's it good for?"

I knew the answer. It was easy. "It helps with indigestion and heartburn."

"Excellent." She smiled, pleased with my progress.

"Oh," I said as an afterthought. "It also helps get rid of gas in your belly." I patted my stomach for emphasis. "Then you fart a lot." I stuck my tongue between my lips and made farting noises, bursting into giggles.

Those cherished moments of my mom and me happened to plop into my brain like a boulder being tossed into the river. The spreading ripples were countless memories pulsing.

Then a bright and clear picture of me in my bedroom rose. With the information I now acquired, I knew this scene was part of the last one after discovering the egg. I had taken it home, knowing I'd have to somehow keep it warm in order for it to hatch and had no idea how. I also worried how to feed the baby bird. Its survival without its mother was bleak, but I'd do my best to beat the odds.

I saw myself sitting on my floor in the center of my bedroom. The sun was dipping into the horizon, creating a soft orange glow through the pane glass window. The teal speckled egg sat on my pillow in front of me as I stared, trying to reach a solution on how to properly care for it. I stroked the top of the egg. "You're safe from predators now, and I promise I'll do what I can to keep you alive," I whispered.

The shell cracked beneath my fingers. I gasped and removed my hand as I watched the egg split apart in a zigzag pattern. A gold, scaly head with a small bump on either side poked out the top. Wide-eyed, I slapped a hand over my mouth.

Oh, my God. It was a baby dragon!

I thought dragons were extinct, but then again I remembered being told they were solitary, private creatures who preferred to be left alone and out of sight.

He opened his eyes. They were orange, reptilian, and looked straight at me while twisting his body back and forth. His tiny wings broke free from its encasement. Bits and pieces of shell fell away, littering the floor around him in shiny chips of teal.

"Hello, there," I said in a soft, gentle voice, still in disbelief over this unusual circumstance. This would make two today. First the unicorn and now the dragon. "I'm not going to hurt you."

He raised his wings that were attached to his arms and talon fingers. He flapped them a few times but wasn't strong enough to fly. There was a bump on the end of his snout and above the inner corner of his eyes all the way to the back of his head was a scaly piece of bone jutting from his face that gave him a permanently angry appearance like they were eyebrows, and he was scowling. He tilted his head to the side, regarding me. His pupils dilated, and his eyes softened. He blinked and there was something different in his gaze than there was a moment ago, a knowing of some sort.

"What are you thinking?" I wondered aloud more to myself than him.

He turned his head upright and stretched his neck. Lifting his wings, he spread his arms out. It looked like he wanted me to pick him up. I moved closer and gingerly lifted him below his wings. At the same time my mother entered the house, calling my name to see if I was home.

I held the dragon up in front of my face, planning on telling him I'd keep him safe, but when our eyes connected, he looked deeply into mine as if he could see every facet of my soul, and the words I was about to say dissolved on my tongue. He opened his mouth, revealing tiny pointy teeth. I wasn't scared he'd bite me. His demeanor was calm, nonthreatening. I wondered, though, if he were hungry and that was his way of asking for food. He then breathed in, making an ahhh sound. His chest rose as he did so. Then he blew into my mouth, and at the same moment, my mother entered my room and screeched. I was immobilized, watching a glittery red tube of air pouring out of the dragon into me, down my lungs, throughout my body. The sensation was warm and tingly. By the time Mom crossed the room, he collapsed in my hand and toppled over, landing in my lap, limp like a rag doll. "No! No! No!" I cried, trying to wake him up, but it was no use, he was dead. I bawled in my mother's arms, feeling like a loser because I had let this little guy down. I should have left him in the forest. I should have–

"Alaris."

A warm hand touched my arm, bringing me back to the present. Brunhild removed her grip from my head. I opened my eyes, my face wet with tears. I looked at Larkin whose hand remained on me, at the same time Brunhild said, "It is done." Concern clouded Larkin's eyes.

A bit rattled, I cleared my throat and wiped at my face with the palms of my hands. The memories that were suppressed a decade ago were now alive and buzzing within me in one giant clusterfuck. I remembered what happened after the dragon died. My mother consoled me, and she was fit to be tied. Each day she grew worrisome. I had no idea why. I was filled with guilt and continued to mourn the loss of the dragon and didn't pay much attention to anything else.

"Alaris," Larkin said again. "Why were you crying?"

I held a finger up. "Hold on a minute. The memories are jumbled. I need to get what I can straight in my head." I closed my eyes and cradled my head in my hands, hearing Merrack and Datura taking seats next to the couch.

My mother always told me she loved me, but during that time, she said it more so than ever before. She hugged me a lot. I thought it was odd but chalked it up to her trying to comfort me. Two weeks later, a visitor arrived at our cottage—a woman by the name of Mardella whom I'd never seen before. I remembered her being nice and pretty in an earthy kind of way. I also thought it was cool she had thin white streaks throughout her dark hair she wore in a bun. Mardella spent the day with us and asked me questions about the dragon. She seemed genuinely interested, so I shared everything, even seeing the unicorn which surprised both her and my mom. With a sparkle in her brown eyes, Mardella said, "The gods are favoring you. Not everyone crosses paths with a unicorn." She then asked to hold my hands. I was apprehensive at first and looked at my mom who smiled gently and told me Mardella would be able to tell if the dragon gave me something before he died. I didn't understand what Mom was talking about, but instead of asking her and Mardella questions, I gave her my hands since I was curious myself.

She bowed her head and closed her eyes. She sucked in a sharp breath and placed her palm on my chest over my heart. Shortly after, she moved it to my forehead. I winced from the heat of her skin on mine. She opened her eyes. They were wide, brimming with shock and surprise. "The dragon is still alive," she said in a haunting voice that caught my attention. How could he be alive? I saw him die. "What I tell you," she continued, "you must not tell anyone this secret. *Ever.*"

"What is it?" My mother was wringing her hands, her face pale, as if she were going to get sick.

Mardella looked at my mom, then me. "His spirit dwells inside you. When he blew into your mouth, it was his essence entering your body." She touched my chest. "You now harbor one of the most important elements of them all . . . fire." She removed her hand and frowned apologetically at my mom. "Alaris now has the ability to find all the other elements, gather them, and become the most powerful person in Atheon."

"It's a myth," my mother said in quick desperation. "The gods and goddesses made sure no one would ever be able to gain that much power."

Mardella's frown deepened. "It doesn't matter. If a Murk were to discover this about Alaris, her life would be in danger *or*," she stressed, "if Alaris becomes corrupt and power-hungry she'll turn into a Murk, and if the myth *is* true, Atheon will perish into chaos and darkness."

I assured Mardella and my mom I'd never do such a thing. I didn't care about power. But I was twelve. They wouldn't listen to me. Instead, they talked among themselves, sometimes in hushed voices. I felt ignored, alone, and longed for Larkin to be home so I could tell him what happened. I was aware I'd promised not to tell anyone my secret, but surely I could tell my best friend, right?

The next day, I noticed my mom had been crying. Her eyes were swollen, face blotchy, and when she hugged me out of the blue, she hugged me tightly, repeatedly telling me how much she loved me. Alarmed, I asked what was wrong, and she told me she was worried sick about me. I tried to reassure her I'd be fine, but she waved it off and said I was a child, innocent and naïve. She then told me Mardella could take care of our problem by casting a spell on me if I were to allow her to do so that night. The charm would hide my secret is all Mom said.

"Fine. I'll let Mardella do what needs to be done," I answered, wanting to end my mother's strife and move on back to our regular lives.

That night, I lay on the wooden floor, shirtless, in the center of the living room in a circle made from salt with four tapered white candles alit on all sides. Mardella sat at the crown of my head while my mother lingered in the background watching. Beside Mardella were copper bowls filled with I didn't know what. Incense burned outside the circle on the floor in a small pewter bowl near me. The smoke was thick with a heady smell that reminded me of smoldering leaves. My eyes were burning and watering so I closed them.

"Keep them closed," Mardella softly told me. Then under her breath, she said words that sounded gibberish to me but having a definite rhythm.

I jumped when her cold wet finger touched my chest. She told me to relax and proceeded to draw a star and swirly designs on my skin. Next, she did the same thing to my head. A sudden exhaustion overtook me. I drifted off to the hum of her voice and the feel of her warm hand cupped over my eyes and–

"Alaris," Merrack calmly said. I lifted my head from my hands and squinted at him. "Who cast the memory spell on you?"

I scratched the back of my head, wondering who that woman was and how did Karrina know her? "Her name was Mardella."

Brunhild was sitting on the coffee table in front of me. Her mouth flopped open, and her eyes grew into saucers which was kind of freaky because of one being blue and the other brown. "*Mardella*," she whispered, drawing the name out in stunned surprise.

Larkin groaned beside me, pulling my attention to him. His jaw was clenched, his face contorted in anger. When he met my gaze, an apologetic sadness softened his features, but then his rage returned as quickly as it left. His hands balled into fists. He rose and stormed out of the room.

"What's wrong with Larkin?" I asked Merrack, not understanding why Larkin was so mad.

He released a heavy sigh. "Mardella is his grandmother."

Chapter Eleven

"What?" I didn't think I heard him right.

"She's a gypsy witch," Datura said, sitting beside me where Larkin sat a few moments ago. "He rarely sees her. I imagine he feels betrayed by her now."

"Wow." I rubbed my temples while trying to absorb everything, including feelings—old and new—in an attempt to sort them out. What happened earlier in the dining room with the water in my glass must have been connected to the baby dragon. According to Mardella, his essence was inside me. Did that mean I had the power of a dragon, like breathing fire? I couldn't imagine a flame coming out of my mouth. It was a silly thought. Besides, did dragons really breathe fire? If so, how would that work? Then I thought of Larkin. His grandmother did this to me, and he had no idea. It wasn't his fault. I hoped he didn't think I blamed him for my life being stolen from me.

"Why would Karrina take drastic measures to have Mardella cast a compulsion spell on you?" Datura asked with great interest.

I remembered my promise to Mardella not to tell anyone about the dragon and what happened to me. I also recalled Larkin telling me about Merrack who wanted to possess all four elements so he could be the most powerful person in Atheon and all that jazz. I decided to stick to my word.

"I don't know." I stared at the floor as if I were trying to remember why. I could feel the weight of everyone's eyes on me. Then a disturbing realization dawned on me, and my heart leaped to my throat: If any of them knew I harbored one of the most important elements of them all and had the ability to find the other three, they'd use me to possess the power Merrack once coveted, or they'd kill me, even though Karrina said it was a myth.

"I think you do know," Brunhild said, regarding me suspiciously, her brown eye glittering in the soft light of the candles.

Merrack sighed, exasperated. "If she says she doesn't–"

"This is what I remember," I said, cutting him off, addressing all of them, hoping my ruse would fool Brunhild. I then launched into my encounter with the unicorn. Of course, I didn't tell them about the dragon egg. I ended my story with him running away.

Merrack rubbed the side of his beard. "Interesting. Unicorns are intelligent, magical beings. In all of my years, I've never heard of a tale such as yours before."

"He didn't show you anything?" Datura asked with an edge to her voice.

"I wasn't close enough to even touch him," I said and rose to my feet. My feelings were all over the place. I needed to sort them out and deal with what I now knew about my life prior to living with the Evergreens. "I'm going to get a drink and then head to my room so I can straighten some things out in my mind." I extended my hand to Brunhild. She took it and slowly squeezed our palms together, intently studying my face, giving me the willies. I kept my thoughts only on the unicorn and shook her hand. "Thank you for your help. I appreciate it."

She didn't say anything, only stared into my eyes and nodded. I pulled my hand away and wiped it on my pants.

"What a splendid idea," Merrack said, rising from his seat. "Maybe once you collect your thoughts, more memories will come to you."

I noticed Brunhild scrutinizing me. "I hope so," I answered, "because I feel there's more, but right now I can't grasp what it is. If I do find out something more, I'll tell you." The corners of her withered lips curled. I shifted my attention to Merrack. He smiled. It was kind, thoughtful, and reached into his eyes.

Datura stood, her expression thoughtful. "We're here if you need to talk about this ordeal you're going through. I'm sure you're feeling quite overwhelmed right now, dear."

"I am," I said as visions flashed in my mind of Karrina and me planting in the garden behind our cottage, of our little community having a party outside beneath the two moons and sparkling stars. There was a huge bonfire and food set out on long wooden tables nearby. Distant laughter rang in my ears, along with music from a violin, and an image of people clapping and dancing. My heart ached. "Goodnight." I clutched my chest as if I could keep all of the broken pieces together and headed to the kitchen, wiping the tears from my eyes, not knowing who the hell I was anymore.

* * *

I sat in my room against my bed, finishing my second glass of wine with the bottle next to me. For an hour and a half, I'd been rolling over all the events in my life that had been suppressed for the past ten years and were now alive and vibrant in my mind, like motion pictures playing behind my eyelids. I was from a village in the midlands called Havenwood. Now I knew where my name came from, which led me to believe the Evergreens were innocent bystanders in this charade. Mardella must have sought a likely couple and placed a charm on them so they believed I was their biological daughter. Regardless, though, if my assumptions were true or not, the Evergreens were my parents—Mom and Dad—and I'd never view them as anything less. Sure Karrina was my birth mother whom I loved dearly and missed, but part of me felt betrayed by her not informing me exactly what Mardella was going to do when I had agreed for her to cast the spell on me.

As I poured myself another glass of wine, there were several friendly knocks at the door. "Yes," I said, too comfortable to get my butt off the floor.

Draylan poked his head in. "Are you okay?" He eyed me putting the bottle down and picking up my wine glass. "Are you having a private party here, or can I join you?"

Draylan, Larkin, and Narik were from Havenwood as well. I knew that now. We all used to play together, along with Draylan's younger sister Lithia and Narik's twin sister Rydia. I waved him in. "Of course." He sat next to me, and I handed him the bottle. "How's Lithia doing?"

He took a swig. The sound of the liquid sloshing against the glass reminded me of Kimmie and me swiping a bottle of Jameson from her parent's liquor cabinet when we were sophomores in high school. It was on a dare at our friend's slumber party whose parents were out of town. All five of us got pretty lit and rowdy that night off the Irish whiskey. Needless to say, Kimmie's parents found out. I was at her house when they confronted her. Not wanting Kimmie to take all the heat, I admitted along with her of stealing the liquor. They told my folks that night. We both got grounded for a month and had to do extra chores around our houses, including cleaning walls. I also was forced to perform an extra day of taekwondo training. We never pulled that stunt again.

He swallowed and made a face. "She's nursing a broken heart."

"Really? Who broke—"

"Larkin."

"Larkin?" I couldn't hide the surprise in my voice. I never even considered Larkin had a girlfriend, but why wouldn't he? He was smokin' hot. I bet he could date anyone. Jealousy I didn't want to feel stabbed my heart. I then reminded myself of my earlier thoughts regarding him. He only considered me as a friend and out of his own guilt was determined to protect me.

"Yes, they dated for roughly two months, but when he received word you might be alive, he dumped her. She's heartbroken and hates you." He let out a bitter laugh, then took another swig of the wine.

"She never liked me," I said, remembering now as we talked how snotty she was to me. One time she tripped me, and I fell into a mud puddle and ruined my pretty dress.

"She's always been jealous of you."

I snorted. "Why? There's nothing to be jealous of."

"For one, you're gorgeous," he said giving me a sideways glance.

I shoved his arm. "Get out. I am not. Datura is gorgeous. I don't even compare to her."

"For two," he said, ignoring my remark, "you were best friends with Larkin."

I drained the last of the contents in my glass and set it aside, opting for the bottle instead. Picking it up, I pointed at him. "I know why you're here in my room, why you brought me that sandwich and tea earlier . . . you're using me to get back at Larkin for hurting your sister." I had a nice buzz going which always enhanced certain qualities I had like being blunt and sassy.

He held his hands up. "Hey, truthfully, yeah I thought about it, but honestly, Datura sent me up here earlier because she was concerned about you. As for right now, I'm here because I enjoy your company. Always have. If Larkin is jealous because of it, so be it. He knows I didn't appreciate him dumping Lithia like he did."

"Why would he even go out with her?" I asked in disgust making a face. "She's impossible." His shoulders tightened, and he looked away. I instantly felt like shit for badmouthing Lithia. "I'm sorry. I know she's your sister." I took a sip from the bottle and handed it to him.

He frowned. "I know she's difficult, and let's say has *issues*"—he did air quotes—"but when Lithia was with Larkin, I'd never seen her so happy."

"I understand," I said. "I just don't get why he dated her. She doesn't seem like his type."

"I think she wore him down, and he finally gave in. I mean, she was always there when he came home. She baked him cookies, showed up at the same parties and pubs he went to. When his mom broke her wrist, Lithia volunteered to help Fiona around the house and with the horses. Basically, and I hate to admit this"—He rubbed his forehead—"she weaseled her way into his life." He took a drink and handed me the wine.

I drank the last bit and raised it between us, grinning. "Gone." I hiccupped and giggled.

"Went quick," he said, laughing.

I nodded. "Yeah, I feel good, though . . . Oh, you pissed me off tonight, ya know?"

"Yeah, I know," he said, toying with a lace on his boot, his brows knitting together. "But I think it's a fruitless act to go after the headhunters when whoever controls them probably punished them for not completing their mission."

"That doesn't matter. They fucking slaughtered my family, and I for one will see to it that they pay for it."

"How?"

I threw my hands up. "Hell if I know, but I'll find a way. Then I'm going back home."

His eyes widened. "You don't want to stay in Atheon after regaining your memory?"

I sighed and ran my fingers through my hair. "I don't know. Maybe. I'm confused right now. I have a life there, though. I'm all set to go back to college and become an archeologist."

"You can build a life here. You belong here," he stressed. "Don'tcha want to know why you caused the water in your glass to boil? There's something different about you."

"Yeah. Maybe."

"Datura told me about the unicorn. What an extraordinary experience."

"It was," I agreed, rubbing the corner of my eye, yawning.

"The unicorn didn't show you anything or communicated with you?"

"No."

"How odd."

"I know. I don't get it." I wasn't lying because I didn't. Why would this magical being lead me to a dragon egg? The gods were favoring me, Mardella told me. Why? Maybe they saw something in me I didn't see. I didn't know, but my head hurt thinking about it.

"Well," Draylan said, rising to his feet while I remained comfortably seated on the floor, "it's getting late, and I have some things to do early tomorrow morning."

"Thanks for stopping by and sharing my wine with me."

He ducked his head. "My pleasure. Sleep well, Princess." The door clicked shut behind him, finalizing my night.

I yawned again. Too lazy to crawl into bed, I curled on my side and closed my eyes, dizzily thinking about Havenwood, thanks to the buzz I had going on. A picture of a wide dark forested area, deep green rolling hills, and marshes, fluttered across my mind. I recalled rolling down those hills, playing in the woods, and going horseback riding with Larkin in the countryside. He mentioned yesterday he had an affinity with horses. It was true. He could communicate with them and made me promise when we were kids never to tell anyone.

Next, the village and cottages floated behind my eyelids in a stream of haziness as I fell into a deep, comfortable sleep. My cottage was made of stone, set back among tall dark oaks. There were flowerboxes on our windowsills, and we had a nice garden in the back.

Home.

I longed to be back there.

I would return to Havenwood I decided right before sleep swept me away into the abyss where darkness and light collided, forming shimmering dreams of a life I once knew and of a massive golden dragon I'd never seen before but felt a strong connection with.

Chapter Twelve

Hiding behind a large oak, I watched in amazement a man under the twin moons shifting into a wolf.

With a start, my eyes popped open. The heel of my hand immediately clapped to my forehead, pressing it hard. A wedge of white light streamed in across my hip through a slit in the curtains. I remained on the floor but somehow acquired a blanket and pillow. I wondered how that happened. I closed my eyes, still seeing the scene in my mind: A dark-haired lanky guy tearing off his clothes and dropping to his knees. His skin bubbled and pulsed. His bones stretched outwards, making awful cracking sounds. He hung his head and swayed it back and forth distractedly. He lifted his chin to the burnt evening sky as his hands and feet stretched, popping more bones. His jaw dislocated, mouth opened in a silent scream, fangs elongating from his gums, coated with blood as his face shifted into a snout. Black hair sprouted everywhere.

I rubbed my eyes and sat up. Wow. I was ten when it happened. A chill crawled up my spine. I hugged myself and wondered if I'd start dreaming of things that happened to me before I was compelled and sent to the Evergreen's house. The thought of my parents twisted my heart in agonizing sadness. Without warning, my mom's decapitated body lying in a heap on the kitchen floor flashed through my mind. I buried my face in my hands and silently cried. Those headhunters would pay for what they'd done. Sniffing, I wiped the tears off my face. I needed to buck up and not allow distractions get in the way of my mission to find those fuckers and rain hellfire down upon them. Crying about my loss wouldn't do me or my parents any good. First thing first: get cleaned up, eat breakfast, and find Larkin so we could devise a plan.

Forty-five minutes later, I was dressed in stretchy jeans, a comfortable white T-shirt, and black gym shoes that reminded me of Vans. With makeup lightly applied and my hair pulled up into a messy bun, I was ready to rock and roll. The palace was strangely quiet as I crossed the hall and went down the stairs. There were muffled voices coming from behind the kitchen door. I opened it and stopped dead in my tracks on the threshold. Merrack and Datura were having a moment—an intimate one. Yuck. His spine was pressed against the counter, his head lolled back, eyes closed as Datura kissed his neck while massaging his member. He moaned in pleasure when she mentioned in a sultry voice how she never tired of their nightly games of master and servant. If he gave her what she wanted, she'd serve him in new and exciting ways tonight.

What the hell was that supposed to mean? It had to be some role playing game. I left the scene, no longer hungry. I decided to explore the grounds instead and see if I could find Larkin. I felt bad for him regarding Mardella and wanted to assure him I didn't blame him for what his grandmother had done.

When I stepped outside, I was surprised to see the sky was overcast— gray and gloomy. It reminded me of Washington. A fierce ache entered my chest to be back home. The temperature, though, felt like the low 70s, and instead of the air smelling like rain, it had a grassy, earthy aroma, like fresh-cut grass in early spring. As I descended the front stairs, my gaze locked onto Larkin's when he looked up from the bottom step. He was wearing what looked like black basketball shorts and a white tank top. He must have been working out because his biceps were pumped. My stomach did several flips. His eyes were both soft and intense. A thrill went through me. Again, I had to remind myself his actions weren't genuine toward me. They were all self-serving. He was my warrior. My protector. Nothing more.

"I was just going to look for you," I told him as I went down the stairs.

"And I you," he answered. "I wanted to apologize for abandoning you last night."

I paused on the step above him so I was almost eye level with him. "I understand. There is no need for you to be sorry about that or Mardella."

He rubbed the back of his neck and tilted his head to the side, squinting at me, clearly annoyed. "I'm not too happy with my grandmother right now."

"I can see that."

He sighed and hung his head, then peeked up at me through long dark lashes. "I need to find out if my mother knew all along about why you were sent away but pretended like she didn't."

"I would like to know that as well," I said, "but honestly, I don't think she did. She wasn't there with us."

"I still need to ask her."

I nodded. "I know."

At the edge of my vision, I saw Draylan heading our way. I waved. He was wearing a similar outfit as Larkin, except for his shorts had a broad white stripe down the center of his thigh, and his tank was black. His arm muscles bulged. I was guessing Narik and Farran were probably still working out which gave me an idea.

"Hey," Draylan said when he reached us, his attention on me. "Did you wake up with a headache?" The corners of his mouth twitched.

Larkin's brows furrowed. I knew what Draylan was doing but figured what was going on between them was their thing, not mine. "Of course not," I answered, smirking. "It wasn't like I got wasted on half a bottle of wine."

"Right, okay." He laughed. "The wine was half gone when I stopped by."

I made a face. "Nu-huh."

"Ya-huh."

"What are you two talking about?" Larkin asked, crossing his arms.

"Draylan stopped by my room last night to see how I was doing," I answered.

"And I found her sitting on the floor with more than half a bottle of wine gone," Draylan interjected.

I jerked my thumb at him while talking to Larkin. "He's embellishing. I didn't drink that much on my own."

Draylan laughed again.

Larkin's eyes danced between Draylan and me. His lips were in a tight line, shoulders tensed. "So you helped her drink the rest of it?"

"You're damn right," Draylan answered. "It was some good shit. Same stuff we had with our dinner"—His gaze swept my body from head to toe, then up again—"I wasn't about to turn her down." He said the last bit in a way that could only suggest if I were to offer myself to him, he wouldn't think twice about it.

Oh, shit. Draylan was seriously pushing Larkin's buttons.

Red-faced, Larkin's arms dropped to his side. He took a step closer to Draylan. "What are you implying?"

Unfazed, Draylan shrugged. "You can interpret it any way you like. I don't give a fuck."

Larkin clenched his teeth. "You shouldn't be cussing in front of royalty. Show some respect."

"Oh, my God. Really?" I pointed at Larkin. "You said the eff word to me yesterday. Don't be a hypocrite."

Draylan gasped, and his hand flew to his neck in mocking shock. "Larkin Vestergaard said the *eff* word to the future queen?"

"I've had enough of you." Larkin shoved Draylan, who in turn pushed back.

I knew this was going to get ugly by the hard, angry look on their faces. I hopped down from the steps. "Stop it," I said. When Draylan moved toward Larkin, totally ignoring me, I positioned myself between them, grabbed his wrist while placing my leg behind his. As I twisted his arm back, I leaned into him, causing him to fall to the ground. I whipped around, ready to subdue Larkin. Wide-eyed, he raised his hands. His eyes darted past me to Draylan. "You two need to get over this *thing* between you." I offered my hand to Draylan, and he accepted it. "So Larkin dumped your sister. Move on."

"How do you know about her?" Larkin wanted to know, his tone pitched in surprise.

"I told her," Draylan said, rubbing his tailbone.

Larkin blanched. "I only went out with Lithia because my mother kept bugging me."

Draylan made a derisive sound and scowled. "Yeah, we already know. Lithia even knew when you first asked her out, but you led her on. You went out with her for two months. I've never seen her as happy and stable as she was then, and then you dumped her when you found out about Alaris. She's heartbroken, and to be honest, there's no tellin' what she might do to Alaris if they ever cross paths."

That caught my attention. I didn't want enemies. Besides, Larkin and I weren't together. "Why would she do something to me? I haven't seen her since I was twelve."

"Because she blames you for Larkin leaving her."

"I'll talk to her," Larkin quickly said to Draylan, "and I'm sorry for hurting Lithia. It wasn't my intention."

Still standing between them, I said, "Where I'm from when people make up, they shake hands." I gestured for them to move closer together. "Come on. You two are on the same team and have to work together. You need to put this behind you."

For a second, by the angry look on Draylan's face, I didn't think he'd make amends.

"I promise," Larkin said, sticking his hand out. "I'll try to make things right between Lithia and me."

Draylan nodded and shook Larkin's hand.

"All right, now that we're all friends again," I said, "I'd like to see where you guys workout and train."

Draylan motioned to Larkin. "Larkin is your warrior. He should show you. By the way, Lithia will have a freaking fit when she finds that out." A short, uncomfortable silence fell between us until an amused expression entered Draylan's face. "Where in the hell did you learn those moves?" he asked me.

"I was wondering the same thing," Larkin chimed in.

"Taekwondo." When they kept staring at me, I continued. "It's the art of self-defense. It's one of the oldest forms of martial arts. I've been practicing it since I was thirteen. I'm a black belt and used to compete in tournaments."

"Impressive," Draylan said, patting my shoulder. "I can almost see you patrolling with us, taking down Murks." He winked and went up the stairs.

I never thought about that and looked at Larkin who in turn shook his head. I rolled my eyes and made for the north side of the palace. He joined my side, deep in thought.

"Show me where you guys workout and train," I said, breaking the silence.

He placed his hand on my arm and tugged me toward a big oak. "I need to tell you something." He looked around as if to make sure no one was spying on us. He even lifted his eyes to the gloomy sky and scanned the treetops.

"Why are you looking up?"

"Pixies. They're not permitted past a certain point on these grounds because some of them like to gossip and stir the pot, so there's a magical ward placed so many yards from the entrance to keep them, Murks, and unfriendly individuals from entering unless invited by Merrack, Datura, and now you. They're clever, though, and I like to be cautious."

"Like vampires," I said. He stared at me expressionless, so I explained. "On my vampire TV shows, they can't enter a house unless invited in by the owner."

"Sort of," he answered, scrunching up the left side of his face, "but in this case the owners and those who stand to inherit the land and house have the power to gain them access to the premises."

My eyes swept the area. There was no one in sight. It reminded me of a ghost town. "I think we're good, so what's up?"

"Last night when I left here, I went patrolling. I needed to blow off some steam, and Merrack had asked me earlier to do so anyway, because a group of weres are–"

"Weres?" I interrupted, my jaw dropping. I was pretty sure I knew what he was talking about, but I needed him to clarify.

"Oh, sorry. Werewolves. But they were in human form and–"

"I saw a man shift into one when I was ten," I piped in. "Out in the forest in Havenwood."

"You never told me," he said, sounding butt hurt. "I thought we told each other everything."

"I'm sorry. I was afraid you'd bitch me out for wandering too far away from home."

"I suppose."

"So the weres," I prompted. "What about them?"

He rubbed the spot above his brow. "Oh, right. Anyway, they've been rowdy lately at the local tavern, not too far from here. Wearing a cloak, I went there last night to check it out. While I was having a pint, a couple of hobgoblins at a nearby table were talking about two revenants and–"

I raised my finger. "Excuse me. Did you just say hobgoblin?" I wasn't sure if I heard him right. I remembered Karrina and the others in our small village talking about them, among other creatures, but to hear Larkin mention a hobgoblin like he was talking about yesterday's weather threw me off.

"Yes, a hobgoblin."

I gestured for him to carry on.

"They were a bit tipsy, but what I gathered from their conversation was earlier in the evening, they were wandering through the woods when they came across a couple revenants who were talking to each other about the earth realm, boasting about . . . ya know . . . what they've done and saying they should have tasted the princess's blood before I showed up since their mistress has denied them a feeding since they've been back."

"Weird and creepy," I said, the hairs on the back of my neck rising.

"Did you approach them to find out more information?"

The corner of his mouth pulled down. "No, I didn't want to blow my cover. If I were to have done so, word would get around I was seeking those headhunters."

"True," I said, chewing on my lip. "Did they say anything else? Why didn't they go and tell Merrack?"

"Hobgoblins aren't too fond of the king, and I got the impression they didn't take the revenants seriously."

"I'm surprised the headhunters didn't know the hobgoblins were there."

"They must have been hidden in the shadow of the trees, and revenants aren't bright."

"Oh." I stared at my feet, not knowing what to think.

"Hey." He lifted my chin with his finger, causing me to look into his bright green eyes. "We have a lead. A female sorceress is controlling them."

"Yeah, but who? I mean, Brunhild is a witch, but I don't think she's powerful enough to control entities like the ones after me."

"Good point," he said, running his fingers through his dark hair, sighing. He stared past me, his thoughts somewhere else. I was about to say something when he jerked his head forward. "C'mon. I want to show you something not many people get to see."

I fell in step with him. "What?"

He gave me a sideways glance. "The armory."

"Really?" I could hear the excitement in my voice. I thought about the weapon looking like a throwing star he used at my house the other night. What other cool ass armament did they have?

"Yes, really," he said, amused.

"How come not many people get to see it?"

"Because most of the fighting tools are infused or marked with some kind of magical properties to take down Murks and other creatures that in your world would be considered supernatural beings," he explained. "We don't want them to fall into the wrong hands. Not to mention we're trained how to use them. We also don't want the Murks to know what weaponry we possess."

"Gotcha," I said. This day was turning out to be full of surprises. I couldn't wait to see what was next.

Chapter Thirteen

We approached a half-timbered building in dark wood and white plaster. It reminded me of something you'd see in a German village. The gabled roof was steeply pitched which added to the charming fairy tale-like structure. When we entered, Narik was punching and kicking a black freestanding heavy bag while Farran was bench pressing, making grunting noises. The large room had different types of shiny equipment to work out every part of your body, and a rack of dumbbells sat in front of a mirrored wall.

Mid-strike, Narik glanced up when we walked in and dropped his hands to his side. Beads of sweat dripped down his face. He appeared both surprised and delighted to see me. "Alaris, what are you doing here?"

"I'm joining the boys' club." I smirked, catching Farran at the edge of my vision, lifting the weights over his head, then lowering them onto a rack behind him with a loud clank.

Narik pulled off his white tank, revealing hard-defined abs. "Well, little girl," he teased while mopping his face and neck, "you need to be able to fight like the boys." He made a clucking sound with his tongue, his brown eyes sparkling with humor.

"I think she can hold her own," Larkin said.

"Really?" Farran joined us, sizing me up. "Scratching, kicking, and biting doesn't qualify. I could show you a few moves if you'd like, but you might break a nail or smudge your makeup."

What an asshat. I squared my shoulders, walked up to him, and did the same thing I'd done to Draylan earlier. Farran's feet flew out from under him, and he fell to the concrete floor.

"Ooooh! You did not just *do* that," Narik said, laughing with Larkin.

Ignoring Narik's remark, I pointed at Farran. "Don't patronize me." He stared at me, dumbstruck. I offered my hand. He took it only to yank me down. I dropped my knee hard on his crouch, rolled, and hopped to my feet. Farran curled into a fetal position and groaned.

"I'm sorry," I said, "but you caught me by surprise."

Narik tossed his shirt on the floor. "I'll spar with you."

"She's a black belt in taekwondo," Larkin warned.

Narik's eyebrows rose to his hairline. "Wow. I've never expected Alaris to be a fighter."

"I'm not," I answered. "My father wanted me to learn martial arts for discipline, confidence, and so I could protect myself." My voice broke on the last few words. I cleared my throat and looked away. My father was a good man. I missed him.

"Are you okay?" Larkin asked, concerned.

"Yeah, I'm fine," I said distractedly, looking at Narik. "I haven't sparred in years, but I'm ready whenever you are."

Farran rose to his feet. "You're not supposed to be here."

"She's the princess," Larkin told him. "She can be wherever she wants, and technically, she owns this place and equipment."

Farran raised his hands. "Point taken; however, she's a princess, and you're her warrior."

I crossed my arms. "Yeah, so?"

"So," he said in a mocking tone, his ice blue eyes burning a hole into mine. "Princesses are not meant to fight. Their job is to be a patron of charities, attend events, host parties, and oversee the welfare of her people."

I stepped in front of Narik and positioned myself into a fighting stance. "I'm not a damsel in distress who needs saving. I'm a wildfire who will burn my enemies to the ground." Farran's pointy ears were peeking through his white blond hair tied back in a ponytail. He had to be a fairy in the same clan as Datura, because now that I thought about it, they did share similar attributes in the looks department. "You're entitled to your opinion, Mr. Spock," I said in a haughty voice to him. "But I have no tolerance or room in my life for your outdated thinking or trying to force it on me."

Grinning, Narik shook his head. "You are a firecracker." He shifted his attention to Larkin who had his elbow on his forearm and his hand covering his mouth. There was laughter in his eyes. "Do you think you're going to be able to handle her? I thought Rydia was unruly, but Ms. Wildfire here is on a level all her own."

Larkin dropped his hand. The corner of his mouth curled, his eyes locking onto mine. "I'll take my chances."

My body flooded with heat. I smiled at Narik. "Poor guy. He doesn't know what he signed up for."

"Everyone knows," Farran said.

"Knows what?" Larkin asked, an edge to his voice.

Farran was studying his hands. The scars on them stood out from his pale skin. "They know Alaris is alive and here."

"How do they know?" Narik asked, stepping closer to Farran, obviously no longer interested in sparring with me. I moved to Larkin's side, a tad disappointed in not being able to practice my moves. I forgot how much I missed taekwondo and how the exercises helped me to focus better. A wave of regret on not sticking with it rushed through me.

"Last night, Datura asked me to inform the people in the nearby villages the rumors were true. Merrack does have a daughter who was formally known as Alaris Yewwand of Havenwood and is indeed a Lockridge. Of course," he said, his eyes sweeping each and every one of us, "the pixies took the information and flew to different parts of Atheon to spread the word. You know how they love drama and to stir up excitement."

"My last name is actually Lockridge?" I still considered myself an Evergreen, but to know what my birth name should have been threw me off guard.

"Yes," Larkin said.

"There's going to be a ceremony in your honor," Farran told me. "You're going to have to be prim and proper. A lady who–"

"Bullshit," I said. "I'm not like that. Never have been."

"A lady who," Farran repeated, ignoring my response, "doesn't swear, speaks eloquently, and has suburb etiquette."

I shook my head, half-laughing out of irritation. "I'm not changing who I am to play a role I'm totally not interested in."

"Tell it to the king and queen." He opened the door, allowing a stream of white light in. "Lunchtime will be in a couple of hours. I'm sure they'll be there. You can tell them then."

"What's his problem?" I asked when he left.

Narik picked up his tank and slipped it back on. "His father is the king of the Solas fairy clan. His mother was Datura's sister," he explained. "Farran's father is making him serve Merrack for four years because Datura is Farran's aunt, and the Solas clan has always been allies with the King of Atheon."

"Okay," I said, thinking my earlier thoughts about Farran and Datura were correct, "but you haven't answered my question."

"His problem is," Narik replied, "he has tunnel vision. He believes everything should be in a certain way. Period. If you do everything digitally, put on a persona people expect from royalty or anyone in a high, respectable position, you in effect create continuity among the populace and a sense of security and trust in your favor."

"All right." I sighed, seeing Farran in a fresh new light. "I understand now why he's the way he is, and I agree with him."

"You do?" both Larkin and Narik asked in surprised unison.

I nodded. "I do; however, I also think by acting that way, you're segregating yourself from others as well as losing sight of who you truly are which eventually will make you one miserable S.O.B." I touched my chest. "I for one refuse to live my life as a cardboard cutout of someone I'm not."

"I don't blame you," Narik said. "I wouldn't want to either, but maybe you can still be you and rule Atheon one day."

I didn't say anything, and neither did Larkin. He and I both knew what my plans were for the future, and it wasn't staying here. That was for sure. Hell, I couldn't even imagine living a life where I ruled a kingdom. It would be like having thousands if not millions of children you'd have to take care of and make sure everyone played nice and got along. Another thing, too: I knew nothing about royalty, who Merrack's allies were besides the Solas clan, and if he had enemies. Did Merrack even have an army?

Narik sprayed light green liquid stuff on the freestanding kicking bag. It had a sharp alcohol smell. He then wiped it top to bottom with a white cloth. "I'm going to go take a shower." He tossed the rag toward a black bucket that sat against the wall across from us, next to a metal shelf stacked with rags. He made it.

"Good shot," I said, suddenly remembering playing basketball with him, Larkin, and a few other guys in Havenwood when we were kids. The only difference between here and earth was the ball's gold, and when it went into the basket, sparkling dust shot out from the top. I recalled us playing at night because the colorful particles were bright and beautiful against the dark sky, like setting off a firework. Huh. Weird, how that memory popped out of nowhere.

"Thanks." He smiled and waved goodbye. "I'll catch you two later."

"I guess I should go do the same thing." Larkin stared at the closed door, talking more to himself than me.

"Do you think the guys would mind if I worked out here, too?" Looking at all the equipment made me realize how neglectful I'd been toward my body. I needed to get back into strength training and regain my flexibility. I'd been ignoring those things for years in favor of having fun and partying with my college buddies.

He considered my question. "Farran and Datura might, but the rest of us wouldn't have a problem with it." He laughed as if he thought of an inside joke.

"What?" His face glowed with happiness. I found it adorable and contagious. I couldn't help but smile.

"You keep surprising me," he said. "The look on Farran's face when you kicked his feet out from under him was priceless." He laughed again. "He's one who rarely gets taken down. Then you come around and pull a cog out of his perfect wheel of life, throwing him off kilter."

"He pissed me off," I said, following him to a wooden door on the other side of the room.

"I know, but your bold and rash behavior concerns me." He opened the door and a puff of stale lavender assaulted my nostrils. It was a linen closet with white towels stacked on shelves. He flipped a switch on the wall, flooding the small room with soft light.

"What do you mean?" I thought he was going to take a towel, but instead, he stepped inside.

"C'mon. I want to show you something, but close the door behind you." He gestured for me to hurry.

My heart skipped several beats. "Are we going to play 'Five Minutes in the Closet'?" I closed the door behind me. He took my hand and positioned me in front of him, facing away.

"I don't know what you're talking about, but I get the feeling it would be something I'd enjoy." I could hear the smile in his voice.

Warm blood rushed to my cheeks. "It's a game we used to play as teenagers. It's fun." He half-turned and reached for something. I would have looked to see what he was doing but didn't want to risk being that close to him in this cramped space. Several buttons beeped in sequence. A black wall slid down, covering the shelves and towels. His hands dropped to my shoulders, cupping them. "What did you do?"

"Hold on." He moved his hands to the top of my arms, tightening his grip. The floor shook. Slowly, it lowered. "I was punching in a code that's needed to gain access to the armory."

"I forgot about the armory," I said, suddenly excited and anxious to see it. "Won't the guys get mad you're showing me this?"

"Farran might, but he'll have to get over it. Like I told him earlier, technically you own everything here. It's yours, and you have a right to know what you're going to inherit someday."

"Um, I'm claustrophobic," I said when we continued to go downward in a black tube with tiny round balls of white light the size of marbles fused throughout its surface. I looked up. Darkness. The floor must have automatically gone back into place, hiding this secret.

"Close your eyes," Larkin whispered next to my ear, his warm breath tickling it, making my pulse race and aware how close his lips were to my neck—a weak spot of mine. "We'll be there in half a minute."

I closed my eyes, noticing a drop in temperature. The air was getting a bit chilly. I wrapped my arms around myself, and we stopped. I opened my eyes. A swishing noise erupted, and the wall in front of us lifted. I blinked as Larkin gently nudged me forward into a room dimly-lit from an unknown source. It smelled dank and musty. When my eyes adjusted to the light, I stood in disbelief, totally not expecting this.

Chapter Fourteen

The room was cut from dark gray stone with four archways on the far wall that were several feet apart and massively carved. On either side were sculpted men in decorative engraved armor standing guard. The contours of their faces and bodies were severe and lifelike, expressionless. I almost expected them to blink because their eyes seemed to follow my every move. Their shields were emblazoned with dragons and mysterious Celtic knots and symbols, exactly like the one I saw on the carriage door the other night. The chambers were cast in shadow. Larkin moved to the first one, his footsteps echoing. I watched his silhouette strike a match and light the torches set in long, scalloped black holders along the walls. The flames flickered across his profile, highlighting the sharp lines of his jaw, nose, and muscular arms. I looked away, not wanting to entertain the thought of being more than friends.

"Each room," Larkin said, stepping out of the one he was in, gesturing to the others, "houses different types of weapons for whatever nasty you need to defend yourself against. This section is mine. The next one is Farran's, then Draylan's, and the last is Narik's."

"This is totally not what I expected," I admitted, my gaze sweeping the area. There was a sitting nook in the far corner from where we stood with a brown couch, two matching chairs, and a round oak table in the center.

"I bet you were thinking of walls lined with weapons." He half-smiled.

"Honestly, I don't know what I was thinking." I paused in front of one of the statues guarding the contents inside. "I saw this coat of arms on the carriage. What does it mean?" Tentatively, I touched it, feeling the deep groves of the stonework beneath my fingertips.

"Gold dragons represents an elemental connection. They're wise, honorable, and brave," he explained. "They have the ability to speak human tongue as well as draconic. Of course, you can't tell the color of the dragon on here, but we revere them for those qualities, and we strive to be like them."

Gold dragon? The one that hatched in my room was gold, and now I have his essence inside me. I also had a dream about one last night, but for the life of me, I can't remember it. A chill went up my spine. I could feel the color draining from my face. I swallowed against the sudden dryness in my mouth.

"Are you okay? You look like you're going to faint." Larkin was studying me. Concern wrinkled his forehead.

I hesitated to blurt the words wanting to spill from my mouth. My eyes danced with his, searching for a reason to trust him besides he was once my best friend. I wanted desperately to tell him about the dragon, to get him to understand why his grandmother helped Karrina take drastic measures to protect me. Maybe he wouldn't be so angry with her.

He frowned and touched my arm. "What is it?"

I opened my mouth to tell him, but then a humming noise erupted from the compartment we came out of earlier.

"Shit," Larkin spat, gritting his teeth.

"What?"

"Someone is coming." He ran his fingers through his hair. "Son-of-a-bitch."

"Are you going to get into trouble?"

"No."

"Has Datura been down here before?"

"No, she has no reason to, and Merrack wouldn't want her to anyway."

"Why?" I thought that was kind of weird. I mean, she was the queen.

If she wanted to see the armory, she had every right.

"Because fighting and weapons isn't her concern."

"Oh, I see," I said, pursing my lips. "She's a woman."

"Merrack holds the same views as Farran," he told me with a hint of disapproval in his voice. "Besides, since she's not blood, she has no entitlement to this unless there is no living heir."

The door lifted, releasing the swishing noise as before and out stepped Draylan wearing black pants and a dark blue T-shirt. "I was wondering if Larkin would take you down here."

"He hasn't showed me anything yet. We just got here," I told him, still rattled about the dragon. Draylan looked like he was up to something or knew a secret. He had that mouth twitchy, anxious energy about him. He rocked on the balls of his feet. I eyed him suspiciously. "What's up?"

"He does appear to be holding something back," Larkin said, scrutinizing him.

Draylan grinned. "There's going to be a dinner party tonight in your honor. Farran's father is going to be a guest and possibly a few other people, as well."

I groaned. "I hate being the center of attention. Besides, I want to go to Havenwood and see the house Karrina and I lived in."

"You mean your house," Larkin corrected.

I didn't say anything. I thought it was too weird to think I owned a house. Hell, I hadn't given much thought to Karrina and the fact I lost another mother. I felt numb toward her for some reason. Maybe because she tricked me into allowing Mardella cast the memory spell on me. I didn't know. I had too much on my plate to allow myself to go there.

"Datura wanted to have a huge party where everyone would be invited," Draylan informed us.

"What changed her mind?" Larkin asked.

Draylan touched the door. The front lifted, revealing the narrow inside compartment. "Merrack. He thought it was too soon for Alaris to be surrounded by a crowd of people, especially ones she's not accustomed to being around."

"How nice of him," I mumbled.

Draylan stepped inside the elevator. He looked at me. "By the way, if Larkin wouldn't have brought you down here, I would have." He winked, and I felt Larkin stiffen next to me. Draylan touched something on the wall. "I suggest you get cleaned up soon, Larkin, lunch is in an hour and half, and Merrack wants us all there." The door slid shut as Draylan moved his fingers up and down in a bye gesture, smirking.

Larkin glared after him. "He's still pissed at me for breaking up with Lithia."

"It was a shitty thing you did," I said, turning back to the dragon on the shield. I tried to imagine seeing one in real life. I think I would laugh and cry at the same time if it ever happened.

He sighed, exasperated. "I told you why. I was never interested in her. My heart has always been–"

"I don't want to hear it," I cut him off. "What is done is done, and it's none of my business anyway."

He frowned. "I hope you don't think I was an asshole for breaking it off with Lithia like I did."

"This is like your third cuss word since we've been here. What will the king think about a warrior cursing in front of his princess?" I asked while entering his room, my voice light with humor. The air was warm and dry and had a metallic leather smell. In the corner was a narrow door made of dark wood. It had to be a closet where he stored his armor. The back wall was lined with shelves and equipment racks, holding various interesting items.

Despite himself, Larkin laughed. "Nothing. He's not here. Besides, I already gave it some thought."

I raised my eyebrows in mock surprise and glanced over my shoulder at him. "Really?"

"Yes, and I came to the conclusion if the princess swears, then she certainly wouldn't mind if I did. Am I correct?"

"Absolutely. You don't need to change who you are in my presence, and I'm under the firm belief one can be both charming and respectful as well as have a propensity to cuss and know how to have a good time. I also read people who cuss are more trustworthy than those who don't." I pointed at a silver set of rings attached to a bar that could fit over the knuckles. There were rows of them on a shelf. I went to pick one up and got zapped like from too much static electricity. My hand flew back. "Ow."

He reached over me and picked it up. "No one can touch that or anything in this room, except for me." I opened my mouth, but before I could respond, he said, "Charmed. Each weapon responds to its rightful owner in here. The only way you can hold it is if I were to hand it to you. However, outside this room you can touch it without my permission." He placed it in my palm. The metal was remarkably light and cool against my skin. "Slip your fingers through the holes."

I did what he said and made a fist. "We have these in my world for hand-to-hand combat. We call them brass knuckles."

"It's used for the same purpose here." He turned my hand to the side. "See the tiny black button here?" I spotted it right away. When I nodded, he said, "Push it with your thumb."

I did, and silver jagged blades shot out of the knuckles part. "Wow. That's badass."

He grinned. "This weapon is a good defense against weres, revenants, wraiths, skinwalkers, and any other beings who can't stand silver."

I jabbed the air like a boxer would, pretending there was a beastie in front of me. "I like this." I pushed the side button. The knuckle blades retracted inside the metal. I handed it to Larkin and pointed at the flat, round, sharp silver star object hanging on the wall rack. There were symbols etched into it. "You used this on the headhunters in my kitchen."

He nodded. "I did. Its function is to send them back to where they came from. Farran has a similar one. Only his will send whomever it strikes straight to the prison world."

"What are these designs? I've seen them in other places here."

"They're elemental alchemy symbols and witches runes. Together, along with the silver, packs a powerful punch. You can't kill a revenant.

They're already dead, but you can do other things to them to make them suffer."

Wow. I was impressed. He then went on to show me the rest of his weaponry, explaining each one, including the iron- and silver-tipped arrows. He told me fairies, elves, among other beings, had weaknesses for iron that I wasn't aware of.

"I better go shower and change," Larkin said when I handed him back the gold disk that had sharp serrated edges around it. It was a Sudarshana Chakra that produced a lot of heat when thrown. The Hindu god Vishnu used the spinning disk for the same reason Larkin and the other guys did—to destroy the enemy.

Larkin whispered something, and as soon as we crossed the threshold, the torches went out, creating a whooshing sound. The aroma of burnt wood wafted in the air, reminding me of a campfire in the forest.

"Magic," Larkin said, his expression bright and happy.

"You know how to cast spells?" We were back in the elevator. I jerked to my right when it lifted. Larkin steadied me from behind. His strong hands gripping my shoulders. I closed my eyes to prevent myself from hyperventilating due to the closed confinement.

"It's in my blood," he simply answered, "but by no means am I a wiz at it. I only know certain ones. On the other hand, my grandmother is proficient at it. My mom can only make healing potions, thanks to your mom and her knowledge she kept record of in books."

We stopped. As the door lifted, a cool draft went across my face. I opened my eyes. I was back in the linen closet surrounded by shelves with white towels neatly folded on them. I realized then anything in this world could be an illusion. I wasn't too fond of that notion and frowned.

"What's wrong?" he asked when we stepped into the gym.

"How would I know if there was a secret room hidden in my bedroom?" The tone of my voice came out high and squeaky from the panic rising in my chest. "I don't like that someone could invade my privacy or listen in on a private conversation without me knowing it. I don't want to be constantly monitored or have the feeling of being watched. I also don't want to go to the dinner party tonight." I took deep breaths to ward off a panic attack. "I'm in awe of the wondrous things in Atheon. I am, but I miss my world."

"I know you do," he said thoughtfully. "To answer your question, your room has no hidden entries. I checked."

The band around my chest loosened. "That makes me feel better. But why would you even think about checking my bedroom?"

His brilliant green eyes were intense on my face. They darted to my lips, then up. My stomach tightened with desire as the energy between us seemed to sizzle, but he answered, and the moment was lost. "I'm your warrior. It's my job to make sure you're safe."

Job.

I nodded and crossed the room, exiting the building. The sky was still gray and gloomy, and the air held the same grassy, earthy smell it did earlier. I waited for him outside the door.

"Did I say something wrong?" he asked when he joined me.

"Job," I said.

Confusion wrinkled his brow. "I don't get it. Why would you be angry about that?"

"I'm not angry," I said. "I'm annoyed."

"Why?"

"Because all I am is a job to you," I told him with a heavy sigh. I hadn't planned on sharing my feelings with him about this but since he asked, I decided to tell him. "The only reason you requested to be my warrior was so you can make up for not protecting me when Mardella cast the spell on me, then placed me in a different realm, which by the way wasn't your fault."

His expression fell into a haunting sadness that I could see ran deep within him. "Yes, it was my fault," he whispered.

I stepped in front of him and gripped his forearms. "It's not. You were away at training camp, and we were only twelve. Besides,"—I lowered my voice—"she had a good reason to do what she did."

He blinked, startled. "What possible reason could that have been?"

I wanted to tell him, to unburden him from this cross he bore. I was even prepared to disclose my secret to him earlier before Draylan appeared, but now as I opened my mouth to reveal the true nature behind Mardella's actions, I found myself telling him the same story about the unicorn as I had to the others last night.

"Extraordinary," he said while pondering my tale. "The unicorn was leading you to something." He regarded me. "Am I right?"

My gaze fell to my feet. I wished my hair was down, so it would shield my surprise at how insightful he was. I had to throw his sniffer off before he figured it out. "Why would a beautiful, magical creature lead me to something?"

Larkin was scrutinizing me. "Did he? Was it a dragon's lair?"

My jaw went slack. My eyes widened. I knew then I needed to quickly recover myself before he discovered the truth. I covered my mouth and coughed to mask my shock. I cleared my throat. "What makes you think of a dragon?"

"I've watched your reaction every time you saw a picture of one."

I crossed my arms. "How did I react?"

"The same way I do with horses . . . in awe and with love."

"I must have an infinity with dragons then."

"It's more." He was deep in thought, and I had a feeling he was getting dangerously close to my secret. He'd figure it out any moment now if I didn't do something about it.

"You know, I don't think you should be my warrior." Larkin's attention snapped on me. "Maybe Draylan should be." I knew it was a low blow, and I hated saying those words, but I wasn't ready for Larkin to pry vital information from me. "At least I'd know his intentions would be pure . . . for me instead of his own selfish reasons."

Hurt flickered across Larkin's face, crushing my heart. "I have genuine intentions toward you," he said, his voice strained. "Your safety means more to me than—"

"Keeping me safe," I abruptly said, touching my chest, "is for your own selfish reasons. I think you feel obligated to be my warrior because you blame yourself for not protecting me from being taken out of this world. It's not your fault, but the guilt you've carried for all of these years has been heavy on your spirit. Now you've found a way to unburden it."

He stared at me, speechless. No comeback. No denial. Nothing. I walked away, disappointed that I was right about his intentions and surprisingly sad over the whole ordeal.

Chapter Fifteen

"We're having a party tonight in your honor," Datura told me with a grin while we were all in the middle of eating lunch in the dining room. I swear if this were a toothpaste commercial, there would be a little sparkle in front of her perfectly straight white teeth, followed by a "ding."

"I think I'd rather get a root canal," I mumbled before taking a bite of my taco salad which I was delightfully surprised to see when I sat for lunch. It was even in a fried tortilla shell.

"Why, dear?" Datura asked.

"Because," I said, "I hate being a spectacle for everyone to gawk at. I was hoping to go to Havenwood instead of participating in . . ." In mid-bite, my fork hovering in front of my mouth, it dawned on me she said "party" as in tons of people. Earlier, Draylan told me we were having dinner tonight with Farran's dad as the guest and maybe a few other people. Datura wanted to have a big shindig, but Merrack talked her out of it. I guessed he changed his mind.

I could feel everyone's eyes pressing on me, except for Larkin's who was sitting across the table, pouring salsa over his salad. He hadn't said one word to me since I walked away from him. I guess I was right about him after all. I looked at Datura. "Wait a minute. Did you say *party* as in crowds of people?"

"Why yes, of course," she said as if what I asked sounded silly. "It will be splendid."

"I think I'll pass." I took a bite, enjoying the taco meat flavor mixed with the sour cream. I chewed slowly, savoring it.

Draylan elbowed me. "It'll be fun. We can drink the wine you like and dance. You know how to dance, right?"

Draylan had no idea about what I said to Larkin earlier regarding Draylan being my warrior instead. It happened to be a coincidence he sat beside me, but by the way Larkin avoided eye contact with us, and the muscle in his jaw twitching, I could tell he didn't like it.

"I know how to move my body to the beat of the music," I answered, "but I'm not interested in going. Besides, you told me we were having a dinner party with Farran's dad instead."

"We were," Datura said. She placed her hand on Merrack's arm. Slowly she slid her palm up and down it. "However, I convinced the king to do this instead." Her voice was low, almost a purr.

I remembered the little peep show I saw this morning with her and Merrack in the kitchen. If he gave her what she wanted, she'd serve him in new and exciting ways tonight. I guessed this had to be what she wanted since Draylan told me earlier Merrack thought it was too soon to put me in that position.

"Have fun," I said. "I'll stay in my room and read while you entertain."

"No one is coming to see Datura," Farran said. He sat between Larkin and Merrack, his features expressionless. I swear he could be a Vulcan. "They want to see you. The future queen."

"I didn't ask them to come," I retorted. I wanted to say staying here to reign over Atheon wasn't in my plans, but I didn't.

On the other side of Draylan, Narik leaned into the table so he could talk to me. There was a jovial glint in his eyes. I recalled when we were kids, we had a lot of fun together, getting into mischief. His twin sister Rydia took part in some of our antics. My heart warmed at those memories and toward Narik as well. "It's only going to be the residents around this part of Atheon. It won't be bad. Everybody already knows you're alive. They just want to meet you, and of course load up on the free food and drinks."

"Nobody is coming from Havenwood?" I asked, hearing the disappointment in my voice. I wanted to reconnect with Rydia and Larkin's mom. I knew Larkin was anxious to talk to her about Mardella, and so was I.

"It's too far to attend on short notice," Merrack said.

"Why can't they teleport here?" If the headhunters and Larkin could jump from this world to mine and back again, I'd think it would be much easier to do the same within their own realm.

"Only certain beings can transfer themselves from point A to point B in Atheon and other parts of this realm unless they're within a prison that has powerful wards around it to prevent them from doing so," Merrack answered. He picked up his glass and went into a coughing fit. It shook, splashing water on the table. Datura took it from him and rubbed his back.

I scooted my chair away from the table and was about to rise when he held a hand up. "Are you okay?"

Datura frowned. "He's been going through these spurts lately. He'll be feeling fine. Then this happens."

His complexion was flushed like he had a fever. I wondered if he had bronchitis, so I asked Datura if he'd been checked by a doctor or healer as they called it here.

"Brunhild gave him some herbs to take," she said. "He took the first dose this morning."

I risked a glance at Larkin and locked eyes with him. My pulse raced, and I think I stopped breathing. Everyone around us seemed to melt away due to the magnetic energy that flowed across the table between us. I swallowed hard and kept staring at him. He had to be thinking along the same lines as me about Brunhild. Though she proved to be thoughtful and kind enough to lift the charm from me, I wondered if her intentions were pure.

"Did she give him anything for the cough like licorice root tea or a ginger peppermint syrup?" I asked. "Honey works, too." Wow. Those words fell out of my mouth without any thought put behind them, and the beauty of it was I knew what I was talking about. Karrina taught me a lot about herbs and natural remedies.

Datura tensed. Her crystal blue eyes were thoughtful, betraying the tightness at the corners of her mouth. "She didn't have any on hand, but I'll see to it we get some."

"I would like to go to Havenwood as soon as possible." I said, breaking a piece of my tortilla shell and dipping it in salsa. "While I'm there, I'll prepare a potion for Merrack to relieve his cough and combat what ails him."

Datura folded her hands on the table. "Are you qualified to handle what could perpetually be a life-threatening task? If you were to make one tiny mistake, it could cost my husband his life." Her voice was conversational with a condescending undertone beneath her spoken words. She sat up straight, evoking an authoritative intimidation I suspected was supposed to cause me to cower. I didn't flinch nor bat an eye. "I'm not comfortable with the idea."

I hated to admit it, but she was right. Since all I had were memories of what Karrina taught me and watching her create healing potions, I realized I wasn't competent enough to make Merrack the medicine he needed to get better.

"You're right," I said, nodding. "Karrina might have schooled me in herbology and what she knew, but I in no way am a healer. Therefore, I propose I go to Havenwood with an escort of course, and hit Fiona up for some"—I held my hands up and wiggled my fingers—"witchy woo stuff."

Narik laughed. "I forgot it's what you used to call your mom's remedies when we were kids."

Despite himself, Larkin smiled, whereas Farran stared at Datura, expressionless. Merrack took a drink of his water and set his glass down. A distant look settled in his eyes at the mention of Karrina—a softness in them only a love for someone could create.

I laughed. "I remember."

"Well," Datura said. "Fiona is the adequate choice, but I suggest we see how Merrack feels in the next few days and then decide what proper measures to take in the matter of his condition. For all we know, he has a virus that needs to run its course."

"I think Datura is right," Draylan said. He looked at Merrack. "How are you feeling now?"

Merrack cleared his throat. "I'm fine, but I'd like to spend some time with my daughter." His gaze shifted to me. "If it's all right with you."

I stared at him, surprised he called me his daughter and wanted to visit with me. "Yes, I would love to." A warm smile crossed his face. "There are things I'd like to ask you, anyway."

"I imagine so," he answered, knowingly. "But back to the party tonight." He drank more of his water and glanced at Datura. I noticed she slipped her hand under the table and was rubbing his thigh. He set his glass down. "Will you please attend and take part in it? I realize this is a lot to ask of you since you only arrived here yesterday. Not to mention, dealing with your misfortune and grief, but as King of Atheon, it's my job to keep an adhesiveness among my people, so they don't feel a strong sense of separation between us and them. Therefore, it would be in the best interest of everyone if you would join in the festivities, say a few words, and mingle with the crowd."

Shit. I hated being put in this position. All I wanted to do was go to Havenwood to reconnect with my past, make the headhunters pay for what they'd done, go back to my old life on earth, and become an archeologist. Was that too much to ask? But Merrack's pleading eyes caused my resolve to waver. Even though we didn't really know each other, I'd hate to disappoint him. Everyone was watching me, waiting for my reply. I stared at my lap, again wishing my hair hung down to veil my face from them.

"I'll make sure you have fun," Narik said. There was a mischievousness in his eyes I remembered quite well, and a familiar excitement rose within me. "Come on. Say yes." He put his hands together as if he were praying and made a silly face. "Please. Please. Please."

I playfully rolled my eyes, my lips curling into a faint smile. "Okay, I'll do it if you promise I'm going to have a good time."

He crossed his heart. "I promise. It'll be like old times. You remember those times now, right?"

"I do," I replied.

Datura clapped her hands together, her expression bright and cheerful. "Then it's settled. The party will start at eight. Farran, you go and make sure everyone in our surrounding area knows about it." He nodded and left the room without a second glance. She placed her hand on mine. "I have the perfect dress for you." She beamed. "I'm looking forward to finally having another female to preen with, and with my beautiful step-daughter is the icing on the cake."

Heat swelled in my cheeks from everyone staring at me and from Datura saying I was beautiful. That praise coming from the most gorgeous woman I'd ever seen in my life.

Datura rose. "I have much to do today, so I will excuse myself." She kissed Merrack on the forehead and whispered something in his ear. A slow, devious smile crossed his lips. When she pulled back to look at him, his eyes were on her. Only her.

"Narik," I said, looking away from Merrack and Datura's intimate moment. "Are you going to pick me up at my room? I don't want to walk outside in front of everyone by myself."

Draylan rose from the table. "I'll go help Farran," he announced to no one in particular. He touched my shoulder and lightly squeezed it. "I'm glad you decided to go tonight. Save me a dance."

Narik moved to Draylan's seat. "Isn't Larkin going to pick you up?" We both looked across the table. Larkin pushed his chair back, stood, and exited the room without even glancing in our direction. "He doesn't look too happy." I stared at my lap, trying not to give into the crushed feeling in my heart. Larkin was my best friend. Those treasured memories with him when we were children were engraved into my soul. Since the spell had been broken, I felt closer to him; however, a decade apart molded us into who we were today. I wasn't sure if I knew him anymore. "Did something happen between you two?"

I leaned next to his ear and whispered, "Yes, I'll tell you later tonight, okay?"

He nodded.

"So will you escort me to the party?" I asked in my normal tone of voice. "You did promise me I'll have a good time."

Narik touched his chest and dipped his head. "It would be my pleasure."

I breathed a sigh of relief, acutely aware of my nerves fraying at the edges and how I dreaded tonight's event. I could get through this. It was one night, I told myself. I thought about my first taekwondo competition and how uneasy I became before I faced my opponent in front of a large crowd. I lost but in a sense won because it made me strive harder, and I got better. Tonight, I would do my best to reflect good will and peace within this kingdom or however Merrack wanted me to present myself. Christ, now that I thought about it, I had no frickin' idea how I was supposed to act or what to say. Oh, well, it wasn't like I was schooled in etiquette behavior, and Merrack knew it. I had no doubt this party would prove to be an unforgettable event.

Chapter Sixteen

"How are you feeling?" I asked Merrack as we strolled outside beneath the cloud-covered sky. There was color back in his face, and he hadn't coughed since lunchtime. Maybe Datura was right about him having a virus that needed to run its course.

"I'm fine," he said, shoving his hands into the pockets of his black trousers. "How are you doing?"

We walked around the craggy, grassy hill the palace sat on—that appeared to me to be brooding against the gray sky—onto a cobblestone path lined with thick tall hedges, flanking us on either side. Ahead a few yards away was a wrought iron bench with an intricately constructed frame of swirling, whimsical patterns. Beyond it stood an archway made of sturdy twigs with dark green leafy vines wrapped around them.

"I'm okay, I suppose," I answered, not really knowing how frank I should be with him.

He stopped and placed his hands on my shoulders. "You don't have to be evasive with me. I see the sadness in your eyes. It overshadows the show of strength you display beyond your private door." His voice was low and caring, matching his sympathetic expression.

Everything that happened in the past couple of days splintered and cracked within me. I bit my lip to stop it from trembling, but without warning, the tears broke free, and my resolve to keep it together shattered into tiny pieces. I wrapped an arm around my stomach and bent over, covering my mouth with my free hand to stifle the sobs raking through my body.

"Come here," Merrack softly said, leading me to the bench. When we sat, he pulled me into his arms and gently stroked the back of my head. "I'm so sorry."

I clung to him, my father who was a stranger to me, yet I felt like a heartbroken child who would accept comfort from any warm and caring person willing to offer it. I had told myself to buck up, so I wouldn't fall apart like this, but for some reason, Merrack broke through the wall I built, and now I was a complete mess.

"It was horrible." I looked up at him through watery eyes. "Can you imagine coming home and seeing your mom's decapitated body?"

He shook his head. "No."

"Then I find out ten years of my life had been a lie, the Evergreens aren't my biological parents, and I'm not even from earth. I'm from a completely different realm. Oh, and I'm of royalty and expected to rule Atheon one day. Not to mention that Karrina betrayed me, and she's dead. I'll never see her again." A fierce warm pressure reemerged around my cheeks and eyes, pushing out another onslaught of tears. I dropped my face into my hands and silently bawled.

"What can I do to help?" Merrack asked. "Do you want me to cancel the party?"

I swiped a palm against my cheeks and sniffed. "I don't want you to do that." My eyes were burning. I blinked and dried them with the end of my shirt. Merrack gave me a weird look as if my actions were crude. "I may have royal blood," I told him harshly, "but my behavior in how I act daily is far from royalty, and I don't plan on changing who I am to play a certain role in someone else's movie."

"I blame your mother for your plight," he calmly said, "but nonetheless, she was my true love, and I strongly believe she had a legitimate reason for her actions."

His admission surprised me. "You forgive her?"

"I do."

"You're still in love with her?" I could see it in his face when we talked about her.

A flicker of a smile passed his lips. "Yes . . . but enough about me." He studied my face. "Are you okay? If you need to talk to someone, I can arrange it."

"No, I'll be fine, especially once those two headhunters get what they deserve."

"If anybody can capture them, Larkin can. It's simply a matter of finding them."

Hearing Larkin's name sent warmth across my chest. I glanced away and rose. I didn't want to think about Larkin or face the bipolar feelings I had toward him. It was too exhausting to deal with the love and bond we once shared as children, as best friends, and my recent disappointment of his disingenuous behavior.

Merrack joined my side. "Don't worry, Larkin will find them and make sure they pay for their heinous crime."

"We need to find out who was controlling them as well," I said as we strolled along the cobblestone path.

"Yes, I'm aware, and I have a feeling it's a Murk." He rubbed the side of his beard in contemplation. "Someone who is well versed in dark magic and deceit."

"Larkin and I were thinking maybe it was Brunhild, but then we thought she's not powerful enough to perform such an act."

"Brunhild," Merrack said, "has many tricks up her sleeve, but she's never done anything to lead me to believe she's evil."

"Whomever it is must be punished."

"Yes, and I'll leave it up to you to be the one to choose the punishment."

I was surprised he'd considered my feelings in the manner and would willingly allow me to make the decision on the fate of this unknown malevolent being. "Thank you. I appreciate it."

His features softened. "You're my daughter and knowing what Datura went through when her family was slaughtered, I'll do anything I can to help you recover from your tragedy."

Not wanting to revisit what happened to my mom and dad, I changed the subject. "Does Atheon have more than four warriors?"

"Yes, but they take care of the villages in other parts of Atheon, and we have soldiers who train, though we haven't been at war for hundreds of years."

"So the warriors are like the elite armed forces on earth such as the Army green berets and Navy SEALs?"

He nodded. "Correct. Also, Atheon doesn't encompass this whole realm. The midlands where you were born is not part of Atheon, though if they need our help, we will assist them."

"For a price, right?" I thought about the politicians and governments on earth. Nothing was free. It was a matter of if you scratched my back, I'll scratch yours. Political favors and corruption had been going on since the beginning.

"Yes," he answered, "but how we do things has worked out perfectly."

"How so?"

"They have an extensive agriculture system for one. Yes, we can supply our own food in Atheon. Enough to sustain us well; however, we prefer to receive it from elsewhere."

"Like the United States buying oil from overseas instead of using their own?" I asked.

"Precisely, and we pay them for their hard work, along with other talents we enjoy. The treaty we have allows us to have a variety of options, and everyone benefits from it. I have no right to tell them how to run their villages and lives unless it effects Atheon. In short, these are self-governing societies. We respect them, and they respect us and the partnership we have with the trade of goods and money."

"Wow," I said, totally impressed. "Too bad earth isn't like that, but most people can't self-govern. Sadly, there's a rampant growth of a sense of self-entitlement that is destructive in nature, and if it continues, it will decay humanity at its very core."

We walked through the arch constructed of twigs into a beautiful garden like I'd never seen before. Awestruck, the first thought that came to mind was Heaven. There was a grove of bright purple, white, and pink flowering trees and colorful shrubbery on either side of us. The lilac aroma welcomed me in its embraced, and a sense of peace followed.

He nodded as if he knew exactly what I was talking about. He followed my wandering eyes as I took in the beauty of this place. "I come here when I want to be alone with my thoughts and relax," he said.

Our path opened and split into a gorgeous wide landscape of dark, plush green grass, knolls, fruit trees, shrubs, ferns, colorful perennials, annuals, and in the distance, wildflowers among oaks and willows. There were alcoves tucked away within the foliage—some with a bench similar to the one we sat on and a few with café tables and chairs.

"This is . . ." I paused, taking it all in. "This is spectacular." I pointed to my left at a two tiered stone fountain with life-size horses below it in midstride. The water on the large bottom bowl flowed gently over the edges behind them. "Wow."

He smiled. "Yes, it's a marvelous piece of work."

I thought about Larkin and his affinity with horses as we continued to stroll throughout the garden and wondered if he ever told anyone about it during the years we were apart. But my attention shifted on Merrack when he asked me what I remembered about this realm. I told him Karrina had sheltered me and kept me in Havenwood, but I admitted I would wander off from time to time. I even shared with him my encounter with a werewolf which spun our conversation onto the Murks. He told me about a prison world connected to this one called Phriosuin Domham. I remembered being told about it when I was younger that there were powerful magical wards surrounding the dark, dismal prison. My friends and I used to tell scary stories about it around the campfire or at sleepovers.

"Did you know Atheon used to be on earth?" Merrack asked me, stopping and sitting on a bench beneath a willow tree.

I joined him. "Yes, Larkin told me before Atlantis there was Atheon, but that was it. I do remember the story about it, but I'd like for you to tell me in your own words."

Merrack went on with the rest of the tale. The gods weren't happy with Atheon's despicable and hedonistic conduct as well as the warring among its people. One day, darkness fell upon them and the air rippled and shimmered. Frightened, the people ran and screamed, knocking each other over to take cover inside buildings and homes. Then it happened. They froze. Still alive and breathing, they were forced to remain still. Several angry booming voices came from above and around them, chastising the residents for their behaviors, warning them of a complete annihilation if they didn't change their ways. Normally, Atheon would have been destroyed like other ancient civilizations before it, but for some reason, the deities took pity on them, and an intra-dimensional shift occurred. They found themselves removed from earth and now in a whole other realm overlapping it, connected to other lands that were dispersed there at the same time for similar reasons. After many heated arguments and wars, they had to learn to coexist and finally reached an agreement between them. They shared a common enemy, the Murks and the Dorchadas clan, which were the dark fairies. Between Atheon and its allies, aside from a few minor upheavals, they'd been able to prevent another bloody war from erupting.

"Karrina told me the same thing," I said when he rose and headed in the direction where we came from. I recalled at the age of eight eating a slice of freshly-baked warm bread with butter at our kitchen table, enjoying the taste and smell of a homemade loaf. I asked her then about Atheon, and she told me.

He didn't say anything, and we walked in silence. I noticed every time I mentioned Karrina, a sad faraway look entered his face. My mind wandered to the what ifs: What if Karrina never broke up with Merrack? Would he be the same man he was today, or would he be corrupt with power? What if I'd been raised in the palace? I wouldn't have the experiences I had living in the midlands or growing up around other children. But then again, I would have never been compelled and ripped from this world, or would I?

Someone giggled by a cluster of colorful pansies to my right beyond the path we strolled. It was the same sound I heard when I first arrived here—light and airy, like a tiny tinkling bell.

I paused. "Did you hear that?"

A warm smile crossed his face. "Have you seen a Deva fairy before?"

I searched my memory and looked at him with wide-eyes. "I actually have. I encountered many as a child in the forest." I put a palm to my forehead. "Oh, my God. Why am I remembering this right now? The dreams of them and the unicorn while I was on earth were memories from here."

"Your recall of past events," Merrack told me, "won't be immediate."

"But a lot of information did come to me," I said.

"Yes, but not everything. It would be too much for the mind to handle. Besides, everyone runs into a situation from time to time reminding them of something from their past they had forgotten. Yours is the same, only more intense."

I thought about what he said as I stared at the pansies. "I suppose you're right." I looked at him. "The giggling I heard was a fairy?"

He nodded. "I know who it is." He released a slow long whistle. "Nalin, Alaris would like to meet you." He whispered out the side of his mouth, "She's shy."

Something jetted out from behind the flowers. It shimmered and sparkled in the air like tiny twinkling lights. As it drew closer, the form took shape into a five-inch girl with pale blue, almost translucent wings, their tips the color of sapphire. My lips parted in wonder.

She hovered in front of me, dipped her head, and said, "Please to meet you, Alaris." She curtsied, her round violet eyes hooded in shyness.

"Please to meet you, Nalin." I smiled, elated I got to meet a small fairy. "How are you?"

She giggled in her hand. A strand of golden hair fell across her face. "Um . . . good. Will you be seeing Larkin tonight?" She peeked at me in anticipation.

"Yes." I was surprised she mentioned Larkin. I wondered if she had a crush on him. I couldn't blame her if she did. He was hot. "Why?"

She hovered above my head. "I think you two make a gorgeous couple." She waved as she flew away. "It was nice meeting you."

"You, too," I called as she disappeared into the distance, a little disappointed she didn't stay longer.

"Nalin is a matchmaker," Merrack said with a comical expression on his face. "She loves to fix up couples and see them happy." He elbowed my arm. "Apparently she has her eyes on you and Larkin."

"Oh, no, I'm in trouble," I joked.

"Her nickname is Giggles, by the way."

"Gee, I wonder why." I flashed him a silly look.

He laughed. "You remind me of your mom. She was strong-willed and kooky at times. She was a lot of fun to be around . . . " His voice trailed off and a cloud of sadness overshadowed his previous sunny mood.

"Tell me about your mother and father, my grandparents, and our family history," I said to get his mind off of Karrina. My ploy worked. He was pleased I asked him and animatedly launched into our family tree, which in the end led me to the edge of a plateau of indecision and confusion about my life.

Chapter Seventeen

After Merrack and I had a light dinner of roast beef sandwiches and potato salad in the kitchen with Datura, I headed to my room to take a shower. My stomach rolled with nerves about tonight, and my head swam with the details of my family tree Merrack shared with me.

Augustus Lockridge was my grandfather's name. He was well-liked among the people, except for the Dorchadas clan, but they despised anyone who wasn't like them. Augustus, along with his father, my great-grandfather, sent many dark fairies from that clan to prison or executed them, and they were still holding a grudge against the Lockridge family because of it. Of course, he also gave swift punishments or killed other malicious beings after they committed a wicked act like the dark elves or whoever else were considered Murks. Therefore, our family would always have enemies to look out for. Not to mention skeletons in our own closets that Merrack wouldn't elaborate on but caused me to question my decision to leave Atheon after the headhunters were taken care of. I wanted to know everything about this side of my family to better understand me and whatever possible darkness I might have dwelling inside.

I closed the door and paused with my hand still on the knob, deep in thought.

Wait a minute.

Darkness.

Maybe someone from the Dorchadas clan or a dark elf was controlling the headhunters, but who? Datura was from the Solas clan, and she had no reason to do such a thing. Besides, they weren't evil, and they were our allies. Brunhild was an elf, but if she were a malevolent being, Merrack wouldn't allow her on these grounds. I longed to talk to Larkin about these racing thoughts and to ask him if he discovered anything since we last spoke. I missed having a cell phone and the ability to contact a person instantly.

My eyes wandered to my desk. The plate with the sandwich on it disappeared, replaced with something else. I crossed the room and laughed when I saw what it was.

A Snickers bar.

The little guy who ate the sandwich yesterday must have left it for me when he took the plate away.

"Thank you," I said grinning while tearing the wrapper off my favorite candy bar. My heart felt a little lighter as I bit into the chocolate, savoring the caramel and nutty taste. For a few moments, the connection between me and this delightful treat was paramount. If I closed my eyes, I could pretend I was back home in a normal life, no longer in Atheon. Then to my chagrin, I realized I would no longer have a normal life, even if I were to leave here and return home, things wouldn't be the way they used to be. I was no longer Haven Evergreen. I was now Princess Alaris Lockridge, heir to the throne, destined to rule.

I threw the wrapper into the wastebasket next to the desk and frowned. Who in their right mind would want to be in the position I was in? I still haven't told Merrack how I felt about the whole thing and decided to keep it to myself for now. He told me earlier after our discussion about his family, I mean *our* family, he was perplexed about what happened over dinner last night. I stressed to him that I'd never caused water to spontaneously boil, and like him and the others who witnessed the phenomenon, I was as dumbfounded as they were and didn't know what to think about it.

I took my shower, trying not to ponder what I did last night since I couldn't come up with a logical explanation for it anyway, and frankly it scared the hell out of me. Instead, I silently gave myself a pep talk about what was expected of me tonight. I'd make an appearance, give a little hello speech to introduce myself, and mingle with the crowd. I could do this. It was only for one night. Narik would be there with me, so at least I'd have a little fun out of the deal.

When I stepped out of the bathroom wrapped in a white fluffy robe, Datura and a woman who appeared to be a few years older than me were entering the room. I remembered Datura told me earlier she'd be bringing someone to do our hair and makeup. She was excited when she mentioned it, and now as I looked at her smiling at me, wearing a dark blue silk wraparound that hugged every curve perfectly, I couldn't help but smile back. Maybe this would be fun getting all dolled up with my stepmother.

"Alaris," she said, "This is Bralana. Bralana, meet Alaris." She gestured between the two of us.

I gave a small wave. "Hi."

Bralana dipped her head. I wished people would stop doing that to me. It made me feel uncomfortable. The only difference between me and her was I happened to be born of royalty. "Please to meet you. I'm looking forward to working with you and Datura this evening."

"Bralana is brilliant," Datura gushed. "She works on me before every event and does a fabulous job." She winked at Bralana, raising a pinkish red stain to her pale skin.

I thought about how gorgeous Datura was anyway and couldn't imagine what she'd look like after Bralana did her handiwork. I visualized a breathtaking goddess who could lure any warm-blooded male to her bed.

"I'm sure she does." I shifted my gaze to Bralana. "I love how glossy your black hair looks. Can you do the same thing to mine?" She also had a cute shoulder-length style that was layered around her face. I would have her create the same look on me but wasn't ready to cut off my long hair and make a drastic change like that. Yeah, I was chicken.

"Thank you," she said, "and yes I can. It would be my pleasure."

* * *

Three hours went by quickly, and I had to admit I enjoyed every minute of it, chatting with the girls and getting pampered. Not only did Bralana do our hair and makeup, she also gave us manicures and pedicures. I found the whole process relaxing. Datura was the first one done, and she was absolutely stunning in her A-line silk lilac floor-length gown that reminded me of a Roman goddess dress. It had the empire waist and cutout arm-length sleeves with a wide shoulder strap embossed with tiny crystals that twinkled with her every movement. The material draped her body perfectly. Her long hair fell down her back in loose waves, the sides pulled back in a sparkling amethyst barrette.

After Bralana was finished with my hair and makeup, Datura told me my dress was hanging in the bathroom and made me promise not to look at it too closely until I slipped it on. She had an anxious excitement about her that reminded me of a child on Christmas morning before opening her presents. I hesitated in the middle of the room. No one had ever picked out a dress for me, and to be honest, I was a bit nervous. What if it was ugly or didn't fit me right?

"Go on," she said, grinning, shooing me in that direction. "Trust me. You'll love it."

Without a word, I entered the bathroom and closed the door. The dress was hanging on a hook on the back of it. When my eyes rested on the gown, the tips of my fingers fell to my lips, pressing them. *Oh, my.* The design and material were absolutely beautiful in a pale mauve color. It had an A-line off the shoulder cap sleeves with beaded crystals, including the entire bodice. There was a delicate sheer see-through material lining the top of the bust. I took the dress off the hook and discovered the same fabric covered the back as well, exposing it. I took my robe off and slipped the dress on, careful not to muss up my hair that was twirled into a bun on the back of my head with a band of baby's breath on my crown.

Holding the front top of my dress, I opened the door. Datura was waiting a few feet away, chatting with Bralana. "Can you zip me up?" I turned my back to her.

"Of course, dear," Datura said. As she raised the zipper, the fabric tightened around my torso and breast but wasn't uncomfortable or too confining. "There." She softly patted my shoulder. "Turn around." When I did, both she and Bralana gasped. "You look . . . I'm at a loss for words." She giggled.

"Enchanting," Bralana breathed in a dreamy voice, placing a hand over her heart.

"Yes, enchanting." Datura took both my hands and pulled my arms in front of me, as if we were going to play London Bridge. "You look like a princess now." She stepped aside and nudged me toward the full-length antique mirror that stood in the corner next to the closet. "What do you think?"

I stared at my reflection, unblinking and wide-eyed. Was this really me? The floor-length dress had a wide band six inches from the bottom in the same crystal beading as the bodice. My makeup was perfect, highlighting my features in a natural way. My dark blue eyes were thinly lined with black liner which caused them to standout beneath dark brows. My face and bare shoulders were dusted with a shimmering neutral color that caused my skin to sparkle with every movement I made. For the first time in my life, I felt beautiful and dare I say, like a princess in a tragic fairy tale that had one night to be free from the heartaches of her life.

Bralana's apprehensive image appeared next to me in the mirror. "What do you think?"

I turned and hugged her, not caring if it was the appropriate thing to do in a position such as mine. "I think you have magical hands that turns ordinary into extraordinary. I love it."

A sigh of relief escaped her lips followed by a grin, her joy reaching her whiskey-colored eyes. "Thank you. It was my pleasure."

"Bralana," Datura said, "why don't you gather your things? It's time for you and me to leave. Narik should be here soon to escort Alaris, and I believe the guest are arriving as I speak."

I imagined a crowd of people waiting to see me with their critical eyes and to quickly pass judgment on the king's daughter who had been lost for many years. Instant fear knotted my stomach. I wrapped my arms around it and sat on the bed, taking deep breaths.

"What's wrong?" Bralana asked as she closed her cosmetic case, concern wrinkling her brows.

"I don't know about being in front of all those people," I moaned. "What will I say?"

"I have it covered, dear." Datura handed me a folded piece of paper. "I wrote you a speech."

I looked at her in surprise as an uneasy feeling stirred within me. "Really?" I wasn't sure about this. Yeah, it was thoughtful of Datura to trouble herself; however, if I didn't like what she wrote, would I still be expected to recite it anyway? I decided not to take a look at it until she left my room.

"All you'll have to do," she said, "is step up on the platform, smile, wave, and read my speech."

"Um, okay." I cast my gaze to my lap. *What in the hell did I get myself into?*

"You'll do fine." Bralana sent me an encouraging smile when I looked doubtfully at her.

"Of course she will," Datura said, watching Bralana pick up her pink and black over-the-shoulder tote and beauty supply cases. "My speech is infallible. All Alaris has to do is read it, be gracious, and everything else will fall perfectly into place."

"Thank you," I said as they exited the room, thinking it was rude Datura didn't even offer to help Bralana carry her stuff out.

Once the door closed, I unfolded the piece of paper and studied Datura's words. My brows creased as I continue to read what she wrote.

You got to be fucking kidding me!

Someone knocked at the door, startling me to my feet. I gave myself a quick onceover in the mirror, stood up straight, and opened it.

Narik stepped back, his brown eyes traveling up and down my body.

"Wow. You look amazing."

I grabbed his hand and pulled him into the room, shutting the door behind us. "Thanks. You look amazing yourself in your black tuxedo and matching bowtie."

"Check it out." He lifted his pant leg, revealing shiny black pointy shoes, the top half white like his shirt. "Pretty spiffy, eh?"

"Yeah, it is," I said. "Since when did you get interested in shoes?"

"I'm not really. This is my little way of rebelling against a system expecting me to conform to its standards on a daily basis." When I raised an eyebrow in piqued curiosity, he continued. "Yes, I signed up for this life to protect the innocent, and I don't mind doing what's expected of me when I'm on duty; however, I'll be damned if I'm going to be a toy soldier and allow the owner to play with me and control my entire existence."

"You sound like me," I said, frowning at the piece of paper in my hand.

"What's that?"

"Datura wrote me a speech."

"You don't look happy about it."

"I'm not."

"Why? What does it say?"

"The bulk of it is mainly about her. How wonderful she is, and when I arrived here I was confused with no memories of this realm or people. If it weren't for Datura's love, compassion, and determination to help me regain my footing in the life stolen from me, I'd be lost." I thrust the paper at him. "Here. Read it."

He took it, and I watched him slowly shake his head. After he was done, he handed it back. "Wow. Talk about stealing your thunder."

"I don't care about that," I said, my voice raising in panic and frustration. "What I care about is being used as a beacon in the name of Datura. This tells me she doesn't give a shit about how I feel. All she cares about is being portrayed in such a light where the people cannot help but adore and follow her. What the fuck?" I waved the speech in the air. "I can't say this. What the hell am I going to do?"

Narik wrapped his hands around my wrists. "Everything will be okay, wildfire. I'll tell you what you need to do."

"What's that?"

A mischievous glint entered his eyes. "Be honest and be yourself."

I lifted my hands, then dropped them heavily to my side. "That's it?"

"Pretty much."

I made a face. "Gee, thanks. You're loads of help." I sat on my bed. "I think I'll stay here. I feel a fever coming on."

He pulled me to my feet. "No, you're not. Here's what you're going to do. You're going to show up, get on the damned stage, act like you're talking to your best friend about what happened to you, and don't hold anything back. Again, be yourself."

"Datura is going to be pissed if I don't recite what she wrote." I didn't want to hurt her feelings, but I suspected it wouldn't be her feelings I'd hurt—more like her ego, instead.

"She'll have to get over it. Besides, even though she's the queen, you outrank her. There's nothing she can do to change it."

"How so?"

"You have royal blood running through your veins. She doesn't."

"Ahhh, yes. I'm sure she's thrilled about that constant reminder since I arrived."

"It doesn't seem to bother her," he said offhandedly and jerked his head toward the door. "C'mon. It's time to go."

I sighed, my stomach rolling with nerves again. "Fine. Let's get this over with."

He opened the door and glanced at me past his shoulder. "Don't be surprised if the werewolves flirt with you."

I stopped in my tracks, my mouth agape. "What? Did you just say–" A vision of the man I saw when I was a child shifting into a were popped in my mind.

He nodded. "I did. They'll be here, and the bachelors won't pass up the opportunity to charm a beautiful woman such as yourself."

I gave him an apprehensive look. "How will I know I'm conversing with wolfman?"

"They have an earthy, woodsy smell, and when they get pissed off their eyes glow." I didn't say anything, only stared at him. He laughed and offered his hand. "It'll be fine. The other warriors and I won't allow anything to happen to you."

I drew in a deep breath and placed my hand in his, wondering what the outcome of this event would be and what other creatures I'd see tonight.

Chapter Eighteen

When Narik and I stepped outside onto the landing, I was amazed at the magical scenery before us. Anchored to the wooden posts, twinkling lights were strung high above the crowd. A medium sized cedar platform stood in the middle with a band of five guys, one playing slow enchanting Celtic music with uilleann pipes while the others stood back—fiddles, a flute, and whistle in hand—chatting with one another. I wondered if they were werewolves. On the north side were several tented awnings. One had what looked like from a distance an oak makeshift bar. The other two from what I could tell had tables, and there were several food vendors like you'd see at a festival or fair.

"Wow. This is great," Narik said, his face bright with excitement. "We haven't had a party like this in a long time. Only on special occasions."

My heart thumped in my ears. My chest tightened, constricting my airways. I placed my hands on my thighs, trying to breathe while bent over.

Narik leaned next to me. "What's wrong?"

"I think," I choked out, "I'm having a panic attack."

He kneeled before me as if he were proposing. "There's no need to freak out. You got this one."

"Easy . . . for . . . you . . . to . . . say," I gasped between breaths.

"Okay, here's what you're going to do." He rose, taking my arms in his hands, causing me to rise with him. He placed my sweaty palm on his chest. "Match your breathing to the beating of my heart and think of nothing else." I nodded and followed his instructions. He waited patiently until I was able to regain my composure. "Now listen to me. I'm going to stand in front of the stage where you can see me. When you speak, look at me and pretend no one else is around. Tune everyone out and act like we're alone in your bedroom, and you're telling me about yourself and what you know of Atheon."

"Okay. I think I can do that." I had no other choice. Well, I did, but I wasn't about to let Merrack down since I agreed to do this for him and our family.

Our family.

How weird that thought crossed my mind without any hesitation. Maybe because I spent time with him today and for the first time since I came back, I felt a connection with him.

"All right," he said. "Let's do this."

We descended the long flight of stairs. I held onto the railing with one hand and the hem of my dress up with the other to prevent myself from falling. As we got close to the bottom steps, heads turned in our direction, people nudging each other. The music stopped. Datura and Merrack climbed the steps to the platform. One of the musicians handed Merrack a wireless microphone. The already tepid temperature grew thick and hot. I immediately chanted a mantra in my head to calm myself, to ignore the pressing eyes on me, and the high whispers of wonder about what I was going to say, what happened to me, and how I felt which gave me an idea. We paused on the second step to the last and as Narik told me we needed to wait until I was called onto the stage, I breathed in the delightful smells of fried food and cooked meat wafting in the air. My heartrate slowed to an even pace. My eyes skimmed the crowd when everyone's attention fell on Merrack, though some were sneaking peeks at me.

"I bet you've never seen the likes of her before," Narik whispered to me when he noticed my surprised reaction to a tall blue-skinned woman with long brown hair, the sides braided and pulled back in 1960s hippy fashion. Her white silky V-neck dress was trimmed in gold, hugging her upper body and flowing freely from her hips down.

"What is she?" I asked as I watched her ambled closer to the stage. Her movements were fluid and graceful, like a ballerina.

"She's a nereid. Her name is Oona."

"What's a nereid?"

"A sea nymph. They're friendly and helpful people."

"Do you know her?"

He nodded. "I do. She's a dancer and singer at the local tavern here."

I was about to ask him to introduce me to her, but Merrack spoke.

"Welcome everyone and thank you for attending this party for my daughter Princess Alaris. As most of you know, I wasn't aware I had an offspring until a couple of months ago. Imagine my surprise and delight when I discovered I indeed had a child who grew into a beautiful woman. The news of her existence was both heartbreaking and at the same time wonderful. Heartbreaking because I was never given the opportunity to be there when she was born, when she said her first word, when she took her first step, and to see her off on her first day of school. I wasn't there to wipe her tears, tell her bedtime stories, and kiss her goodnight. However, she's with me now, and your queen and I are thrilled to have her. I'm sure once you get to know Alaris, you will be thrilled, as well." He looked at me above the crowd, kissed his fingertips, and showed them to me. Everyone turned to stare. I wanted to shrink into the shadows and hide, but instead, I mirrored his gesture.

Datura took the mic from Merrack and cleared her throat so everyone's attention would fall on her. It worked. "Alaris is a fine young lady who went through some hardships and is now coping with them. With my help she's doing an excellent job recovering from the unfortunate circumstances Karrina had deceptively thrown her into."

"What the hell is she doing?" I whispered to Narik, gritting my teeth.

"She's spotlighting herself to make sure you don't outshine her," he answered, casting a disapproving look in her direction. "She's also tearing your mother down without giving her the benefit of the doubt . . .

your mother, Alaris"—His eyes captured mine. They were serious and unrelenting—"was a good person and well-loved in Havenwood. I remember her quite fondly. I have no doubt her intentions to take such drastic measures to hide you was for a good reason."

"In her mind, I'm sure it was," I said, holding back the tears that threatened to spill.

"No mother," Datura went on, her tone filled with disgust, then anger, "should ever betray her child like Karrina had done, keeping the identity of Alaris' father a secret and transporting her to a different place away from where she belonged." Some people were glancing at each other in surprise while others stared up at Datura in glory and sympathy. "And then we have your king who always wanted a child to love and cherish. He had no idea Karrina was pregnant when she left him. With the help of a powerful witch, she hid Alaris from him, and succeeded until now." She paused long enough to look at the faces staring at her and placed a hand over her heart. "I was the one who found a way to get Alaris back to us, and I'm helping her regain her footing here in Atheon. She's a lovely person. The daughter I always wanted." She turned toward me and stretched her hand out. "I'd like you to meet Princess Alaris."

Again, all eyes were on me. I wanted to shrink and disappear in a hole. Heat rose to my face. I imagined my complexion was beet red. Narik nudged me to move forward while at the same time he reminded me to only pay attention to him when I addressed the crowd and to be myself.

As we approached the swarm of bodies, they stepped aside to give me a clear path to the stage. Heads dipped in respect. A few women curtsied. Dotted among them were elves, dwarfs, fairies—I was guessing from the Solas clan since they looked similar in appearance to Datura and Farran. Tiny lights fluttered above us. One flew to me, stopped midair, and giggled. Nalin. She smiled and pointed to my right. I glanced where she was indicating and didn't see anything except for new faces. When we reached the steps, Narik told me he'd be in front where I could see him and not to worry. I'd be great. He kissed me on the cheek before disappearing into the crowd. My heart pounded painfully against my chest. My hands shook. I clasped them together and drew in a deep breath.

"Here she is," Datura said into the mic, following Merrack who took my hand when I stepped onto the platform, kissed it, and turned us both to our audience. Datura moved to the other side of me. "Ladies and gentlemen, meet Alaris." Immediate applause surrounded me. Datura pressed the microphone into my sweaty palm, pecked me on the cheek, and joined Merrack on the other end of the stage. My pulse thumped on the side of my neck, and the air in my lungs thickened. Everyone was looking up at me expectantly. My mind drew a blank. What the hell was I going to say? I took cleansing breaths to calm my nerves while scanning the crowd in front of me and pasting a faint smile on my face. *I will not go into another panic attack*, I silently chanted to myself.

I caught a twinkling light out the corner of my eye. Nalin. She was hovering above Larkin, pointing downward. She flew away into the bright starry night. Larkin was staring at me with an expression of tenderness, determination, and something else I wasn't sure about or had time to ponder. I was a nervous wreck, but to my relief I spotted Narik standing near the stage. He mouthed to be myself and gestured to begin.

"Hello, everyone," I said in a shaky voice. I focused on Narik, taking his advice to speak only to him and no one else. "As you already know I'm Alaris. I was born and raised in Havenwood . . . well, until I turned twelve after Karrina, my mother, had a memory spell cast upon me for reasons that still elude me to this day. The next thing I remember, I'm Haven Evergreen, living on earth as an only child with no recollection of my life in Havenwood. My parents were loving, caring, supportive, and . . ." A lump formed in my throat, and my eyes stung. I blinked to ward off the tears. " . . . and fun," I continued. "By no means were they rich, but they gave me a good life and lots of love." I decided to be brave and shifted my gaze from Narik and onto the masses. I had their undivided attention. What stood out the most in that moment was the tapestry of expressions of compassion, sympathy, curiosity, and interest in a diverse tribe—human and non-human.

I gripped the microphone as a sudden strength and boldness rose within me. A drive to share my convictions overrode my fear of being the center of attention. "I know what it's like to have to work," I said, knowing most of the people here were working class. "For years I held down a job at a café called Full Moon. I served and waited on people. I was paying my way through college since the Evergreens couldn't afford to foot the bill for my tuition without going into debt, which I refused to allow them to do." I paused and rested my gaze back on Narik. "If I were on earth right now, I'd be settling into my next year of college, but here I am in Atheon a princess. Your princess. Imagine my surprise when I discovered I was one. I didn't believe it at first. I mean, I was raised a commoner with strong values of working hard and earning your keep. Now I'm of royalty where everything is handed to me? There was no way in hell I could be a princess . . . so I thought." Someone gasped behind me. It sounded like Datura. So I said "hell"—big fucking deal. "But then the pieces came together, and the charm was lifted. Honestly, I'm still coming to terms with this new station in my life. I mean, this dress I'm wearing . . . isn't it beautiful?" People nodded. A few wolf whistles issued from the crowd. "I love it, and don't get me wrong, I appreciate Datura getting this for me, but this outfit would have cost me six months or more of my wages if I were to have purchased it where I came from. To be honest, I wouldn't have. Instead, I would have used my money a lot more wisely.

"Anyway . . ." I swept my gaze among the people who appeared to be hanging on my every word. Thoughts raced through my mind if what I said made me appear like a babbling dork. Was I supposed to be regal and refine instead of coming across as one of their peers? Did I fuck up? I glanced over my shoulder. Datura stood near the band members with her arms firmly across her chest, her mouth in a tight line. Merrack was nowhere to be seen.

Shit.

I must have pissed him off because clearly Datura wasn't pleased with my speech. Why had I listened to Narik? I should have played along like I had originally intended. The speech Datura gave me earlier was bogus, though. I couldn't bring myself to read it, I reminded myself. Besides, if I wasn't being true to who I was and instead threw up a false persona that I'd have to follow on a daily basis, I'd be sacrificing my happiness and handing it over to Datura, which I refused to do.

I turned back to the audience and smiled as the idea I had earlier when I was waiting to come up here popped into my head. "Do any of you have any questions for me?"

Datura appeared by my side and said in a high, strained whisper, "I don't think it's a good idea. You need to end this *now*!"

"Don't worry," I said out the corner of my mouth. "I got this."

She narrowed her eyes, gave me a curt nod, and went back to where she was standing only a few moments ago.

"I have a question," a female voice called out. The blue-skinned gal moved closer to the stage so I could see her. If I remembered correctly, Narik told me her name was Oona.

"Go ahead." I gestured for her to continue.

"Were the Evergreens compelled to think you were their biological daughter?"

I frowned. "I don't know, but I think they were."

"Does it bother you," she went on, "that they're probably distraught over your sudden disappearance and probably has everyone looking for you?"

I glanced away. A sudden pressure formed around my eyes at the thought I wished that were the case. I turned my attention back to Oona. A tear slipped down my cheek. I swallowed hard. "They're . . . they're dead." My voice cracked.

Oona's beautiful features crumbled into sympathy. "I'm sorry. I didn't know. Please accept my condolences."

I sniffed and cleared my throat. "Thanks."

"How did they die?" A coarse, raspy voice asked. It came from a short guy about four feet tall with a bald, sloping, knobby forehead. His long pointy ears stuck out from his dark scraggly hair. His elongated nose and pale yellowish skin gave me no doubt he was a goblin.

"They were murdered," I said plainly. Sharp intakes of breaths echoed around me.

His glittery, dark beady eyes widened with interest. "Ahhh, who would perform such a wicked act and why?"

I opened my mouth to respond when Datura answered instead. "It's under investigation." She held another microphone and stepped beside me. "On earth, there are thousands of horrible crimes committed on a daily basis. The Evergreens were victims of one of many. Thankfully,"— she looked at me. Anger flashed in her eyes like bolts of lightning, threatening to storm in its wake. She forced a smile and placed an arm around my shoulders—"Alaris wasn't around when the Evergreens met their demise. Shortly after, I had Larkin collect Alaris, sparing her the danger that more than likely would have befallen her, and now she's here." A swarm of hands popped up in the crowd, wanting to ask more questions. "I think it's time to have some fun. Eat, drink, and be merry." She threw her hands above her head in a hooray gesture.

"Thank you, everyone, for coming here. Enjoy your night," I said, bracing myself for Datura's wrath. Applause broke free, louder than before. I waved as I followed Datura off the stage. She led me away from the party next to a group of trees. I didn't know what she planned on saying to me, but I was ready to state my case and not allow her to intimidate me.

Chapter Nineteen

"How can you behave in such an ill manner?" Datura demanded, her eyes flashing with anger. "I wrote you a perfectly fine speech, and you disregarded it. You might as well have thrown it in my face and spat on me for good measure!"

"You're being overdramatic," I said with a heavy sigh. "I didn't mean to insult you by not reading your speech. I wanted to face my fear of publicly speaking and do it on my own."

"You spoke like a simpleton," she said between tight lips.

"Gee, thanks. Don't try to build up my self-esteem or anything."

"You're a princess. You need to start acting like one. Your behavior is a direct reflection on us and our kingdom."

"I am who I am," I said, touching my chest. "A few days ago I didn't even know I was an heir to a throne. I was perfectly happy with my life, and now I'm in a different realm surrounded by beings straight out of a Grimm Brother's story, expected to be something I'm not. I don't think so."

"I'm not asking you to be any different."

"Yes, you are. According to what you just said, I'm a simpleton because how I acted on stage was me."

"I didn't suggest you're one of those people. What I mean is you lowered yourself to their level instead of elevating yourself above them. Docking your IQ points in order to communicate with them will diminish your role as their superior. You must separate yourself from their class."

I placed my hands on my hips. "*Those* people? Do you even hear yourself? You're a snob. Do you realize that?"

She glared at me. "I rather be a snob than a half-wit, and right now you're acting like one."

"Okay, then, let me tell you what this half-wit knows, and if I'm wrong, do enlighten me because you know"—I slapped the side of my head with the palm of my hand—"I'm a little slow . . . I realized after I said a few words I should have been more regal. I could have turned it around then, but I didn't. You know why?" She didn't answer, only stared at me with her arms crossed. "Because by doing so, I'd be sacrificing my happiness, and I'm not willing to do that. I also felt if the people here got to know the real me, they'd feel–"

"Sorry to intrude on your conversation," Narik interrupted, "but I'm hearing nothing but great things from our guest about Alaris."

"What are they saying?" I asked.

"How bad they feel for you, and they respect how honest and straightforward you were with them. They also loved you encouraging them to ask you questions. No one has ever done something like it before. They're hoping you do it again. They feel like you understand them because of what you told them about you working at a café."

I turned to Datura. Her lips were pursed. "See? I didn't ruin anything. Oh, and for the record, I wasn't going to tell them about the headhunters. I know you thought I was, but I wasn't."

"Very well," she abruptly said, her posture rigid, her expression cold. "I'm going to attend to my king."

My head snapped up. "What do you mean? Is he okay?"

"He was a bit fatigued, so he went to go lie down."

"I'll come with you." I made a move to go, but she held a hand up, stopping me.

"He'll be fine. He did too much today, and it wore him out. Enjoy your party. I'm sure everyone is anxious to be in your presence since you won them over with your charm." She said the last part as if she had a bad taste in her mouth. She turned on her heel and hurried off.

"My half-witted charm," I announced, not hiding the annoyance in my voice.

"Don't tell me she called you a half-wit," Narik said.

"She did," I answered, "but I said she's a snob, so I guess we're even."

He laughed. "You didn't?"

I nodded. "Yeah, I did."

"C'mon," he said. "Let's eat and have some fun." He jerked his head toward the food tent where groups of people were stuffing their faces and chatting with one another, listening to the beautiful Celtic music the band was playing.

I linked my arm with his, determined not to allow Datura's insults and sour mood affect me. I understood her point of view. I did. Yes, my behavior reflected directly on our monarch. I was aware of it and even questioned my own behavior; however, I knew what it was like to be one of *those* people as Datura so rudely classified them. What she didn't understand was I could reach them in a way she and Merrack could never do. Loyalty shouldn't be bred from fear. It was earned through mutual respect. If it weren't for the working class, Merrack and Datura wouldn't be where they were today. I may be a cherry in this kingdom and make mistakes, but that was how we learn, and as long as I was here, I'd do my best to be true to myself and create changes that would benefit everyone in the long run.

As we approached the food vendors with lit signs advertising steak hoagies, hot sausage, hamburgers, French fries, and drinks, people stopped us, one after the other:

"I'm sorry about what happened to your family."

"Your speech was quite touching. I daresay it's time for a change, and I feel you're it."

"You're lovely, and I think you make a fine princess."

"Oh, my. I can't believe I'm actually talking to you. Hi, Princess. It's nice to meet you."

"What a pleasure to see you."

"Welcome back, Princess Alaris. My name is Lucy," a light green skin girl said who appeared to be around my age. There were tiny scales on her pretty heart-shaped face framed by long dirty-blonde hair. Her big blue-green eyes gave me pause due to their deep reflective color.

"Thank you," I replied. "I have to say, you have extraordinary eyes."

She grinned. "Wowzers. That means a lot coming from you."

I shook my head, feeling a bit uncomfortable. "I'm really no different than you are."

She laughed. It was a light, playful sound. "Um, yeah, you are." She made a sweeping gesture in front of her body and held up her hand, showing her webbed fingers. "We're totally different."

"Oh, my God. I didn't mean how we look." I touched her arm. "What I meant was I just found out I'm a princess, and this is all new to me. As you now know, I grew up in a working class family, so it's weird to me how people treat me differently when really I'm like them. If that makes sense." The words flew out of my mouth before I could put any thought to them. I wondered if I should have said those things. Would I lose her respect?

"It does," she said. "You are a princess but one who can relate to the lower class. I think the majority here appreciates it. I know I do."

"She's one of a kind." Narik bumped my elbow with his.

"Thank you," I said to Lucy, ignoring Narik's comment, feeling relieved what I said didn't tarnish the Lockridge name by me admitting I was no different than her.

An elderly man and woman who looked like shriveled prunes and couldn't be more than five feet tall approached me. I immediately thought of hobbits. "It's an honor to meet you."

"Thank you."

They dipped their heads and left.

"I'm starving." Narik nudged me toward the vendor in front of us.

"Me, too." There was a menu beside the glass window written on a whiteboard. I was surprised at all the things they offered. "Fish on a stick. Raw and still breathing for your enjoyment." I wrinkled my nose.

"It's to cater to our aquatic friends," Narik said. "And then we have the bloody liver sandwich for the weres."

"Yum. Yum." I made a face, and he laughed. "I think I'll get a cheeseburger and fries."

"I'm going to order the hot sausage on a hard roll with fried onions and mustard."

"That sounds good, too, but I'll stick to my all American meal."

We ordered our food, and while we waited, we chatted with a guy with brown moppy hair and sideburns who I thought might be a werewolf. He had that earthy smell Narik mentioned to me earlier. The aroma reminded me of being in the woods. The guy told us his name was Wyatt, and for some reason as the light conversation progressed, mostly with he and Narik, I felt strangely attracted to him. At one point, Wyatt's hazel eyes held mine. His pupils dilated, and then he shifted his attention back to Narik. Wow, what the hell was that? Thankfully, our food was ready.

After we got our drinks, Narik and I sat at one of the long tables beneath a white tented canopy. We were fortunate enough to claim the end among the swarm of people who already parked themselves here and were happily stuffing their faces while animatedly conversing with one another. I hoped they'd ignore me and wondered if there was an invisibility cloak in this world. I was totally out of my comfort zone with all the attention I'd been getting.

"You're a rock star tonight," Narik said. "Can I be one of your groupies?" He took a swig of his ale and waggled his eyebrows.

I playfully slapped him on the shoulder. "Stop it. I'm more of a curiosity than anything else." I took a bite of my cheeseburger. "Oh, my God, this is the best burger I've ever had," I exclaimed while still chewing. The meat had a wonderful flavor with a hint of garlic powder in it.

Narik made a face. "It's rat meat."

I stopped swallowing and made a choking sound. Just the thought of eating a rodent made me want to vomit. I turned to spit out what was left in my mouth when Narik quickly stopped me.

"I was kidding." He laughed. "You're eating cow."

I glared at him. "Asshole. You freaked me the fuck out." There was no anger in my tone, only a sharp annoyance like a sister would have toward a pesky brother.

"Sorry. I won't do it again." He was still laughing. "You should have seen the look on your face. Hilarious."

I pinched his arm. "You're going to pay for that one mister."

Someone coughed, pulling my gaze from Narik to the people eating at the table. Dozens of eyes were staring at us. A burning sensation filled my cheeks. Datura would have a shit fit if she knew I was behaving this way in front of everyone.

Wait a minute.

She talked me into doing this when she knew damn well I didn't want to. A sudden stab of guilt pierced me. To my surprise, I realized the people I'd met so far I liked, and a part of me struggled with being true to myself or putting up a false front to fit the mold as a proper princess so these people would feel secure about their lives and future.

On a whim much like a panicked outburst, I rose from the table. "If anyone of you have a problem with my behavior, speak now. I'm your princess, and I ask for you to take into account this title was recently bestowed on me. This is who I am. In time, you will know more about me and what I plan to do for this kingdom."

"What are your plans for Atheon?" A gruff guy with red bushy hair and a scruffy beard asked.

"Yes, what are your plans, Princess?"

Farran. I recognized his smooth, condescending voice. I glanced over my shoulder to where his voice came from. He stood with his arms folded across his chest, his pale blue eyes imploring me to go on.

He hated me.

My heart hammered against my chest. What should I say? I never thought about the actions I'd take to make everyone's lives better. My mind quickly searched for past information I could use that would be satisfactory. The humanities and political science classes I attended in college came to mind. I loved them and aced both courses.

I straightened my back and addressed Mr. Red. "I plan to go to each village and spend a week or maybe longer there to get a taste of what life is like. I want to encounter the daily struggles, listen and converse with the people who live there, as well as find out what they like and don't like. When I'm done, I'll take the information I gathered and create a plan to benefit all of us . . . of course, I can't appease every individual. However, the majority will be pleased with the changes."

A plump woman with jowls, holding a half-eaten chicken leg in her hand gaped at me. "What an extraordinary idea."

"Interesting," a gray-haired man said who was wearing a black bowler hat. "I like the idea."

People nodded, including Mr. Red.

I looked at Farran. He had an unreadable expression. I sat and finished my meal while fielding questions being thrown at me one after the other. Narik bumped my arm several times, giving me his "You're a rock star" look. I rolled my eyes. This wasn't how I imagined tonight to be, and I had a newfound appreciation for my college courses and parents who made a point to interest me in politics and the news.

Finally, Narik rose. "Okay, people," he said, "enough with these questions. Let's have some fun." He took my hand and pulled me to my feet. "Will you dance with me?"

"I want another rum and Coke first." My shoulders were tense, and I'd like to get a good buzz going.

"Only if you promise to have fun; otherwise, I'm slinging you over my shoulder and hauling your ass to where everyone is dancing."

I laughed and crossed my heart. "I promise."

We got another round of drinks and slugged them down. The music picked up to an upbeat Celtic tempo with flutes and a fiddle playing. Narik led me to where everyone was dancing and moved his feet in an Irish step dance. Grinning, I attempted to follow his feet. After a few times of fouling up, I stopped and decided to perform my own wacky dance. Narik shifted gears and emulated my moves in an exaggerated sweep of his arms and legs, causing me to burst out in laughter.

"May I have the next dance?" Wyatt asked after the music stopped and rolled into an equally lively tune.

"Go ahead," Narik said to me. "I want to ask Oona for a whirl, anyway. I'm sure she can keep up with me." He flashed me a goofy smile.

"Brat." I swatted him on the back of the shoulder as he walked by me.

"I really don't know how to dance to this music," I confessed to Wyatt, feeling a bit self-conscious.

He put his hands on his hips. "It's okay. Watch me." He moved his feet in time with the music, back and forth, then crossing them and so forth. I followed his movements the best I could but felt awkward and clumsy. "You're doing fine," he reassured as if he sensed what I was feeling.

I kept my eyes on his steps until I got confident enough to follow along without looking. I was having so much fun, I couldn't help but grin. When Narik jumped beside me and hopped on his feet like what we were doing, perfectly mimicking our moves, I laughed. He had a silly look on his face, making me laugh even more. A few minutes later, the music stopped.

"See, I told you you'd have fun tonight," Narik told me.

"You were right. I'm having a blast." I turned to Wyatt. "Thank you for teaching me the moves."

"My pleasure," he said. "Would you like to—"

"It's my turn to dance with the lovely princess," a guy about an inch shorter than Wyatt with an athletic muscular built said, stepping beside me as the music began to play.

I looked up into his tawny eyes. They appeared a bit wild and held a glint of arrogance that immediately put me off. He had a similar woodsy scent as Wyatt, only his was much stronger. "No, thank you. I'm going to stay with Wyatt."

He half-smiled. "Aw, come on, sweetheart. I'm much better on my feet than him."

Wyatt took a couple of steps forward. "Alaris said no."

"You'll have more fun with me. I guarantee it. My name is Nash, by the way."

Such cockiness!

I held a hand up. "I'm good." I wondered where Narik disappeared to. I scanned the area and spotted him at the bar tent ordering a drink.

A low guttural growl issued deep from within Wyatt's chest, and his hazel eyes glowed. I could feel the shock on my face and was too stunned to move. "Take a hint and leave. *Now!*"

Nash's lips curled, and a sharp snarling noise issued from him. His nose and jaw transformed into a snout. Long canines protruded from his mouth, strings of saliva hanging from them.

I jerked back—or so I thought—until I realized warm, strong hands were pulling me away from the scene, and I wondered whose they were.

Chapter Twenty

The high-spirited music was still playing. People were dancing, oblivious to the standoff between the two weres, but there were some I noticed who gathered on their own in groups, drinking, nudging each other, and pointing in my direction.

"Stay here," a rough voice said from behind.

Larkin.

I turned, not catching his eyes. They were focused on Wyatt and Nash instead. Narik, Farran, and Draylan circled them, swords drawn.

Where did they get those?

Larkin had on the silver knuckles he'd shown me earlier. I thought he should have a sword as well and worried about him getting into close combat with those powerful creatures. He ran to the group before I could say anything. Nash was already backing away with his hands raised shoulder high, surrendering. He turned and caught me staring at him. His eyes glowed and narrowed. He bit the air and hurried off in quick strides. I stared after him as he headed for the forest. Once he was safely away from everyone, he ran and as he did so, to my astonishment, dropped onto four legs as he shifted into a sandy blond wolf, the same color as his shaggy hair. Chills broke across my skin.

"Are you okay?" Larkin asked, his voice still rough.

I shrugged. "I guess so."

"I would like to talk to you if you don't mind."

That was unexpected. "Okay." I had no idea what he had to say and didn't even entertain random guessing on what it could be. I was still reeling from what had just happened. If I told Kimmie about this and everything else, she'd surely think I was off my rocker.

I missed her.

Just the thought of Kimmie and my life before it all came crashing down sent a tremor of sadness through me.

I followed Larkin to the north side of the palace, near the path to the beautiful garden. The music wasn't as loud where we stopped, and my guests in the distance appeared to be enjoying themselves.

Larkin stopped beneath a large gnarled tree. For the first time tonight I was able to get a good look at him. Like Narik and the rest of the warriors, he wore a black tuxedo, but he ditched the tie. His white shirt had a few buttons undone as if he got warm and had to cool himself. He looked hot, and I had the sudden urge to run my fingers through his dark, spiky hair.

"I've been doing a lot of thinking," he said, meeting my eyes. "Soul searching," he added, his expression serious yet thoughtful.

"Okay, and what did you discover?" I had no idea what he was going to say. No clue. He'd been distant toward me since I told him I didn't want him to be my warrior. Maybe he realized he didn't want to be, and I was doing him a favor by releasing him from his duty to protect me.

My heart sank.

I dropped my gaze to the ground, preparing a speech in my mind to tell him he'd still have to honor his oath to me in finding those headhunters and making them pay for what they'd done to my parents.

"I'm in love with you."

"What?" I looked at him, stunned, my lips slightly parted. I knew what he said, but for some stupid ass reason that word fell out of my mouth.

His green eyes softened into a pool of unabashed honesty, causing my pulse to race. "I'm in love with you. I have been since we were kids."

"But I'm not the same person as I was back then," I said, thinking he might have this fantasy version of me from long ago and didn't really love me for who I was now. "A lot has changed. I've changed."

"I know," he agreed, "and I thought hard about it; however, being around you, seeing the type of person you've become and the life you've led away from here makes me love you even more."

"But what about the guilt?"

"I admit," he said, "the guilt of you being taken away from Havenwood has been weighing on me for many years, and now knowing my own grandmother was the one who orchestrated the whole thing added to it; however, I came to the painful realization that even if I were home during that time, I wouldn't have been able to do anything about it. My grandmother is a powerful witch. Obviously, she had solid reasons for doing what she had done. Otherwise she wouldn't have." He sighed, suddenly disturbed and rested his hand on the back of his neck. "I wish I knew what they were, though. It would ease my mind if I did."

"I know," I softly said, thinking back to when I was going to tell him anyway because he was my best friend, even though I told Mardella I wouldn't. Telling him now wouldn't hurt. He was my warrior and now confessed his love for me.

The skin between his eyes wrinkled. "What do you mean?"

I looked about to make sure we were alone. The twin white moons weren't quite full yet but bright enough for me to see if anyone happened to be lurking nearby. I cast a glance at the branches above us and into the sky. No pixies. I moved closer to him, hyperaware of the way my body reacted like it always did when we were almost touching, like the silly flips my stomach did and the burning desire to have him rub his hands all over my naked body. "If I tell you, you have to swear not to tell a soul."

"Of course, I'll guard your secret with my life," he said with a sincerity that left no reason for me to doubt his word.

I told him everything, and when I was done, he did something I didn't expect. He pulled me into a tight embrace. I wrapped my arms around him and told him I was sorry.

"For what?" He pulled back and cradled my cheek with the palm of his hand.

"I should have sent word to you that I needed to see you."

"We were twelve, Alaris. You had no idea of the severity of the situation. Your mom and my grandmother did, so they took drastic measures to protect you." His thumb gently rubbed soft circles around my cheek, causing my stomach to tighten with desire.

"They did and succeeded until now," I said in a breathy voice. He was staring at my mouth. Was he going to—

Before I could finish my thought, his lips were on mine, soft, sweet, and unsure at first, but when I threw my arms around his shoulders and pressed my body into his, his kiss deepened. I parted my lips and darted my tongue into his mouth. I was wet and ached for him to be inside me, but I held back and enjoyed making out with him instead, our breaths huffing into each other's mouths. He was a great kisser, and when I sucked on his bottom lip, he groaned, making me wetter.

He broke away. "You're so beautiful," he whispered in my ear. He kissed my forehead. His lips rested there for a few seconds, then his eyes met mine. "I realize you might not be in love with me, but I'm willing to wait and take the risk of you turning your back on me and Atheon. In all honesty, all I want is for you to be safe and happy . . . I hope it's with me."

I softly stroked his cheek. "I do love you. I always have, but right now there's so much going on in my life. I don't even know how I feel about my own self. I need some time to figure things out."

"I understand," he said, taking my hand and placing soft kisses on my knuckles. "Do you still not want me to be your warrior?"

I shook my head. "No. I only said it because I didn't want to be a charity case. I wanted your intentions to be pure and not self-serving."

He threaded his fingers with mine and gently squeezed my hand. "I assure you my intentions are pure, but I have to be honest with you . . ." He leveled his eyes with mine, and my breath got caught in my throat. "Me being your warrior is self-serving but only in the sense I don't want to lose you again, and I will protect you with my life." There was a fierce passion in his voice that made my stomach flutter. I wanted to kiss him again, but he continued to speak. "Now knowing the reason behind my grandmother's and your mom's extreme actions to protect you, my mind has been eased. Thank you. But the severity of your situation has me on high alert; therefore, I'm going to have to take extra precautions to protect you."

"Like what?"

"I don't want you leaving these grounds on your own. You're safe here. There are magical wards up to keep the Murks away."

"But I want to go to Havenwood," I said, frowning.

"I'll take you myself." He let go of my hand to rub the side of his face. "You not only have a powerful element inside of you but the spirit of a dragon, as well. I'm at a loss to why the unicorn would lead you to the dragon egg and why what happened to you did, but whomever is controlling the headhunters knows your secret."

"The only two people who knew were Karrina and Mardella. Karrina is no longer with us, and I can't believe Mardella would do this to me," I said, sounding exasperated.

He nodded. "I agree, but somehow someone else knows, and we got to find out who." His gaze drifted to the party that was still in full swing. "I say we put this matter aside for tonight and have some fun."

"Yes, I can use another drink." I went to place my hand in his, but he stopped me.

"We shouldn't display our intimate affection openly quite yet, especially now when people are discovering who you are."

"But we kissed," I said with an undercurrent of annoyance in my tone. I didn't care if they had a problem with their princess being more than friends with her warrior. It was my life not theirs. They could either accept it or not.

"True," he answered. "However, we're at a safe distance away from them. It's unlikely anyone saw us."

"I really don't give a flying fu–"

He placed a finger on my lips, and the corner of his mouth lifted. "I know you don't, but being a princess and one day queen, there are certain behaviors you're going to have to tame."

"Why? If they can't accept me for who I am, then they can go live somewhere else."

"I love your spunk," he said, smiling, "and most of them will accept you for who you are, but there's a certain time and place to do things. You can't be careless. You need to exhibit strength, honor, wit, and proper behavior, so they'll look up to you and be secure knowing they have a leader who has their best interest at heart."

What he said made sense. If I were to stay here and eventually rule Atheon, I'd have to take my actions and what I say more into consideration for the sake of the kingdom. I'm sure Farron's father wouldn't appreciate my spunk or loose tongue, and he was one of our greatest allies, someone I didn't want to lose. At that moment, I made a promise to myself to sanitize parts of my erroneous behavior while in the presence of others outside my inner circle. I could still be myself; however, on certain occasions I'd have to adjust my behavior accordingly, get the shit done, and call it a day.

"You're right," I finally said, staring at my guests who appeared to be having a good time. "Let's go party."

Chapter Twenty-One

I woke up the next morning to the delightful aroma of bacon, and for a second, thought I was back home, but when I opened my eyes, I realized I was in someone else's bed. I peeked beneath the covers. Oh, God, I was wearing a long, white button-up shirt.

Where was my dress?

What the hell did I do last night? Where was I?

By the masculine rustic furniture and décor, I was in a man's bedroom. I thought about last night, remembering everything clearly up until I think it was my fifth, maybe sixth drink. First I had rum and Coke, but I switched it up to Singapore slings. Those babies went down nicely. After I want to say the fifth drink, my memory became a bit hazy. I recalled dancing with Larkin, then a group of us performing an Irish step dance, including Oona, a goblin, and a fairy from the Solas clan. Wyatt must have left after the confrontation with Nash, because I didn't see him the rest of the night. I vaguely remembered saying goodnight to my new friends and blowing kisses at them while Narik lit some fireworks as a grand finale to a fun-filled night. My arm was slung over Larkin's shoulders, and I kept saying . . . oh, no . . . I kept saying how hot he was, and I wanted to kiss him from head to toe.

Did I really say that?

Maybe I was misremembering.

I wasn't sure, but from there, the rest of the night faded into the dark abyss of intoxication. I must be in Larkin's room, I guessed, then wondered if we had sex. I hoped not. I mean, it wasn't like I didn't want to, but I'd like to have remembered it.

The door across from me opened. In came Larkin, holding a tray with a plate of food, and a steamy cup of something. He was wearing black sweat pants and a dark blue T-shirt. "You're up. Good." He looked happy, and for the first time since we reconnected, at peace, as well. "I made you bacon, pancakes, and tea with cream and sugar." I sat up, and he set the tray over my lap. As he did so, his eyes poured a fountain of sweet and heartwarming love into mine. His lips were inches from my mouth, inviting me to kiss them. I wanted to but was still trying to piece together what exactly happened last night. "We didn't have sex," he said in a low sensual voice that made me want to grab him. He pulled back and sat beside me.

I sighed with relief. "Thank God." When he shot me a funny look as if he were saying, *Gee, thanks* in a joking manner, my face heated up. "You know what I mean."

"I do," he said, slowly running the tip of his finger down my burning cheek, causing my skin to tingle beneath his soft touch. "I don't take advantage of women who are unconscious."

I covered my face. "I'm so embarrassed."

He laughed. "Don't be. Besides, you were coherent enough to undress yourself while I waited in the hallway. You crashed afterward."

I dropped my hands. "You didn't undress me?"

He shook his head. "Nope."

"Thank you," I said, once again relieved and grateful for Larkin taking care of me. I looked down at the delicious breakfast he made me. The pancakes had no maple syrup on them, only butter, just how I liked them. "And thank you for taking the trouble of making me something to eat. I appreciate it. This looks yummy." I picked up a fork and tried the pancakes. The fluffy texture and buttery flavor burst in my mouth, awakening each taste bud with pleasure. "Mmmm, this is awesome." I cut off another mouthful with the side of my fork.

"No trouble at all. It was my pleasure. I'm glad you like it."

"Not like. Love," I said, between bites. "How did you know I rather have butter than maple syrup?"

His green eyes sparkled. "It was your preference when we were kids, so I took a chance you still enjoyed them the same way as before."

I smiled. "Good guess." He rose and turned to leave. "Where are you going?"

"I need to clean up my mess." He nodded to a door on his right. "Your dress and shoes are in the bathroom. You're welcome to take a shower; however, I think you should start training with us after you're done eating."

"Really?" I took a sip of the warm tea. It tasted like chai with the cinnamon and ginger flavors. Larkin was scoring some serious points here. Chai was one of my favorite drinks. "You want me to train with you? How come?" I loved the idea but curious to find out his reasons behind it.

"You impressed me when you took Farran down, and since your unfortunate situation is so volatile, I think it would be wise for you to clock in some one-on-one combat training."

"I'd feel better if I did," I admitted. "I need to brush up my martial arts skills anyway."

I ate the last piece of my bacon and finished off the tea. I sat up straighter and attempted to move the tray.

"Here . . . let me get it for you." Larkin lifted it off me and stepped back, allowing me room to slip out of bed. I stood before him in his white buttoned-up shirt, except the top three were undone, revealing the cleavage between my round breasts. His gaze dipped to the length of my body, then up to my face, all the while his eyes filling with desire. I wanted him to touch me, but he turned and crossed the room, his shoulders tight in a straight line. "I'll be in the kitchen."

After the door clicked shut, I got dressed, perplexed about why he didn't kiss me. I knew he wanted to. He did last night, and it was amazing. Then I remembered he told me he was in love with me, and I didn't return his exact sentiment. Instead, I told him I loved him, but I needed more time since my life was out of sorts or something along those lines. Larkin was only doing the right thing and giving me some space, which spoke volumes for his character and gave me a newfound respect for him. All the guys I'd ever dated only thought of their own needs and not mine, except for on special occasions like my birthday or if they were in deep shit. Larkin was different. I liked it and looked forward to spending more time with him and getting down to business, so I could move on with my life and see what direction I wanted to take. For now, however, I wanted to learn how to kick some ass and find out who was controlling the headhunters.

* * *

"Show me the block again," Narik said after I countered his attack when he tried to kick my stomach. Larkin was watching closely. He wanted to see how well I did and my fighting techniques so he could determine what type of training I'd need.

"Okay, let's move into an open stance." I positioned my body across from Narik's with my feet apart. He did the same. "Now kick me like before but slowly." He did. I deflected it with my left hand, lightly punched his stomach with my right, and kicked his side with my front leg. My kick wasn't as high as it used to be, which didn't surprise me since I'd been out of practice for a while. "I'm a bit rusty," I said, tilting my head to the side, scratching it.

Narik hopped back and rubbed his forehead. "You could have fooled me."

"I can see what Alaris is talking about," Larkin said. "She needs to stretch and limber up some more, but in no time she'll be back on her game."

"I agree, because I'm not as flexible as I used to be, and I need to do whatever I can to prevent injury or at least reduce it." I turned to Narik. "I'll show you a low, middle, and high block."

"Okay, wildfire. What do I need to do?" He raised his fists as if he were in a boxing match.

"You don't need to do anything. I'm going to demonstrate them for you and Larkin." He stepped aside when I changed my stance, getting into position. As I moved my arm up by my shoulder, I told them this was my blocking arm. The arm below it was the chamber arm. As I executed the counter motion, the blocking arm came downward, protecting my abdomen and upper leg. I continued showing them the moves, aware that Farran had entered the building. He was watching me with his back leaning against the wall and a stony expression on his pale face.

"This is some cool shit," Narik said after I finished my routine. "I like learning new fighting techniques."

"We haven't even scratched the surface yet." I shifted my attention to Larkin who appeared deep in thought. He must have sensed me staring at him because he met my gaze with a half-smile. "What do you think?"

"I think we should get Draylan here and have you teach us what you know and in return we'll train you the basics on what we know."

"Where is Draylan?" I asked. I hadn't seen him since yesterday. He probably had the brown bottle flu, but then again I didn't see him drink last night.

"He was on patrol duty at the party," Larkin answered. "I imagine he's giving a report to Merrack."

"Did Datura say anything to you this morning?" Narik asked me. "I know she was pissed off about you not reading her speech, which by the way I'm glad you didn't."

Larkin's eyebrows knitted together. "What speech?"

"She wrote a *terrible* one for Alaris," Narik said.

Larkin's eyes darted between Narik and me. "What do you mean? In what way?"

"Narcissistic," I answered.

Narik draped his arm around my shoulders. "She wanted to steal Alaris' thunder."

I shook my head. "I don't care about that. What annoyed me was she had the audacity to expect me to give a speech singing her praises and how wonderful she was for helping me get through this rough time in my life, and I wouldn't have been able to do it without her."

"Doesn't surprise me," Larkin said.

Farran stepped away from the wall. "Why do you say that?" He sounded bored, but his words were lined with interest. "Don't you trust her?"

Larkin narrowed his eyes at Farran. "Do you want to know because Datura is your aunt?"

I gawked at them both. "She's your aunt?" Then I recalled Larkin mentioned they were related. I waved a hand back and forth. "Never mind. I knew that."

Farran had a sour expression on his face. "My mother was her sister." He turned and left.

"Was?" I wondered why he spoke in past tense as if she no longer existed.

A solemn look entered Larkin's face. "The Murks not only slaughtered her mother, father, and brother but her sister, as well . . . Farran's mother. He was close to her as was his father. Farran's demeanor has grown detached from others since then. He used to be a cool guy, but after his mother was murdered, he's cold and distant."

I covered my mouth, my heart going out to him and Datura. Now I understood why Farran was standoffish and stoic. He must have shut off his emotions so he could keep his grief at bay. All three of us shared a common tragedy. Why then was he not tolerant of me? Why did he hate me so? My mother's decapitated head flashed through my mind. A wave of sadness washed over me, and my eyes welled.

"What's wrong?" Larkin asked, alarmed. He took my hand in his.

I bit my lip and squeezed my eyes shut, feeling the tears trail down my cheeks. My stomach caved in on me as if someone suckered punched it. I wrapped an arm around myself and dropped to the floor.

"Alaris?" Narik knelt beside me, his hand on my shoulder.

Larkin sat behind me and embraced me, pushing his chest into my back, his chin next to my ear. "Shhh, it's okay." He rocked in a soothing manner.

"What's wrong with her?" Narik sounded concerned.

I held tight to Larkin's arms, feeling safe and secure and lowered my chin as I silently cried. I missed my parents and didn't think I'd ever get over their gruesome death.

"What I told Alaris about Farran's mother triggered the events of her own horror regarding the Evergreens," Larkin told him.

"I'm sorry," Narik said to me. "If I can do anything to help you, let me know, and I will."

I looked at him with watery eyes. "Help me catch the bastard or bitch who's responsible for my parents' death."

He nodded. "Of course, whatever you need for me to do . . . I'm there for you."

"Thank you," I whispered.

"Hey," Larkin softly said, kissing me on the cheek, his lips warm and soft against my skin. "I promise we will find the person who is behind all of this, but for now, you need to train. It'll help your mind, body, and spirit. It'll also build your confidence and endurance."

He was right. Throughout my childhood, when I trained and competed in competitions, I felt strong, alert, and in the moment. We rose from the floor and spent the rest of the day teaching each other fighting techniques, and he was right. I was able to channel all of my hurt and anguish into physical activity and could feel the fluidity of my movements and strength of my muscles returning to the glory they once were.

Chapter Twenty-Two

Earlier this morning when I went back to the palace to change into workout sweats, Datura stepped out of the kitchen wearing a long, powder blue silky robe and silver ballerina type slippers. Her hair was in a braid draped around her shoulder.

How could someone look so beautiful this early? She didn't even have makeup on. Darkness flashed in her eyes when they caught mine, momentarily casting a shadow over her perfect face. But then she blinked and greeted me with a sunny smile. Something was a bit off with her. Jealousy. Oh, and I had no doubt she was still pissed off about me not reading her lame-ass speech. I decided to apologize to her, not because I wanted to. I wasn't sorry in the least bit, but I expressed regret to keep the peace and for Merrack. Datura accepted my apology but not without saying how hurt she was I didn't read what she wrote and how much trouble she went through to write it . . . blah, blah, blah. I played along as best I could to pretend I felt bad even though I knew she was trying to manipulate my feelings to satisfy some twisted need.

Fast forward to now, and I felt like shit after being reminded of her whole family being slaughtered. The sun had already set behind the horizon, and I was beat from training the entire day. All I wanted to do was grab something to eat, take a hot shower, and go to bed. I went to the kitchen and made a ham and cheese sandwich. I ate it while I made a peanut butter and jelly one to leave for the little guy who ate my chicken salad sandwich the other day. I never met anyone who didn't like PB & J, so I thought what the hell, he might enjoy it. I wrapped it in a napkin and poured a glass of chocolate milk to go with it.

No one was around, and that was fine with me, although I wondered how Merrack was feeling. When I'd asked Datura this morning how he was, she told me he was asleep but seemed to be doing well. As I walked near their bedroom on the way to mine, I heard Datura giggling behind their closed door and Merrack laughing. Good. He must be feeling bet–

He went into a coughing fit.

I paused and leaned my ear near the door, thinking I should go to Havenwood and get him some medicine.

"Here you go, darling. Drink this," Datura said.

The coughing stopped. Merrack cleared his throat. "Thank you, my queen." A brief silence fell between them. "Now come here and do that trick with your mouth again."

I made a face. Gross. I didn't even want to entertain thoughts of what he meant by that. I hurried down the hall. The flames in the gas lanterns anchored to the walls flickered, casting shadows around me. They seemed to stretch and move, as if following me. Larkin said there were wards around the palace, and I'd be safe, but I couldn't help shake the haunting feeling I was being watched. I wished Larkin were here, but he had to patrol for a few hours tonight.

Once in my room, I set the sandwich on my desk along with its beverage and took a much needed and well deserved shower. Afterward, I noticed the food and drink remained untouched. I sank into my comfy bed, hoping I didn't offend the brownie. If I did, he'd leave, and Merrack and Datura would be pissed off at me, something I'd like to avoid. My mind conjured dramatic scenarios on the matter and what I would do and say if they were to happen. I was about ready to get up and throw it away, but sleep captured me into a dark, dreamless void.

* * *

The next morning, when I pushed the sheer curtain around the bed aside, I discovered my offerings on the desk were gone. The brownie must have liked what I made him, and it brought a smile to my face. Rubbing the sleep from my eyes, I stepped out of bed, noticing a folded piece of paper where I had placed the sandwich. I picked it up and unfolded it. It was a hand-drawn picture of what looked like tunnels beneath the palace and rooms.

"What the hell?" I said to myself.

"It's a map," a scratchy and withered voice said behind me, causing me to jump and whirl.

My eyes widened at the short guy standing but a few feet from me. I was able to quickly recover and replied in a span of a heartbeat, "I figured as much."

The brownie poked himself in the chest with his thumb. "Me name is Brulin, and if I could be so bold, I suggest you follow it tomorrow night when the two moons are full."

I looked at the drawing. "Why? What's down there?"

He peered up at me from beneath the folds of wrinkles on his face, his oily eyes shining like black ice. "What you've been seeking, you will find, but do not go alone. Take Larkin and Farran with you."

Headhunters!

My heart leaped to my throat. They were here? How could that be? Larkin told me there were wards around the palace, and the only way they could be breached was if Merrack, Datura, or I temporarily broke the spell to allow a Murk in. I certainly didn't know how to lower our magical shields, and I couldn't fathom why Merrack or Datura would. I wondered if a witch like Brunhild could.

I swallowed against the sudden dryness in my mouth and attempted to speak. "I seek the headhunters. Are you telling me they're here?" I nervously looked around as if one had been hiding in my room all along and would suddenly appear.

He pointed a long, knobby finger at me. "You must find out for yourself, Princess, but do not go alone."

The paper shook in my hand. How could I stay here one more night knowing I hadn't been safe all along and didn't know whom to trust? He wanted me to take Larkin along which I would anyway but Farran? "Larkin is my warrior. He'll go with me."

"You must take Farran, as well," he said.

I shook my head in objection. "No, he hates me. Besides, he's Datura's nephew. I don't know if I can trust him."

Brulin drew closer to me. One eye bulged pleadingly beneath his bushy brow, the other half closed. "He needs to *see*," he hissed.

I bent with my hands on my knees so I was eye-level with him. "See what?"

"Brulin cannot tell you." His gnome-like features fell in apology. "I am bound to keep secrets by the owners of the household where I live and work. I can only direct you and offer some advice . . . but nothing more."

"Why did you give me this map?" I raised it between us, still disturbed about all of this. "You're risking a lot for me. Why?"

He reached gnarled fingers to softly touch my face. "This," he said, his voice sad, confusing me, but I remained still and allowed him to do so. "You don't look at me with disgust or as a lesser being. You didn't even flinch when I touched you. Nobody ever displayed such behavior toward me before. You're also"—he dropped his hand, and his eyes shone with tears—"kind to me, leaving me delights to eat and drink. All that's ever been left for me was cream and porridge out of a duty to do so, not out of the kindness of one's heart. Not like you, Princess. Not like you."

"I want to be your friend," I said, moved by his words. I slipped the map between the mattresses to hide it until tomorrow night and turned back to him.

"That you are, Princess." He pulled a faded red handkerchief out of his pocket and wiped his watery eyes. "That you are."

"Good." I got on my knees and held my arms out. "Can I give you a hug?"

He put a hand on his chest in astonishment. Oh, no, I hoped I didn't offend him or broke some code I didn't know about. "You want to embrace Brulin?"

I dropped my arms. Maybe this wasn't a good idea after all. "I'm sorry if I crossed the line. I'm still learning how I'm supposed to act in certain situations here. I just . . . I just thought you needed a hug, and it would make you feel better."

"Nobody other than my own kind ever wanted to hug Brulin before." His dark eyes were wide with wonder and welled with fresh tears. He quickly wiped them away, shoved the handkerchief into his front pocket, and opened his arms to me.

I leaned forward and wrapped mine around his small, round body. He smelled like pumpkins and cinnamon. I bet he baked last night. I wouldn't be surprised if there were fresh muffins in the kitchen this morning.

A friendly knock resounded from the door, startling me.

Pop!

Brulin was gone, causing me to fall forward. Luckily, my palms met the floor instead of my face. I pushed myself up and opened the door.

"Good morning." Draylan examined his fingernails. "I heard a rumor you're training with Larkin and Narik. Is it true?" His honey-colored eyes met mine.

I yawned, trying to hide how rattled I was inside from the news Brulin gave me. "It is, and I'm going to be late if I don't get movin'. I still need to eat breakfast." I left him standing in the threshold while I grabbed for my workout clothes, then headed to the bathroom. "You can come in if you like," I called over my shoulder before I closed the bathroom door behind me.

"I don't think training is a good idea," Draylan said, "and Merrack won't approve."

"Well, too bad," I said while slipping a T-shirt over my tank top. "He doesn't rule me. Besides, I need to learn how to protect myself against the Murks."

"You have Larkin for that," he answered with a hint of sarcasm in his tone. I didn't say anything because I was in the middle of brushing my teeth. "He can protect you," Draylan added.

I spit out the toothpaste and made a face. "I can't rely on Larkin to protect me all of the time. Besides, I was raised to be self-sufficient."

"Yes, but you didn't know at the time you were an heir to a throne. You must be cautious with your life. You have the rare opportunity to make a huge difference here and to do great things."

I opened the door and stepped out. Draylan was leaning against the doorframe. "I plan to do amazing things with my life, but right now, I'm going to learn how to kick some ass and find out who the asshole is controlling the headhunters."

Draylan pushed himself off the wall. "I think you're wasting your time."

I pulled my hair into a ponytail and turned to him. The thought that the headhunters were dwelling beneath my feet, and Draylan wanting me to stop pursuing them consumed my mind. I balled my hands into fists as hot anger and frustration rose within me. "How can you think that? What if it was your family instead of mine?" Gritting my teeth, I moved closer to him, causing him to take a step back. "What if you found your mother headless or Lithia? Would you feel the same fucking way as you do now?"

Draylan's lips parted in surprise. "There's smoke rising from your fists."

I looked down, and sure enough, tendrils of gray smoke rose above my knuckles.

What the fuck?

I opened my hand and a pea-sized ball of red glowed in the middle of my palm. It felt warm but not hot like it should. Wide-eyed, I looked up at Draylan who stared at me with the same shocked expression on his face.

He pointed at me. "You harbor the fire element. Now it's clear why your mom and Mardella hid you from Atheon!"

I took several deep breaths to calm myself and closed my palm. I opened it, and the tiny ball of fire had disappeared. "Don't be silly," I snapped, pushing him aside, heading for the door. "I have no such thing inside me." I left him standing in the center of the room baffled, hoping he'd chalk this up as a weird occurrence but knowing in my gut he wouldn't. Soon my secret would be discovered.

Chapter Twenty-Three

I ran to Larkin's house, my long dark ponytail swinging behind me. The sky was milky gray with thin vapors of clouds crisscrossing, forming diamond shapes. It reminded me of a cage, creeping me out.

What if we were being locked in by the gods and goddesses?

I ran faster, my heart thumping hard against my chest. When I reached Larkin's front door, I banged on it in quick, hard knocks while trying to catch my breath.

He opened it, his expression alarmed. "Alaris. What's wrong?" He pulled me inside.

"He . . . he . . . knows." My chest was tight. I placed my hand on it and tried to slow my breathing.

"Who?"

"Draylan."

"Draylan knows what?" Farran asked from the far corner of the room, his tone dry. He'd been standing there all along, but I was too preoccupied to notice.

What the hell is he doing here? Then I reminded myself he and Larkin trained and worked together. This wasn't something out of the ordinary, although they did have their differences.

"I'm not telling you," I harshly said. "I can't trust you."

"You can trust him," Larkin said, his voice even with assurance.

I snorted. "Yeah, right. Whatever. He doesn't even like me and has been rude to me since day one."

"At first I didn't like you," Farran admitted. "I thought you were a disrespectful, self-centered girl raised as an earth child who acted like one."

"Well, for your information," I retorted, "this is who I am. If you don't like it, you can kiss this earth child's ass." I had no time for his narrow-minded ideologies, and Brulin wants me to take Farran along tomorrow night with Larkin and me to search the underground tunnels. He was practically begging me to do so. I didn't get it. I didn't get it at all.

Farran's mouth twitched into a faint smile. "I said at first."

Frustrated, I threw my hands up. "What's that supposed to mean . . . you like me now? Or does it depend upon which mood you're in or which pill you take to decide how you feel about me that day?"

"I can see why you feel the way you do," Farran said, "and I deserve it; however, despite how I felt about your outlandish behavior, I've recently come to realize something since you arrived here."

I blew out an impatient sigh. I was anxious to tell Larkin what transpired this morning and wanted Farran to go away. "What?"

"Our ways are outdated." In thought he twisted a silver decorative ring around his finger. It looked similar to the one Larkin had on. A teleport ring. "My father would surely disagree with the statement as I would have a few days ago." He paused and met my gaze. Something flickered across his face. Emotion. The hard edges of his sharp features softened. "When you were onstage last night, you spoke from the heart. The people in Atheon felt it. They were touched by your words. *I* was touched by your words. I saw hope for positive change in their eyes and felt it myself." His pale-blue eyes sparkled. "I've never encountered such a response from a crowd before."

"Well," I said feeling a bit awkward at the compliment he gave me because he was the last person I'd ever expected to hear that from, "Datura gave me a speech she wrote and wanted me to read it aloud. I couldn't bring myself to do it. Instead, I took Narik's advice to be myself."

Farran arched an eyebrow. "And my aunt didn't take too kindly to you ignoring her written words." It wasn't a question. It was a statement with a hint of humor.

I nodded. "She was pissed."

He laughed.

"Why are you laughing?" I asked. "I didn't think you could other than to mock."

"Would you rather I not?" His shoulders shook in silent laughter, betraying his usual stony self.

"Oh, no, please." I waved my hands as if in a panic to tell someone to stop. "I don't want you to go back to Vulcan mode. I like you better this way. Nice to see you smile."

Larkin took me by the shoulders and turned me to face him. "Draylan knows what?"

I shot Farran a wary look. I still wasn't sure if I could trust him, but Brulin and Larkin did.

"Alaris," Farran said, now serious. He placed his hand over his heart and inclined his head. "I give you my word of my trust."

I stuck my pinky out and curled it like Kimmie and I always did. "Pinky swear." It sounded childish, but it gave me comfort.

He eyed it like I was giving hand signals to natives. "I don't understand."

"It's an earth thing," I told him. "A pledge. My best friend Kimmie and I do this to assure each other we'll keep our promise."

"What am I to do?" he asked, confused.

"Put your little finger up like mine." Once he did, I hooked mine with his. "Now swear what I tell you will remain our secret."

His eyes locked with mine. They were serious and shone deep with a fierce loyalty that struck me in the chest and melted reservations I had. "I promise."

"I have the fire element inside me, and he knows," I blurted and proceeded to tell them what happened.

"How could this be?" Farran wondered aloud, puzzled. At the same time, Larkin ran his fingers through his hair and cursed.

"I can tell you how," I said to Farran, "but I want something in exchange." Both Farran and Larkin looked at me in surprise. "The information I share with you is top secret. In fact, I wasn't supposed to tell Larkin, but I did anyway."

"Of course, Princess." Farran bowed in a meaningful stately manner. "Whatever you require of me, I'll do my best to suit your needs."

I rolled my eyes. "Okay, stop it. It makes me feel uncomfortable when you do that, especially since you've been rude to me until today."

"Yes, but you now know why my behavior was standoffish, and my opinion of you has changed."

"Okay, well," I said, twirling my ponytail around my fingers, then tossing it aside. "Tell me why you don't have respect for Datura. I mean, she's your aunt. You're all about honor and loyalty."

"I'm loyal to those who have earned it," he simple stated. "Datura has not."

"How come?"

"I don't trust her."

"Why?"

He stuck his pinky out and curled it. "I guess, Princess, both of us have secrets we must swear not to tell another soul."

I hooked my little finger with his. "Stop calling me Princess. Call me Alaris, and I promise not to breath a word of what you're about to tell me to anyone except present company." I glanced at Larkin. "What about him. He needs to–"

"I know," Larkin said. "I've known all along."

I should have been surprised, but I wasn't. Larkin once told me Farran used to be a fun and easygoing guy, but after his mom died, his demeanor changed to brooding and stoical. Regardless, though, they'd always been friends.

My stomach pinched with hunger, and I could use some coffee. "Since you already know, can I trouble you for a cup of coffee and something to eat? I'm starving."

"Of course." Larkin headed toward the kitchen. He paused. "Do you mind a spice muffin? The brownie must have made them last night because they were on my counter this morning."

I was right. Brulin did bake last night. Not calling him by name told me Larkin didn't know Brulin. I smiled to myself thinking about talking to him this morning and becoming friends. I wondered if Brulin would care if I were to tell these two about giving me the map. "I love spice cake, and it'll taste even better with coffee," I said.

I sat on the couch and gestured for Farran to sit with me. He opted for the loveseat across from me. "Why don't you trust Datura?"

Steepling his fingers, he answered, "Datura has always been different than the others in our clan. She resented my mother, Eris, because she married well, and her brother Flax because of his close relationship with my mother. She also had a turbulent relationship with my grandparents under the belief they favored the other two over her. Datura spent many years away from home. No one knew where she was or what she'd been up to. One day, my grandmother Phira went home from spending the day with us to Datura waiting for her. Datura said angry and hurtful words that to this day remains a mystery. All we know is Phira was rattled when she fled back to us that evening. In tears and broken sobs, she repeated she made a mistake and now was paying for it."

My eyebrows creased. "Mistake? I wonder what she meant."

Farran frowned. "I don't know. I don't even think my grandfather Trevan knew." He fell silent and stared at the floor, lost in thought.

I didn't say anything and went into my own speculation about what could have happened until Larkin brought us our coffee and muffin. I thanked him, and when he sat beside me, I took his hand and kissed it, meeting his eyes. They softened in such a way that made my heart skip several beats.

"My parents used to look at each other in the same manner as you two," Farran said, his voice filled with sadness. "My father is still not over my mother's death, and even though the Murks who slaughtered my family are dead, he's under the belief one escaped and is in hiding."

"How did the Murks die, and why does your father think there's still one more to kill?" I asked, biting into my muffin, tasting the yummy cinnamon, cloves, and brown sugar.

Farran clenched his jaw. Hatred and vengeance flashed in his pale blue eyes. "We killed some that night and spent months hunting down the rest. We let it be known throughout this realm anyone harboring one would die, as well. There were six in total. Once we found those who escaped, we showed no mercy." He drew in a deep breath as if he were trying to calm himself. Slowly he released it. "Several witnesses told my father they saw a cloaked figure on a black stallion riding through the forest a mile or so away from our village. Trailing behind were two ghouls, three Dralks, and–"

"Dralks?" I should know what they were, but I couldn't remember. "Sorry, I didn't mean to interrupt you, but I can't recall ever hearing the word before."

"They're dark elves," Larkin said.

"Are they tall or short?" I asked. "When I envision an elf, a picture of Santa Claus' helpers pops in my mind."

"The males are tall." Farran's voice was flat, but I could hear the anger behind it. "The females are shorter than you."

"Like Brunhild."

Farran nodded. "Yes."

"What was the sixth Murk?" I could tell he was having a hard time recounting the worst night of his life, so I wanted to hurry him along to spare him what grief I could.

"A troll." He clenched his hands into his lap and continued. "These Murks were following the lone rider on their own horses. What we found odd about it was how did the leader gather a diverse group to do its bidding and why?"

"Do you think it's Datura?" I could hear the doubt in my tone, feel it on my face. She might be a narcissistic attention whore, but her being the cliché evil queen like in the fairy tale stories I grew up with on earth was hard for me to swallow.

Farran was in the middle of taking a sip of his coffee when I asked him. He set the mug on the end table and met my questioning eyes. "My father Alder sent me here to Atheon after Merrack and Datura wed, two years after the attack on my family. My father did so for two reasons. One, because he and Merrack are allies and friends. The second is because he's never trusted Datura and wants me to keep a close eye on her. He finds it both disturbing and fortunate Datura happened to be conveniently scarce during the attack."

"Datura," I said, trying to make sense of the situation, "was angry with your grandmother and probably left. I mean, you said there were years when she was gone, and no one knew where she went. It seems to me she liked to travel and not stay in one place for long. She needed to get it out of her system before she settled down."

"It's possible," Farran agreed, "but my duty to my father is to make sure Datura is free of blame, and confirm her feelings toward Merrack are pure." I nodded, and he gave me a rueful smile. "Now you know my secret, one weighing heavily on my shoulders." He did a sweeping gestured toward me. "The floor is all yours, Alaris."

Chapter Twenty-Four

After I told Farran my secret, he paced the room, voicing his thoughts punctuated with simple hand gestures. "There's a myth," he said. "A unicorn won't allow someone near it unless the person is pure of heart."

"I don't know. I don't understand any of it." I could hear the frustration in my voice. I had no idea why a unicorn would lead me to a dragon egg and why the dragon's essence resided inside of me.

Farran moved around the room, throwing ideas as if he drank five cups of espresso. "Maybe because you were a child and nearby. You happened to be at the right place at the right time."

"I'll go with that," I said.

Larkin slung his arm around my shoulders. "I'm thinking the unicorn knew your mom was a healer. Who better to care for a dragon than the daughter of a healer?"

"If what you're saying is true," I said, "why didn't the unicorn lead Karrina to it?"

Farran stopped in the middle of the room and looked at me. "Karrina was already tainted with life. You weren't."

I shrugged. "I suppose." My thoughts were scattered with all kinds of different reasons the unicorn chose me and why the baby dragon breathed his life into me. I couldn't come up with a logical answer, only speculation. The subject grew tiresome. I opened my mouth to say as much when Farran spoke first.

"I think you have special abilities only a dragon has," he said, sounding shocked as if he hadn't realized what he was saying until he heard his own words.

"I think you're right." Larkin rose, leaving me sitting on the couch in stunned silence. He spun and pointed at me, excited. "You made the glass of water boil when you were angry at Draylan. Then this morning he pissed you off yet again, and a smoldering ember appeared in the palm of your hand. Holy, shit!" He gaped at me. "Do you realize what an advantage it is to possess the same fire element as a dragon?"

"What's the difference?" I asked. "I mean, are there different fire elements?"

Farran shook his head. "No. However, not only do you have it in you, but what I think Larkin meant was you harbor the same special abilities as a dragon, which would make you a powerful person."

I laughed. "Okay, I don't really see myself as powerful."

"It's because," Larkin said, "you have no idea what you can do and what abilities you have. We need to find out."

Farran snapped his fingers and pointed to Larkin. "Great idea."

"If you do have the power of the dragon," Larkin continued as if he didn't hear Farran's comment, "we need to keep it between us and guard it with our lives."

A haunting feeling emerged in the pit of my stomach. "Why? Does it have to do with having the ability to obtain all of the other elements like I was told?"

Larkin shook his head. "No, it's impossible to gather all of them. The gods and goddesses made sure of it. My grandmother was wrong."

"How do you–"

"Know?" he interjected. "After our ride here in the carriage, I researched the myth people latch onto as reality, but in all truth, the gods and goddesses decreed no one could possess all four elements."

"Karrina said the same thing to Mardella," I shared and thought about Merrack. I mentioned his name, and Larkin knew exactly what I meant. Darkness had latched onto Merrack when he attempted to become all powerful.

He nodded. "I have a theory: He dabbled in the dark arts to aid him on his quest which explains his demeanor at the time. He was lucky to break free of its grasp before it was too late."

I mused his point. It made complete sense. Then a wave of sadness washed over me when the thought of Karrina and Mardella sending me away from Havenwood based on Mardella's belief of a myth came to mind. My shoulders slumped. "So I was sent to earth for nothing?"

"No," Farran was adamant. "The wards around the prison in Phriosuin Domhan are partly created from the fire of a dragon."

I gave him a weird look. "Phiriosuin Domhan?" After the words flew out of my mouth, I remembered what it meant: prison world. "Never mind. I know what it is," I blurted when Farran opened his mouth to respond. "So what? The wards have dragon fire infused within them. What's the big deal?"

Farran's expression turned serious, and there was a caveat ring to his voice that sent chills up my spine. "The big deal is you have the ability to lower the ward for a certain amount of time to allow Murks to escape. If the wrong person discovers you harbor the spirit of the dragon within you, he's going to do everything in his power to get you to free the Murks from their imprisonment."

My stomach clenched. If what he said proved true, I could probably never go back to my old life and more than likely be forced to keep myself out of harm's way, which meant seclusion. Living a life behind closed doors wasn't what I envisioned for myself. I had the sudden desperate urge to talk to Mardella. She'd know what to do. Too bad I had no idea where the hell she was.

Larkin rubbed his temple in thought. "We need to think of a safe place where we can see what powers if any reside in you."

They were deciding for me. At least it felt like it. They didn't even ask for my opinion on the matter, or if I wanted to do what they were talking about. They assumed I was onboard. I didn't like it, so I changed the subject, knowing they'd drop this one. "I have another secret, and again it stays among us three. No one else."

Farran's eyebrows shot up. "More?"

"What is it?" Larkin asked, concerned.

"You two swear you won't tell anyone?"

"Yes," they said in unison.

"Okay, then." I shot them a clandestine smile. They moved closer. My plan worked. All had been forgotten about discovering what dragon powers I might be harboring within. "Did you know there are tunnels beneath the palace?"

"My father knows a lot about this kingdom," Farran said, "but he's never mentioned what you speak of."

Larkin shook his head. "My father served under your grandfather, Augustus, and he's never said a word about it." He searched my face, curious as to what I was about to say.

"I was given a map this morning and–"

Larkin stiffened and gave me a guarded look. "By whom?"

"I can't tell you," I said. When he opened his mouth to object, I raised my hand, halting him. "When I see this person again, I'll ask if I can tell you two, but for right now, I don't want to betray a confidence."

"Fair enough." Farran sat on the coffee table in front of me while Larkin chose to sit beside me, both huddling around as if we were team members in a ballgame discussing our next play.

"Anyway," I went on, "it's a map of tunnels beneath the palace. I was told to bring only you two with me tomorrow night when the twin moons are full. In fact,"—I shifted my gaze on Farran—"it stressed to me to bring you along, and after hearing your story I wonder if it has to do with the leader of the Murks you told me about."

Farran's pale skin turned whiter, translucent, to where spidery purple veins appeared. "Two years," he whispered more to himself than us, staring past me. "Two years of misery, seeking the leader who had my innocent family slaughtered and the reason such a heinous and cruel act occurred. Those answers could possibly have been within my grasp all along."

I touched his hand, startling him. He jerked back, but when he realized what I was doing, he relaxed and allowed me to place my hand over his. His skin was cold and smooth. "Listen, I know what you're going through. My family, the Evergreens, were brutally slayed, as well. That's why I will not stop until justice is served. My objectives are to find the two headhunters who killed my parents and who controlled them." I rubbed my thumb over the scars on his hand, and surprisingly, he allowed me to do so, his eyes never wavering from mine. I could see the hurt in them. My throat tightened with emotion. He and I shared a common tragedy, so it seemed fitting we banded together to make things right again. "I don't have a clue what we're going to discover tomorrow night, so don't get your hopes up. All I know is it's important I take you with me."

He looked down at our hands. "I'm sorry I was an asshole when you first arrived," he softly said. "Of all people, I should have been sympathetic to your situation and had the decency to share my story with you. However,"—he released a regretful sigh—"I buried my emotions in duty to my father and Merrack and to not blemish my perfect record of following orders as a warrior. Those things changed last night when you told your story to everyone."

I squeezed his hand, then released it. "It's okay. We're in this together now, wanting the same outcome—to find the asshole who destroyed our families."

A muscle in his jaw twitched. The color returned to his face, but his expression contorted into the same angry revenge that had been burning inside of me since the headhunters entered my life. "I swear on my bleeding soul," he said between gritted teeth, "The Murk will wish he were dead after I'm through with him."

"For sure." I tapped his knee and rose. "In the meantime, I need to continue with my training and see how Merrack is doing."

"Where's the map?" Larkin asked, rising to his feet, following me and Farran to the front door. "I'd like to see it."

The corners of my mouth turned up mischievously. "In a safe place.

I'll show you and Farran tomorrow night." The question about how we were going to pull this off without being conspicuous entered my mind. "Where should we meet without bringing attention to ourselves?"

"Let's meet here at eight tomorrow night," Farran said, "so we can go over the map, then make our move."

"Sounds good to me," Larkin replied. "I'll cook dinner, and you and Farran will have a reason to come over."

"What about Draylan?" I asked as I recalled the shocked expression on his face. His words that I harbored the fire element rang in my ears. I twisted my fingers at the thought of him telling everyone about his discovery.

Larkin brushed a stray hair off my face that must have escaped my ponytail. The soft butterfly touch of his fingers caused my heart to race and a warm sensation between my legs. "I'll take care of it."

I was swimming in the heated emotions he stirred in me. I wanted to kiss him but bit my bottom lip instead and nodded.

"With any luck, Draylan will keep his mouth shut," Farran said, reaching for the doorknob. "I'm sure he's smart enough to know your life could be compromised if word got out."

We stepped beneath the dreary sky—a beautiful purplish gray, I thought. The clouds had shifted from their earlier cage-like disturbing form to thin wisps snaking above us in all directions.

Narik was jogging toward us in black basketball shorts and a white T-shirt. He must have been at the gym expecting us since he was running from that direction. A stab of guilt went through me. I hated keeping people waiting for me when I was supposed to meet them at a certain time and place. What happened this morning, though, had been unexpected, I told myself. It wasn't as if I planned it or anything. I hugged myself against the cool breeze. Farran and Larkin were on either side of me, watching Narik. Larkin noticed me holding my arms tight against my body and wrapped his arm around my shoulders. We stopped until Narik reached us.

He had an anxious look on his face. Beads of sweat dotted his forehead.

"Hey," he said, his chest rising and falling as he caught his breath.

His urgent energy alarmed me, and a cold feeling developed in the pit of my stomach. "What's wrong?"

He pulled the bottom of his T-shirt up to wipe his face and ran his fingers through his messy brown hair, causing it to be even more unruly. "Is it true?"

I played dumb because I really wasn't too sure what he meant and didn't want to admit to something until he clarified himself. "Is what true?"

"Do you have the fire element in you?" His eyes darted to Larkin, then Farran, and back to me. His curious expression deepened.

I kept my gaze steady on his. "Why do you ask?"

"Draylan told me," he answered. "He told me about what happened in your room earlier. In fact," he went on, "he told Merrack and Datura. They want to see you right away and sent me to go fetch you."

"Son-of-a-bitch," Larkin huffed under his breath. "The weasel better not go blabbing this information around–"

"He won't," Narik abruptly said. "He's under strict orders not to . . . so it's true?"

I sighed. "Yes."

Narik's eyes widened, his mouth forming an O. "Wow. Why didn't you tell me?"

"Because I didn't know," I said. "Not until this morning."

He scratched his head and nodded. "You need to go back to the palace and see Merrack and Datura. They're waiting for you in their bedroom."

"Why there?" I asked. They should be having breakfast and doing their morning routine, whatever it was, I thought.

The corners of Narik's mouth turned down. "Merrack isn't doing so well."

"He was fine last night," I told him, worried.

"He's not now."

Larkin slipped his arm off my shoulders and turned me to where we were facing each other. "It'll be okay," he told me in a soft, reassuring voice. "We'll go to Havenwood in a couple of days and have my mother cook up a remedy for him."

Farran had been silent this whole time, deep in thought, his face smooth. I could tell he was mulling something by the contemplative look in his eyes. It reminded me of someone playing chess, pondering his opponent's strategy before making his own move. I wondered what exactly he was thinking. I imagined he had a complex mind which explained his quiet nature whenever he observed a situation on the sidelines.

"Okay," I said to Larkin. "I better go since they're waiting."

"We'll accompany you," Farran said.

I tried to smile, but it was weak. "Thank you. I'd appreciate it."

As we headed toward the palace, all I could think about was the events that had taken place, changing my world after I returned home from Vegas. Since then, every part of my life had been in disarray. I didn't like it one bit. I liked structure, continuity, and organization. Sure I was an adventurous soul who a few days ago planned on becoming an archeologist and seeing the world, but now those hopes and dreams were evaporating with each passing day. I had to resign myself to the fact this was my life now, and if Merrack took a turn for the worse, I'd be given the throne and would be the new ruler of Atheon—something I dreaded with every fiber of my being.

Chapter Twenty-Five

"Alaris," Merrack said after he took a drink of water and placed it on his bedside table. He was propped up on some pillows in his four-poster bed. His voice sounded scratchy and weak. It concerned me a lot. Not to mention that his complexion was sickly pale except for the tiny dark bags forming below his dull chestnut eyes. "Come sit by me." I sat next to him while Larkin and Farran stood quietly nearby. Datura hovered next to me like an attentive nurse waiting to lend a hand. I could tell she was still upset about me not reading her speech because she didn't look at me unless she had to, and when she did, her lips were in a tight line, her eyes like chipped ice. "Draylan told us about what happened earlier in your room."

"Yeah," I said. "It's the first time it's ever happened. Just like the other day in the dining room." I slowly shook my head. "I don't know what to think of it."

A weak smile formed on his face. "You have the fire element in you, child." He brushed my cheek with his fingertips. "It's a curse but at the same time a gift. You must learn about it and how to use . . . " He closed his eyes, and his hand fell heavily to his side.

I gasped and grabbed his wrist to check for a pulse. A slow throbbing sensation beat against my fingertips. Larkin and Farran crossed the room as I placed my palm on Merrack's damp forehead. Warmth radiated off his skin. He had a slight fever, I guessed. "I think he's okay," I told no one in particular but was aware Datura abruptly left the room.

"He's exhausted and needs medical attention," Farran said, sounding perturbed.

Merrack opened his eyes. "Brunhild," he croaked. He looked about wildly, then at me. "Brunhild, can help you."

"I don't know. I–"

The door swung open, and in walked Brunhild followed by Datura. "I'm here." Brunhild's brown watery eye darted to me and the pale blue one followed. I forgot how freaky they were but couldn't stop staring at her. The guys stepped back as Brunhild and Datura charged in, but I remained by Merrack's side. "Move out of the way, girly." Brunhild made a shooing gesture.

I looked at Merrack, worried—on a crossroad of what to do. I mean, really, Brunhild had her opportunity to help him, and whatever she gave him obviously didn't work. What we needed was a healer like Larkin's mom Fiona to cure him.

"It's okay," Merrack said and patted my hand reassuringly.

"Do you even know what's wrong with him?" I asked Brunhild who was shifting her weight impatiently next to me. "I'm not a doctor," I continued, "but I've had pneumonia before, and his symptoms are similar to what mine were."

Brunhild reached inside her tan cloak and pulled out a long, glass tube full of purple glowing liquid. She raised it. "This is an elixir that'll help him rest while the potion I gave him earlier works through his system."

I glanced at Larkin and Farran, unsure. In all reality, I grew up on earth which was different from this realm, so I had reservations on what she was offering. In my world, Merrack would be given a prescription or admitted to a hospital. I was clueless about how they handled situations like this here, except for the memories of Karrina leaving our house to care for a patient. Maybe I was stepping out of line questioning Brunhild's tactics. Hell, I didn't know.

Farran glanced at Datura who stood within a few feet of me and Brunhild, pursing her lips. "I suggest we allow Brunhild do her job and then see if she can help you discover what abilities you harbor." When I shot him a wary look, he went on, "If Merrack doesn't get any better within a few days, you can go to Havenwood and have Fiona whip up something to cure him."

"I'll give it two days." I rose from the bed, taken aback by Farran's Team Brunhild attitude. Brunhild didn't waste any time giving Merrack the elixir. Datura handed him a glass of water, her back to me as if she were shielding him. "If he shows no signs of improvement by then, I'm going to Havenwood." My voice was stiff. I could hear the stubbornness in it. I wasn't going to bend on this issue, and I had no doubt they knew it.

Farran and Larkin nodded in agreement while Datura seemed to ignore me and didn't even acknowledge what I said. If she wanted to give me the silent treatment so be it. I didn't give a damn.

"Alaris," Brunhild said as I headed out the room. I turned and met her gaze. "I'll expect you at my house at two today."

Wow. They weren't going to waste any time. I didn't know how I felt about it, and I still wasn't sure if I could trust Brunhild. "I don't–"

"Larkin can take you," she said, scratching the side of her long, hooked nose.

"Very well then." I turned on my heel and left not knowing what to think about another weird-ass situation I fell into.

* * *

I spent the rest of the morning training with Larkin, Narik, and now Farran. When we left the palace, I confronted Farran about his support of Brunhild helping me. I didn't trust her and thought he felt the same way. He confirmed he did agree with me; however, if he objected like he wanted to, he would have raised eyebrows. Right now, Datura and the others believed Farran was in their court, and he wanted to keep it that way so they wouldn't grow suspicious of him. I could see his point. Datura was his aunt and had the power to send him home if she desired. If she were to do that, he wouldn't have the opportunity to find out if she had any involvement in the slaughter of his family. So yeah, I got it.

I enjoyed training with the guys this morning because Farran was now involved. Narik was surprised and delighted Farran decided to be onboard with us in the matter of me learning how to fight and protect myself just in case I ran into a situation where I happened to be alone and someone or something attacked me.

"I thought you objected to what we're doing here," Narik said to Farran when we were limbering muscles in the gym. His face showed a sheen of sweat, and his white T-shirt had a large round wet spot over his chest. I noticed his biceps were larger than normal and thought he must have been lifting weights while we were gone. "What changed your mind?"

Farran stretched his arm over his head and leaned sideways. "My mother," he simply stated.

Narik screwed up his face. "Your mother? But she's—"

Farran dropped his arm to his side and clenched his jaw. "Dead," he finished Narik's sentence. "I'm well aware, but last night when Alaris was between those two weres, and the pushy one, Nash, wouldn't take no for an answer, I was forced to take a hard look at the ideologies I held fast. If my mother would have had the ability to protect herself and fight back, she might still be with us." He glanced at me. "Alaris is our princess, and I don't want the same fate to befall her, and I want to at least give her a chance to stand her ground. It's why I was at Larkin's house this morning . . . to tell him I had a change of heart."

"Awesome." Narik smiled. "I'm glad you came around. Now we need to get Draylan in on this."

I extended my leg in front of me and bent forward, feeling the pull in the muscle. "Where is Draylan?" My opinion of Draylan had changed since this morning when he ran to Merrack and Datura and told them what had happened. Really? It was like he couldn't wait to be the one to tell them I had the fire element in me, like it would gain him brownie points or something. What an ass kisser. You'd think he would have talked to me about it. Yeah, I took off on him but still. If he were honorable, he would have taken a step back and thought things through first. Just sayin'.

"He's jogging outside," Narik replied offhandedly, then changed the subject. "I think we should teach you how to use our weapons and find one that'll work best for you."

"Great idea," I said. My mind quickly thought of what weapon I could see myself using: a crossbow, a sword, maybe a spear. No, not a spear. It would be too awkward to handle.

Larkin groaned and shook his head. "Bad idea."

"Why?" I asked as the vision of me being a warrior princess in a sword fight with a Dralk faded.

He leveled his eyes with mine. The sternness in them was unquestionable, but so was his unwavering protectiveness toward me. A warm sensation filled my chest. He was worried and didn't want me to get hurt. It was plain on his face. My heart fluttered, and oh, man, did he look hot in his black sweat shorts and gray T-shirt that hugged his well-defined chest just right. "It takes years to learn how to wield the weapons we have and use them to protect ourselves and the lives of others. We've been training since childhood. It's our calling. Do you understand?"

"I do," I said, unable to break away from his gaze.

Narik clapped his hands. "Okay, then, let's get busy." He looked at me. "I want to show you how to get out of the full nelson."

I was anxious to learn everything they could show me and in turn, teach them what I knew. For the next hour, we did one-on-one training. It was tough but energizing, as well. I could feel my body, muscles, and movements readjusting to what they once were when I competed in taekwondo competitions. I forgot how much I loved the feel of my body and mind after a good workout—the strength, energy, and ability to focus better were awesome. Again, I silently chastised myself for not listening to my mom who wanted me to continue my martial arts training after high school. I guessed parents did know best, which brought my thoughts to Merrack. He wanted Brunhild to help me, and although I didn't feel comfortable with the arrangement, maybe he knew best. I had to trust his judgment. Besides, what was the worst that could happen?

Chapter Twenty-Six

After I took my shower and slipped on a pair of brown stretchy jeans, a long sleeve white peasant blouse, and black suede knee-high boots, I put my hair up in a ponytail and met Larkin outside, feeling relieved I hadn't seen Datura since I'd been back from the gym. I wasn't in the mood for her pettiness. It would blow over eventually, I told myself, and we'd move on, but for now, wherever she happened to be suited me just fine, as long as it was away from me. Family drama sucked.

Larkin stood next to a beautiful white horse with large black spots on its body. The mane and tail were black, but the feathering hairy hoofs were white. The chest was broad and muscular.

"Wow," I said. "What a gorgeous horse." I reached my hand out to pet its head and stopped. "Is it okay if I touch her or him?"

"Of course, I've already told *her* about you."

"You have an affinity with horses," I said. "You told me you did when I first arrived. I also remember when we were kids you shared this secret with me." I paused and squinted my eyes playfully. "So you can talk to horses like the horse whisperer?"

"I don't know what a horse whisperer is," he said, running his fingers through the wavy mane, "but I can communicate with them." The corner of his mouth tilted upward. "It's a gift . . . one I appreciate."

An idea popped into my head. "Oh, my God," I gasped, touching my lips with my fingers, causing Larkin to stop what he was doing and look at me in alarm. "The stallion the leader of the Murks was riding the night of the raid on Farran's and Datura's family . . . have you thought about finding it so you can talk to it or perhaps ask the other horses about that night?"

He nodded. "Yes, but we don't know where the stallion is, and I asked the other horses. They don't know anything about it."

"That sucks." I softly petted Larkin's horse. "You're so beautiful," I told her. I glanced at Larkin who was watching me with a contented expression on his handsome face. "What's her name and what type of breed is she?"

"Her name is Gypsy," he answered, "because you know . . . she's a gypsy horse." He laughed when I cocked an eyebrow, like asking really? "I know it's not original, but I'm no good at naming animals, and most human names shouldn't be used on them. Do you know what I mean, or am I being weird?"

"I know exactly what you mean." I patted Gypsy's head while watching Larkin put his black boot in the stirrup and pull himself into the saddle. There were brown leather saddlebags that matched it hanging from the side. They reminded me of a messenger bag with long thin straps and antique brass buckles. "I'm the same way. Naming a cat like Mary or Mike bugs me for some reason. Now Max or Salem is a good human name for a pet."

"I agree." He leaned forward and whispered something in Gypsy's ear. She bent her front legs to kneel, and he offered me his hand. There was a twinkle in his eyes. "Are you ready to go for a ride?"

I grinned, took his hand, and mounted behind him. "I was born ready."

"Hold on," he said as Gypsy rose.

I wrapped my arms around his waist, feeling his muscles tighten beneath me. I had the sudden urge to slip my hand under his T-shirt and run them along the hard planes of his abs. "How far does Brunhild live?" I asked to distract myself from sexy thoughts on the verge of exploding into fantasies.

"About a half hour or so." He made a clicking sound and shook the reins.

I jerked forward when Gypsy took off and held tighter to Larkin. The clopping of hooves surrounded me when we reached the cobblestone path lined with the regal bronze gas lamps I had admired when I first arrived. After we went through the gray stone gateway, I glanced over my shoulder, watching the black metal latticed gate lower. The thick hedges along the path whizzed by, and I couldn't help but smile, feeling free and alive. We traveled on a narrow road between a sloping mountainous valley carpeted on either side of us in deep green grass and foliage. There were rocky, jagged plateaus high above.

Larkin veered off the tree-lined path and into the forest. We slowed down and rode north among the towering, thick oaks. I breathed in the rich, earthy smells and sighed. Contentment filled my spirit while I admired the bright green ferns and different shrubs, some in colors of pink and purple. There were clusters of sagebrush we passed that I recognized were used for medicinal purposes. A distant memory of Karrina and me picking leaves and placing them in a satchel fluttered across my mind. She was teaching me about the plants and what purpose each one served. My heart squeezed, and I realized with a start, I missed being with her. She was my mom. I loved her. Yeah, she tricked me into allowing Mardella to cast a spell on me, then sent me to a different realm and placed me with a couple who I thought were my biological parents. I lived a false life and lost years without Larkin, my friends, and growing up in Havenwood, but despite the resentment I had toward Karrina, part of me understood her hasty decision. It didn't make what she'd done right, but she paid for it with her life. She died of a broken heart. My eyes stung with tears.

The air grew cooler, and I shivered against Larkin.

"Are you cold?" he asked.

"A little." My voice cracked with emotion. I cleared it and tried again. "Yes, but I'll be fine."

He leaned forward, and we stopped. He dismounted and turned to me, his forehead creased with worry. "What's wrong?"

I slipped off Gypsy and hugged myself, aware of a lone tear slowly trailing down my cheek. Larkin gently wiped it with his fingertip. "I was thinking of Karrina and how we used to go to the forest and collect herbs . . . I miss her."

He pulled me into his arms, and I sank into him, welcoming his comfort. "I'm sorry. I didn't think about us being here would remind you of your mom. We should have taken another route."

I pulled back and looked at him. "Don't be sorry. I love it here. This"—I indicated the forest with a wave of my hand—"makes me happy. Besides, we can't prevent triggering another memory of Karrina and me. It is what it is." I sniffed and wiped the corners of my eyes.

He nodded and hugged me again. "I hate seeing you cry, though. I always have. I don't want you to ever be sad." His voice was low and caring. He kissed my forehead. His lips were warm against my skin. I tightened my arms around his waist, wanting to get as close to him as possible. "I brought us lunch," he said. "It's why I took this route to Brunhild's house instead of following the road. I wanted to surprise you."

"You did?" He released his arms and went to the saddlebags. He pulled a red hooded cape out of one of them and handed it to me. "You brought this for me?" I could hear the surprise in my voice, and my heart melted when I thought how thoughtful and attentive he was, and I found myself wanting to only be with him.

He moved to a brown leather bag behind my seat that I hadn't realized was there until now. "I thought you might get cold. It tends to be cooler in the forest." He handed me a folded blue and black checkered cloth. "See the grassy spot between the trees over there?" He pointed to my right. "Can you spread this out between them?"

"Sure." I did what he asked and sat on the blanket, watching him gingerly feed Gypsy apple slices. He looked happy and content as she ate from the palm of his hand. I found myself being even more attracted to him as I observed his caring actions. Ya gotta love a man who treated animals with such kindness as Larkin did.

"I made us ham and cheese sandwiches," he said, handing me mine.

"Thank you. You're sweet for doing this." I unwrapped the thin brown paper and took a bite of what looked like twelve grain bread. The cheese was sharp cheddar, and the ham had a smoky taste to it. The combination along with mayo tasted really good. I took another bite, not realizing until now how hungry I was.

He sat beside me and followed suit. "You're welcome. It looks like you're enjoying it." He handed me a round brown container that reminded me of a canteen. "It's water."

I took a swig. The cool liquid tasted like it came from a spring. I gave it back to him and finished my sandwich. "This is yummy," I said between bites.

"Thanks. I like to cook, so I'm glad you're enjoying it."

"We balance each other," I said, grinning. "I don't like to cook, and you do." I placed my finger on my chin. "Hmmm, what else would make us a perfect pair?" I eyed Larkin playfully, and the corner of his mouth lifted. "My strengths, your weakness, and vice versa. What would they be?"

He brushed his fingers down the side of my face. His feathery touch sent a delicious thrill through me. "You're my weakness." His voice was husky and serious. Desire tightened my stomach. His gaze fell to my lips. We both leaned forward, only to be interrupted by a giggle that sounded like wind chimes.

We looked up. Nalin was hovering above us. Her violet eyes widened. Her hand went to her mouth, her round face turning scarlet. "Sorry," she said between her fingers. "I didn't mean to disturb you." She flapped her wings faster and rose higher, disappearing above the treetops before we could respond.

"It's okay," I called out, wondering if she'd been following us. I didn't mind really. I liked Nalin. She was harmless. I thought she was cute playing little matchmaker and wanting everyone to be happy and in love. Our little cupid. I turned to Larkin. "Now where were we?"

His hand cradled the back of my head, and he gently pulled me toward him. "We were here," he half-whispered, his warm breath brushing my lips.

The next thing I knew, we were kissing, deeply, passionately, our tongues intertwining. I wanted him. I needed to feel him inside me, to get as close to him as I possibly could. I never felt this way toward another guy before, but I think I'd fallen in love with Larkin. I grabbed a fistful of his shirt, and he wrapped his arms around me. We were breathing heavily. A small neigh issued from Gypsy. Her hoof scratched the dirt, causing our lips to part.

"Is she jealous?" I asked, finding it both weird and comical if she were.

Larkin rose and pulled me up with him. He gathered our stuff and stuck them back in the saddlebags. "No," he said, his expression bright and cheerful. "She's letting me know we need to go, or we're going to be late. Brunhild doesn't take too kindly to tardiness."

"Then, we better get moving." I mounted Gypsy behind him, and as soon as I wrapped my arms around his waist, she took off. Her skill and knowledge of this forest amazed me. Never once did she stumble through the foliage or bracken. When we came across a fallen tree in our path, she jumped it with ease. I decided then that I wanted my own horse. I didn't know much about them, but Larkin could teach me and help me pick the right one. We could ride alongside each other, and I could go off on my own wherever I wanted. But would I be allowed to since I was Princess of Atheon?

We emerged from the forest into a small wooded, hilly valley with patches of green and yellow grass carpeting the ground. A stone cottage constructed of river rock sat on top of a grassy knoll in front of more forested land that trailed up into the foggy distant mountains.

"It's show time," Larkin said, rubbing my forearm as we headed across the valley toward Brunhild's cottage.

My shoulders tensed. My mouth became dry. What if Brunhild was the one controlling the headhunters? Merrack trusted her, but I didn't know him long enough to trust his judgment. I knew I should because he was my father, but I couldn't shake the sick feeling I had in the pit of my stomach toward her. Merrack might have sent us into the lion's den, and if that were the case, I hoped Larkin knew what the hell he was doing. Otherwise, we were screwed.

Chapter Twenty-Seven

"Listen," Larkin said in a low voice when we headed up the knoll to Brunhild's cottage, "try not to use your elemental power."

"I don't even know how," I answered. "That's the whole point of being here."

"I know, but she's going to provoke you, so you'll get the same reaction as before. Don't allow her to. Pretend you don't know why nothing is happening. Can you?"

"I think so. Why? Do you not trust her, either?"

"Ever since the night she broke the compulsion spell on you, I haven't trusted her one bit," he admitted.

I sighed, feeling relieved he felt the same, and that he came up with a plan to hopefully throw her off our trail. I hugged his waist and pressed my cheek against his back. "Thank you."

"For what."

"For feeling exactly the way I do."

He lifted my hand and kissed it. His lips sent a wave of heat throughout my body.

"You're ten minutes late," Brunhild said when we rode to her front door.

We dismounted, and Gypsy moseyed to the backyard where a timber-framed gray stone building stood, reminding me of a barn straight out of medieval times. Larkin and I shared a look. He raised his eyebrows, and the silent message was clear: *See? I told you she'd have a fit if we weren't on time.*

Brunhild waved her hand in annoyance. "Never mind. You're here. Let's get to work." She went inside, and we followed.

The interior of her cottage was simple but cozy. I liked it. The wooden floors and heavy oak beams along with the stone fireplace on the back wall was charming. A brown couch and a matching chair were placed in a half circle around it with a large trunk made from dark timber in front. The air was coated with the smell of cinnamon and orange. I breathed it in, wondering if she just got done making her cinnamon buns and Orange Bliss. My mouth watered as she led us to the left, through an arched doorway, into her kitchen.

"Wow. You have a cool house," I said, admiring the stone recess on the far wall with an apothecary shelf set inside it filled with odd-shaped glass jars, brimming with all kinds of different herbs, liquids, and God knows what. "Your kitchen kind of reminds me of the one in the palace, but I like yours better."

Brunhild turned and looked up at me. Her brown eye glistened, while her pale blue one looked like a dull marble worn with age. "Why is that you say?"

I gestured around me. "It's awesome in here. What you have is organic and real. I love it. I bet you Datura copied the look of this room to make her kitchen identical to it."

Brunhild's lips twitched into a goofy smile, revealing her front black tooth. "She did."

"I thought so," I said, glad her rotten mood seemed to wane, "because the sink, the counters, the herbs hanging from the ceiling . . . everything is totally similar to what we have at the palace."

She cocked an eyebrow. "So you like my home, eh?"

I nodded. "I do. I recall my house in Havenwood is decorated in a similar style as yours since Karrina was a healer and all; however, your taste is much better."

She blinked and touched her heart. "No one has ever given me such a compliment."

"Really?" She was up there in age. I couldn't believe no one ever had. "Not even Datura?"

"Datura has thanked me for my services and has put her trust in me. It's enough, I suppose." She headed to the back of the room. We followed her through an open doorway, down a short hall lit by torches to a heavy polished oak door. She tugged on the round metal handle. With a loud creek it opened. I took Larkin's hand into mine and gave him an apprehensive look. He intertwined our fingers and lightly squeezed them, mouthing everything would be okay.

We stepped into an octagon room. There was a large black pentagram on the floor with weird symbols around it and a crude wooden table in the corner. A crystal ball sat in the center of the table on a silver stand. There were tapered candles in different colors around it in brass holders. The ceiling had a round skylight above the circle, allowing the afternoon light to shine into the room in a ray of white light.

Brunhild bent down outside the pentagram and lifted a board. Beneath it was another round handle. She pulled it up, revealing a square gap in the floor. A whooshing sound issued from the depths of the dark abyss, followed by a noise that reminded me of popcorn cooking in the microwave. An array of colorful bubbles: blue, pink, yellow, and orange rose, then snapped. A soft light followed in their wake. "Come," Brunhild said. "It's safe to practice down here."

We trailed behind her down a narrow stone stairwell. I wrinkled my nose at the pungent mildew odor, wondering if there were rats here. I doubt it, though, since there were no point of entry except for where we came from. Besides, were there rodents in this realm? I didn't recall ever seeing one, but that didn't necessarily mean–

"Alaris," Brunhild said, interrupting my internal chatter, "I was told your anger is what triggers this gift you have."

We were now standing in the center of the room. It was empty except for a rickety table against the far wall with a pewter pitcher and four tall glasses on it. Larkin's gaze swept the room. I wondered if he thought the same thing I did—we could be held as prisoners here with no hope of escape. My stomach churned uneasily, and I had the sudden urge to race up the stairs and get the hell out of here.

Brunhild eyed me, taking in the apprehensive expression I could feel on my face. The corners of her mouth twitched in amusement. "Don't worry, girly. The king and queen know you're here. You're safe. No need to be frightened."

I nodded. "I guess I've read too many dark fairy tales, and my imagination got the best of me."

A wicked grin crossed her face. "There's truth to those tales."

"I've told her already," Larkin said, his voice stiff. "I think we should get on with this because Alaris and I have plans afterward."

He'd never mentioned to me about what we were going to do later. I wondered if he only said that so we could get out of here as soon as possible. He watched her closely with his arms tight across his chest.

"Very well." She filled a glass with water and handed it to me. "Your anger is the key to unlocking the power that resides within you. Your job is to make this water boil like you did the other night."

"It was a freak occurrence," I said. "I don't know if I can do it again."

She pushed her bushy brown hair off her shoulders and straightened her back. "The headhunters killed your family." She leaned forward in front of me, and in a hateful tone, she spat, "They cut off your mother's head." My heart dropped. My face felt cold from the blood draining from it. "They might even have it in a shadow box, displayed nicely with their other treasures."

My hand shook at the image she projected in my mind. I never even thought about something like that. What if what she said was correct? I gasped. "What?"

Larkin took my free hand and squeezed it. "It's okay." He glared at Brunhild. "She's been through enough. Adding to it is not the right approach to what you're trying to achieve."

"I know what I'm doing," she snapped and turned her attention back to me. "Draylan sees no point in you seeking the headhunters who murdered your family. How do you feel about his lack of caring?"

I know Larkin told me to try not to display my elemental power, to play it like for some reason it wasn't working; however, the rage within me could not be contained. The entities who murdered my family must pay for their heinous crime.

I suddenly felt hot. Beads of sweat formed on my forehead, exactly like the night when we were having dinner. My palms were burning. Bubbling sounds came from the water glass I held. Thick puffs of smoke rose to the top.

"Alaris," Larkin whispered next to me under his breath. "Don't."

He wanted me to stop. I knew that. Brunhild didn't need to know what I was capable of, let alone teach me how to wield it. I breathed through my nose to calm myself, trying to think of something else, but Brunhild opened her mouth and continued jabbing at me.

"Yes. Yes. Allow your hate to overtake you," Brunhild said. "The headhunters are getting away with murdering your family, and who's to say they won't go after Kimmie and her family?"

"No," I said, gritting my teeth. She was playing on my fear, using it to piss me off, to get a reaction out of me. I knew this, but even so, the thought of a revenant harming the people I loved enraged me.

"They're not going to touch her," Larkin said in a low voice out the corner of his mouth. "Relax."

I glanced at him. He gave me an infinitesimal nod, his green eyes silently telling me to trust him. My attention swung back to Brunhild. She was watching the water boil in the glass I held. I had to admit I was curious to see what would happen if I allowed my rage to overtake me, but I trusted Larkin. The way Brunhild was testing my elemental power, using hurtful reminders along with horrific images to provoke me wasn't the right tactic. Anger shouldn't be used to trigger it. I wasn't the fucking Incredible Hulk.

"The headhunters enjoyed taking your parents' lives. After they decapitated them, they laughed while licking up their blood. Now they're going to get away with it."

I tuned her sick words out and thought about Larkin and me riding our horses side-by-side through a prairie, then making love beneath the stars and twin moons where no one could disturb us. I wondered if there was such a place here because it seemed like no matter where we went, there was someone around like the fairy at our picnic. I'd have to remember to ask Larkin.

The water stopped boiling, and the smoke above it dissipated, like before when Larkin was there beside me helping. All I had to do was calm myself to stop it.

"What's going on?" Brunhild took the glass and snatched my hand, turning it over to where the palm was facing upward. The lines in it glistened with sweat. "Why did it stop?" She eyed me suspiciously. Her brown watery eye widened, while her pale blue one was all squinty. "What did you do, girly?"

I pulled my hand out of her grasp. "I didn't do anything."

Brunhild snorted and shuffled across the room, mumbling something under her breath I couldn't make out. She put the glass back on the table and faced us. "Your life is never going to be the same again."

"I know," I said. "I'm coming to terms with it."

"No, you don't understand." She crossed the room and once again stood in front of me. "You have the fire element which means eventually you will be forced to seek the other ones: earth, air, water. There are Murks who are obsessed with being the most powerful beings in this realm, not just in Atheon, and you, girly, are the one who can make it happen."

Larkin's muscles tightened. "It's a myth. The gods and goddesses made sure no one would obtain such power when they put us all together here."

"Is it so?" Brunhild hissed. "Are you sure?"

"Completely," he said without hesitation. He took my hand. "C'mon. Let's go."

"So soon? We were just getting warmed up." She cackled at her obvious pun.

"I don't agree with how you're handling this," Larkin said, annoyed. "It's unkind. Alaris doesn't need to be reminded about the tragedies of her family. She's still vulnerable, and toying with her emotions like you were doing is unacceptable."

"You may see it as such," Brunhild answered, "but those feelings are what triggers the elemental power within her. As cruel as it may be, it has to be done to see what she's capable of, then teach her how to control and use it to her benefit."

Larkin narrowed his eyes. "There's a better way."

She moved her head from side-to-side reminding me of a snake. "Like what?" she asked and cupped her long pointy ears with her hands as if she were trying to hear something. "I'm all ears." Her tone was low and raspy with a hint of amusement.

Having the sudden urge to get a drink of water, I released Larkin's hand and crossed the room, but when I approached the table, I noticed a ton of dead flies on the floor that were shadowed from the light.

I drew in a sharp breath, and my blood ran cold.

"I don't kno–" Larkin started to say but stopped when his eyes locked onto mine, then widened in response to the horror on my face.

I moved toward him in hurried steps, hoping he had a weapon on him. "Let's go." I grabbed his hand and led him to the stairs in a rush.

"Alaris," Brunhild called.

I turned, losing contact with Larkin and stepped around him, prepared to tell her I appreciated her breaking the memory spell and trying to help me, but I had to do this on my own. In all honesty, what I really wanted to tell her was to fuck off, but I didn't want to cause any trouble, especially since we were on her turf. I opened my mouth to rattle off my prepared speech, feeling a bead of cold sweat trickle down my back. At the same time, she raised her closed fist to her lips, opened her hand, and blew across her palm. Shimmering particles flew across the room between us at lightning speed. As soon as they touched me, I lost my breath and took a step back. An image of a dragon from the neck up emerged from my chest. It was holographic and wicked looking with its horns and scales. It opened its mouth, revealing large pointy teeth, and snapped at Brunhild. She clutched her chest and stumbled backward, panting, her expression twisted in fear.

"It's okay," Larkin whispered in my ear, his tone rattled. "She's not going to hurt us now. Let's go."

The dragon disappeared, and when it did, I turned and rested my hands on my knees, gulping in large amounts of air, trying to catch my breath. Larkin moved behind me, sheltering my body from Brunhild and nudged me toward the stairs. I tripped and tipped forward but caught myself on the third step.

"Sorry," he said and stuck his hands beneath my armpits, raising me to my feet. "Are you okay?"

The room spun. "I feel a bit dizzy, but I'll be all right."

His strong hands braced my arms, and he placed his chest against my back. "I got you. Lift your foot and step up."

Feeling a bit shaky as if I hadn't eaten in days, I did what he wanted. "I can do this," I said to myself, focusing on what I was doing instead of what just happened.

As we made our way up the stairs, Brunhild's voice boomed behind us. "I knew it! I knew there was something you were hiding. Now your story makes sense about the unicorn and Karrina and Mardella going to great lengths to hide you. But how did you get the spirit of the dragon in you and why . . . why you?"

That was a question I'd been wondering about all along and unfortunately had no answer to.

Chapter Twenty-Eight

"What the hell am I going to do?" I asked Larkin. We were on Gypsy, racing through the forest to get as much distance as quickly as possible from Brunhild's house. It still amazed me how Gypsy flawlessly maneuvered over parts of the rough terrain without stumbling. "And the flies." I shivered against him, my backside bouncing from Gypsy's gallop. Two large squirrels darted out of our path.

"What's with the flies? I don't know what you're talking about."

"When I came home the night you showed up at my house, there were dead flies everywhere. Then the headhunters appeared." The image of that night popped in my mind—bright and clear. I shook my head to dislodge it. "I think Brunhild is the one who is controlling them."

We exited the cover of the trees, but instead of heading back to the palace, Gypsy crossed the dirt road and entered another stretch of forest similar to the one we left. She slowed to where I could relax against Larkin and loosen my grip around his waist. The earthy organic smell of plants and dirt enveloped me. We were on a clear, windy path surrounded by moss-covered oaks. The ground on either side of us was carpeted in lush green foliage.

"I think you're right," Larkin said.

"Where are we going?" I wondered what Brunhild was doing at the moment and if she would tell Merrack and Datura about what happened.

"I told Farran to meet us at The Blue Fairy."

"What's that?" A picture of a tiny blue-skinned creature with wings entered my mind. It wouldn't surprise me if there was one.

"It's a club," Larkin told me. "Oona works there. She dances and sometimes sings. I thought we could have a drink and get a bite to eat while discussing matters with Farran."

"Good idea. I can use a cocktail, and maybe Farran will know what to do." I was hoping he would because I was clueless about what actions to take regarding my situation.

"I think he will. He's a resourceful guy."

Twigs crunched beneath Gypsy's hooves. Berry bushes dotted our path. Huge twisted roots were spread across the mossy ground. The sky was slowly darkening, and high above the majestic treetops, the outlines of the twin moons were forming.

"Why are you so calm?" I asked, thinking he hadn't seemed freaked out in the least, even when the dragon emerged from my chest. Instead of bolting up the stairs, Larkin told me it was okay and Brunhild wasn't going to hurt us. Anyone else would have backed away or run out of the room. Not him.

"I'm not," he said. "I'm concerned about your safety more so now than ever before."

"But you weren't afraid of the dragon."

He laughed. "You didn't see my face when it happened."

"True. You did sound rattled when you spoke to me."

"I was and still am." His chest rose and fell into a heavy sigh. "Let's talk more about this with Farran, in case there are pixies around listening to us."

My eyes swept the area, but I didn't see anything out of the ordinary. There was a pool of standing water on our far right in a wide open space between the trees. The light of the rising moons glinted off the surface, giving the illusion of an oval mirror framed by twigs and leaves. A couple yards ahead was a large tree split in half. Both sides formed an arch in an M fashion. Jagged pieces of bark were poking up, revealing the fleshy part of the oak. I thought it was bizarre and stared in wonder when we rode by.

As night approached, the air grew chilly. I pulled the sleeves of the red cloak Larkin gave me over my cold hands. It was woven from wool and some other type of material that kept me warm. The ground sloped downward and then up. When we reached the top of the grassy hill, we were near the edge of the forest. The aroma of burning wood hung in the air. A two-story medieval building constructed from timber, stone, and a grayish white stucco stood a few yards away from us. It had three pitched roofs. The two in front were attached to the side of the long building with shuttered windows and weathered perpendicular wooden slats. Gypsy's hooves clopped against the flagstone as we approached the tavern. A wrought iron sign that said: THE BLUE FAIRY hung on a wooden pole in front. A dozen horses or so stood on the far side of the building.

We dismounted, and Larkin pulled a dark brown cloak from one of the saddlebags. He slipped it on and the hood over his head. He then dug into the cargo pocket of his pants while Gypsy joined the other horses. "Here, keep this with you." He handed me a small tan cloth sack in the shape of a teardrop due to a piece of twine wrapped around the corners.

I bounced it on the palm of my hand. It was heavy like there was sand inside. "What is it?"

"It's magical dust," he answered in a low voice, his head bent next to mine. "If someone gives you any trouble when I'm not around, throw some at him. A wall of thick smoke will appear between the two of you, which will give you time to escape."

"Why did you wait until now to give this to me?" I thought it was cool this would give me the ability to hold off my attacker but was a bit perturbed all the same.

"Because I thought you were safe until now."

I slipped the sack in the front pocket of my cape. "I don't think I ever was, but I can see why you thought that since there are wards around the palace."

"They might have been breached," he said while scanning the area. He pointed at a grayish white horse with dark gray speckles hanging out with Gypsy. "Farran is here." He made a move to go, but I placed a hand on his arm to stop him.

"I think there's a good possibility the headhunters who killed my family are dwelling beneath the palace." The thought of it being true unnerved me. I took a deep breath and continued. "When I was given the map, I was told I'd find what I'd been seeking." I shook my head. "I honestly have no clue what we'll discover, but I fear those murdering bastards have been near me since I've been here."

Larkin embraced me. "If it's true, we'll catch them, and they will pay for their horrendous crime."

He was right. We might get our chance tomorrow night. I sighed against his chest, feeling safe and secure in his arms. I wanted nothing more than to be wrapped in them for the rest of the night, but Farran was waiting, and I was anxious to know his thoughts about what happened at Brunhild's house. "You're right," I said, "but in the meantime, let's see what Farran has to say."

Larkin softly kissed my forehead and released his arms. Without saying a word, we crossed the short distance to the building and entered the tavern through the heavy oak door. The smell of alcohol and cherry pipe tobacco engulfed us, along with the sound of easy chatter and laughter. Chandeliers with lit candles hung from thick wooden beams. The whole place was rustic. The stairs to our left went up to another floor that made a half circle around the room with ornate carvings on the railings. A stone fireplace was lit near the bar. I felt as if I stepped back into medieval times—only the patrons here were goblins, dwarves, elves, fairies, and nymphs. There also could have been weres at some of the tables—normal looking guys, talking among themselves—but I wasn't close enough to tell. Larkin nudged my arm. "There's Farran." He jerked his head toward a table in the far corner.

Farran had his back to the wall and held a pewter mug in his hand. He nodded at us in acknowledgment. Keeping my head bent and the sides of my hood shielding my face, I followed Larkin, staying to the back of the room so we wouldn't draw too much attention to ourselves, though I was highly aware of the curious looks thrown our way.

"What happened?" Farran asked as we took our seats. Larkin and I exchanged a look. "That bad?" Farran took a swig of his drink and set his mug down.

"We should get a drink and a bowl of stew before we fill you in on the details," Larkin said.

As if he summoned a waitress, right on cue a fairy with dark shoulder-length hair and green eyes flew to our table. She hovered between Larkin and me. "Hello, my name is Nissa. What do you two fancy tonight?"

"Two bowls of stew," Larkin said. "A dark ale for me." He looked at me and so did Nissa.

"Um." I didn't care for beer, not after playing quarters when I was nineteen at a party with Kimmie, and I ended up hurling in the trash can. "What do you have other than beer?"

"Whatever your heart desires, sweetie." Nissa smiled and gestured toward the long hardwood bar to the far right of the round stage. A ghostly woman with long hair, wearing a dressing gown was pouring blue liquid from a gooseneck bottle into a tall thin glass. A burst of red rose from the bottom.

"I'll have a Singapore sling. Do you know what it is?"

"No, but I'm sure Appara will," Nissa said. "Her hobby is to learn about drinks in every realm she can enter. It's a challenge for her."

"Okay, well," I answered. "If she doesn't know, I'll take a cabernet sauvignon."

Nissa half-nodded. "Will do. Your order will be here in two shakes of a lamb's tail." She flew off to the bar and hovered near Appara's ear, giving her our order I guessed. I was too far away to see her face, but I think she was looking at me.

"What is Appara?" I asked Larkin, realizing even though I gained most of my memory back (The rest will come in time, I know), there was a lot I didn't know about in this realm. Karrina had sheltered me from a lot of things.

Larkin folded his hands on the table and leaned forward. His eyes flicked to her, then back to me. "She's an echo, which is a spirit who is caught between the living and dead."

"Oh," is all I said. I wanted to know more about Appara and echoes, but Farran cleared his throat, snapping me back to the reason why we were here.

Larkin and I moved our chairs closer to him. With bent heads and low voices, we proceeded to tell Farran what happened. Toward the end of our story, a light green-skinned gal with long dirty-blonde hair and tiny scales on her heart-shaped face came to our table. She carried a platter with two bowls of stew, thick white buttered bread, and our drinks. I recognized her right away from the party.

Lucy.

"Thank you, Lucy," I said, pleased Appara was able to make the Singapore sling.

She smiled. "You remembered my name." She sounded surprised and happy that I did.

I forgot how deep and reflective her big blue-green eyes were. I thought they were amazingly cool but made an effort not to stare too much into them. I didn't want to make her self-conscious.

"Well, to be honest," I said, "I'm usually horrible remembering names of people I've met, but for some reason I remembered yours. I think it's your eyes. I find them extraordinary."

A brownish color bloomed in her cheeks. "Thank you." She held the empty platter to her chest. "Enjoy your meal and drinks. If you need anything else, let me know."

Farran folded his arms on the table and leaned forward when Lucy left. "Finish your story. What happened when you were about to leave Brunhild's house?"

With hands cupping my mouth, I told him in a high whisper what Brunhild had done and the dragon's head that emerged from my chest.

His eyes widened, and his lips parted. He leaned back, covering his mouth, his expression clearly saying, *Oh, shit.*

I nodded. "Yeah, what the hell are we going to do? My goose is cooked because we all know Brunhild is not going to let this go. Larkin and I are thinking maybe she's the one who was controlling the headhunters."

"Do you have any ideas on what plan of action we should take?" Larkin asked as I scooped some stew into my spoon. There were chunks of meat and vegetables in a thick brown gravy that looked yummy. I took a bite, and the beefy flavor burst in my mouth delightfully.

Farran drummed his fingers on the table and the bottom corner of his mouth twisted in contemplation. His eyes flicked to mine. Fear and sadness glistened in them. My throat tightened. I didn't want him to feel that way about me. We were becoming friends and sharing similar tragedies. I took a long drink of my cocktail to stop myself from getting emotional. It tasted awesome, like fruit punch with cherry undertone. When I set my glass down, Farran reached out and placed his hand on my wrist, surprising me. "I'm not afraid of you," he said, as if he could read my thoughts. "I fear if this information gets out, your life will be compromised." He looked at Larkin. "I think after we follow the map tomorrow night, we should take Alaris to see my father and tell him everything."

"Why your father?" I asked, not sure if I liked the idea and thought maybe my own father would know what to do if Brunhild told him, which I was sure she did. Then I thought about him being power hungry years ago. It almost destroyed him. Would he return to his old behavior?

Larkin nodded. "You're probably right," he told Farran and frowned. "I wish I can find Mardella. She would have the answers we seek." Right when I opened my mouth to repeat my question, Larkin's gaze dropped to mine. "Alder is a wise man. He's not only king of the Solas clan, he's also a historian, among other things."

"Good evening, ladies and gentlemen," a sultry female voice rang above the chatter, catching our attention. It was Oona. She was onstage holding a wireless microphone. Her metallic purple mini dress clung to her tall, lanky form. The color stood out against her bluish skin beautifully. "I hope you're enjoying yourselves," she continued.

"Yeah, baby," a gruff voice called out, raising a beer glass. He sat at a table near the center of the room. His scraggly black hair reached his shoulders, and the tip of his pointy ears curled away from his head. He had a long hooked nose with a rather large mole on the side, and his yellowish-green skin looked tough and rock-like. "I want to see you dance tonight."

I leaned next to Larkin's ear. "What type of creature is that guy?"

"A trow," he said. When I gave him a funny look, he corrected his statement. "A troll."

"Oh, wow. I always thought of trolls as cute and little. I don't think Karrina ever told me about them. At least his kind."

Farran leaned into the table. "Why would you think they're cute and little?"

"Because in my realm," I told him, "there are small naked troll dolls with adorable faces and colorful wild hair that stands up on end. I actually have a few of them in my bedroom on a shelf."

Farran pointed at the guy staring at Oona as she told him tomorrow night she'd be dancing, but tonight she'd sing the siren's song. "As you can see, he's nothing like what you described. He's probably seven feet tall."

I gaped. "Are you serious?"

Farran nodded. "Yes, I am, Princess." He smirked and took a swig of his ale, obviously enjoying my reaction.

"Okay, on that note, I need to use the restroom." My bladder was aching from holding it so long. I had to go now or risk having an accident. "Where is it?"

Larkin's chair scraped against the hardwood when he pushed it back. He rose. "I'll show you."

I was going to object to him shadowing me until I considered my current situation and thought maybe it would be best he did. Little did I know, though our plans for tonight would dramatically change within the next ten minutes of us leaving the table.

Chapter Twenty-Nine

Neither of the two restrooms in an alcove was marked for men or women. Instead, dangling from a nail on the wall dividing them was a hand-carved sign that said: WATER CLOSET. Nothing fancy was inside, only the basics: a toilet, sink, mirror, and a brown towel that hung from a rack between the sink and the john. After I did my business, I washed my hands, and as I was drying them, Brulin appeared gripping the map, scaring the crap out of me.

"Sorry, Princess," he said when I placed a hand over my racing heart. "I didn't mean to frighten you." He gave me the map, surprising me because I hid it under the mattress of my bed, but then I recalled he was there when I did. "You need to follow this tonight." His words came out fast and insistent.

I stuck it in my pocket. "Why, and what are you doing here?"

"I'm here to help you," he said without hesitation. "You're precarious situation changed the plans. It must be tonight. It must."

"When?"

Beads of sweat stood out on his wrinkled forehead. When he spoke it was in an urgent high whisper. "The witching hour, Princess. The witching hour."

"Alaris, are you okay?" Larkin asked on the other side of the door. At the same time Brulin disappeared with a *pop*, similar to uncorking a wine bottle.

I opened the door and pulled Larkin inside, locking it behind him.

"What's wrong?" He looked worried.

"We have to go tonight at midnight," I said, breathing heavier than normal. My chest was tightening. I think I was on the verge of having an anxiety attack. I knew we needed to do this, but I wasn't mentally prepared for tonight, and after what happened at Brunhild's house, I had no clue on what would await me at the palace.

He placed his hands on my shoulders. "It's okay. Whatever this is, we'll get through it together." I took a couple deep breaths and nodded. "Now what are you talking about?"

I reached in my pocket. "It just gave me this and told me we have to go tonight instead of tomorrow night." I handed the map to him. "What time is it?"

He unfolded it and looked at the drawings. "Tunnels," he murmured, "beneath the palace." He continued to examine the sketches. "The entrance is in the wine cellar. I'll be damned."

"You didn't believe me?"

He glanced up, his expression full of wonder and curiosity. "I did, but holding this brings what you told me and Farran into reality."

I shifted my weight and chewed on my fingernail. "What time is it?"

"Um, after six, I think." He folded the map and gave it to me. "We need to tell Farran about this and head back to the palace as if nothing ever happened."

"Okay, but Brunhild probably already told Merrack and Datura my secret."

"There's only one way to find out," Larkin said, opening the door.

We exited the restroom and made our way back to our table. Oona was singing about the ocean and being set free in a land with sparkling white sand and deep blue waters as far as the eyes could see. Her voice was hauntingly captivating—beautiful and tranquil. A symphony of instruments played, though there wasn't a band behind her. I wanted to sit at our table and listen like everyone else was doing, staring at her as if in a magical trance.

"C'mon. We have to leave," Larkin said to Farran, snapping him out of his dreamy daze. "I'll go pay and–"

Farran rose from the table, an alarmed expression on his face. I'm sure he could feel or sense our anxious energy. "I already did."

"Thanks." I took one last swig of my Singapore sling and followed Farran.

We kept to the back of the room in the shadows, single file with me in the middle, Farran in front, and Larkin in the back, not that anyone would notice with Oona singing, but nonetheless we did. Once we stepped outside into the brisk night and reached our horses, Larkin and I quietly filled Farran in on what happened. He wanted to see the map but knew he should wait until we were back at the palace and in a safe place for him to observe it. We mounted and took off into the woods, Farran leading the way.

The twin moons were almost full. Their white light filtered through the branches in bright rays around us. I held onto Larkin's waist as we rode at an even pace. A large sandy blond wolf stood to our right between the trees. His sharp, penetrating eyes stared at us. Nash. I recognized him from my party. I wondered if he knew my secret. There were more wolves standing along our path, watching us intently.

"Look to your left," Larkin said to me out the corner of his mouth near his shoulder.

I did. There was another pack of wolves mirroring the same stance as the others across from them. I caught the gaze of a brown one. He ducked his head as if bowing. I had a strong feeling it was Wyatt.

"What are they doing?" I asked.

"They're fighting over territory. Farran, Narik, Draylan, and I have been talking to them to try to prevent a war between the two."

We passed more of the pack, emerging out of the shadows: gray, white, black, and brown wolves. We were flanked by weres, but I could tell by their nonthreatening postures they had no interest in harming us. They were more curious than anything else. "It doesn't look like it's working."

"We know about this meeting," Larkin informed me.

"Shouldn't all four of you and maybe more warriors, be here in case a fight breaks out?"

"We can't babysit everyone; however, Narik and Draylan are supposed to be on patrol duty tonight along with some other warriors you haven't met yet. I'm sure they'll check on them."

"How come I haven't met them?"

"They're not the elite." I could hear the smile in his voice. "We're like the special forces on earth, except for we do a lot of patrolling."

The chilly breeze was nipping at my nose and cheeks. I nuzzled my face against Larkin's back and closed my eyes, listening to the rustling of the leaves. The sound was soothing, lulling me into a state between sleep and awake. Moving pictures drifted through my mind of Kimmie and me dancing among a group of people at a club in Vegas, having movie night with my parents (the Evergreens), eating pizza, and of me at the age of twelve, quietly listening outside our kitchen to Mardella telling Karrina why she thought the unicorn chose me. Then the clattering of hooves on rock jarred me out of the scene.

My lids snapped open. Bleary eyed, I looked about. High on the grassy hill the palace loomed in the moonlight like a dark creature observing its next prey. Buttery light glowed through the turret's arched window and on one of the peaked towers on the south side of the building. The rest of the windows were like black gaping holes glaring down at us. The treetops of the forested sloping landscape behind the palace were bathed in white light that gradually faded into darkness. We rode past my new home straight to Larkin's cottage. Once we dismounted and were safely inside, I discarded my cape and handed the map to Farran.

"This is amazing and a bit disconcerting," he said, placing the drawing on the kitchen table and taking a seat. "I wonder if my father knows about this but never told me."

Larkin shook his head. "I don't think he does, but I'm sure Merrack knows."

I leaned beside Farran and tapped my fingertip on the paper. "How far do these tunnels go and to where? Some of them branch off, and if you look here"—I pointed to a drawing of a room on the north end of the palace. The square was drawn below the building with the word: *cellar* inside the box. On the bottom was a word written between what looked like rows of barrels: trapdoor—"the entrance is in the wine cellar. That's what Larkin said. I didn't even know we had a wine cellar." When Brulin first gave me the map, I was too stunned to examine it closely. Otherwise, I would have noticed that detail we needed to enter the tunnels.

"I see that," he said, his tone full of interest. He looked up and squinted at me. "How do you know the person who gave you this is trustworthy? What if it's a setup?"

Larkin rubbed the back of his neck as if he were loosening a tight muscle. "I was thinking the same thing."

"It's not a plan to trick us," I told them.

"How do you know?" Farran asked, still skeptical.

"I just do," I sighed. Doubt weighed heavily in their expressions. "Look," I went on, "I'd tell you how I acquired the map, but I'm not sure if I can. Besides, I'm your princess, so you have to listen to me and do what I say." I wasn't planning on playing that card, but the words tumbled out of my mouth before I realized what I was saying. It felt kind of good and almost comical that I, Haven . . . Alaris, was their superior. I smirked.

Larkin barked out a laugh and in good humor said, "Now I know how this is going to be."

I crossed my arms and smiled. "You're damn right."

Farran's expression turned serious. "I think we should go to the armory, put on our armor, and grab some weapons. I have a bad feeling about this."

"You think my contact is leading us into a trap?" I asked, having the urge to defend Brulin.

Farran folded the map, handed it to me, and rose. "No, but I think there's something down there we might need to defend ourselves against, and I'd feel better if we were prepared."

"I agree," Larkin said, "but let's wait until an hour before we're supposed to go."

"Sounds like a plan." I looped my arm with his and hugged it. The gesture felt natural, and he returned it by wrapping his arm around me. I knew one thing for sure during this whole mess: Larkin wouldn't let anything happen to me, and the thought of it warmed my heart.

To pass the time, we decided to chat in the living room while drinking coffee. I remembered to tell them both about the dream of me eavesdropping on Karrina and Mardella when I was twelve. All three of us came to the conclusion it was a memory, and any time now, I'd recall the rest. The charm Mardella had cast on me was a son-of-a-bitch. I was grateful Brunhild broke through it but wished all of my past memories came to me at once instead of resurfacing one, maybe two at a time when I least expected it.

We talked about going to the palace before we headed to the armory but decided to stay put since we didn't know if Brunhild told Datura and Merrack about my secret. We'd deal with that issue tomorrow morning and focus all of our energies on our mission at hand. All three of us were anxious about tonight. It was obvious by the lively chatter we exchanged and how we bounced from one topic to the other. Farran wanted to know why I didn't call Karrina "Mom." He found it odd. To him, your birth mother was your mother, unless she'd proven not to be a fit parent, which in my case, Karrina was. He pointed out when I talked about my memories of her and me, there was love and happiness in my tone. I did my best to explain to him I wasn't ready to acknowledge her in that manner, because by doing so would release a flood of emotions I wasn't ready to deal with. I already lost one mother. I wasn't in the right frame of mind to deal with the loss of another or revisit all of the memories of her and me. I think he understood, because he thoughtfully nodded, and we moved onto another topic—thanks to Larkin—about fighting techniques. The next thing we knew, we blew through a few hours, and it was time for the guys to arm themselves and to find out why Brulin was so insistent we go through the tunnels tonight.

Chapter Thirty

Larkin and Farran didn't waste any time putting on their armor while I waited on the couch in the armory, biting my fingernails. When they stepped out of the dark gray stone archways that led to their separate rooms, they both were wearing black hooded robes. I rose and met them in the center of the room, noticing Larkin had a brown leather sheath in his hand with a knife attached to a belt.

"I want you to wear this," he told me. He pulled the knife out of the sheath. Only it wasn't a knife: it was a short sword. "The blade is made out of pure silver and can harm a revenant, among other creatures." The metal was shiny, appearing almost fluid when he angled it toward me. He opened his palm, balancing the weapon on it to show me the wooden grip. It had two wide bands of silver with what looked like Celtic designs. The ball on the end had a ruby in the center. He pressed the handle into my hand, wrapped my fingers around it, and as he did so, he said, "I'm gifting you this short sword. It belongs to you now." My hand gripping the handle tingled, and a starburst of light flashed between my knuckles, then disappeared as quickly as it came. "The only way I or another person can use this," Larkin went on, "is if you give your permission."

I bit my lip. "But I don't know how to use a sword."

"Don't worry," Farran said, stepping beside me, "it's only for your protection. If you do have to use it, I'm sure your defensive fighting instincts will kick in, and you'll know what to do."

I blanched with the sudden onslaught of doubt and fear. "Um . . . I don't know if I feel comfortable carrying this or using it for that matter." A vision of me being confronted by a seven-foot trow who happened to be a Murk with the intention of doing harm, and me being clumsy with the sword to where he swiped it out of my hand popped inside my head.

Larkin gently brushed a stray strand of hair off my cheek, his touch warming my blood, calming me. "It'll be okay. If I thought otherwise, trust me, I wouldn't have given this to you." He lifted my chin with his finger so I had to look him in the eyes. There was confidence and adoration in them. "I'd never give you a weapon I thought you couldn't handle."

My gaze kept darting from his lips to his face. I really wanted him to kiss me but knew he probably wouldn't since Farran was present. "All right," I said, not knowing what else to say because my thoughts were all mushy with him touching me and looking at me the way he was—like I was his whole world.

"Are we all settled now?" Farran asked. "It's almost the witching hour. We have to get going."

"Just one sec." Larkin held the leather belt in front of me. "You need to put this on."

I handed him the knife, pushed my cape behind my shoulders, and took the belt from him. After it was secured around my waist, I sheathed the blade and adjusted my cape. "I'm ready."

"Can I have the map?" Larkin asked. "I want us to look at it one more time before we head out."

I took it out of my pocket and handed it him.

All three of us gathered in a circle and pored over it. We already knew we had to go to the wine cellar since that was where the entrance was. We decided from there, once we were inside the tunnel, we'd figure out which way to go.

Larkin kept the map and tucked it away in his front pants pocket beneath his robe. He took a deep breath and released it. He looked at Farran and me. "Are we ready?"

"Let's do this," Farran said.

I stuck my hand out. When they stared at me in question, I half-smiled. "This is what we do on earth when members of a group support each other, like a brotherhood . . . Larkin, place your hand on mine and Farran place yours on Larkin's." They did what I told them. "All for one and one for all. The three musketeers." I grinned.

"You and your silly ways," Farran said, shaking his head with a hint of a smile. "But I have to admit, it's refreshing."

Larkin wrapped his arm around my shoulders and pulled me into him. He kissed my temple, then released me. The corner of his mouth curled. "My wildfire."

Farran headed toward the elevator that led back up to the gym. "Our time for dawdling is up."

Tonight one of two things would happen, I thought. Either justice would be served, or we were sent on a wild goose chase and would be back to where we started.

* * *

The twin moons were like white glowing orbs in the star-filled night. We hurried along, and as a precaution, we kept to the shadows like in the tavern. When we reached the north side of the palace, there were two doors. I opened the one on the far left and was met with a ramp. Darkness flowed downward, ending in a square faint of golden light far below. Larkin told me the ramp was used to roll barrels into the underground room. The light concerned us, because no one had any reason to be here at this time of night, except for us of course.

"Be on guard," Larkin told me as Farran opened the door on our right. "I have a feeling whomever is down there is up to no good."

Farran glanced over his shoulder at us and cocked an eyebrow. "It could be a trap."

I rolled my eyes and sighed. "For the millionth time . . . it's not."

"If it is," Larkin said behind me, "there will be hell to pay."

I nudged Farran's back. "Go. I want to get this over with so I can hopefully move on with my life."

Farran took the first step, his frame swallowed in darkness.

Crack!

I flinched and felt Larkin's comforting hands on my shoulders from behind. I opened my mouth but closed it when Farran raised what looked like a stick glowing the color of blue, brightly illuminating the stairwell. He handed it to me, and I in turn gave it to Larkin. A couple of cracks later, all three of us had light sources to aid us through the shaft of darkness.

As we descended the stairs, the pungent odor of mold and dirt grew along with the chill in the air, causing goose bumps to rise on my skin beneath my red cape. When we reached the domed room constructed from rough gray stone, I wrapped an arm around myself to stave off the cold. Two balls of light on twisted wire hung from the ceiling, casting a soft glow in this dungeon-type room. Like the map drawing, there were rows of barrels on shelves on either side of us. Behind me, a few yards away, appeared to be a round alcove—another room, maybe, but I wasn't sure since our limited light didn't reach that far. At the other end of the row, were four chairs around a rough wooden table with a rusty lantern in the center. Large squares of flagstone covered the floor with no trace of a trapdoor.

I bent and held my glow stick over the floor, dousing it in blue light while swiping the layer of dirt aside with my other hand. "I don't see an entrance here."

Larkin spread the map on the table. He turned and pointed to the left of me, a few feet in front. "It looks like in the picture it should be over there."

Farran and I moved to where Larkin indicated. We brushed our fingers against the flagstone, checking for a crack or flaw. Nothing.

Farran shook his head and stood while I remained on my knees still inspecting the area. "The entrance to the tunnels isn't here."

"It has to be," Larkin said. "Why would the map lie?"

Farran looked at me, and I knew what he was going to say by the I-told-you-so expression on his face, but before he could say anything, I shot back, "It's not a trap."

He shrugged. "Maybe not, but it might be a ploy to distract us from whatever underhandedness might be taking place here."

I ignored him and returned to what I was doing. He joined Larkin at the table and while they were discussing what to do next, I continued my search.

I was good at finding things. I knew I could do this. Granted, I'd never been in a situation like this before. In the past, the things I found that turned up missing were trivial such as car keys or Kimmie's term paper, but still . . . I wasn't giving up. Then an idea came to me as if it fell into my head. I unsheathed the short sword, held the grip tightly, and mentally asked it to help me find the trapdoor. With the tip pointed to the flagstones, on its own accord, my hand holding onto it moved in a straight line in front of me. At the same time, a slow stream of silvery liquid flowed from the tip. My grip on the hilt moved to the right, then behind me and to my left, creating a perfect square of pearly glowing light.

Holy shit! I'd been kneeling on the entrance to the tunnels all along.

"Alaris," Larkin said, sounding alarmed, walking toward me in quick strides with Farran close behind. "What did you do?"

I rose to my feet and showed him the blade that was no longer weeping. He took my free hand, and as I stepped outside the square, the top lifted and fell backward, revealing stairs down a gaping hole of darkness.

"What possessed you to use your weapon?" Farran asked. "I would have never thought of such a thing."

"This wildfire," I answered with a smirk as I slid the short sword back into the sheath, "don't fuck around."

Larkin laughed.

"I'm impressed." There was a smile in Farran's pale blue eyes, something that was rare to see, and it warmed my heart. He lowered himself onto the first step. "The stairs are steep, but there's a railing you can hold onto." He held his glow stick in front of him—a blue hue lighting the way as he went down into the bowels of Atheon.

Larkin made a sweeping gesture. "After you, Princess, and don't worry. I'll protect you." He winked.

I followed Farran, mimicking his gestures, holding onto the railing with my free hand and my glow stick with the other. I could feel Larkin's tall frame behind me, its heat pressed against my upper back and shoulders. As I cautiously moved my way downward, the cool air bit at the tip of my nose and ears. A thick musty earthy smell enveloped me as I continued, careful not to slip on the loose pebbles and chipped stone worn with age.

When we reached the bottom, we were in a central location. There were a network of tunnels to choose from. The one on our right was lit with rusty gas lanterns anchored to the wall several feet apart, creating dark pockets between them. The realization that someone was down here finally sank in.

Larkin turned to Farran and me. "I guess we don't have to question which route to take."

A haunting feeling grew in the pit of my stomach, causing it to twist with anxiety. I reminded myself I had two elite warriors with me. I'd be fine. They knew what they were doing and wouldn't allow anything to happen to me. Besides, I knew how to fight. If it came down to it, I could defend myself, right?

Farran slipped his glow stick into a pocket inside his robe, we did the same as he swung his attention on us. "We move in silence, single file. I'll be in front, Alaris in the middle, and Larkin behind. Got it?"

We nodded and followed Farran through the tunnel. Our shadows stretched against the dimly lit walls in a ghostly fashion that set my nerves on edge. Farran's posture was stiff and alert, his right hand resting on his hip. We walked in silence between the ancient stone walls lit with the lanterns to lead us deeper into the bowels of this subterranean place, each of us caught in our own thoughts. I was beginning to think we should have brought a backpack full of supplies to sustain us during this seemly long trek until we heard a noise like someone would make during sex—a pleasurable sound. It was coming from the corridor in front of us, to our left.

Farran stopped and turned—a mixture of curiosity and surprise in his expression. I mouthed the word "sex" thinking maybe there was some kinky shit going on in Atheon we weren't aware of. I didn't know, but it sure sounded like a female getting off. I looked at Larkin who appeared equally perplexed. He motioned with his finger for us to move to the other side. We crossed the hall, and as we crept closer to the source, we became aware we were approaching a room the lanterns didn't illuminate. It was hidden in shadow, and we would have missed it if we kept to the other side. It made me wonder if there were others we didn't see.

I went back to the opposite wall, because I had to know if my assumption was correct, earning a whispered, "Where you going!" from Larkin. I mouthed "I'll be back." When I looked across at him and Farran, I couldn't see the room at all.

Magic.

It had to be some sort of camouflage spell to hide the chamber under the guise of a stone wall. The trick was a clever thing to do but disconcerting, as well.

I rejoined Larkin and Farran and in a low whisper I said, "Magic." I wanted to say more to answer their questioning expressions, but now wasn't the time to do so.

The pleasurable sounds escalated.

Slowly, we edged toward the entrance and peeked inside. What we witnessed was beyond anything I could have imaged.

Chapter Thirty-One

Datura was kneeling on a plush crimson rug in the center of the room, her back arched, chin tilted up, arms spread apart behind her. Two cloaked ghostly skeletal entities with black holes for eyes were feeding on her. One at her neck, the other on her breast that had escaped her silk robe.

Her eyes were closed, and her lips parted as she moaned. "Yes, my sweets," she said in a breathy voice. "Drink from me."

We pulled back with shocked expressions on our faces.

Datura.

Oh, my God!

She was the one controlling the headhunters.

That bitch!

My parents were dead because of her, but why? Why would she do such a thing?

Heat rose from the back of my neck. It spread across my shoulders, down my arms, to my hands. I balled them into fists, clenching my teeth.

Larkin looked at me, his forehead creased, his shocked expression now worried. He took hold of my arm and turned me to him. "Try to stay calm," he whispered. "We don't want to do anything rash." His gaze dropped to my fists. Tendrils of smoke rose from them. I opened my palms, and like in my bedroom with Draylan, a small ember sat in the middle of each one. I wondered what would happen if I continued to be angry, but Larkin's distraction temporarily dulled my biting rage.

Farran eyed my hands, then his gaze met mine. "Listen to Larkin," he said in a low voice. "Whatever powers you behold are unstable due to the lack of knowledge and control you have. Instead, we need to break up this sick lovefest in a swift manner and subdue Datura."

"What do you propose?" Larkin asked. "We don't have time to ponder and discuss a clever strategy."

"I say we hose the bitch," I said and at the same time thought about Merrack. Did he know this about Datura and didn't care what she did in order to find a way to obtain all four elements? Because honestly, at one time, Merrack set out to do the same thing. I didn't know what to think at this point.

Farran shook his head. "No, we need her. I want to interrogate her or at least find out if she knows who slaughtered my family."

Farran made a good point. I would also like to ask Datura questions. However, the headhunters were going to get what they deserved as far as I was concern. I told the guys that, and they agreed. They needed to go on trial for their heinous acts, and now that we knew Datura was the one controlling them, the revenant's admission would surely smoke Datura and whatever diabolical plan she had concerning me. It was obvious to all three of us that she'd targeted me from the beginning. We didn't have time to discuss the whys and the hows. Datura's sensual moans and endearments to her pets were dying down. We had to take action now.

Farran and Larkin decided to go into the room first while I stayed behind them. Larkin preferred for me to remain out of it altogether, but I refused to go along with his suggestion. I wanted the bitch to know that I knew what she'd done and to see on my face the promise that I'd make damn sure she'd pay for all of her wrongdoings.

Before they made their move, Farran signed quick hand gestures to Larkin. I wasn't getting what he was communicating, but it was obvious they'd worked together long enough to know what the other was saying. Larkin gently pushed me behind him, turned his back, and reached for something inside his robe. I withdrew my sword and held it next to my side. The next thing I knew, a horrible high-pitched screech poured from the room. Larkin rushed in, and I followed, noticing right away the dead flies on the floor.

Datura was on her feet. Her eyes were black as coal. Dark spidery veins webbed across her pale face. She held her hand out in front of her, palm facing Larkin, too focused on him to have noticed my presence. She was saying words I'd never heard before. Larkin flew backward, then stopped. Datura repeated what she said, frustration coloring her wicked tone.

"You're too weak," Farran said from across the chamber. The revenants were standing, frozen in place with a silvery netting over their cloaked bodies. He regarded them with disdain. "Five, four, three, two, one. Bye." He waved, and they disappeared.

"I'm not," Brunhild said behind me, making me jump and whirl.

The next thing I knew, my sword clattered to the floor as I was flung across the room, along with Larkin and Farran. Our backs pressed against the cold stone wall like squished bugs. I couldn't move my limbs, only my head. I opened my mouth and tried to speak, but the words came without sound.

Datura blinked, her crystal blue eyes and flawless ivory skin back to normal. A bead of blood trailed down her neck. Surprise and contempt marred her beautiful features when she saw me. She looked at Brunhild and smiled sweetly. "Thank you for your assistance."

"I have something to tell you," Brunhild said in a scratchy tone. She glanced at me before returning her attention to Datura. "Alaris not only harbors the fire element but also the spirit of the dragon."

I would have never guessed both Brunhild and Datura were partners in a diabolical plan to ruin my life and use me to possess all four elements. They had to have known it was a myth. According to Larkin and Karrina, the gods and goddesses made sure no one could gain that much power.

Datura's eyes widened in delight. She looked at me and crossed the room, kicking my sword aside. Her expression darkened. Larkin shot her a warning look, but she didn't notice. Her attention was on me and me alone. "I had a feeling," she said through tight lips, "after the spell was broken you knew more than what you were letting on. Why?"

I opened my mouth to show her I couldn't speak.

She rolled her eyes and glanced over her shoulder at Brunhild who stood near the entrance, appearing like she had more to say. "I'd like to talk to Alaris."

Brunhild moved her fingers in a circular motion and jerked them in my direction. There was a tickle in my throat. I coughed, wishing I had some water. My hand tried to move up in an automatic response to cover my mouth, but it remained plastered on the cold stone.

"Well?" Datura asked, crossing her arms, glaring at me.

"Well, what?" I choked out.

She snatched my chin, her grip tight around my jaw, fingers pinching my skin. Her eyes narrowed to slits. "Why didn't you tell me you possess the spirit of the dragon? After all I've done for you, you ungrateful little bitch!" With a jerk of her hand, she released my face.

I smirked. "You're still sore about me not reading your speech, aren'tcha? Well, get the fuck over it, you murderer!" I knew I shouldn't provoke her, but she was the reason my parents were dead, and I wasn't about to cower before her.

The muscles in her face tightened. She gritted her teeth, and in one swift move the palm of her hand met my cheek, producing a loud slapping sound. My skin burned from her harsh blow, stunning me. I glanced at Larkin. His face was red, eyes blazing, throwing Datura a venomous look.

"I went to great lengths to bring you here," Datura snapped. "Your parents' death was not by my design. The revenants took it upon themselves to eliminate them. Not me!" She paused. The corners of her mouth slowly turned up. In a syrupy sweet voice laced with poison, she continued, "Although I did tell them whomever stood in the way of their mission, they were free to do what they desired if such a situation arose."

She shrugged like it was no big deal. "The Evergreens were simply at the wrong place at the wrong time."

My temper flared. If I could reach out and strangle her, I would. She was a conniving, psychotic, cunt, and I didn't use the C-word lightly. But at the same time, the thought of my earthly mom and dad being dead caused a shattering punch to my stomach, reducing me to tears, watering down my anger. I didn't say anything, only stared at her.

Her finger swiped a tear off my cheek. She showed me the wetness on its tip. "The Evergreens weren't your parents. They don't deserve your remorse and neither does Karrina. She betrayed you, like my own mother betrayed me."

"The Evergreens thought they were my parents," I choked out. "They were compelled to believe so. They raised me as their own flesh and blood. They were loving and kind." A sob escaped my lips. A new wave of emotions I didn't know I had gripped me.

Datura waved her hand dismissively. "No matter." She turned and went to where Farran was. "I don't know how you three discovered these tunnels or knew I'd be down here, but you," she seethed, "you're my nephew. I'd done nothing to you but made sure you'd have a bright future, and you betrayed me!" She spat on him. I couldn't see Farran, but I gathered it was in his face. "Brunhild," she said. "Release Alaris but leave the other two bound to the wall."

I dropped to the floor on my hands and knees. My whole body prickled with numbness. Datura grabbed me under the arm and yanked me up, turning me around so I faced Larkin. A torrent of emotions flickered across his face: fear, sadness, rage.

"Take a good hard look at the object of your affection," she told him. I blinked to dry my weeping eyes. I didn't know what would become of me, what Datura and Burnhild's plans were, but an overwhelming warmth of love for Larkin filled my chest. I knew then I was in love with him because the thought of never seeing him again crushed my heart. "This might be the last time you see her."

"I love you," I told him as she pulled me out of the room.

Brunhild stood in the hall, waiting for Datura like an obedient servant. The flames from the gas lamps flickered. "Your father wants to speak to you," she said to Datura.

Her father? I thought, confused because I was told he died when the Murks attacked her family.

Datura's demeanor brightened as we walked down the long corridor. She released her grip on my arm and smiled. "Excellent. His timing could not be any better." She shot me a warning look. "Don't even think about escaping. If you do, you'll rot down here unless you're lucky enough to find your way out. If that's the case, the wolves will get a hold of you and won't be as gracious as I am."

I swallowed against the dryness in my throat and wiped the tears off my face. I was at her mercy. Datura's magic was useless at the moment, but I had no idea when she'd gain it back. I wasn't about to risk causing a fight with two evil witches with the odds stacked against me. I made up my mind then that if I were to survive this, I'd make damn sure to discover what powers I had and learn how to wield them.

We neared the area where Larkin, Farran, and I entered, but instead of going that way, we veered off into another tunnel. This one was pitch black. Datura placed her hand on my shoulder to stop me.

"Aduro," Brunhild said. A whooshing sound followed. Flames lit the glass lanterns anchored in rusty metal sconces along the stone wall, like the ones in the previous tunnel.

Datura released my arm. I walked beside her, wondering how far we had to go. The air was cold with a thick musty stench I didn't care for. It coated my whole body like a second skin. I bet my clothes would reek once we left this place. I hoped not. It was weird how the mind worked during a time like this. Here I was a prisoner, not knowing what would become of me, yet I was fretting over a stinky smell. My thoughts then jumped to Datura's father wanting to talk to her. It didn't make sense to me. He was dead . . . or was he?

We halted in front of a rough wooden door. My stomach clenched, and my pulse pounded in my throat. Brunhild opened the door, the hinges protesting with a long drawn-out tired groan. Soft light shone, creating a wide wedge in front of me.

"Two things," Datura said to me before we entered. "Don't disrespect my father, and if he asks you a question, answer him. Got it?"

"What about my father?" I snapped not hiding my hatred toward her. "Is he part of this scheme to obtain the elements and become all-powerful?"

"We'll talk about your father later," she said dismissively. She fixed her eyes on mine. They turned cold, and her voice dropped into a scathing warning. "Do you understand what I told you not to do?"

I nodded, refusing to look away or allow her to intimidate me.

She smiled, her face now bright with happiness. "Good girl." She playfully nudged me with her elbow as if we were old friends. "Come now. I want you to meet my daddy. He's the best."

With a racing heart, I took a deep breath, and stepped into the room.

Chapter Thirty-Two

The chamber was small, no bigger than an average bedroom. I was surprised there was no one in there except for us, and the only pieces of furniture were a wooden table and four chairs, much like the one in the wine cellar. On the table propped on a metal stand, was a round shiny black object about seven by five inches long. The intricate designs on its edges reminded me of a vintage picture frame.

Datura sat in front of it and gestured for me to stand next to her. Then it clicked what the object she stared into was.

A scrying mirror.

At least that was what it reminded me of. Witches used it as a powerful metaphysical tool to see into the past, present, and future. I knew this from watching my paranormal TV shows.

"Father, are you still there? Brunhild tells me you want to speak to me," Datura said.

Brunhild moved to the other side of Datura. Her shoulders were relaxed like she had no worries and was waiting for a friend to meet her.

The dark surface rippled, and several rings appeared like throwing a stone into a pool of ebony water. They expanded outward. As they disappeared, a shadowy face emerged. The outline was masculine with a strong square jawline, a well-define nose, and almond shaped eyes. His features were shaded as if an artist had drawn a rough pencil sketch of him.

What the hell?

Was her dead father communicating with Datura from the spiritual realm? Was this a tool to connect with our loved ones who crossed over to the other side? If so, I wanted to use it to contact my parents and would find a way to do so if that were the case.

He smiled. "Datura, thank you for taking the time to visit with me."

Datura grinned. "Anytime, Daddy." Her tone was childlike, which I thought was weird. "Brunhild told me you wanted to see me." She mindlessly curled a lock of hair around her finger.

"Yes, dear," he said. "Brunhild told me about Alaris." He looked up at me. "Is this her?"

Datura slightly turned and placed her hand on the back of my arm, urging me forward. "Yes, Daddy, it is. Meet, Alaris."

I raised a hand. "Hi."

"Please to meet you, Princess. Brunhild told be earlier you harbor the fire element as well as the spirit of the dragon. Is this true?"

"It is." I decided not to lie because what would be the point? Brunhild witnessed both things first hand, and lying would only gain me more trouble than good.

His eyebrows lifted. "I see. Do you know what this means?"

"Yeah," I answered without thought. "If word gets around about it, I'm fucked."

Datura cleared her throat and shot me a reproachful look, clearly saying to watch my tongue.

Her father laughed quietly. "Indeed."

Feeling bold and spurred by curiosity, I blurted, "May I ask you a question?"

"Certainly."

"I thought you were dead. How can we be communicating with you?"

His gaze shifted to Datura. "Do you want to tell her, or shall I?"

"Whatever you wish, Daddy, I will do."

"Why don't you tell her, sweetheart?"

Datura turned to me, beaming. She was nuts. Plain and simple. Her demeanor and moods shifted from one extreme to the next, and this *thing*, whatever it was she felt for her father was both weird and creepy. All I could do to possibly save my own hide was to play along, and to be honest, I was anxious to hear what she had to say. "This is Aven Blackwald, my biological father. Trevan who died, wasn't my father."

I scratched my head. "I don't understand."

"Of course not," she answered, her tone patronizing, making me bristle. Her neck was within my reach. I could easily step behind her and snap it. "My mother," she went on, "had an affair with Aven who is from the Dorchadas clan. When she discovered she was pregnant with me, she panicked, which resulted in her lying, accusing Aven of assaulting her. Because he was a dark fairy who displayed evil behavior, he was automatically judged as a Murk. He was then sentenced to Phirosuin Domhan by your grandfather—Merrack's father."

"Aven was wrongfully accused," I stated, immediately feeling bad for him. "How heartbreaking and so unfair."

Datura smiled. "Yes, and my mother hid this from me most of my life. I happened to stumble onto this information by accident."

"How did you find out about your mom's betrayal?" I hoped I wasn't prying too much, but I was sure Farran would want to know about this. I know I did.

"A diary," she said.

"It was the day you got into an argument with your mom, right before she died. Am I correct?"

"Alaris," Aven interrupted, pulling my attention back to him. "I rather we not talk about Phira."

"I'm sorry," I said and meant it. I couldn't imagine being betrayed by my lover, wrongfully accused of a crime I never committed, and then sentenced to prison. I looked at Datura. "Why didn't you use the diary as evidence of Aven's innocence?"

Darkness flicked crossed her eyes, and she clenched her teeth. "Because when I confronted her about it, the bitch snatched the diary from my hands and tossed it into the fireplace."

I shot her an accusing look. "So in retaliation you had your family slaughtered?"

She glared at me. "The *Murks* killed them."

"But weren't you the one who coaxed them into it?"

"Alaris," Aven said, interrupting me. "How did you get the spirit of the dragon inside you?"

I sighed. "Does it matter?"

"It does," he answered, "very much so."

"How can you be communicating with us when there's no magic inside the prison you're in?" I asked, deliberately changing the subject as he had because for one, I did want to know that and two, I didn't feel like talking about the whole unicorn-dragon-egg tale again.

"He's doing it through his dreams," Brunhild said, shifting her dark watery brown eye on me. "Right now he's asleep. When he wakes, he'll remember everything that transpired here."

I twisted my lips to the side. "Interesting." I wondered how that could be and was about to ask, but Aven spoke first.

"I'm going to tell you about something I did before I was sentenced here," he said to me. "Because I have a feeling it's connected to what happened to you."

That got my attention. "What?"

He rubbed his chin and squeezed it in thought. "I'm going to get to the point. I want all four elements. I have for a long time–"

"It's a myth," I interrupted.

"I don't think so. The gods and goddesses abandoned us a long time ago. They no longer care what we do unless we affect the Axis—a conduit through which the deities and their children can travel along the outer planes. I will make sure that doesn't happen and so will my daughter."

I glanced at Datura. She was grinning. I wanted to slap it off her face.

"I don't–" I started to say, but he cleared his throat, signaling he wasn't done.

"We can talk about it later. Back to what I wanted to say to you . . . before I was captured and sentenced to Phriosuin Domhan, I found a female dragon who just laid an egg. I knew I needed the fire element naturally residing in a dragon, so I used magic to bind the mother, which immobilized her and sent her into a deep sleep. I then placed a charm on the egg so the baby inside wouldn't expire, because I knew I had to obtain the other three elements and use them all together in order to cast the spell and become all-powerful in this realm. The same day while trekking through the forest, I ran into some trouble and tossed the egg aside. I was then captured and not too long after, I was sent here."

I was dumbfounded. A dragon still existed. Not just any dragon but the mother of the baby I tried to save.

Wait a minute.

The dream I had when I first arrived here but couldn't remember it all was of a large golden dragon. Was it her? Was she trying to communicate with me? Then something in my brain clicked like a key unlocking a door, but nothing came to me, only the strong sense it was her.

"So the mother is still alive, sort of like in cyrosleep?"

"Yes. Now, I'd like to know how you were able to harbor the spirit of a dragon inside of you. Is it the same one I spoke of?"

I nodded. "It is." I launched into the whole story.

"Fascinating," he said when I was done, obviously intrigued.

"I still have no idea why the unicorn would choose me," I told him.

"I have my theories," he answered offhandedly, "but right now it's not important. I'm running out of time. Soon I'll be waking." He leveled his eyes with mine. "Because you have the power of the dragon inside of you, you can lower the magical wards in this prison for a short period of time and release me. If you do so, I'll take you to the dragon and break the spell."

I shifted my weight back and forth and bit my nails. I'd love for him to free the dragon because in a way, she was in her own prison. However, in no way did I want him or Datura to take full control of Atheon. Not to mention that more than likely he was full of shit. It wasn't likely he'd release the spell and risk facing a pissed-off dragon, *if* he were telling me the truth. "I don't think so," I finally said, earning a dirty look from

Datura. "I feel bad you were wrongfully accused of a crime you didn't commit, but I can't have you and Datura take control of Atheon. It's fine how it is, and one day I'll rule. I believe I can do great things here." I couldn't believe I was saying this. I mean, I wasn't planning on staying. I missed my old life, but I knew now it would never be the same. There was Larkin, and I was a princess. I could do well here and help other people. Of course, there was no way I'd sit back and lead a pampered life. That wasn't me. I wanted to explore and learn about other creatures and their ways of living, among other things.

Aven rubbed the side of his jaw, not hiding his disapproval. "I see."

"I'll handle this, Daddy," Datura looked at me calmly and simply said, "If you don't release him from prison, your father will remain in a coma."

I blinked at her. "What?"

A shitty expression crossed her face. "I said," she raised her voice, "that—"

I spoke louder to shut her piehole. "I know what you said. When did he fall into a coma?"

"This evening," she answered. "And I'll make sure he remains in it unless you help us."

"He might wake up from it tonight or tomorrow," I said.

Brunhild shook her head. "He won't. We made sure of it."

I gaped at her, then shot an accusing look at her and Datura. "All this time he's been sick because of you two? Why? Why would you do that to him?" I was more shocked and hurt than mad, because I thought all along they were trying to help him when really the herbs they were giving him was for their own demented purposes.

Datura flashed me a wicked smile. "Insurance." She turned back to her father. "I'll meet you again tomorrow to let you know when we're on our way."

I pressed my lips together to prevent telling them I didn't agree to anything. Instead, I decided to play along until I could come up with a reasonable plan to get out of this situation, save Larkin and Farran, and get them to help me find a way to cure Merrack.

"Alaris," Aven said. "Come closer to me." I gave him a wary look. "I'm not going to bite." I moved to the table and bent next to Datura. He fixed his eyes on mine. "Trust me."

There was something in his face and tone that almost caused me to doubt my conviction not to help them. It was like an undercurrent of meaning hidden from what he had spoken aloud.

I rose to my feet. "You're a dark fairy. A Murk. How am I supposed to trust you?"

He didn't respond, only nodded, but his gaze never left mine. There was a message in it he was trying to convey to me alone. I thought of the Jedi mind trick and looked away. Not that he could actually bend my will, but I couldn't grasp what he was silently telling me. Besides, he could be a sociopath who had a knack for manipulating people. I wasn't about to risk finding out. There were lives at stake, and I needed to figure out a way to save them—but how?

Chapter Thirty-Three

We left the tunnels the same way Larkin, Farran, and I came in. To add weight to her claim regarding Merrack's state, Datura wanted to take me to him. I guess it was her way to motivate me into doing her bidding.

I walked in silence beside Datura while we headed toward the palace, ignoring her jubilant mood. She gushed about her daddy and how great a man he was. I wanted to gag. Ignoring her and Brunhild, I admired the twin moons bleeding brilliant light onto a dark canvas, then fading into black again. I wondered how Larkin and Farran were going to get out of their imprisonment or how I could help them. The only answer I came up with was to visit Havenwood and talk to Larkin's mom to see if she could get hold of Mardella who could not only help Larkin and Farran but Merrack, as well. It was a good plan, and I bet Mardella could help me discover what powers I possessed and how to use them, but how would I escape my current situation? I no longer had my sword, and if I did I probably wouldn't use the weapon anyway since it would be foolish to take on two evil witches with one short blade. Then it hit me, causing me to almost gasp when I remembered the magical dust Larkin gave me at The Blue Fairy. I stuck my hand in the pocket of my cape and felt the small cloth sack with the piece of twine wrapped around it. I glanced to my left. The forest wasn't too far from us, but I remembered what Datura said about the weres getting me.

Shit.

I could dash to the stables and grab a horse. However, that would take too much time. My best bet would be to take my chances and find help along the way.

I bit my lip, weighing my options. If I didn't use all of the dust, I'd have some to protect me if trouble were to cross my path. I also had a good sense of direction and could hightail it to The Blue Fairy and ask for help. I'd have to hide along the way because Datura and Brunhild would surely be hot on my trail. If I were to follow along with what they wanted, maybe there would be a better opportunity than now to escape. Maybe. My heart sank when the realization came I'd be playing Russian roulette if I were to hoof it into the trees with a slim chance of reaching Havenwood on my own. I should probably–

A silhouette of a man riding a horse emerged from the forest. I squinted to see who it was. As the horse galloped toward us, the guy's appearance came into focus: brown hair, messy on top, muscular frame, and chocolate eyes that were looking at us with frank curiosity. He was probably wondering what I was doing with Datura and Brunhild at this hour.

Narik.

Datura and Brunhild were still idly chatting. They glanced at him, paying no mind. I was relieved to see him, knowing now what to do. I halted, allowing Datura and Brunhild to walk several feet ahead of me. I motioned for Narik to come closer. When confusion entered his face, I mouthed, *Help me.* Before I gave him the opportunity to react to my plea, I pulled the sack from my pocket, tugged on the string while cupping my hand around it, took a healthy pinch, and right when Datura and Brunhild turned to look at me, I took a step forward and tossed the dust at them. They screeched and threw up their arms as a wall of gray smoke engulfed both women. I dashed to Narik, grabbed his outstretched hand, and swung onto the saddle behind him.

"Let's go," I said. "We need to get out of here as fast as possible and to Havenwood."

He made a clicking sound, and we leaned forward like jockeys in a race. I held onto him as we galloped through the forest, feeling the tightness in his muscles, knowing he had no idea what was going on, but it had to be bad in order for me to do what I'd done.

"How far to Havenwood?" I asked, closing my eyes because the cold air was causing them to water.

Right when I asked him, his horse reared on his hind legs and neighed. I slipped backward but was able to swing my leg around and jump off. Narik did the same. A large brown wolf stood in front of us, baring his teeth in a menacing growl. Narik reached inside his jacket across his chest and withdrew a silver and copper antique pistol with a large barrel and a small grip. It was nothing like I'd ever seen on earth before. It was sort of steam punkish with a filigree and scroll style pattern on the handle and sides. Narik pushed me behind him and pointed the weapon at the wolf who immediately stopped growling.

"No need to brandish your weapon," a male voice said. I stepped out from behind Narik and made eye contact with Nash—the were who wanted to dance with me at my party. He smirked. "Nice to see you again, Princess. What brings you to these parts at such an hour as this?"

"It's top secret royal business," I answered, grabbing the first thought that came to mind.

He touched his chest as if he were impressed, but his snarky tone suggested otherwise. "Oh, really? Well, then, I should let you go off on your merry way." The wolf next to him kept his gaze steady on the pistol Narik still directed at him.

"I think it would be a good idea," Narik said. "I already dealt with you and your pack tonight. I'm not in the mood to do so again." He motioned for me to get back on the horse.

I could feel Nash's eyes on me as I mounted. When I turned to look at him, he flashed me a devilish grin that sent a chill up my spine.

Narik hopped on in front of me. "Hold on tight," he told me under his breath, still aiming his weapon at the were.

I leaned forward and wrapped my arms around his waist. Nash

turned up the collar of his black trench coat. "I'm still waiting for that dance, Princess."

"Another time," I said as we passed him, not intending to follow through with it.

My bottom bounced against the saddle as we raced through the woods. Soft golden rays of light beamed through the tall trees, kissing the ferns, the bright colorful wildflowers, and foliage. When we slowed to an even pace, I rested my cheek against Narik's back and yawned. The inside of my ears were thumping, which was a signal I needed to sleep. There was no time for it, I told myself. People's lives were in my hands, and I had yet to tell Narik what was going on. He needed to know but not here.

"How much longer to Havenwood?" I asked.

"An hour. Why? Are you tired?"

"Are you?"

"Yeah, I am, but if you want to keep going, I'm fine with it."

"No," I said. "I'm exhausted, and I'm sure you are, too. Is there a safe place around here where we can go to get a few hours of sleep?"

"Actually, there is, and it's not far."

He pulled the reins to the left, and we headed west. I blinked several times to prevent my heavy lids from falling. It was no use. I had to close them, if only for a moment. The next thing I knew, I was in a lush green valley surrounded by black jagged smoky mountains.

"Alaris," A female voice said from behind.

I turned and gasped at the colossal golden dragon standing before me on legs spread broadly apart to support her massive body. Her length and wingspan must have been hundred feet. Two long horns protruded from the top of her head, and a short one stuck out on her snout and chin. Her gills flapped open and closed as she breathed. Saliva dripped from her long teeth as her orange reptilian eyes captured mine. They softened, and the sudden fear and shock I felt a moment ago disappeared, replaced with an intense connection.

"Alaris," she said again. "My name is Shalnal, the mother of the wyrmling you discovered years ago and whose essence now dwells within you."

"I'm . . . I'm sorry for not being able to save him. I . . . I tried." A lump formed in my throat as the events of that time sprang forth in my mind.

"No blame is placed on you," she said. "It is the way of things. Besides, he chose to live on inside of you."

"Why?" I swiped the tears off my face. "Why me?"

Narik nudged me and told me we were here, breaking my connection with Shalnal. My eyes snapped open, and the dream I had shattered and faded away. I couldn't remember shit, except for the awesome feeling of being with a dragon. We stopped in front of a two-story stone building with a brown thatched roof. There was a wooden sign hanging between two four foot poles in front that said: *Goblin Inn*.

Narik dismounted. "Put your hood up and look at your feet so the innkeeper can't see who you are." He pointed to the round oak door. "I'm going to go inside and get us a room. Stay here. I shouldn't be too long."

I nodded and pulled my hood over my head, tugging it down so it would cover the side of my face. I was a bit nervous sitting here in the middle of nowhere by myself, but I trusted Narik and knew even though he wasn't my warrior, he'd protect me with his life. He hadn't even asked me what was going on, probably because he was waiting until we were in a place where no one could hear us, but nevertheless, he did what I asked of him without question. He was a good friend, just like he was when we were kids before I was taken out of Havenwood. I appreciated him and would make a point to tell him so. As I waited, I tried to bring back the dream I just had, but all I could recall was the warm feeling of being with a dragon.

"I got us a room," he said, taking the reins and hopping up in front of me.

"Does a goblin actually own this place?" I asked as we headed to the back of the building and toward a large timbered barn that was worn and gray from age.

"Yes, his name is Ghoub. He's good shit and highly intelligent. The room we're staying in has a magical ward that'll keep us safe."

We dismounted when we entered the barn. The sharp smell of hay and earth assaulted my nostrils, which reminded me . . . I sniffed my cape. There was a hint of a musty aroma but not bad enough to wrinkle my nose at.

As Narik led his gray thoroughbred into a stall with hay on the ground and water in the trough, I marveled at the heavy arched beams and the enormous length of this structure. A couple of horses in separate stables ahead of us made low rumbling sounds in their throats, like they knew they had a visitor and were greeting him.

Once outside, the sky was a swath of burnish orange and pinkish colors highlighting the ribbons of clouds across it, reminding me of jet contrails. A sad longing for home tugged at my heart. I shook it off as best I could, telling myself I couldn't go back in time. I had to move forward. This was my life now.

We entered a door in the back of the building and went up steep steps illuminated by lanterns of yellow warped glass composed of heavy wrought iron and anchored to the wall. When we reached the top, we went down a short hallway. At the end was a plain iron door. There was nothing fancy about it, except the knob looked like it was fashioned from pure silver.

I pointed at the door. "Is this made of–"

"Yes, it's iron and silver," Narik said, sticking the key into the lock. He turned it, and a sharp click followed. He opened the door and gestured for me to go in first. "I told you we'd be safe in here." He closed the door behind us and continued, "Fairies, elves, witches, spirits, and other various beings all have a weakness when exposed to those two metal elements. Not to mention for extra security, Ghoub has a magical ward up around this room, but I already told you that." A tired smile crossed his face.

"Yes, you did," I said, yawning. I waved a hand in front of my face to stave off my sleepiness. I took my cape off and draped it on a high-backed walnut chair. Its top and base were finely carved in a swirly pattern, and the cushions appeared to be constructed of red leather. Fancy, I thought, planting myself on one of the twin beds with patchwork quilts on them, while Narik picked up a pewter pitcher from the nightstand between the two and poured water into a pair of amber drinking glasses. He handed me one. "Thank you." In no time, I drank the cool liquid down, not realizing how parched I was until now.

Narik sat across from me. "What's going on?" he asked while shrugging out of his coat.

I took off my boots and slipped under the covers. "Do you want the short version or the long one?"

He settled onto the other bed and propped himself up on his elbow. Although his brown eyes appeared dull from lack of sleep, a humorous spark entered them. "The short version first. If I have any questions afterward, then you can elaborate."

"Fair enough." I turned on my side, facing him. "Datura is an evil bitch, and Brunhild is not much better." That got his attention. A renewed energy entered his face, but before he could voice his surprise and interest, I continued, "Datura is the one controlling the headhunters who slaughtered my family."

"How do you know this, and where's Larkin? I thought he'd be with you."

I shook my head and sighed, then told him everything, including me harboring the spirit of the dragon and Datura's father wanting me to bust him out of prison so he could resume his mission to gather all four elements. I must have fallen asleep toward the end of my story because the next thing I knew I was with Shalnal again in the lush green valley, and amazingly enough, I remembered everything from our last visit.

"Welcome back," she said. Her orange reptilian eyes were intense, but there was warmth in them, the same kind a child received from her mother.

I rubbed the spot above my brow. "How come you're now entering my dreams, and I can't remember anything when I wake up?"

"One question at a time, my dear." She turned her massive body around. It was covered in curved armor-like scales. Small horns trailed down her spine and long tail, and the tip ended in the shape of a spade. She walked on her knuckles, which caused her enormous wings to stick up, their jagged edges giving them a feathered look that was wicked. I was in total awe, and the happiness I felt being with her reflected through my smile and the bounce in my steps.

"Okay, then, why me?"

"I know about the unicorn," she abruptly said. "We've been friends for a long time. His name is Olwen."

"How do you know about the unicorn?"

"Mardella, but we don't have time to go off topic and onto a new one." She paused as if collecting her thoughts. "Except," she continued carefully, "Mardella told me Olwen had been observing you in secret and saw an adventurous, kind, and caring spirit in you. He also knew you were the daughter of a healer and of royalty. Those qualities bottled into one being was worthy enough to discover my wyrmling and take him home."

"I was a child, though."

"Yes," she agreed, "a young one yourself, and you still are. However, simply because the body is of a certain age, doesn't mean the spirit is. The two are separate."

I twisted my lips to the side. "Hmmm. I've never thought about that, but it makes sense."

"My wyrmling was going to expire anyway." Her tone was low and filled with an emotional sadness that broke my heart. "The spell Aven cast on him had a time limit. Olwen led you to my egg, knowing this. He also suspected, in his last attempt to survive, the wyrmling would transfer his spirit into you and would live on through you, but then Mardella placed a memory charm on you that not only affected you but the dragon as well since your spirits are intertwined."

"Alaris," Narik said, gently shaking me. "Get up. It's almost lunchtime, and we should be heading out soon."

Eyes still closed, I held a hand up. "Okay, I'm up." My voice sounded groggy, and I had a strong desire to roll over and pull the covers above my head, but then Narik told me he bought us ham sandwiches. My hunger roused me enough to sit up and wipe the sleep from my eyes. I realized then I'd been having another dream about a dragon. What was her name?

"You must have been tired. You didn't move a muscle until now. I thought for sure I'd wake you while I was taking a shower." He handed me a cup of coffee. "I doctored it like I do mine with cream and sugar. I hope it's how you take it."

"Perfect," I said and sipped the coffee. The slightly sweet, creamy flavor was wonderful. "Mmmm, this is good. Thank you."

The corner of his mouth turned up. He handed me my sandwich. "You're very welcome."

We ate and drank our coffee, revisiting the events I shared with him last night. He admitted he never cared for Datura because her intentions seemed false to him, but Merrack seemed happy with her, and they were his employers, so he kept his opinions to himself. Not in a million years had he thought Datura was the conniving bitch that she turned out to be. He was pissed about what she and Brunhild did to Merrack, Larkin, and Farran, and was anxious to get to Havenwood as soon as possible. I was, too, so I took a quick shower and cleaned myself up as best I could.

"Are you ready to revisit your home?" Narik asked me before we headed out.

"As ready as I'll ever be," I said, slipping into my cape and pulling my hood up. All I remembered of Havenwood were distant memories, like a reoccurring dream you had as a child that stuck with you throughout the years, but in my case the recall was hidden until recently. Now I was both excited and nervous to go there: excited to be back in my old house and village but nervous as hell that this would be a waste of our time and my emotions would get the best of me regarding Karrina. I took a deep breath and followed Narik from the room, silently praying things would work out in my favor.

Chapter Thirty-Four

Havenwood.

Home.

Narik pulled the reins back, causing his horse to stop near the edge of the forest. We were in the shadow of the trees on a hilltop, looking upon a sweeping view of lush rolling green hills, golden fields in the west with structures that looked like barns and farm houses. Nestled in the hilly valley was the village, dotted with fairy tale type cottages and windy cobblestone paths. I couldn't see everything the idyllic small town held and offered, but the memories trampled through my brain like a herd of elephants. I recalled everything, and at the same time, my heart soared and warmed like never before.

Yes, I was home.

"We better keep inside the tree line for now," Narik said. "We can reach Larkin's house and yours in privacy this way."

"Sounds good." I had a stupid, silly grin on my face, temporarily forgetting my troubles. I couldn't stop smiling; the twelve-year-old child in me—the one compelled and yanked from Havenwood—was elated. Then as the forest sloped downward, and we neared the honey-colored stone cottage with a pitched roof, a lump formed in my throat.

Karrina.

Mom.

She used to spend a lot of time here with Larkin's mom, Fiona. They were besties, and Karrina taught Fiona about medicinal herbs and how to make healing potions with them. In return, Fiona taught Mom about horses that she bred, raised, and sold.

We approached the house and dismounted. We paused when a gal with long, straight brown hair came riding up on a black and white spotted horse. She took one look at me and pursed her lips. I knew who it was, though I hadn't seen her for ten years, but she still carried the same sour look on her face as she always had.

Lithia.

Oh, goodie.

I wondered what she was doing here, and I was sure she was wondering the same about me. The thought of her sucking up to Larkin's mom in an attempt to win back his heart unsettled me. My muscles stiffened.

"Hi, Lithia," Narik said in a friendly voice, but the corners of his eyes were tight. He didn't much care for her either.

"Hi." Her expression held a caution one gets when unsure about something. I took that as a silent affirmation of my earlier thought that she didn't have a clue why we were at Larkin's house. "Is Larkin with you?" She looked about and frowned when she didn't see him.

"No, he's not," Narik answered. "Is Fiona home?"

"I'd like to say I'm happy to see you back after all of these years," she said to me, ignoring Narik's question, "but–"

"You're not," I answered for her.

She shook her head. "I can't help how I feel. I've never really liked you, ya know?"

"The feeling is mutual." I turned to Narik. "Let's see if Fiona is home."

"She is," Lithia piped up, "but she's caring for Mardella at the moment."

Narik and I looked at each other in surprise. She was here. Oh, my God, she was here! I needed to speak to her now.

"Mardella is here?" Narik asked as I took his hand and pulled him toward the door, anxious to see her.

"She's dying," Lithia answered in a flat tone, halting me, forcing me to pay attention to her. "She doesn't have long to live." There was no emotion in her words. She obviously didn't care, so what the hell was she doing here?

Narik eyed her, unsure whether to believe her or not. "Are you serious?"

"I am." She gestured toward the door. "See for yourself if you don't believe me. "

Narik knocked on the door and poked his head in. "Hello, it's Narik. I have someone who wants to see you. May we come in?" We stepped into a small entryway. "We don't mean to intrude, but it's important."

"Narik?" a female voice said. "What's wrong?" She sounded tired, and when I lowered my hood as she came around the corner, she gasped. Her hand touched her mouth, then dropped to her side. "Alaris," she whispered, tears glistening in her hazel eyes. A heavy emotion shook me at the sight of her—a feeling of reconnecting with a beloved relative you thought you lost. Fiona was like a second mother to me. I remembered it clearly now and bit my lip to prevent it from trembling and to keep me from crying like a fool. She threw her arms around me and hugged me tightly. A delicate lavender scent permeated from her that was comforting, like a warm blanket on a cold night. "We've missed you so much." She pulled back and held me at arm's length. "Look at you. You've grown into such a beautiful woman."

"Thank you," I said, wiping the tears from my eyes.

She held my cheeks in her cool hands and kissed my forehead. "Did Larkin come with you? I sent a messenger fairy to Atheon this morning to give him the news about his grandmother, and he needed to hurry home."

"No," Narik answered. "We have to see Mardella, if we may."

Fiona paled, and she clutched her heart. "Is Larkin in trouble?"

"We all are if we don't get Mardella's help," I said.

Fiona gestured for us to follow her, then stopped in the middle of the living room. "Does this have to do with the spirit of the dragon in you?"

"How do you know about that?" I asked.

"Mother told me last night when she arrived here. She heard you were back, and the spell she cast had been broken. She felt the need to confide in me." She rubbed her forehead and sighed. The sound was long and heavy like she was at her wits end and on the verge of accepting defeat. "She's dying, and there's nothing I can do to stop it."

"Why?" My hands shook from nerves. I clasped them to try to keep my composure under control. Silently, I prayed for Mardella to be okay. This realm needed her. I needed her, not only to help us with our problems, but I needed her guidance and friendship more than ever now. Sure, I was still a bit upset about her tricking me into allowing her to compel me, but I understood why she did it. She and Mom thought they were doing the right thing at the time, and maybe they had. I didn't know or at the moment care.

"Her body is shutting down," Fiona finally said. "No magical potion can stop it."

"How come?" I wanted to know.

A bittersweet smile crossed her face, confusing me even more. "I'll let her tell you."

We followed Fiona across the living room and down a hallway to the back guest room. The door was cracked. She signaled for us to wait and slipped inside, closing the door behind her. I pressed my ear against it. Narik did the same.

"I wonder what Fiona was talking about?" he whispered.

I placed my finger on my lips and listened.

"Mom, are you up for some company?"

"No, darling, leave me be unless it's Larkin. I'd like to speak to him," a low rough voice said—croaky, as if she had a sore throat.

"Larkin should be here soon, but are you sure about having no visitors? It's Narik and Alaris. They really–"

"Alaris? Bring her in. Bring her to me."

We moved away from the door right when Fiona opened it. She waved us in. Mardella was propped up on pillows against a carved walnut headboard that looked Victorian to me. Like Fiona, her dark hair was in a bun, only Mardella had white panels of gray heavier than the last time I'd seen her. Her face was marked with few wrinkles, but her complexion was pallid, and her brown eyes were worn, tired. She was clutching the blanket to her chest but let go and wildly gestured for me to sit next to her on the bed. I noticed each of her fingers was adorned with a jeweled ring.

"Hi," I said, my lips pressed into a weak smile. I didn't like how frail she looked, and she couldn't be all that old, maybe early seventies. I hated to bother her with our problems, but I had no choice.

"Alaris." Despite her condition, Mardella's expression was bright and happy to see me. "I heard you were back."

"I am, but I'm in serious trouble, and I need your help." I didn't have time for idle chatter or pleasantries. Merrack was under some sort of sick sleeping spell, the queen and her sidekick were after me, and Larkin and Farran were held in compromising positions. I needed to save them and figure out how to stop Datura and Brunhild.

Mardella looked at Narik. He nodded to confirm what I said to be true. She sat up straighter against her pillows and planted her attention back on me. "What's troubling you?"

I told her and Fiona everything, right down to the weres, including Nash, giving us grief on the way here. Not that I thought it had to do with anything, but once I started talking I couldn't stop, even when Fiona gasped when I got to the part about Larkin and Farran. Mardella gestured for her to be quiet and returned her full concentration to me. I resumed rushing through my story. To my ears, I sounded like I was babbling, and once I finished, I stared at her expectantly, hoping she soaked up every word I said.

"Larkin," Fiona said, her features twisted in worry. "What are we going to do about my poor boy? He needs us." She paced the room, twisting her fingers in a state of nervous energy.

"Larkin is fine," Mardella said.

Fiona paused in the middle of the room. "What do you mean?"

"How do you know?" Narik and I asked in unison.

Mardella yawned. She looked exhausted. Bags formed below her eyes and the hollows beneath her high cheekbones were sharper than what they were when I first stepped into this room. "The magical dust you threw at Datura and Brunhild has iron in it, among other things. Witches have weaknesses to all ferrous metals. Both Datura and Brunhild's powers will be out of commission for twenty-four hours or more . . . the charm Brunhild cast on Larkin and Farran only last for a few hours, maybe a bit longer, but I have no doubt they're free now."

I let out a sigh of relief, noticing Fiona's tense posture relaxing. "I thought the weapon Larkin gave me was to temporarily distract the enemy so I could escape."

"It depends on who your adversary is."

"What about Merrack?" I asked.

She frowned. "I don't know the extent of the charm they cast on him or what components were used to create the state he's under. Tell me his ailments."

"He goes into coughing fits," I answered, "and sometimes he gets tired easily. I was thinking he had bronchitis or was getting pneumonia, but now I know that's not the case. Apparently, at the moment he's under some sort of sleeping spell."

In thought, Mardella tapped her lips with her finger. "What you're describing to me sounds like he'd been slowly poisoned to make him appear like he suffers from a virus so no one will suspect otherwise, then through dark magic, he's been rendered into a state between sleep and awake. I'm guessing Datura was the one who cast it, and Brunhild provided her with the ingredients to administer them to him orally in a form of a drink maybe."

"Yes." I glanced at Narik. He nodded in agreement. "Datura gave him tea. So how do we break the spell?" I thought how horrible it would be to end up in a comatose type state where you were partly aware of what was going on around you, yet you couldn't do a damn thing about it. Then it dawned on me. The blood drained from my face. Datura had no intention of waking Merrack up. If she were to do so, he'd have her thrown in prison.

My heart dropped.

I had to get rid of Datura.

There was no other way.

My body swayed from the realization of the act I must perform in order to save Merrack and the kingdom. I placed my hand on the bed, steadying myself. Horrified, I looked at Mardella.

She knew what I was thinking. There was a glint in her eyes, and they weighed heavily on mine. It was that knowing look you get from another who was attuned with you. "Dark magic was at play and still is," she said. "The revenants are bound to her, and now Merrack is in a fragile state. I'm not sure what type of charm Datura used, but I could have Fiona whip up a potion that might counteract it."

I bit my fingernail. "But you're not sure it's going to work."

She shook her head. "No, I'm not."

"Then–" I started to say, but she continued, her tone low and foreboding.

"If Datura doesn't release the spell, I'm afraid the only other thing you can do to save Merrack and the kingdom is kill her."

I tried to lick my lips, but there was no moisture on my tongue. My mouth was bone dry. "Why?" is all I could say. There had to be another way. The thought of me murdering someone made me sick to my stomach.

"Anything now bound to her," Mardella said, "will be released once her heart stops beating. You see, she created a spell that chains them to her. I suspect Merrack is one of them; however, I could be wrong. Thus, we could try the potion to possibly counteract the charm."

"What happened to the headhunters?" Fiona wanted to know.

Narik had his arms crossed against his chest, quietly taking in what we were saying. His gaze went to Fiona. "The weapon Farran used," he explained, "is designed specifically for entities such as them, similar to the one Larkin used to save Alaris. As I'm sure you know, they can't be killed since they're already dead. I'm guessing since Farran was certain he'd cross paths with these malevolent beings, he armed himself with a weapon that would send them directly to a holding cell until a decision could be made on their punishment."

"How can you punish a being such as them?" I asked. "They're already dead."

"The dead can still be punished," Mardella said.

I understood what they were saying now and blurted, "Like Purgatory or Hell."

Mardella placed her hand over mine. It was cold and limp. "Yes." She paused and took a deep breath. A light whizzing sound escaped her cracked lips. I hadn't notice how dry and chapped they were until now. It was almost like she was wasting away before my eyes. It struck me then: I'd been surrounded by death since I arrived home from my Vegas trip. It seemed to follow me, and now according to Mardella, I'd have to commit murder in order to save lives. I pushed that thought out of my mind, telling myself there had to be another way, and instead, I sat biting my lip. Mardella's fingers squeezed around mine. The pressure was weak, and my heart broke knowing soon she'd no longer be with us. Finally, she continued, "I'm sorry for tricking you into allowing me to cast a memory spell on you and for taking you away from your home. At the time, both your mother and I thought it was the right thing to do. The panic we felt spurred that decision. Whether it was the right thing to do or not, I'm still unsure. However, I've spent almost a decade searching for the unicorn and the dragon who laid that egg, to assuage my curiosity and get answers. Recently, I came across the unicorn. I suspect he'd been watching me all along without me knowing it and realized my intentions were pure. He led me to the mountains northwest of Havenwood. On horseback, I followed him up a narrow trail until my mare could go no more. I resumed the trek on foot until I felt a wall of magical energy before me. Going on experience and the vibes I received, I knew a cloaking spell stood before me. To anyone else, they'd continue by, unaware they were passing a cave that held a dragon inside. Even the trolls were clueless."

"What did you do?" I asked.

A ghost of a smile crossed her face. "I broke through it using my own glamour to create a doorway that I could pass through, yet keep the cloaking spell intact."

Narik sat on the foot of the bed. "Why would you do that?"

"To protect the dragon, of course." Mardella said.

"Weren't you scared?" I imagined going into a dark creepy cave and then facing a dragon. Oh, my God, I'd probably shit my pants, but then again the thought of it thrilled me.

The dreams.

I encountered a dragon in them. I was elated being with her.

Her.

Think, Alaris.

She laughed and nodded. "I'd be lying if I told you I wasn't, but I hadn't gone this far for so many years only to allow my fear stop me from my mission."

I could see her point, and honestly I'd be the same way. "I understand, but what did you do when you saw the dragon?"

"With a lighted stick in hand, I went deep into the cave and when I found her, I let out a sharp gasp. Not only because I'd never seen let alone faced a dragon before, but she was bound by a black fluid cord that shimmered against her enormous golden body, and she was fast asleep. She'd been that way for decades."

I covered my mouth, and my vision blurred from the fierce emotion of sadness that suddenly took hold of me. Aven was telling me the truth. He'd admitted to doing this. "Aven," I said behind my fingers, then dropped them. "He's the one who enslaved this dragon through a binding spell. He confessed to me he did so, just like I told you earlier when I shared what's been going on since I arrived in Atheon."

She nodded. "Yes, I know. I was able to telepathically communicate with her through a spell I performed, and she relayed to me the details of her unfortunate situation. I then told her what happened to her baby and that his spirit now dwelled inside you."

"What did she say?" Narik asked, intrigued, while I gaped at Mardella, almost afraid to hear her answer.

"I showed her a mental picture of Alaris. Of course, it was when Alaris was twelve since that was the last time I'd seen her. The dragon told me her name was Shalnal, and an outpouring of love flowed from her when she saw Alaris' image." Mardella fixed her gaze on mine. "You're her daughter, Alaris. You may not be physically a dragon, but when the wyrmling breathed his essence into your mouth, you two became one. Therefore, she considers you her offspring."

My mind went totally blank. I stopped breathing. All I could do was stare at her.

"Wow," Narik said, breaking me free from my momentarily disconnection. "How cool is that?"

My heart thudded against my chest. "You're telling me Shalnal loves me?" My hands shook, and my chest tightened. I wrapped my arms around my stomach, trying to get air into my lungs. At the same time, something inside me clicked, and the dreams I had came to me all at once. Holy shit! Shalnal was her name.

Narik scooted closer to me and rubbed my back.

Fiona moved to my side. "What's wrong with her?" she asked, alarmed.

Mardella patted my hand.

"She's having an anxiety attack," Narik said.

I raised a hand, gulping air into my lungs. "I'll be okay. I'm prone to these when I get wound up with nerves."

"There's no need to be nervous," Mardella told me, lying back on her pillows. She looked exhausted. A stab of guilt went through me. I should say goodbye to her and go on my way so she could rest. But before I could gather myself to leave, Mardella continued to speak, "And yes, to your question."

"I have to tell you about the vivid dreams I've been having about Shalnal and what she told me," I said in between breaths. "For some reason, I'm remembering them now." I launched into my encounter with Shalnal, and when I was done, Mardella confirmed what Shalnal told me to be true. She made sure the magic she used to communicate with the dragon would also give her the ability to reach me when I was in a dream state.

"You couldn't recall them until now," Mardella told me, "because they got caught in the web of memories that have yet to step forth into your conscious mind. What triggered it was me saying her name."

"That makes sense," I said, "but what do I do about my situation, and how do I break the charm Aven cast on Shalnal?"

"I was getting to the solution," Mardella answered, "but you're not going to like what I have to say."

Oh, God, I thought. Now what?

Chapter Thirty-Five

Fiona brought us some water. I gulped it down and handed her back the glass, thanking her. I wasn't sure what Mardella had to say, but whether I'd like it or not, I wanted to know.

After Mardella placed her drink on the nightstand, she narrowed her attention on me. *Shit, this must be serious.* "Aven is the only one who can break the spell, which means you're–"

There was an urgent knock at the front door. "Mom, are you there? Open the door. I don't have my key."

"Larkin!" I gasped and bounced to my feet, ready to go to him, but Fiona held her hands out, halting me. "What's wrong?"

"Stay here. I'll bring him to you." Though her expression held a sense of relief her son was home, the worry line between her eyes deepened, making me even more nervous.

I glanced at Narik. He stood near the foot of the bed and shrugged. My gaze shifted to Mardella. She pulled the covers to her chest and rested her arms on top of them, releasing a heavy sigh as if the whole act exhausted her.

"Do you want me to help you get more comfortable?" I smoothed and tucked the blanket around her.

She shook her head. "No. There's no need for you to fuss over me, but my time is waning."

"She's here?" I heard Larkin say, his tone pitched in surprise with a note of panic. The door swung open with a bang. I turned from tending to Mardella. When my eyes locked onto his, a moment of pure joy swept through me. His shoulders sagged, and he sighed. "Thank God." My stomach dipped, releasing a swarm of butterflies. We crossed the room, and I fell into his arms. His embrace was strong and protective. He rested his cheek against the side of my head and whispered, "I thought I might have lost you."

I pulled back and smiled. "Because of Narik, you didn't."

He looked at Narik. "Thank you for taking care of Alaris. I owe you one."

"You don't owe me anything," Narik said. "Alaris is not only our princess but a good friend, as well."

"What happened?" A low, bored voice asked from behind me. Farran.

I placed my hand in Larkin's and turned to Farran. "It's a long story, and Mardella was just about to tell me something important."

"What's wrong, Grandmother?" Larkin asked, looking at her for the first time since he entered the room. We moved to her bedside, and he sat next to her while I stood watching the boy inside him emerge through his heartfelt expressions of love and concern for her.

"I'm dying," she bluntly said. "I won't survive the night."

Larkin swallowed hard and cleared his throat. "Why?"

"I haven't been well for a while," she answered, "and I overexerted my magic when I used it to communicate with the dragon and to get back home, which caused my health to quickly deteriorate."

"Dragon?" Farrran asked. "The one who laid the egg Alaris found?"

"Yes," I said, then rehashed everything that had happened after Datura kidnapped me. During that time Fiona fed us pizza—the best I'd ever had. The crust was buttery with cheese melted into it. Yum— while I answered their questions.

Farran's hands were balled into fists, and the muscle in his jaw twitched. "Datura is the one who had my family slaughtered."

"You don't know that for sure," I said, even though I had a gut feeling she had.

"After what you told me, I have no doubt in my mind," he seethed.

"Did you guys see her after you escaped?" I asked.

"Yes," Larkin said. "She and Brunhild were asleep on the ground. I think they'll be out for a while." The corner of his mouth lifted and humor sparkled in his eyes. "How much dust did you throw on them?"

"Apparently enough," I said with a laugh, then turned serious. "Did either one of you check on Merrack?"

"No," Farran answered, his hands still clenched.

"I was too worried about you," Larkin replied when I looked at him with a Are-you-kidding-me? expression on my face. "Nothing else mattered to me. I had to find you." He trailed his finger slowly down my cheek, igniting a burning desire to kiss him.

"We ran into Draylan as we came across Datura and Brunhild," Farran said. "He just returned from patrolling. We told him what happened and to go check on Merrack and keep an eye on him while we get him some help."

I felt a little bit better that Draylan would care for Merrack, but my anxiousness to break the charm he was under remained.

Mardella took a drink of water and cleared her throat to get everyone's attention. "I need to finish what I was telling Alaris before you two arrived." She paused and shifted her attention on me. "Aven is the one who cast the binding spell on Shalnal. Therefore, he's the only one who can undo it—by his own hand or death. I suggest you find Datura and release him like she wants you to."

Larkin stiffened beside me. "Absolutely not. I won't jeopardize Alaris' life on the off chance Aven will keep his word. He and Datura are not to be trusted and want to use Alaris as a tool to reach ultimate power." He scrubbed the side of his face and gritted his teeth. "I can't believe you'd propose such a thing. Why? Aven is an old man now and not all binding spells are linked to the castor. There's got to be another way."

"I have to get rid of Datura, too," I said weakly, my stomach churning. I wrapped an arm around it, hoping not to lose the pizza I ate earlier.

"I'll do it," Farran said without hesitation. When we looked at him, he continued. "I have no problem taking Datura's life . . . or Aven's for that matter. If I have to gather an army from my Solas clan, I will, but first I need to speak to my father. I'm sure after I tell him what happened, he'll be onboard."

The room was slowly darkening, which meant Mardella didn't have much time left, and I was sure she wanted to spend the rest of it with her family.

Fiona turned the bedside table lamp on. "I've been quiet throughout most of the conversations you've had since you arrived here," she said, "but I think you should let Mother finish what she has to say before you make a decision."

Larkin sat beside Mardella, took her limp hand and kissed the back of it. "I'm sorry for my outburst. Please continue."

She reached for her water. Her arm fell to her side like dead weight. I moved to the other side of the bed and held the glass to her lips so she could take a drink. Once she was done, she thanked me. I resumed my position next to Larkin, swallowing back the tears that threatened to spill.

"Aven," she said, "is an old man, though once he steps out of prison, he will regain his vitality, but his magic will take a while to recharge. How long? I don't know. However, this window of time should give you the opportunity to eliminate him and Datura. If you don't, he'll expect you to find the elements before he breaks the spell over Shalnal . . . if he does at all. Personally, I don't think he will, which unfortunately means his death by your hands or another is imminent. There is no other way."

The weight of her words fell heavy on my thoughts. She was right. Locking Datura away with her father would do no good. Both Merrack and Shalnal would remain as they were at this moment, neither dead nor alive, simply existing.

"What about the powers of the fire element Alaris has?" Narik asked, breaking the brief silence between us. "Who can teach her what they are and how to wield them?"

A tired smile crossed Mardella's face. "Shalnal is the only one who can teach her. Even if I were on top of my game, I wouldn't be able to help. Only Shalnal can since the powers derives from her . . . now, if I can please have some time alone with my daughter and grandson, I'd appreciate it."

This was it. I had to say goodbye to her and make it quick. Choking back tears, I moved to the other side of the bed. I gave her a hug and a kiss on the cheek. "Thank you for finding Shalnal and telling her about me. I'll never forget you."

"It's the least I can do for my trickery," she said.

I wiped the tears from my eyes. "If you see my mom, please tell her I said hi, and I love her."

Mardella smiled. "I will."

"I'm going to take Alaris to her house," Narik told Larkin.

Larkin's eyes were red and glassy. He nodded. "Please," his voice cracked. He cleared his throat. "Please watch over her and keep her safe. I'll be there as soon as I can."

"Of course," Narik answered. He turned to Mardella, bent his head in acknowledgment, and blew her a kiss. "Farewell, sweet witch. May your journey across the rainbow bridge and to Summerland be an enjoyable one."

"Thank you, Narik," she replied.

We left the room as Farran was saying his goodbye and waited for him in the living room. It didn't take him long, and when he met us, his expression was locked in determination, his energy drenched in anger.

"I'm going to go pay my father a visit." He crossed the room in quick strides.

Narik stepped in front of him and took hold of his shoulders. "You need to calm down and think things through before you decide which recourse to take."

Farran's lips tightened. He nodded, broke away from Narik's grasp, and left.

Narik raised his eyebrows, and I shrugged. I figured Farran was a big boy. I was told his dad was an intelligent man. If anyone could reason with Farran, it would be him. I mean, I understood why Farran felt the way he did. Hell, I felt the same way; however, we needed to be smart about what actions to take. Right now, though, I found myself being a bit nervous about reentering my old life, stepping into the house I shared with my mom. From what I was told earlier, Fiona had left everything the way it was—a shrine she'd taken care of due to a promise she kept for a dying friend, just in case I returned or maybe to preserve the life's energy that once flowed between those walls. I didn't know. All I knew was there was another hurdle I had to overcome, and I hoped my emotions wouldn't get the best of me.

Chapter Thirty-Six

O n Narik's horse, we approached the stone cottage I lived in with my mom, once upon a time ago. It was set back among tall dark oaks. Empty flower boxes were built under the window sills, and if memory served me right, a garden lay in back. My heart squeezed and warmed at the flood of memories that poured over me. I wanted to laugh and cry at the same time but managed to keep my emotions together in front of Narik—at least for now.

When we entered my house, the aroma of apples and cinnamon welcomed me like an old friend. People on earth used candles and plug-in air fresheners to get their house to smell yummy, whereas here, Mom created a simple spell out of her herbs and cast it to give our house the delicious scent like she was baking an apple pie. I remembered her doing it. I remembered everything.

I paused at the edge of the foyer and glanced around the living room, taking in the heavy wooden beams, the stone fireplace on the far wall, the comfortable couches and chairs in a plush forest green color, and the oak coffee and end tables with antique lamps on top of them. A deep sadness gripped my heart as a vision of me sitting next to my mom and reading a book aloud to her came to me. I covered my mouth and looked at Narik. He placed a comforting hand on my shoulder and told me if I needed anything, he'd be outside. Blinking back the tears, I nodded, appreciating he knew what I wanted without having to tell him.

I spent a couple of hours wandering through the house. I came across several pictures of me and my mom, smiling in each one. I picked up a humorous photograph off the bookshelf in the sitting room of us laughing, wiping mud on each other's faces. I pressed the frame to my chest and plopped into a chair. Bending over on my knees, I rested my forehead on my palm and sobbed. The grief of losing the Evergreens, the life I had on earth, the life I had here, and my birth mother ran deep. The muscles in my stomach ached along with my heart. I wanted to crawl into a hole and disappear.

"Alaris?"

I looked up to the sound of Larkin's concerned voice, tears trailing down my face. I sat straight and hastily wiped them off. He stood in the doorway, his eyes raw with an emotional sadness that mirrored my own. I set the picture down on the small table next to the chair and hugged myself. I didn't want him to see me like this. He had his own loss to deal with and didn't need to shoulder my burdens, as well.

I cleared my throat to prevent my voice from sounding hoarse. "I'm sorry about your grandmother. I . . . I think you should be with your mom instead of with me. I'll be okay. Narik will watch over me."

"I told Narik to go home and spend time with his family tonight," he said, slowly crossing the room in even steps. His gaze turned serious, his jaw set in determination. He paused a few feet away from where I sat and rubbed the back of his neck, peeking at me through long dark eyelashes. The corner of his mouth curled, and a bittersweet expression entered his face. Despite my sorrow, my stomach fluttered. I wanted nothing more than to be in his warm embrace, to be held, to feel comfort, and secure . . . to be loved. "My grandmother told me many things tonight," he went on, "but one of them really struck a chord with me."

"What's that?" He was looking at me in a way that caused my pulse to race and a warmth between my legs. His gaze was steady, intense, filled with desire and resolution.

He stepped closer to me and reached his hand out for mine. I took it and rose. His hand cupped the side of my cheek, his thumb slowly stroking it in a circular motion. "She told me if you love something or someone that brings you joy, and you're harming no one, you'd be a fool to allow other people's opinions or your own fear get in the way of your own happiness. She then told me to go to you because you needed me and to not mourn her. Her body may be dead to this world, but her spirit is alive and vibrant." He placed his free hand on my other cheek and gently lifted my chin. I think I stopped breathing as a shock of heat went through me. "She knew."

"She knew what?" I whispered breathlessly.

He skimmed his thumb across my lips. I parted them slightly, staring into his green eyes. "How much I'm in love with you. Nothing means more to me than you, Alaris, and now after what Mardella said, I don't care if the people in Atheon know it, whereas before I was trying to adhere to the image a warrior plays in the eyes of the public."

"I'm in love with you, too," I said.

His lips pressed against mine, searing me with their heat. A tiny whimper issued from me as I kissed him back. All of the pent up desire I had for Larkin since he reentered my life exploded, and my kiss turned urgent. I parted my mouth and intertwined my tongue with his. He was like a balm to my aching heart, soothing it with his touch. I ran my fingers up the back of his neck and through his hair, crushing my body against his, feeling the hardness straining against his pants. There was a wet throbbing sensation between my legs that ached for him to penetrate deep inside me.

"Please make love to me," I said.

He pulled back, his eyes hooded with desire. A spark of concern entered them. "Are you sure? I don't want to take advantage of you at your most vulnerable state."

I nodded. "I'm positive. I want you . . . unless you don't want me."

The look in his eyes turned serious with a burning yearning in them that matched his husky voice—the same tone I found unbelievably sexy from day one. "I've always wanted you and have dreamed of this very moment for more times than I can count." He skimmed his fingers over my swollen lips. I parted them, releasing a slow breath as I ran a hand up beneath his shirt, feeling the ripples of his tight abs contract. He took his shirt off, revealing his muscular frame. I followed suit, never taking my eyes off of him, leaving on my white lacy bra. Then I pulled the elastic out from my ponytail, allowing my hair to cascade around my shoulders and back. "God, you're beautiful," he whispered.

He picked me up, and I wrapped my legs around his waist while kissing him deeply. He pushed my back against the wall in the hallway, his lips trailing down and up my neck, driving me crazy. I pointed to the spare bedroom. When we entered, he set me on my feet and unhooked the front of my bra, releasing my perky breasts. He cupped one of them into his warm hand, bent his head, and took my erect nipple into his mouth. He sucked on it and gently pinched the bud between his teeth, sending pleasurable electroshocks throughout my body. With his free hand, he undid my pants, and pulled them down along with my panties. I stepped out of them, and with my back against the wall, his mouth still on my nipple, his fingers went between my legs. They slid up and down my slick folds, over my clitoris, then inside me in a repetitive motion, slowly at first, but when a soft moan escaped me, he quickened his pace, his fingers sliding in me faster, deeper, then over my sex and clit. I moved my hips in time with his motion. My breath grew shorter and coarser, my moans louder. He moved to my next breast and paid the same attention as he had done to the other one, his fingers still working me. I couldn't take it anymore. I had to have him.

"I want you inside of me," I huffed.

His hand and mouth stopped for a split second in hesitation, giving me the opportunity to reach down and undo his pants. He took them off, grabbed my hand, and led me toward the bed. I crawled onto it and pulled him down on top of me. Placing my hands above my head, he passionately kissed me, whispering he loved me against my lips.

"I love you, too," I said, then made a sound between a whimper and a sigh when he entered me and slowly moved in and out. I gyrated my hips in time with his.

He groaned. "God, you feel good."

The room was bathed in moonlight from the twin moons being full tonight, and the sounds of our short quick breaths and pleasures encompassed us, temporarily blocking out the outside world and what lay ahead of us.

He reached down and stroked and rubbed my clit, and at the same time, his warm lips kissed down my neck, followed by his teeth scraping slowly across my collarbone. My body tensed. My stomach and vaginal walls tightened with a violent pulsing heat that radiated upward and across my body. I arched my back and cried out as my body twitched and shuddered, releasing its juices. He was still inside me, his hips still in motion. There was a coy, sexy smile on his lips, and his eyes were filled with desire. His black hair was messy, and his muscular body rippled in the bright white light, gleaming with sheens of sweat.

"Now it's my turn," I said, pushing myself up, rolling over on top of him, our connection never broken. I teased and pleasured him, driving him to the precipice of a mind-blowing orgasm, only to pull back long enough for him to slow his breathing. I straddled him and moved my hips in circles, then rocked them. A deep throaty groan rumbled in his throat. His fingers went to my sweet spot, once again, stroking and rubbing it. I quickened my pace and felt the fluttering inside me, the hot pressure exploding the same time his did, his body buckling and jerking. I fell into his arms, happy for the first time in I didn't know how long. He kissed my temple and tightened his embrace. For the next few hours we talked. Not about death or our family or what we were forced to face tomorrow but about us. We revisited our childhood memories we had together and compared how we were back then to today. We laughed and found we still had a lot in common. I fell asleep in his arms, more blissful than ever before.

* * *

I awoke in the middle of the night to my name being called in a whisper. It came from the hallway. I glanced at Larkin. He was on his side, sound asleep. I reached out to wake him but pulled my hand away. He needed his rest. Besides, if this were Brunhild calling me, like she'd done when Kimmie and I were in that abandoned farmhouse, big deal. She found me. She'd eventually would anyway.

"Alaris," the whispery voice said again. A gal with long hair and a dressing gown floated through the door and stopped near the foot of the bed. I recognized her from The Blue Fairy.

Appara.

She was an echo who bartended there.

Although her milky white form was transparent, her heart-shaped face and big round eyes were well-defined. She placed a finger on her lips, and her gaze darted to Larkin. For some reason she didn't want me to wake him. He did seem like he was in a peaceful sleep. She beckoned for me to follow her and glided across the room and through the wall.

I hesitated, wondering if I should disturb Larkin. Why would Appara not want me to? But my curiosity got the best of me. I stepped out of bed, careful not to wake Larkin, and slipped on my clothes and shoes, thankful the moonlight was bright enough in the room so I could locate them on the floor. I found Appara near the front door waiting for me.

"What do you want?" I asked.

"Draylan wants to talk to you," she said in a soft breathy voice. "Alone," she added.

I yawned. "He can talk to me in the morning." I turned to go back to bed. Her hand touched my arm. It was cold and clammy, sending a chill to my bones. I shivered. "What?"

"It cannot wait. It's urgent."

"Is he in trouble?" The first thought that came to my mind was Datura and Brunhild did something to Merrack, and Draylan was able to get away to tell me.

"No, but if you don't meet him now, Havenwood will be."

My heart dropped.

Datura.

Draylan probably came here to warn me about her. He and Larkin weren't on good terms, so that would make sense for him not wanting me to bring Larkin along.

I shrugged into my cape and followed Appara outside. A silhouette of a male figure stood at the edge of the forest. I could tell it was Draylan by the shape of his form.

Appara gave me an apologetic look. "I'm sorry, but I was summoned to retrieve you and would not be released until I did so." She pushed back the lace around her wrist. Shiny spiral black lines were wrapped around it. She pulled down her high frilly collar. It was the same thing but around her neck. "I hope you don't hold this against me . . . if you go to him, I'll be free from being controlled."

I was at a loss for words. My mind seemed to shift out of place. I rubbed the spot between my eyes and looked at her. "Did Draylan do this to you?"

"No," she said, "Datura did."

"I take it she's in the forest waiting for me?"

"She is, and she's not alone."

I looked at Draylan who like a soldier was standing at attention. "Who's with her, and why doesn't Draylan come to talk to me?"

"You must go now," she said with a desperate urgency that made me fear for her. "I was only given so much time to retrieve you. If you don't meet him now, she might not release me."

I chewed on my lower lip, trying to figure out what was really going on. I was confused about Draylan being here and came to the conclusion Datura must be controlling him, as well. I didn't want Appara to be Datura's slave and lose her freedom. Mardella told me I should go with Datura and release Aven, then eliminate them both. My stomach churned. How in the hell was I supposed to do that? I had no weapons, nor was I a murderer. I had no choice because if I were to turn back, there would be no telling what Datura would do to Havenwood. Knowing her, she'd probably burn it to the ground. I also had to think of Merrack,

Shalnal, and Appara.

I took a deep breath and released it. "Alright, I'll go, but do me a favor."

"Yes, Princess," Appara said, shooting nervous glances at Draylan. He tapped his wrist, indicating time.

"Tell Larkin what happened. Can you do that for me?"

Her head bobbed. "Yes. Yes. I will." She nudged my shoulder toward the forest. "Now go." She looked up. In the moonlit sky were large red numbers, like you'd see on a stopwatch, ticking away: fifty . . . forty-nine . . . forty-eight . . . "Run!"

I turned and ran as fast as I could to Draylan, telling myself at least I'd have one ally with me, and maybe he could help me end Datura and Aven.

Maybe.

Chapter Thirty-Seven

"You need to come with me," Draylan said when I reached him. He grabbed my arm and tried to steer me into the trees, his fingers biting into my skin.

"What the hell?" I jerked out of his grasp. "What's wrong with you? Are you under Datura's control?"

"No, he's not," Datura said, stepping out from behind a large oak, along with Lithia whose puke green eyes held a haughtiness in them that matched her expression.

Holy. Mother. Fucking. Shit!

My mouth flopped open, and the hair on the back of my neck rose.

"Look at her," Lithia squealed, then laughed and pointed at me. "The dumb bitch didn't have a clue you two were involved."

I swung my attention on her. "What?"

"See?" she asked still laughing.

I snatched her raised wrist and with my other hand, pushed on that shoulder and kicked her foot out from under her. She yelped and fell to the ground. "Don't test me, Lithia," I warned, leaning over her, secretly delighted when she raised her hands in fear I wasn't through attacking her. An invisible force yanked me backward, my heels scraping against the dirt. Without my doing, I spun toward Datura as if on a turntable.

"Enough!" she spat. She motioned to Draylan. "Check to see if she's unarmed."

Draylan reached for me. I smacked his hand away. "Don't you fucking touch me! Traitor."

Datura sighed heavily. "If you continue to be difficult, the people of Havenwood will suffer." Her eyes turned black, causing her beautiful face to appear demonic. She raised her palms heavenward and chanted in a bizarre language. Several colorful lightning bolts webbed across the night sky, and the thick smell of wet earth surrounded me. Sheets of rain poured hard and fast over my village but not us. "I'll drown them if you don't behave and do what you're told. Are we clear?"

I nodded. "We are. I promise to be good and to release Aven. Please don't harm Havenwood."

"Good girl," she said. She raised her hands above her head and once again said some words I didn't understand. The rain stopped. "Draylan, check Alaris now."

I heard a tinkling sound to my right, but when I looked, I didn't see anything. I stiffened at Draylan's touch and glared at him the whole time he patted me down. He found the remaining magical dust in my pocket and placed it in Datura's hand. She carefully dumped it out and tossed the bag to the ground.

"She didn't have anything else on her person," Draylan told her.

"Thank you, my sweet." Datura threw her arms around his broad shoulders and kissed him. He pulled her against his chest and responded with the same enthusiasm as a horned-up teenager. Placing her hand on his crotch, she gently squeezed as she broke their kiss. "We'll resume this later, my love."

I was appalled and disgusted with the both of them. I wanted to call her a cheating, lying whore along with a few other colorful words, but I refrained due to my promise to behave. I tightened my lips and glanced at Lithia who was standing quietly with a shitty look on her face. The sounds of horses grunting nearby told me we were to travel on horseback and made me wonder how far we had to go. The milky dark sky was slowly bleeding into a faint pinkish orange hue. Soon, dawn would raise its head, offering another day to us all. The question was: What type of day would I have?

"Don't worry about Larkin," Lithia said to me, giving me a wide berth as she walked past toward my house. "I'll keep him warm in your bed."

Datura laughed. I gritted my teeth and fought the urge to pounce on Lithia. Heat crept up my neck, but at the same time, an insecurity tugged at me heart, diluting my anger. Larkin had a longer history with Lithia than me. They grew up together and had recently dated. I pushed those thoughts out of my mind and told myself I needed to trust Larkin's declaration of his love was true. Another tinkling noise had me looking about.

Nalin flew in front of Lithia's face, and the tiny fairy placed her hands on her hips. "You keep away from Larkin. He belongs with the princess, not you."

Lithia swatted at her. "Get away from me."

Nalin zipped out of reach to move behind Lithia. Grabbing a tiny fistful of hair, Nalin pulled as hard as she could, yanking Lithia's head back. "Ow!" She threw her hand behind her and clutched the air trying to snatch Nalin. "Stop it!"

"No, not until you–"

"Ante mortem somno."

Nalin stiffened and fell, but I was quick enough to catch her in my hands. Her eyes were closed, body motionless. "What did you do?" I gasped.

Datura flicked her hand toward Nalin as if she were annoyed. "She's still alive . . . for now."

I placed the pad of my fingertip on top of Nalin's chest and felt a heartbeat. Thank, God.

Datura whistled. "Sela, Coral, Plume, Rill."

Four fairy-like figures the size of Nalin swooped in from above. They hovered in front of Datura with their hands behind their backs, waiting to be addressed.

"Take Nalin to a place where she can rest," Datura ordered. "Oh, and if I discover you started any rumors about what's taking place, I'll clip your wings and see to it you never fly again."

When she said that, I realized they weren't fairies. They were pixies.

The dark-haired one in a knee-high form-fitted blue dress ducked her head. "Yes, Queen." The other three mirrored her gesture.

I stuck my hand out in offering. "Please be careful, and take good care of her."

"We will, Princess," a blonde pixie promised, taking Nalin's wrist while a redheaded one took the other. The other two grabbed Nalin's ankles. They flew her away, disappearing into the forest.

Lithia smoothed her hair, turned on her heels, and left without saying another word. I hated that she was going to Larkin. I should be in bed with him, fast asleep by his side. Now she was going to take my place. I didn't even want her in my house. It bugged the shit out of me.

"Come. Come," Datura said, clapping. "We're wasting time. I'm anxious to see my daddy, and I'm sure he's sitting on the edge of his seat, waiting for you to free him and to finally get to be with his gorgeous daughter."

Draylan had been quiet this whole time, probably because he knew what a piece of shit I thought he was. I followed him and Datura into the forest. Brunhild was waiting for us on a black horse which was fitting since now I knew she was a dark elf or dralk as they were known here. Two appaloosas with saddles and leather bags that hung from them waited for us nearby.

"You're riding with Draylan," Datura told me.

I figured that and didn't like it one bit, but I sucked it up and hopped on his horse behind him. I looked at Brunhild who was cautiously watching me. "So what do you get out of this deal?"

"Beauty," she answered.

"You're a witch," I said. "Surely you could come up with a potion for that."

"Only for a short while," she responded, maneuvering her horse behind us while Datura took the lead. "When one possesses the power of all four elements, the person becomes god-like and will be able to tap into universal magic."

I glanced over my shoulder at her and rolled my eyes. "It's a myth. The gods and goddesses made sure no one would ever have the opportunity to become like them." Begrudgingly, I slipped my arms around Draylan's waist as we rode at a steady pace through the forest.

Brunhild laughed. It was deep and gravelly. "Like Aven has told you, they don't care about us anymore. We're on our own."

"They do if it affects them, and it would," I shot back.

Brunhild snorted.

"It's not a myth," Draylan said.

"You finally speak." My voice dripped with sarcasm and disgust. "I don't associate with traitors. Just sayin'."

His back muscles tightened. "I fell in love with her. It wasn't as if I planned it."

"Yeah, whatever," I snapped.

I decided not to engage in further conversation. Instead, I allowed my thoughts to wander as I took in the beautiful terrain we were traveling on, like stone bridges arching over the small bodies of water, bright green foliage, and brilliant colorful flowers. Morning had arrived, and the sky was a dreary milky gray. The temperature was cool but not uncomfortable, although I was grateful I had the presence of mind earlier to grab my cape. I wondered what Larkin was doing at the moment and if Fiona could help Merrack. I didn't expect her to hightail it to Atheon. She had the death of her mother to deal with. I wondered if she'd hand over the potion to Narik and have him go in her stead. All of those thoughts kept me occupied for what seemed like hours since we left Havenwood. We stopped near a fallen oak and sat on it while we ate roast beef sandwiches and drank water from a glass container that reminded me of a flask. I remained silent while listening to the three of them chatting away about having a huge party after Aven was free. It would be in his and Datura's honor. Yeah, I thought, Datura had no plans to release Merrack.

"I need to take a leak," I announced, rising to my feet.

Datura sighed and shot me a stern, disapproving look, "A princess would never talk in such a manner as you. You need to learn to speak properly, Alaris. It's so unbecoming of you when you choose not to."

I stuck my hip out and placed my hand on it. "Enlighten me then. How am I supposed to say it? Oh, and what if I have to take a shit? What words would I use to frame it in such a way to sound posh?"

Draylan laughed, then coughed in his hands to stifle it.

Datura grimaced. She cleared her throat in the annoying way some people do, sat up straight, and folded her hands in her lap. "All you have to say for either bodily function you must do is, 'Pardon me while I go to the lavatory.'"

Dramatically, I looked around, gesturing to the trees and vegetation. "Ahh, there's no lavatory here."

"Well, then you say, 'Pardon me while I go relieve myself.'"

"Pardon me while I go relieve myself," I echoed.

She smiled, too dumb to realize the hidden sarcasm. "Splendid. There's a roll of toilet paper in the back saddlebag." She looked at Draylan. "Go with her." When I opened my mouth to protest, she raised a hand. "I'm not taking any chances of you running off, Alaris."

"I promised you I wouldn't."

"It doesn't matter. Draylan will stand behind you with his back to you. Your dignity will still remain intact. By the way . . ." she leaned forward on her knees, and her eyes turned black again. Dark spider veins pulsed beneath her porcelain skin. "I'm still angry about what you did to Brunhild and me at the palace. The only way for you to make up for it is to be a good girl and free my father."

I blanched, and my body tensed. Datura's normal beautiful self—dressed in brown rider's pants and a dark blue velvet waistcoat—cloaked the evil that stirred within her. I mustn't forget that beauty was hiding the beast within. "You need not worry about me escaping, and I will retrieve your father as promised."

She blinked. The darkness disappeared, her crystal blue eyes now bright and cheerful along with her flawless complexion. "Excellent!"

I grabbed a roll of toilet paper out of the saddlebag, not happy about Draylan being my shadow. He followed me a few yards away where I found a clump of bushes I could get in between and squat.

"Don't worry," he said in a low voice. "I'm not going to watch."

I glared at him, then stepped into the bushes to do my business, careful not to piss on myself.

As we headed back, the jolly sound of singing and laughter caught my attention. I stopped and looked at Draylan questionably.

"Fairies," he said. "They like to have a good time."

"I want to see."

"We have to get going if we want to make it there within the hour."

I sighed. "Fine." I stomped past him, not even giving him a second glance.

When we reached our resting spot, Datura and Brunhild were already on their horses. Once Draylan and I were settled on his, we took off, and then it hit me. He said we'd be there within the hour. *Within the hour*, I repeated in my head. A haunting feeling emerged in the pit of my stomach that I'd be entering a prison world soon. What would it be like? Not only that, Datura was forcing my hand to release a Murk and possibly others, as well. If I had balls, I'd say she had me by them. Oh, and how in the hell did she expect me to lower the ward? I never even thought of asking her that. I opened my mouth, then closed it. She was too far ahead to even hear me. I rested my cheek on Draylan's back and closed my eyes. The gentle swaying and the hooves striking rocky terrain was soothing.

"You better stay awake," Draylan said.

My lids snapped open, and I sat up. "Why?"

"Because soon we're going into a dark region, and you wouldn't want to be asleep through it."

My stomach clenched.

What the hell did I get myself into? I had no weapons to protect myself. Nothing. For the first time in a while I wished I were back in Washington—in my own world, hanging out with Kimmie, living a normal life where things made sense. I'd be starting my college classes now. I'd have a routine I'd follow each day and would look forward to weekends with my friends. Not here. Here I was stuck in a dark fairy tale. One that might not have a happy ending.

Chapter Thirty-Eight

Ten minutes later, we came across a large ebony tree arching over our path. Datura stopped in front of it, and we joined her. Darkness loomed within its depth. The outer surface rippled in a fluid motion.

"This is the entrance to Phriosuin Domhan," Datura told me.

I didn't say anything. I merely stared at her. I was speechless and apprehensive to cross the threshold. My face felt cold, probably from the blood draining from it. I was sure I looked as white as a ghost.

"We must go now," Brunhild said. "I have a feeling we'll be getting company soon."

Company? I wondered what she meant.

Datura nodded and entered first, disappearing into the darkness. Draylan urged his horse forward. I squeezed my arms around his waist and buried my face into his back, feeling like a little girl going on a haunted rollercoaster ride. Frigid air swept over us. Goose bumps rose on my arms. The cloying sweet stench of rotten meat made me gag. The two quickly past, replaced with cool air and the thick, moldy smell of damp earth and decaying vegetation. I lifted my head. We were in a forest at the edge of a misty swamp. The branches of gnarled trees hovered above the water like arthritic fingers. They stood on a small sloping hill covered with composted foliage. We followed Datura up the short mound and ambled among the thick timber on a rocky dirt path. A series of loud caws startled me. Perched high above on a moss-covered branch was the largest crow I'd ever seen. It had to have been three times the size of the ones on earth.

"He's announcing our arrival," Brunhild said from behind.

I glanced over my shoulder at her. "How do you know?"

Her dark watery-brown eye focused on me while her pale-blue one stared straight ahead. "A few days ago, I cast a spell to have the crow call when we're close to the prison, and Aven will telepathically hear it."

"As of this moment," Datura excitedly said, "he's getting ready to vacate the premises and be free." She lifted her shoulders in quick jerks and grinned. "Soon, I'll get to see my daddy in person for the first time ever. Weeee!"

I leaned next to Draylan's ear and whispered, "She's fucking nuts. You betrayed my kingdom for a fruitcake." His head twitched away from me. I sat back and thought about trying him for treason. If I got through this alive, I'd make sure he'd be punished for his betrayal, I decided.

When we exited the woods, I was amazed at the huge castle-like monstrosity not far from where we halted. The dreary lime-green sky made the glossy black structure appear ominous with its multiple jagged spires, narrow arched windows, and the red vapors that surrounded it. Nothing else was around the prison except for deep forest as far as the eyes could see.

Datura wheeled her horse to speak directly at us. "As you can tell, the wards are up." She gestured toward the red vapors and settled her attention on me. "Once you bring them down, Daddy will be able to walk outside."

"Where are the guards?" I asked.

"There's no need for them to be outside since the magical wards were put into place," she answered.

"How am I supposed to lower them?"

Brunhild grinned, revealing her front black tooth. "You bleed on it."

Horror struck my heart. In panic, words tumbled out of my mouth. "I'm not fond of pain or blood loss. There has to be another way. I'm not going to allow you to cut and bleed me."

Datura raised her eyebrows. I was ready for her eyes to turn black again, but they didn't. "Oh, really? If you don't do what I say and perform the task to free my daddy, I will not only destroy Havenwood, I'll also see to it that Merrack never recovers, and Nalin will die. Do you want to shoulder the guilt of their demise for the rest of your life?"

"No," I said, loathing her even more. "How much blood do you need?"

"Not much." She acted like it was no big deal and turned her horse around before I could answer back. "Let's go!"

My stomach churned as we headed toward the prison, my bottom smacking hard against the saddle as Draylan's horse galloped along with the other two. Datura was ahead of us. I watched her stop and dismount in front of the red vapors. We followed suit, joining her side. A loud whistling noise echoed from the forest. Simultaneously, all four of us turned our heads to that direction.

"I think we have company," Brunhild said. "We must hurry."

I wondered if it was Larkin. My pulse raced, my chest tightened, and my breaths were coming out labored. I placed my hands on my knees in an attempt to calm down.

"What's wrong with you?" Datura snapped, glaring.

"She appears to be having an anxiety attack," Brunhild answered.

Datura marched to me and snatched my wrist, hauling me upright. "For fuck's sake! We don't have time for such nonsense!" She yanked me toward the red vapor, causing me to stumble forward as I slowly gained control of my breathing.

Draylan handed her a pocket knife, and before my mind could register what she was about to do, she slit the palms of my hands. The sharp pain caused me to yelp and pull back. Draylan moved behind me, grabbed my arms, and forced my bleeding hands to lie flat against the ward. My instincts from years of martial arts training was to take him down but coupled with barely recovering from an anxiety attack and Datura's threats ringing through my head, I behaved as promised.

"Alaris!" Larkin called in the far distance.

My body was anchored in place. I couldn't move to see if he actually called my name or some delusional part of my mind wishing for it. A sweltering rush of heat ignited within my body, and a whooshing sound exploded in my ears along with muffling hooves hitting the ground at top speed behind me. The arched door to the building swung open. A tall, slender man with long salt and pepper hair tied behind his neck walked out.

"Daddy!" Datura shrieked happily, jumping up and down, clapping her hands.

"Scutum Protegens," Brunhild said behind us.

Aven paused on the top step. He smiled, tilted his chin to the sky, and threw his hands above his head. Other Murks stepped outside in his wake.

Oh, God, what the hell did I do?

As I was stuck in what seemed like suspended animation, I watched in horror as each creature came out of the prison: The first one had a round bald head, a flat nose, beady eyes that were too close together, and a greenish tinge to his skin.

A ghoul.

The next one was a noble-looking dark-haired guy with a rich face, long nose, and pointy ears.

A dralk.

Next, an extremely tall man with brown tangled hair that fell to his shoulders, a hooked nose, and a face that had a rocky type structure to his yellowish-green skin emerged.

A trow.

Behind him were two hooded beings who appeared to be the revenants that killed my family.

They all lined in single file behind Aven. If there were more, I couldn't tell. Then by their own accord, my hands moved upward, lifting the red vapor with them, creating a gap between it and the ground. Numerous people shouted behind me, but their voices were garbled. I tried to move my head to glance behind me but couldn't. My hands shook as a heaviness pressed into them and down my arms, straining my muscles.

"Hurry, Daddy, before the ward drops!" Datura shouted.

Aven and the other Murks rushed down the flight of stairs and ran toward me. My heart hammered in my chest as each one drew closer. Aven was the first. His sky-blue eyes caught mine. They were lined with thin wrinkles that webbed across his handsome face. Something deep and heartbreaking passed through them that stole my breath. It reminded me of people who never recovered from great losses in their lives. A wave of sympathy washed over me. He had to have been in his early twenties when he was sentenced and locked up here. For forty plus years, he'd been in prison, accused of a crime he'd never committed. I couldn't even imagine what that would have been like. He dipped his head in respect, thanked me, and crouched, slipping through the gap. I tried to force my hands to fall to quickly shut the ward, but they remained locked into position. The ghoul grinned at me, revealing yellow pointy teeth, then bent through the opening. Next, the dralk was in such a hurry he didn't bother acknowledging me when he squatted to get to the other side. The ward kept lowering. The trow dropped to the ground and rolled beneath the closing gap at the same time the headhunters tried to crawl their way out, their white skeletal fingers clawing at the dirt in an attempt to pull their way through. My arms dropped and a high-pitched scream of pain echoed before me. The revenants were yanked backward, the front of their bodies folding in response, reminding me of demons being yanked back to Hell. They flew through the stone stairs, disappearing from sight.

"We need weapons," a gravelly voice said.

Shaking my hands out from the heaviness in them, I examined my palms. There was no evidence of them ever being cut. The ward must have healed them, I thought as I turned and gaped at the bluish white bubble we were inside. Wow, it had to be a protective force shield, I guessed. Larkin kept trying to penetrate the barrier with his sword but after each blow to the surface, his blade would bounce backward. As if he felt the weight of my eyes on him, he looked up, locking his gaze with mine. The frustration on his face softened. He opened his mouth and said something, but the sound was garbled. I pointed to my ears and shook my head. Behind him on horses were Narik, Farran, an older gentleman who had similar features as Farran, and what looked like twenty or so fairies who appeared to be from the Solas clan. Farran raised his bow and shot arrows at the force shield. When the tips struck it, a burst of blue and red waves washed over the bubble, temporarily distorting their images in a watery fashion.

"You won't need weapons," Aven said, pulling my attention to him. Datura was hugging his arm, beaming up at him like a little girl. "My magic is coming back. I can feel it recharging."

The ghoul grunted in dissatisfaction and joined the other two Murks who were talking among themselves in low voices, probably devising a plan on how to elude the warriors.

Aven cradled Datura's face into his hands, kissed her forehead, and embraced her. "Brunhild," he said, "when I point at you, I want you to lift the sound barrier so we're able to communicate with my rivals while still being protected."

She nodded obediently. "As you wish."

Aven held Datura at arm's length. "I'm going to ask you a question, and I want you to tell me the truth. Okay, sweetheart?"

"Yes, Daddy," she answered.

Aven pointed at Brunhild who then did a swirling motion with her finger above her head. "Audite hoc!"

A tangle of voices surrounded us. Larkin was telling me to get away from them, and the Solas warriors were throwing out ideas on what to do. Farran, his dad Alder, and Narik approached our bubble on foot, weapons in hand. They halted next to Larkin.

Aven wrapped his arm around Datura's shoulders and led her to the four men. Draylan, Brunhild, and I followed while the Murks kept their distance.

"Alaris," Larkin said. "Get on the other side of Draylan."

"He's not going to protect me," I answered. "He's a traitor. He's on Datura's side. He's in love with her." I made a face.

"What?" Narik said in shocked disbelief.

Larkin's face twisted in anger. "You son-of-a-bitch!" His fist hit the barrier and flew back.

Draylan laughed. "Like I'm scared of you. You don't know shit, Larkin!"

"Silence!" Aven said. "Datura has something to tell Alder and Farran." He placed his hands on her arms. "Tell them what you did and then we can be on our way."

"What did you do, Datura?" Alder asked, his brow furrowing. I think in his heart he knew since he'd been suspicious of her enough to have sent Farran to Atheon to keep a close eye on her, but his mind would not fully accept the truth until it was spoken from her own lips.

Datura's hands balled into fists. She faced Alder. "To avenge my father, I had my bitch of a mother killed! The others, including your wife"—she looked at Farran whose eyes were blazing with rage—"and your mother were added bonuses because none of them ever treated me well. They all deserved what they got, because I think they knew," she spat, jabbing a finger in the air. "They knew I had Dorchadas blood running through my veins, and my biological father was a Murk. They. Lied. To. Me! They've made me feel like an outcast my whole damn life!"

Angry tears rolled down Farran's face, causing my own eyes to water. Alder hung his head and covered his face with his hands. His shoulders shook from his silent sobs.

"You're going to pay for what you've done not only to Farran's family but to Alaris' as well," Larkin promised.

Datura let out a ridiculous laugh. "Idiot! My daddy and I are going to be the most powerful people in this realm. There's nothing you'll be able to do to me, so you best mind your tongue!"

"Did Brunhild have any part in slaughtering our families?" I asked Datura.

She looked at me. Her eyes were black, and her entire face was webbed with dark spidery veins again. "Brunhild has been teaching me magic for years. The only hand she has in any of this was mentoring me, giving me the tools to carry out my plans . . . and finding you because we knew there was something special about you that would be useful to us."

Brunhild nodded. "We did."

"Why did you have the headhunters go after me?"

Datura smirked. "I wanted you to myself for a while, but Merrack ruined it for me when he sent Larkin to retrieve you while I was spending time with Brunhild."

"What's in it for you?" Narik asked Brunhild.

"I asked her the same question," I told him. "She said beauty. Once Datura and Aven possesses all four elements, Datura promised to make her beautiful."

"It's not going to happen," Aven said.

"What do you mean?" Brunhild choked out. "She . . . she promised."

Datura turned to Aven, her eyes and face were back to normal. In a childlike voice, she said, "I did, Daddy. She's helped me out a lot throughout my life."

Aven shook his head. "It doesn't matter. Your mother was the love of my life. She saved me from myself by having me imprisoned. Our secret affair continued while I remained segregated from the outside world. Throughout the years, she assisted me in finding my soul. She made me a better man and silenced my demons. I hold no ill will toward her, but you I do for having her killed." He threw his hand out toward Draylan's boot. A knife flew from the side pocket and into Aven's hand. In one swift move, he grabbed Datura's wrists, spun her to where she was facing Alder, and slit her throat in front of him.

Chapter Thirty-Nine

"Nooo!" Draylan hollered. He moved to strike Aven, but Datura's father threw his hand out, mumbled something under his breath, and Draylan froze with his fist suspended in the air. Aven turned to Brunhild who stood like the rest of us, gaping in shock. He said something under his breath, and Brunhild became motionless like Draylan. Only her eyes could move, which was a bit freaky. Aven then stuck his palm out toward her breast, curled his fingers, and slowly pulled back. A tube of black and red sparkling particles came out and went right into his chest.

Oh, shit!

Aven turned to me, and my breath got caught in my throat. The thought of wanting to end my life due to me harboring the fire element entered my mind unless he planned on still using me to feed his unfounded obsession of obtaining all four elements to become all-powerful. It could go either way.

"Please don't hurt her," Larkin begged. "She's done nothing wrong. She's a victim."

"Aven," Alder said, "Alaris is an innocent. There's no need to harm her."

"I have no intentions of doing so," Aven told him, then looked at me. A warm, compassionate smile crossed his face. "I'm sorry about what happened to you and your family. If this gives you any solace, know Datura can no longer harm you or the people you love. Also, the revenants who took the Evergreen's life are now imprisoned here. Her death made it so, and the binding spells she'd cast have been lifted."

"Merrack," I whispered.

He nodded. "Yes, the king will be fine. As for me, it's time to go, and my promise to you will be kept." He turned his attention to Alder and motioned toward the creatures who were keeping their distance from us. "These Murks need to be given a second chance. They paid for their crimes and are not the same monsters they were when they came here."

"Your request will be granted," Alder said, placing a fist over his heart, bowing his head.

Aven took my hand and kissed the back of it. "Goodbye, sweet Princess."

I had no idea what he was about to do. A shock of fear and panic went through me. When he dropped my hand and turned, I reached for him. "Wait!" But it was too late. His arm jerked back as he slit his own throat, and he fell to the ground. Draylan stumbled forward. Brunhild shook her body, and the force shield disappeared. Alder was already beside Aven's still form. He gently turned him over onto his back. Aven's eyes were closed. A gaping gash ran across his throat with blood pouring out. Datura was but a few feet away, face smashed into the ground. Larkin pulled me into his arms and held me tightly as Narik and a few of the Solas warriors apprehended Draylan. Three more went to Brunhild. She threw her hands out in an attempt to use magic to stop them, but they kept going. She tried again. Nothing.

"He took my magic!" she squeaked in horror.

A tall Solas fairy with white blond wavy hair that touched his shoulders grabbed her hands and slapped a dark, rusty metal cuff on each wrist that appeared antique with mysterious symbols. "Your magic will return," he told her. "However, these will prevent you from using it."

"No, you can't take away my powers and send me to prison," she cried. In desperation she looked at me. "Princess, please don't let them do this to me. I broke your memory spell. If it wasn't for me, you wouldn't have remembered Larkin."

I stepped out of Larkin's embrace and moved closer to her. "I promise you will get a fair trial."

"All I wanted was to be beautiful," her voice cracked, breaking my heart, even though she supported and fueled Datura's wickedness. Fat tears ran down her puckered face. Maroon blotches rose beneath the grayish tint in her skin. A drop of snot hung on the tip of her long hooked nose.

I refused to stare into her eyes. They were unnerving anyway, but to see the sorrow and brokenness from her soul reflecting through them weakened my resolve to allow justice to be served. Instead, I focused on her trembling lip. "I know, but you went about it the wrong way, and now you have to take responsibility for your actions." I turned to leave but as an afterthought, I said, "By the way, you asked why me? Why was I chosen by the unicorn and dragon to harbor the fire element?" She tearfully nodded. "It's not because I'm special. It's because the unicorn saw an adventurous, kind, and caring spirit in me, and of course because my mother was a healer and my father is of royalty. The wyrmling chose for probably the same reasons and to continue to survive through me. That is all." I walked away before she could reply and allowed the fairies to do their jobs.

"Are you okay?" Larkin asked, cradling my face in his hands.

I took a deep breath and released it. A mingling of relief and sadness gnawed at me. Honestly, I was on the brink of bursting into tears, but I told myself now wasn't the time to fall apart. "Um . . . as well as expected, I suppose."

He kissed my forehead and hugged me again. "I see the turmoil in your eyes," he whispered in my ear. "You're holding it together in front of the others because it's your job as a princess . . . but tonight I shall hold you in my arms, and when you break, I'll pick up your pieces, dust them off, and put them back in place."

I swallowed back the tears. "I love you."

"I love you, too," he said in a low husky voice that made my stomach flip.

Alder cleared his throat. "Sorry to interrupt, but I suggest you head back to Atheon as soon as possible to tell Merrack the news. I'll be there as soon as I can to pay him a much needed visit, but first I need to take care of this." He gestured to the two black thoroughbreds ridden by Solas warriors, emerging from behind the prison, towing a large metal cage. Narik opened the door. We watched as Draylan hesitantly stepped inside. Then the three Murks followed. Brunhild was already on a brown horse sitting behind a muscular fairy with golden hair tied at the nape of his neck. The others were on their horses, except for two who were taking care of the bodies, wrapping them in gauze-like material. "I promised Aven," he continued, "to give the Murks another chance. They will be reevaluated."

"I'd like for Larkin and me to take part in the whole process if we may," I said.

He smiled, and though it was sad, it was also genuine. "I wouldn't want it any other way." He folded his hands in front of him and tilted his head to the side, regarding me. "May I ask you a question before we take our leave?"

"Sure," I said, wondering what it might be.

"Do you plan on staying in Atheon and taking on the role as princess? The reason I ask is Farran told me a lot about you." I must have had an uneasy look on my face, because he raised a hand and quietly chuckled. "Nothing bad, although he did share his first impression of you." He paused, then continued. "He informed me about what you said to the people in Atheon when you spoke to them at your party and how taken they were by you. Because of your experiences on earth, raised in a working class family, and you yourself having to serve the people in order to provide for yourself is an extreme benefit in your royal position. I admire the fact you're willing to go to each village and take part in their duties to gain a deeper understanding of what's going on in your kingdom and then bring it to the table afterward in an attempt to fix what is broken. By doing so, not only will you gain loyalty from the people, but you'll also strengthen Atheon in a way that's never been done before."

"Wow, that's a huge compliment coming from someone of your caliber," I said, feeling the heat in my cheeks. "But to answer your question, I did plan on returning to earth, to my old life, but I decided to stay here instead."

"What changed your mind?"

I squeezed Larkin's hand. "Larkin, Havenwood, and the opportunity to do amazing things for people and for my kingdom."

"Those are good reasons, but if I may be so bold, Farran has shared with me your aptitude for fighting and your usage of colorful language."

I tilted my head to the side and rubbed it, making a face. "Yeah, well, it's who I am. I understand I need to tame my behavior for the good of Atheon, and I will when necessary. To be honest, though, I'm not going to sacrifice the real me to appease a certain class of people. Do you know what I mean?"

He laughed. "I appreciate you being forthright with me, but would you be opposed to one of my people going to your palace to teach you the proper etiquette you'd need to adopt when the situation calls for it?"

"No, that would be cool," I said and meant it. I didn't want to have to worry about what fork or spoon to use at a dinner party or struggle with the proper way to handle myself when mingling with other royalty.

"Splendid," he said. "I will arrange a time for your classes and send word to you."

I shifted my weight, unsure if I should tell him what was on my mind, but before I could make a decision, my mouth decided for me. "I'm not going to quit training in hand-to-hand combat, and I'd like to learn how to handle the weapons the warriors use to take down a Murk."

He rubbed his chin in thought. "Normally I'd be against a princess or queen learning the ways of a warrior; however, I have to admit if my wife would have been trained to defend herself on her own, she might be alive today."

We headed toward the horses. Larkin's Gypsy was there, patiently waiting.

"So what are you saying?" I asked as he swung his leg over his horse.

"I'm going to make it mandatory for all females to learn how to defend themselves. Not extensively but enough to protect themselves."

"Awesome!" I really liked Farran's dad. In fact, I was looking forward to getting to know him better and felt a fatherly connection with him. "You don't disagree with my desire to fight like a warrior then?"

He looked down at me from his horse. "I don't agree with you handling weapons. It's your warrior's job. He's there to protect you at all cost. Your duties are to assure your kingdom runs smoothly and to forge peaceful relations with neighbors of Atheon."

I frowned. "I understand, but I have other things I want to accomplish, and I plan on splitting my time between Havenwood and Atheon."

He nodded. "We have a lot to iron out, Princess. We can address your wants and duties when I pay a visit."

"Fair enough," I said. "Until then, safe travels to you and your companions."

"And you and Larkin, as well." He dipped his head, turned his stallion around, and made a clicking noise. The horse took off. The other fairies followed. The wheels on the cage housing the Murks and Draylan clanked as it trailed behind them. Larkin and I watched until they were dots in the distance.

Chapter Forty

Larkin and I headed back to Atheon on Gypsy. We took a different route than the one I did with Datura. I learned there were several gateways to enter this realm from ours, and one of them wasn't too far from the palace, so we rode that way and made it to Atheon within an hour. When we neared the exit of the forest by the palace, five tiny balls of light danced and zigzagged around us. The one in front giggled. Gypsy grunted and stopped.

"Nalin," I gasped and grinned when she hovered next to me. "You're okay. I was so worried about you."

"Good to see you," Larkin told her.

Nalin giggled again. "Thank you. I feel fabulous!" With her arms spread, she twirled, then stopped. "I don't know what you did to help me, but I appreciate it." She looked around. "Where's that bitch?" Her eyes widened, and she slapped a hand over her mouth.

Laughter erupted from the tiny balls of light still flitting about.

"It's taken care of," I said. "She won't be bothering you guys anymore."

Nalin's hand slipped from her lips. "What happened?"

"I'll answer your question later," I told her. "Now isn't the time."

She nodded. "I understand." She blew me a kiss. "I'm so happy you and Larkin are together. See ya!" She took off, and the balls of light followed her high above, their illumination causing the branches on the trees to twinkle against the darkening sky.

"I'm so glad she's okay," I said to Larkin as we headed out of the forest.

"Same here. I think you have a new best friend." I could hear the smile in his voice.

"Maybe," I answered, enjoying the idea of being BFFs with a tiny fairy, but then wondered what Merrack was doing, hoping he was actually okay. He had to be since Nalin was, right?

When we reached the front of the palace, we hurried inside. Merrack's voice poured from the kitchen, and my heart skipped several beats.

He sounded fine!

When we entered the room, he was sitting at the table wearing what looked like red plaid flannel pajamas, drinking a cup of tea with Bralana, the gal who had done my hair and makeup for my party. He stood when he saw me.

"Alaris, I'm so glad you're all right."

"Ditto," I said, feeling all warm and fuzzy inside. "You look great." And he did. His chestnut eyes were bright, though I could detect sadness in them, and he had good color in his complexion. "I was so worried about you." I threw my arms around him and sighed against his chest when he hugged me tighter. The genuine love he had for me as his daughter poured from it, generating an overwhelming warmth from me to him. He was my father. The only biological parent I had left. It was about time for me to allow him into my heart, and then with a start, the realization came: he was already there. I'd loved him since the day I strolled through the garden with him.

He pulled back and studied my face, worry creasing his brow. "Are you sure you're all right?"

"I am." I paused and chewed on my lip. "I have to break some bad news to you."

"If it's about Datura, I know what she did to me, why, and the plans she and Brunhild aimed to carry out."

"How?" Larkin wanted to know, handing me a cup of tea. I wrapped my hands around it, enjoying the warmth against my cold fingers. The aroma of vanilla, nutmeg, and cinnamon were delightful.

Merrack sighed heavily. "When my body was asleep, my mind and ears were alert. I heard their conversations in the room. It frustrated me that I was powerless to stop them, and the fear I had for your life was insufferable, a living Hell."

Bralana rose from the table. "You three sit. I'm going to take my leave. Have a good night."

Merrack kissed Bralana's hand. "Thank you for watching over me. Your loyalty and kindness will not be forgotten."

Her pale cheeks blossomed red. "My pleasure."

After she left, we gathered around the table and told my father everything. He covered his face several times, much like what Alder had done, and wept, breaking my heart. He kept apologizing for Datura's behavior and for him being a blind fool. Numerous times, I tried to reassure him it wasn't his fault, but I could see the guilt he felt. What Datura had done would take some time to get over, if he would at all. The same regarding Draylan and Brunhild. He trusted them, and they betrayed us. He was visibly upset and excused himself from our company.

I looked at Larkin. "Can I ask you a personal question?"

"Sure. You can ask me anything."

I shifted in my seat and bit the corner of my lip. "Did Lithia crawl into bed with you this morning?"

"No, she didn't," he said honestly, "but she came into the bedroom as I was getting up, calling your name." He shook his head in disbelief. "I was shocked she had the nerve to walk into your house and approach me like she did. She's nuts, and Draylan . . . don't even get me started on him. Like you said, he's a traitor and needs to be punished."

I twisted a lock of hair absently around my finger as a vision of Lithia walking into my spare bedroom with Larkin naked came to me. I didn't like it. At all. "What did you say to Lithia?"

"I asked her where you were. At first she wouldn't tell me and opted to convince me she and I belonged together. I had to literally take her by the shoulders, look her dead in the eyes, and tell her I didn't love her." He ran his hand through his hair and to the back of his neck. "I hated seeing the hurt in her eyes, but she wouldn't quit. She got angry. Scary angry. She vowed I'd pay for breaking her heart, and she hoped after you freed Datura's father, one of them would kill you. It's how I found out where you were, and Appara filled me in on the rest."

"Wow." I said, staring at him. "I don't think anybody has ever hated me like Lithia does."

"She has issues. She always did."

"I think I want to lie down," I said, no longer wanting to think about her. "Will you join me?"

"Of course, but I'm not ready to go to sleep yet."

"Neither am I." I pushed the chair back and took his hand. "I just want you to hold me for a while, and if I break, like you said earlier, you'll be there to put me back together."

Sometimes all a girl needs is to be held so she can feel safe and loved.

"It would be an honor to do so, your highness." He bowed his head and flashed me a crooked smile. God, he was hot.

I playfully rolled my eyes. "Whatever, ya goof. C'mon."

When we reached my bedroom, the light was on, and Brunlin was standing near my nightstand with a king-sized Snickers bar in his hand. It looked huge in his small hand. To my surprise, he didn't pop out of the room, instead he smiled, the folds on his face bunching below his black eyes. "The princess is safe. Brunlin is pleased."

"A brownie," Larkin whispered next to my ear in shock. "They never reveal themselves to anybody except for the owner of the house."

"He's my friend," I whispered out the side of my mouth. "Yes, I'm okay, Brunlin." I bent down and opened my arms. "I can use a hug from a friend."

His smile deepened, and he hurried to me, throwing his small arms around me. "Brulin was worried he'd lose his princess who is his friend."

I patted his back. "Nope, I'm still here. Thank you for the map. I'm sorry I lost it."

"He's the one who gave you the map?" Larkin asked. He laughed. "I would have never guessed in a million years."

Brunlin stepped back and cocked his head to the side. "You didn't tell your warrior Brulin was the one who–"

I touched his cheek. "No, I didn't tell a soul."

His eyes grew wide. "Why?"

"Because I didn't want to get you into trouble. I was protecting you."

"You were protecting Brunlin?"

I smiled. "Yes."

His bottom lip trembled. He handed me the Snickers. "Here."

"Thank you." I tore the wrapper open and broke off a piece. "Have you ever tried this?" I handed it to him when he shook his head. "It's super yummy." I handed some to Larkin. "You try it, too."

Brunlin looked at it curiously.

I bit off a chunk and chewed it. "Go on," I urged. "I think you'll like it."

"This is really good," Larkin said.

Hesitantly, Brunlin took a bite. His bushy eyebrows knitted, then he looked up at me wide-eyed. "Mmmm, Brunlin likes this. Brunlin likes this a lot." He popped the rest into his mouth. I gave him more.

I laughed. "See? I told you so."

He dug into his pocket and pulled out the map. "Brunlin was worried about you and went looking for you. This was lying on the ground in the tunnel."

I licked the chocolate from my fingers and took it. "Thank you. This might come in handy." I gave it to Larkin.

"You're most welcome, Princess. Brunlin must go now. Lots of work to do."

"Before you disappear," I said. "I want you to know the queen is no longer with us. You won't be seeing her again."

"Good news. Good news indeed," he answered, then vanished.

Larkin sat on the bed and slipped his boots off while I threw the candy wrapper away and took off my own shoes. "You keep amazing me." He pulled me onto the bed with him.

"Why, because I made friends with a brownie?"

"Yes, and how you are." He yanked the edge of the blanket on the other side of the bed over us and spooned me. "Your strength and kindness are inspiring. I want to become a better person because of you."

I tucked my hand in his and kissed it, suddenly tired. I yawned. "You're sweet to say those things to me, but I am who I am, and I'll never pretend to be any different."

He pulled me closer to him. "It's one of the many things I love about you. You won't sacrifice your real self in order to fit into the herd. Whether you recognize it or not, you're a leader. Atheon has been starving for one like you since its inception."

"Yeah, okay." I laughed. "Whatever you say. You realize I have to learn how to conduct myself in front of the big wigs?"

"Having proper manners when required is not abandoning your beliefs," he pointed out. "Or selling yourself out."

I yawned again and closed my eyes. "I know that now. My brief conversation with Alder has put it all into prospective. I really like him. He's a good man."

"He is," Larkin said. "I have nothing but respect for him."

"Uh-huh," I mumbled, feeling myself slipping into the dark abyss where dreams took form. I was sinking deeper and deeper. I gave into it, and in the far distance, I heard Larkin whispering goodnight to me and warm lips softly touching my cheek.

* * *

The next morning, Larkin went home to take a shower. After I finished taking mine, I threw on a pair of jeans, a gray sweater, and black suede knee-high boots. I left my hair down since we decided not to train today. I found Larkin in the kitchen eating pancakes and sausage. He met me with an endearing smile and told me my plate was in the oven keeping warm.

"Who made breakfast?" I asked while I poured a cup of coffee and doctored it with cream and sugar.

"Merrack."

I slipped a pair of oven mitts on and took my plate to the table next to Larkin. "Where is he?"

"He went to see Alder. He told me he had to get some fresh air and clear his head. Alder is a good friend of his, and he needs one right now."

Piercing a piece of buttery pancake with my fork, I frowned. "I hope he's going to be okay."

"He will," Larkin reassured. "He has a lot to think about."

"That's for sure," I said and proceeded to eat my breakfast. For some reason Mardella crossed my mind. I wondered what she was doing at this moment. I touched Larkin's arm. "I'm sorry about your grandmother. How are you doing?"

He looked down and ran his thumb along the edge of the table. "I'm okay . . . oh, I forgot to tell you"—he fixed his eyes on mine—"what she told me to relay to you. The Evergreens *were* compelled to believe you to be their biological daughter. They were innocent in Karrina's and Mardella's scheme."

I looked away and stared at nothing in particular. The corner of my eyes prickled, and I blinked away tears. "I was right," I whispered.

Larkin's warm hand slipped into mine. "I'm sorry, but I thought you'd want to know."

"Yes, thank you." With my free hand, I wiped the tears away and told myself the Evergreens wouldn't want me to dwell on their loss. However, I found myself silently apologizing to them for everything. They were dead because of me, and the guilt I felt the night I discovered my mom's headless body was still fucking there.

"Mardella has some things in a trunk she was adamant I have."

I sat up, intrigued, thankful he changed the subject because I needed a distraction from the dark thoughts threatening to encompass me. "Really? I wonder what's in it."

"Who knows? Probably old family photos or trinkets she'd collect during her travels."

"I would love those. In fact," I said, "I want to go on many adventures."

I rose, took our plates, and set them in the sink. "I want to explore."

He laughed. "I bet my grandmother said the same thing when she was younger."

I took his hand and pulled him to his feet. "And she eventually did it." I led him out of the kitchen. "C'mon. Let's go outside. We can start my adventure here. You can show me things I haven't seen yet."

"There's a wide-open field past the gardens where a bunch of us practice fighting moves on horses," Larkin said. "Want to check it out?"

"Yes." I couldn't wait to see it and everything else around the palace I hadn't seen yet and should. I intertwined my fingers with his, happy to be in Atheon for the first time.

* * *

"Here it is," he said when we reached an enormous grassy meadow with thick forest bordering it. "I've spent countless hours here training and riding on Gypsy."

I pictured him and a dozen or more of his comrades on horseback practicing together, like knights in armor. I was about to say something when a large dark shadow passed across us. I looked up thinking it was the clouds but there were none.

I gasped and pointed at the huge golden creature with a wing span of about a hundred feet, circling us. "Oh, my God! It's a dragon! Shalnal."

Larkin grabbed my hand. "We need to get out of here."

I stopped him. "No, it's okay. She's not going to hurt us." I knew she wouldn't and was elated to finally get to see her in person instead of in a dream state. I let go of his hand and waved her down.

"Alaris, what the hell are you doing? We need to leave now. I've never dealt with a dragon before. None of us have." He tried to take my hand again, but I moved it away.

"Then you go. I'm staying. Besides, I've already met her. Remember the dreams I told you about and what Mardella said?"

Shalnal was moving closer. My pulse raced at her enormous size.

Goose bumps rose on my arms. A strong gust of wind from her flapping wings blew my hair back. As she got closer, Larkin and I backed away. She glided downward and landed right in front of us. Just like in my dreams, there were two long horns on the top of her head and a short one on her snout and chin. Large gills on the sides of her neck opened and closed when she breathed, and her massive body was covered in curved armor-like scales.

An overwhelming emotion came over me. I covered my mouth and burst into tears.

"There is no need to cry," Shalnal said, her orange reptilian eyes capturing mine. Her voice was soft and musical. "I am fine now."

I sniffed and nodded. "I'm just so happy to see you. It's much better when I'm awake than asleep."

"Yes, I agree." Her gaze flicked to Larkin who was cautiously watching her. "You need not worry about me. I will do no harm to your people, and I'll protect Alaris with my life if circumstances ever arise where I need to."

"If word gets out about Alaris harboring the fire element and the spirit of a dragon," Larkin said, his forehead wrinkling, "her life will be in danger. I'm also concerned about people knowing about you. I'm sure you've already been spotted by some." He sounded nervous, like he didn't know how to take her.

"I'm aware of those dangers, but Alaris is a part of me, and I will do what needs to be done to ensure she receives the knowledge I have to give her and her safety."

"What about your safety?" I didn't want crazy ass trolls attempting to slay her or a bunch of Murks for that matter.

"There's no need to worry about me. I'm clever enough to evade them or if forced to, destroy them."

"But Aven was able to outwit you," I pointed out.

"He did," she said, "but I birthed a child and was at my weakest stage."

I chewed on my nail. "That makes sense."

"Are you going to teach Alaris how to use her elemental power?" Larkin wanted to know.

"Alaris is human with the spirit of a wyrmling," she told us, "which means she cannot produce fire, only heat when angry. However, she possesses the fire element allowing her the ability to lower the ward around the prison, make cold water hot, burn another with the touch of her hand, and so forth. The caveat is if her secret gets exposed, her life will be in danger."

Larkin rubbed the back of his neck and moved it around. "I was afraid of the last part."

"Maybe we can have something done to the people who already know about it," I said, not wanting Larkin to worry, but honestly, I was concerned myself, "like compel them to forget."

Shalnal nodded. "Talk to Alder and your father about it. I'm sure a solution will present itself, but in the meantime, you need to take care of your kingdom."

"I suppose you're right." I knew she was, but I wanted to resolve the problem now and planned on addressing it as soon as possible.

Larkin slipped his hand in mine. "We'll take your advice. Thank you."

Shalnal looked at me, and her eyes softened. "We are connected, you and me. Over time, our connection will grow stronger to where we'll be able to communicate across vast distances, through thought and feelings . . . and know this, as long as I'm alive, you'll never be alone. I'll be your shadow when you need me, your strength when you are weak, and the light to see you through the darkness."

My throat tightened, and my eyes welled. I lifted my hand toward her face. She lowered it to where I could touch the side of the horn on her snout. It felt rough and scaly, but I didn't cringe or pull away. Instead, I continued to stroke it.

"I must go now and retreat into the mountains. I haven't fully regained my strength yet," she admitted.

"But I don't want you to go," my voice cracked. "When will I see you again? What mountain is your lair in?"

"When the time is right, you'll see me again," she reassured me. "And my lair can only be found by a clever witch or one who possesses magic."

"I'll miss you."

"And I you, but I can also visit you in your dreams, thanks to Mardella." She lifted on her hind legs. Larkin and I backed up when she flapped her enormous wings. She struggled to get the momentum of them and had me worried at first. I could tell she was still weak. Then she picked up speed, and a gust of wind blew us from her even further. The sound reminded me of a jet engine. Finally, she pushed off with her feet and went airborne, disappearing into the distance. Larkin wrapped his arms around me from behind, and we stared after her, deep in our own thoughts.

Chapter Forty-One

~Two Days Later~

"It is done," Alder told me when I opened the front door to let him into the palace. Rain blew sideways into the entryway, and the wind howled something fierce. I hurried and closed the door behind him. Drops of water were dripping from the hood of his forest green cloak. He lowered it, his sharp sky blue eyes capturing mine. "The memory spell has been cast on each and every one of them."

"Even Father and Narik?" I asked, watching him shrug out of his cloak and hang it on the coat tree in the corner of the entryway.

"Yes, everyone who knew except for myself, Larkin, Farran, and"— he gestured to me—"yourself."

I nodded, briefly thinking about my father. He had struggled with the decision whether to keep the knowledge of my secret alive within him or to euthanize it all together. With a lot of soul searching, he chose the latter due to the poor decisions he made in the past. To add more troubles, Datura's betrayal, along with Brunhild's and Draylan's, shook his confidence in trusting not only others but also himself. Then I thought of Narik whom I trusted as much as Farran. I hated this had to be done to him, but he'd agreed to having the spell cast on him with no reservations. Even so, I felt guilty about it.

"Your father will be along shortly," Alder informed me. "He wanted to stop at The Blue Fairy with Farran to have a drink and see Oona perform."

"Oh, that reminds me," I said as we stepped into the main room and headed into the kitchen. "The people of Atheon need to know what happened to Datura, and I was thinking of inviting everyone to The Blue Fairy for an important announcement concerning their queen. What do you think?"

He sat at the table while I filled a teapot with water. "Your idea is unconventional." He rubbed his hands together and blew on them. "It's not the proper way to address your kingdom."

I turned the burner on and frowned. "I know, but think about it, what a—"

"Is she telling you her idea about inviting everyone to The Blue Fairy to inform them about Datura?" Larkin asked, smiling at me. His dark hair was sticking up on top, and he had on a pair of gray sweatpants and a white T-shirt that hugged his muscular frame perfectly.

I returned his smile and watched him get the cream out of the refrigerator. He placed it on the table next to a bowl of sugar and took a seat next to Alder. "I am, but he's against it; however, I haven't stated my case yet." I handed Alder and Larkin a teacup.

"Indeed she hasn't," Alder said, "and I'm rather curious to find out why she wants to deviate from what's considered common practice in her station here in Atheon."

"I'll tell ya why," I answered. "It's the same reason I was myself at the party and did a question and answer with the crowd. They loved it. Even Farran was blown away by the response."

Alder rubbed the side of his chin. It was smooth and pale like the rest of his face. I wondered if fairies from the Solas clan didn't have facial hair. So far, every one of them I'd seen didn't. "Yes, he was taken by the outcome of your bold move to disregard protocol in favor of your earth's contemporary line of thinking."

"I know," I said, taking a seat next to Larkin and pouring tea into our cups, "and the response was amazing."

"It was," Larkin agreed.

Alder took a thoughtful sip of his tea, then set the cup down. "I'm not convinced and find it rather distasteful to give an important public announcement at a club. You're their princess, not their peer."

"I am their peer," I told him and sighed. "I know I have to help run this kingdom, and one day I'll rule, but I hate the whole caste system, and I want the people of Atheon to know that, yeah, I was born of royalty. Yeah, I'm their princess, but we all bleed and share the same fate . . . death, unless there are immortals here I'm not aware of, but that's beside the point. The point is I want to close the division between us and them. Of course, I can't do it completely but enough to show them that in the end, we're all the same."

Alder folded his hands on the table and leaned forward, his expression stern yet his words were gentle. "A mother can be a friend to her child, but she'll always be their mother first and act accordingly as one."

I pinched my bottom lip in consideration. What he said did put it all into perspective. I hated to be forced into a position to where I couldn't just be their friend, that there had to be boundaries, and I was now their matriarch. "I see your point," I finally said, sounding dejected. "I guess that wouldn't be a good idea." I frowned at the table. "What do you suggest then?"

"I recommend," he said, "for you to get together with the pixies first thing in the morning and tell them to spread the word to the people of Atheon that an important announcement will be made at the palace. They're invited to hear Princess Alaris speak about the recent unfortunate events that occurred within the kingdom. By doing so, you'll pique their interest and set them up for the news about Datura."

I held my head in my hands and moan. "Ugh! I hate speaking in front of crowds."

A warm hand touched my arm, causing me to look up to Larkin's smile. "You'll be fine," he assured me. "All you have to do is write a speech about what you want to tell them regarding Datura and how you're moving on."

"You know, people are going to ask about her funeral," I said as I thought the words. "What are we going to do about that? Are we going to have one for her and Aven?"

"The Dorchadas fairies will take care of them both," Alder simply answered.

I blinked at him in surprise. "Why won't the Solas clan take care of Datura's body?"

Anger flashed in Alder's eyes, and his lips turned into a thin line. "Because she was the driving force in the murder of my family. The Dorchadas lot can decide what to do with her remains."

"Sounds like a plan," I said, my tone light in an attempt to break through the sudden dark cloud that rolled into Alder's mood and took form in his clenched fists and set jaw. "I will take your advice and have the pixies send word to the people of Atheon about a speech I'll be giving here regarding their kingdom."

Alder's posture relaxed as if he released an internal sigh. His tight expression softened. "Splendid. I think that's a wise decision. Now if you two will excuse me, I'm going to retreat to the library and immerse myself into some fine literature while I wait for my son and Merrack to arrive."

"Of course," Larkin said as Alder rose from the table.

"See ya." I turned to Larkin when Alder left the kitchen. "He's having a hard time with Datura's betrayal. I feel bad for him."

"I do, too, but at least he has our support, his family, and Merrack who is going through his own similar troubles."

"True." I scooted back my chair. "Let's go to my room and work on the speech together."

The corner of his mouth curled, stirring the affections I had for him. I bit my lip as the heat between us sizzled. A vision of when we made love surfaced. It was erotic, passionate, and hot. I collected the teacups and set them in the sink to distract myself from the desire tightening my stomach. Now wasn't the time to act on it, I told myself. "Sure. I'd love to help," he finally answered.

That night we worked on my speech until my father and Farran came home. My father was stumbling drunk, which concerned me since he had a history of alcohol abuse. With Alder's help, he made it up the stairs and into bed. Farran filled Larkin and me in on Draylan, Brunhild, and the Murks Aven wanted to be reevaluated. Their trials would begin in a week. In the meantime, they were in individual holding cells with only their thoughts to keep them company. He also confirmed their memories about me harboring the fire element and the spirit of a dragon were magically wiped cleaned by a Solas fairy witch whom Farran and Alder held in high regard. The next morning, Larkin and I took a stroll in the forest outside the protective ward around the palace's grounds. The cool air had a crisp clean smell only rainfall from the previous night could bring. I called out to the pixies: Sela, Coral, Plume, and Rill. Four twinkling balls of light came at us from every direction. As they neared, the pixies took form. They all stopped shoulder to shoulder, in front of me.

"Hello," I said. "I'd like for you to introduce yourselves to me so I know one from the other."

A girl on the far left with long dark hair and who was wearing a red knee-high form-fitted dress moved forward. "I'm Sela."

The blonde with short pigtail braids in tight brown pants and a white poet blouse moved next to Sela. "I'm Coral."

"I'm Plume," said the redhead whose hair was layered around her round face. She had on a dark green mini dress that tied over one shoulder, leaving the other one bare. I noticed she sported black combat boots, and I thought she had a cool style to her.

The last one had deep blue eyes, and her black hair was in a high bun. She wore a similar dress as Sela, only it was lavender. "I'm Rill."

I smiled. "Please to officially meet you. As you know, I'm Alaris, and I have an important job for you to do for me."

Their eyes widened.

"What would you like for us to do?" Sela asked, giving me the impression she was the leader of this group.

"I need you to spread the word to all Atheonians that I'll be giving an important speech regarding their queen tonight. They're invited to come here to the palace. Due to the circumstances I'll be addressing, no festivities will follow."

Coral gasped. "What happened?"

"You'll find out tonight," I replied. "Now, go spread the word so people can make last-minute arrangements to be here at eight o'clock."

"Yes, Princess," they said in unison and then took off.

Larkin pulled me into his strong arms. I melted against him, loving being enfolded into his embrace. "You're a natural at this."

I laughed. "We'll see how I do tonight. I hate giving speeches." I thought of Narik and how much he helped me the last time I had to speak in front of a crowd. "What's Narik doing today?"

"He's dealing with the weres. Nash and his pack are being obstinate regarding territory."

"Should I be worried about this?" I thought of Wyatt and his group. I didn't want anything to happen to them, but to be honest, I had no knowledge of what was really going on and would like to be involved in it.

Larkin pulled back and held me at arm's length. "Not at the moment."

"Okay, well," I said, "I want to be informed on what's happening between the two packs."

Holding my gaze, he slowly nodded. "After tonight, you can brief Narik on all the details."

"After tonight," I echoed as he lowered his face to mine and kissed me.

* * *

The hour finally arrived to give the speech. I was a nervous wreck. Like last time, Bralana came to my room to do my hair and makeup. Only on this occasion, she brought with her the dress I was to wear. The bodice was a beautiful baby blue lined with delicate lace and had a wraparound off-white crochet in a swirling pattern below the breasts with ribbons in the back that laced up. The skirt came away from the hips and was made out of tulle material and featured vertical tatters of raw ragged fraying at the bottom. It reminded me of something a fairy would wear. I loved it. To set the look, I wore a white lace choker around my neck. I stepped onto the platform after my father, their king, told our people I'd be the one to give an important announcement. I told myself I could do this as he pressed the microphone into my sweaty palm. I realized when I turned to the sea of curious faces that I'd left my speech in the drawer of my nightstand.

Dammit.

I even had mentally reminded myself. I was looking in the mirror at the loose bun Bralana fashioned, admiring how the double thin crystal headband sparkled when I turned. I remembered telling myself then not to forget it. Now what was I going to do? My mind went blank as my eyes scanned the different creatures in the crowd. There were a lot of them: fairies, goblins, sea nymphs, the seven-foot troll with the rock-like skin and long black scraggly hair was even here. I saw Oona. The warm yellow dress she had on made her blue skin more striking. She was in the front. When I caught her gaze, she dipped her head, and the corners of her mouth formed into a warm smile. I mouthed, hi, then gave my attention to the crowd and grinned when I spotted Narik weaving his way to the front. He gestured for me to begin.

Taking a deep breath, I decided to relax and be myself. "Hello, everyone. I wrote a speech last night for this occasion, but to be honest, I accidently left it in my room." I let out a nervous laugh.

Larkin was only a few feet away from me on the platform performing his warrior duty to protect me. He moved to my side and whispered in my ear, "I can have someone fetch it for you if you like."

I waved it off. "No, I'm fine."

"As you wish, Princess," he said. His voice was low and sensual, his breath feathering against my ear.

I slightly turned toward him to where our lips were almost touching.

His bright green eyes were locked onto mine. "Thank you." The intoxicating energy between us caused my pulse to race. He dipped his head and stepped back, never taking his eyes off me. I shifted my attention to my audience. "Since I don't have my speech, I'm going to tell you why you're here . . . Due to unfortunate circumstances, your queen is no longer with us."

Gasps issued from the crowd.

"What do you mean?" a gravelly voice asked. It came from a short yellowed skin guy with a knobby forehead. He had a black top hat on, and his long pointy ears were sticking out the sides. A goblin. "What happened?"

I frowned. "She turned dark." More gasps. "You see, years ago she discovered her biological father was from the Dorchadas clan. Her mother had an affair with one and covered it up."

"Oh, my!" A female said from the crowd.

"Long story short," I continued, "Datura and Brunhild—"

"Brunhild!" I followed where the voice came from. It was Lucy, the sea nymph with the big reflective blue-green eyes. "I thought she was good."

"Yeah, well, apparently not," I told her. "Anyway, Datura and Brunhild were poisoning your king. They then kidnapped me and forced me to go to Phriosuin Domhan, which all of you know is the prison world. She had me watch as her father and a few Murks escaped."

"How could they have escaped?" a male asked from somewhere in the crowd. "There are magical wards around it infused with elemental magic."

"Yes, I know," I answered. "But with Brunhild's assistance, Datura conjured some powerful dark magic that briefly allowed the ward to lift long enough for them to escape. When her father was released, he killed her and then himself." I paused at the sharp intakes of breaths and the shocked expressions staring at me. "The Murks have been apprehended and so have Brunhild and Draylan."

"Why Draylan?" a familiar male voice asked. Wyatt. I scanned the crowd and found him in the middle. His hazel eyes were full of questions. "He was one of your trusted warriors."

I cleared my throat. "Draylan and Datura were having an affair. He sided with her, and by doing so, he betrayed us all. Now he has to face the consequences."

"Tell them about me," a bright voice rang inside my head. Female. I recognized the lilt of her tone. Shalnal. *"I will be there shortly."*

My heart thudded in my chest. She'd told me we'd be able to eventually communicate across vast distances, but I didn't put much thought into how it would happen. It was cool, but I feared for her life. There were trolls in this crowd. What was she thinking?

"It'll be fine. Tell them about the spell Aven cast on me. Tell them I befriended you and by doing so, I'll protect both you and Atheon."

"I have one more announcement to make." I glanced over my shoulder at my father and Larkin who both looked confused. "Datura's dad was Aven. Before he was sent to prison, he cast a binding spell on a dragon. When he perished, the spell broke, freeing her. The next day, she approached me. We became friends, and she gave me her word she'd protect me and Atheon."

"A dragon," someone scoffed. "They've been extinct for hundreds of years."

A large dark shadow passed over the bright twin moons. Heads tilted skyward. People quickly backed away. Some ran toward the forest. Larkin, my father, and Alder were instantly by my side.

"Don't be afraid," I called. "Stop!" The people who were about to reach the forest, halted. I waved my hand to the left. "Everyone, move over here so she can land."

"Alaris, this is madness!" my father seethed. "This dragon is putting our kingdom in disarray! Why didn't you tell me you made friends with this creature?"

I did, but since his memory of it was wiped clean, I needed to come up with a quick response to his answer. "You had too much on your plate. I didn't want to add to it. I was only protecting your feelings."

"I hope you know what you're doing," Alder said to me as a colossal golden dragon became visible above us. The sight of her sent a thrill through me.

The force of the flapping of her wings created gusts, forcing everyone to step back a few feet and flipping hats to the ground.

"It's okay," I assured everyone. "She's not going to harm you."

Shalnal landed beside the stage and stood on her hind legs, her massive wings tucked behind her. The curved armor-like scales rippled and glistened a golden hue beneath the moonlight. Her orange reptilian eyes flicked to me. "I would like to speak to the people if I may."

I walked to the far edge of the stage and held the microphone for her.

"What Alaris told you was true," she said. "I give you my word. I will not only protect her, but I'll also protect Atheon. No harm will be done to you by me," She paused, lowered her chin to where the two long, pointy horns on her head were directed at the group of trolls who were feverishly whispering to one another. "Unless you threaten my life or the princess's." She lifted her head and smiled, revealing long sharp teeth, then glanced at me, silently telling me she was done.

I went to my original spot on stage, glad to see the expressions on most of the faces staring at me and Shalnal were unafraid. Realizing I was about to speak, they moved closer to the wooden platform. "Darkness had unknowingly crept into the heart of Atheon," I said, "but it's been eradicated, and justice will continue to be served. We now have a dragon on our side, something that has never happened here before, so rest peacefully in your beds and know we have your best interest at heart."

Heads nodded. Someone clapped, another followed. A thunderous beat of clapping surrounded me, and although the trolls and a few hobgoblins were off in their own tight group conversing with one another while shooting glances at Shalnal, I felt good about everything. This wasn't the life I'd envisioned or wanted when I first arrived here, but sometimes fate had other ideas. At first you might not like the hand that you were dealt or the path your life veered onto, but I realized through all of this, that I had to trust in the universe and know there was a bigger plan for me. I was now at peace with it and ready to embark on this new life with a hot warrior on one side and a badass dragon on the other. Life here wasn't too terrible after all, if I do say so myself.

The End.

Author Note

If you enjoyed Legends of Deceit, I'd appreciate it if you took the time to leave a review on Amazon.com and Goodreads. Your review doesn't have to be long.

Thank you for your support. I appreciate it. ☺
You rock!

About the Author

Rebekkah Ford is an award-winning author who writes paranormal fiction. She believes her fascination with the unknown derives from her childhood. When her parents were married, they were the directors of the UFO Investigator's League. They also investigated ghost hauntings and Bigfoot sightings in addition to extraterrestrial cases. Rebekkah's upbringing, knowledge, and experiences with the paranormal world, along with her colorful imagination, aids her in creating her stories.

Rebekkah has an irreverent sense of humor and believes having a dirty mind makes boring conversations more interesting.

Find Rebekkah Ford

Facebook: www.Facebook.com/RebekkahFord2012

Twitter: www.twitter.com/RebekkahFord

Website: http://rebekkahford.com/

Blog: http://themusingwriter.blogspot.com/

Amazon Author Page. Follow it to get notified of new releases: www.amazon.com/Rebekkah-Ford/e/B00896OMB0/

Goodreads: www.goodreads.com/author/show/6180865.Rebekkah_Ford

Pinterest: www.pinterest.com/rebekkahford/